BEST BRITISH HORROR
2018

BEST BRITISH HORROR 2018

Edited by Johnny Mains

NewCon Press
England

First edition, published in the UK October 2018 by NewCon Press

NCP 172 (hardback)
NCP 173 (softback)

10 9 8 7 6 5 4 3 2 1

CONTENTS

Introduction – Johnny Mains   7

Paymon's Trio – Colette De Curzon   9

Love and Death – Reggie Oliver   19

In the Light of St. Ives – Ray Cluley   37

The Book of Dreems – Georgina Bruce   53

The Affair – James Everington   65

Fragments of a Broken Doll – Cate Gardner   75

The Lies We Tell – Charlotte Bond   81

Ting-A-Ling-A-Ling – Daniel McGachey   97

Tools of the Trade – Paul Finch   127

Departures – A.K. Benedict   153

The Taste of Her – Mark West   167

Sun Dogs – Laura Mauro   175

Dispossession – Nicholas Royle   193

Shell Baby – V.H. Leslie   199

The Unwish – Claire Dean   217

A Day With the Delusionists – Reggie Oliver   227

We Who Sing Beneath the Ground – Mark Morris   235

About the Authors   249

Editor's Thanks and Acknowledgements   253

Editor's Dedication

For my wife, Lou – 'we'll do it all, everything, on our own'.
Remembering Richard Dalby and Carl Ford

INTRODUCTION

Johnny Mains

Welcome back to *Best British Horror*, it's been a while. I didn't know if BBH would or could ever be resurrected, and the hiatus gave me time to write and complete my first novel. After that was finished, I realised that I missed reading short stories by my peers. I truly believe that we are entering a new 'golden age' – where the anxieties of living in a period of fake news, extreme nuclear terror, poverty akin to Victorian times, the wholesale destruction of morale at the hands of a morally void government, *has* to filter through into the fiction that's being written, no matter how subconsciously it might appear.

It was with this in mind I approached Ian Whates from Newcon Press and told him my idea to bring *Best British Horror* back from the dead. He was immediately on board, and my utmost thanks for letting me dive back into a world I truly love.

Now it's time to see what diabolical tales are in store for you, and what tales! I'm really excited by this volume, and I hope you are too, it was an absolute hoot to do, lots of stories read, and with this volume, I wish I could have reprinted another ten stories from last year – the quality coming from this small island is *that* good. I am so proud to be part of a community that never stops experimenting with the short form.

Johnny Mains,
Third Circle of Hell,
2018

PAYMON'S TRIO

Colette De Curzon

I had always been fond of music: it was a kind of passion in me, around which I centred my whole existence, and in the beauty of which I derived all the pleasures I required from life. I was well up in anything and everything connected with music, from the earliest and most primitive of rondos to the latest symphonies and concertos. I played the violin passing well, though my ability of execution fell far short of my desires. I had played second violin in various concerts, provincial ones, of course, for a natural shyness prevented me from daring to launch my meagre talent into higher spheres. Besides which, the violin for me was not a profession: it was merely a friend in whom I confided all the thoughts and emotions of my soul, which I could not have expressed in any other way. For even the most retired of men needs to express himself in one way or another.

I had always connected music with the beautiful side of life. In this, for my fifty-odd years, I was strangely naïve. The experience I went through shook the rock-solid foundation of my innocent belief. It will, no doubt, be hard for anyone reading this story to believe it all, or even any part of it; but I am here to testify that every word of it is true, I and my two very dearest and noblest of friends, for we all three went through the same experience, and all three unanimously declare that every word of it is solid fact. A few years have elapsed since the evil day that brought a passing shadow on my life's passion, but the memory of it is still fresh in my mind.

I will start at the beginning and try to impart all its vividness up to you.

It was on a raw November's evening, with dusk swiftly descending on windswept London, as I was returning from Hyde Park, where I had taken my dog, Angus, for his afternoon exercise, that I suddenly remembered I had gone out for a double purpose: the first already mentioned, the second a half-hearted quest for a second-hand copy of Burton's Anatomy of

Melancholy. To say that I was interested in that work would be a great exaggeration. I had heard various reports about it that did not rouse my enthusiasm, but as it had got a new vogue and was much talked of, I wished to acquaint myself of its content, so as to know, roughly, at any rate, what it was about.

I prided myself on being erudite – such puny accomplishments are very satisfactory – and my ignorance concerning Burton's work was a serious lapse in my literary learning. So, Melancholy bound, I made my way down some narrow side streets, ill-lit by bleary lampposts, where I knew I would find a number of barrows of second-hand books, and where I hoped to find the work in question. The first two barrows revealed a great deal in the nature of melancholy, but not Burton's. At the third, which was overshadowed by the towering bulk of a surly woman vendor, who eyed me as suspiciously as though I were a notorious nihilist, I found the book I was looking for. Or books – for it was in three volumes. But they were wedged behind a tall black volume which I found necessary to remove in order to reach them.

I daresay I was clumsy, or perhaps Angus chose that particular moment to tug on his leash and jerk my arm. At any rate, Angus or no Angus, my hand slipped from the black book which, having been dislodged, fell with a thud on to the muddy pavement, its binding being badly stained in the process. I remember thinking, in spite of my vexation, that the fat woman was no doubt proud of having suspected me of evil intentions from the start, for I was certainly proving myself to be no ordinary customer.

I picked up the book, and seeing how badly damaged it was, I thought it only civil of me to buy it off her, though many of her books were in more distressing conditions. She accepted my offer grudgingly, and had the impudence to charge me an extra *6d* on the original two shillings. Being hardly in a position to argue, I allowed her to engulf my half crown and departed with my new acquisition under my arm… and the Anatomy still skulking dismally in its barrow.

When I got home to my flat – which I shared with my most faithful and congenial of friends, Arnold Barker, with whom I had seen two wars and a prison camp in Germany – I inspected the book I had just purchased. Arnold was out at the time, so I had the flat all to myself. I dreaded so the fearful trash which would have disgraced my library – some cheap romance that would make me shudder. But the binding calmed my fears: no romantic author would have chosen thick black leather to garb his story.

The title in gold print was hardly discernible.

I opened the book and felt a little shiver of pleasant anticipation run down my spine. In bold black lettering, ornamented with fantastic arabesques à la Cruikshank, the title displayed itself to my eyes: *Le Dictionnaire Infernal* by J Collin de Plancy, 1864. It was in French, which pleased me all the more, as my knowledge of that language was more than fair, and it was full of weird, humoristic and infinitely varied engravings by some artist of the middle of the last century.

I perused it avidly and rapidly acquainted myself of its contents. An Infernal Dictionary it was, written in a semi-serious, semi-comical style, giving full details concerning the nether regions, rites, inhabitants, spiritualism, stars reading, fortune telling etc, which, as the author informed us, all had to be taken *cum granu salis*. I hasten to say that I in no way dabbled in demonology, but this book, though certainly dealing with the black arts, was harmless to so experienced a reader as myself. And I looked forward to several days of pleasant entertainment with my unusual discovery. I pictured Arnold's face as I would show him my find, for the occult had always fascinated him.

I skimmed the pages once more, smoothing out those which had been crushed in the fall – or perhaps before – when my fingers encountered a bulky irregular thickness in the top cover of the book. The fly leaf had been stuck back over this irregularity, and gummed down with exceedingly dirty fingers.

To say that I was puzzled would of course be true. But I was more than puzzled: I was very intrigued. Without a moment's hesitation, I slipped my penknife along the gummed fly leaf and cut it right out; a thin piece of folded paper slipped out and fell onto the carpet at my feet. What made me hesitate just then to pick it up? Nothing apparently, and yet fully ten seconds elapsed before I took it in my hand and unfolded it. And then my enthusiasm was fired, for the folded sheets – there were three of them – were covered with music: music written in a neat, precise hand, in very small characters, and which to my experienced eyes appeared very difficult to decipher.

Each sheet contained the three different parts of a trio – piano, violin and cello. That was as far as I was able to see – for the characters being very small and my eyes not so good as they had been, I could not read very much of it. I was, however, thrilled; childishly, I must confess, I hoped – even grown men can be foolish – that this might be some unknown work from a great composer's hand. But on second perusal, I was quickly disillusioned. The author of this music had signed his name: *P Everard,*

1865, which told me exactly nothing, for P Everard was quite unknown to me.

The only thing that intrigued me considerably was the title of the trio. Still in the same neat hand, I saw the skilfully drawn figure of a naked man seated on the back of a dromedary, and read, *'In worship of Paymon'* underlining the picture.

It may have been a trick of the light, or my imagination, but the face of the man was incredibly evil, and I hastily looked away.

Well, this was a find! However obscure the composer, it was interesting to find a document dating back to the nineteenth century, so well preserved and under such unusual circumstances. Perhaps its very age would make it valuable? I would have to interview some authorities on old manuscripts and ascertain the fact. In the meanwhile, the temptation being very great, I set about playing the violin part on my fiddle. My fingers literally ached to feel the polished wood of my instrument between them and I was keenly interested at having something entirely new to decipher.

Propping up the violin part on my stand – the paper, though thin, was very stiff and needed no support – I attacked the opening bars. They were incredibly difficult and at first I thought I would not be able to play them, although I can say without boasting that I am more than a mere amateur in that respect. But gradually I got used to the peculiar rhythm of the piece and made my way through it. Strangely enough, however, I felt intense displeasure at the sounds that were springing from my bow. The melody was beautiful, worthy of Handel's *Messiah*, or Berlioz's *L'Enfance du Christ*, for it was religious. Yes, religious: and at the same time it seemed only to be a parody of religion, with an underlying current of something infinitely evil.

How could music express that, you may wonder. I do not know, but I felt in every fibre of my body that what I was playing was 'impure' and I hated as much as I admired the music I was rendering.

As I attacked the last bar, Arnold Barker's startled voice broke in my ear. 'Good God, Greville, what on Earth is that you're playing? It's terrible!'

Arnold, in all his six-foot-three of ageing manhood, brought me out of my trance with his very material and down-to-earth remark. I was grateful to him. I lowered my fiddle.

'Well, I daresay it could be better played,' said I, 'but it is amazingly difficult.'

'I don't mean you played it badly,' Arnold hastily interposed. 'Not by a long chalk. But... but... it's the music. It's wonderful, but extraordinarily unpleasant. Who on Earth wrote it?' He took off his mist-sodden coat and hat, and picked up one of the two remaining sheets of music.

As he scanned it, I explained my little adventure, and how I had come into possession of the unusual manuscript.

The book did not appear to rouse much interest in him: his whole attention was centred on the sheet of paper he was holding. As I was finishing speaking, he said, 'This appears to be the piano part: I could try my hand at it, and accompany you. Though, as you say, it appears to be extraordinarily difficult... the rhythm is unusual.'

He was puzzled as I had been, and I watched him as he seated himself at the piano and played the first opening bars. He was a born pianist: these short competent hands, as they stretched nimbly over the keys, were sufficient proof of that. The only defect in his talent that had prevented him from making a career of it was his deplorable memory and total incapacity to play anything without the music under his eyes. Now, he did not appear to find his part difficult – not as I had done. Of course, the piano, in this trio, merely featured as an accompaniment, a subdued monotone which now and then picked up the main theme of the piece and exercised variations upon it.

Arnold played the piece half-way through, then stopped abruptly. 'Of course my part is rather dull,' said he. 'It needs the violin and the cello to bring it out. But, well... I don't mind admitting that I don't like it. It's... uncanny...'

I nodded in agreement.

'What do you make of the man's name?'

'Nothing.'

'As far as I can tell, the name Everard has never become famous in the music world, and yet the man was gifted, for this piece has rare qualities. It reminds one of some strains of *The Messiah*, and yet... well, there's just that something in it that makes it all wrong.'

'It's peculiar,' I admitted. 'Extraordinary luck my finding it. I suppose it has been in the binding of that book since the date when it was written. But why was it... well... I should say "concealed"? I can't think. And what about that dedication? Who is Paymon?'

Arnold bent closer to the picture, and I noticed him suck in his breath as in some surprise. He straightened himself up and cast me rather a furtive look. 'I don't know,' he mused. 'Paymon... and "in worship" too. Somebody this fellow Everard must have been frightfully fond of. But have you noticed the expression on the man's face? It's rather unpleasant.'

'Evil is more like it – the man was an artist as well as a musician. It's very odd. I will have to take this manuscript to old Mason's tomorrow and see what he can make of it. It may have worldwide interest for all we know.'

But, the following day being a Sunday, I did not care to trouble my old friend with my mysterious manuscript, and I spent my time, much to my reluctance, practising my part of the trio. It fascinated me, and yet repelled me in every note I drew across the strings. When I looked at that small, hideous picture, I felt as though a cunning little devil had got inside my fingers and compelled me to play against my will, with the notes dancing and jumbling before my eyes, and the weird strains of the music filling my head and making me loathe myself for yielding to that strange force.

Late in the afternoon, Arnold, who had been strangely moody as he listened to me from the depths of his favourite armchair, rose to his feet and came over to where I was playing. 'Look here, Greville,' said he. 'There is something definitely wrong with that music. I feel it, and I know you do too. I can't analyse it, but it is there all the same. We ought to get rid of it somehow. Take it to Mason's and tell him to do what he likes with it, or burn it, but don't keep it.'

I was stubborn. 'It may have its value, you know,' I remonstrated. 'And, after all... it's really beautiful.' And I wondered at myself for praising something which I loathed with all my heart.

'Yes, it's beautiful. But it's bad. Don't lie to yourself – you think so too. I have been watching you all the time you were playing, and by Heaven, if anyone seemed to be in absolute terror of something, that person was you. That thing's infernal – I've a good mind to destroy it here and now!'

He seized the three sheets that were lying on the violin stand and made as though to throw them into the fire. But I stayed his hand and murmured quite feverishly (and quite, it seemed, against my will), 'No! Not just yet. After all, it's a trio, and we have only played two parts of it. If we could get Ian McDonald to come round this evening with his cello, we could play the whole thing together – just once, to hear it as it should be played. And then... well... we can destroy it.'

'Ian? That boy will be scared stiff!'

'Scared? Of what? Of a few notes on a sheet of paper eighty-five years old? You're being foolish, Arnold. We both are. There's nothing wrong with the music at all. It's weird, uncanny perhaps, but that's all that's to be said against it. So is Peer Gynt for that matter, and yet no one would dream of being scared by it, as we are by this trio...'

Arnold still looked very doubtful, so I pressed my point.

Why, I wonder now... why was I so eagerly enthusiastic about my find, when deep down in my mind I felt a lurking fear of it, as of an evil thing that polluted whatever it touched? I detested it, and yet that little naked figure on the dromedary's back held my senses in a kind of spell and made me talk as I was now doing: without my being able to control my thoughts and voice as I wished.

'After all,' I argued, 'this is my discovery, and it's only natural that I should wish to know what the whole effect of the trio is like. As we've played it – you and I – it was, well, lop-sided. It needs the cello to complete it. And, you said yourself when you first heard it that it was beautiful!'

'And ghastly,' Arnold added sulkily, but he was clearly mollified. He perused his part of the trio once more.

On the three sheets was repeated the detestable little figure, and I noticed that Arnold kept his hand carefully over the wicked face, and on replacing the sheet on the music stand, he averted his eyes. So, that drawing held that strange influence over him, too? Perhaps... perhaps... there was something after all.

But Arnold prevented any further speculation.

'All right,' he said, in a resigned voice. 'I'll go round and collect young Ian. But remember, I take no responsibility.'

'Responsibility? What responsibility?' I asked.

Arnold looked embarrassed. 'Oh, I don't know. But if... well... if this blasted trio upsets the lot of us, I want you to know that I wash my hands of the whole thing from this very minute.'

'Don't be a damned idiot, Arnold,' I said with some heat. 'I never knew you to be so ridiculously impressed by a piece of music. You're as silly as a five-year-old child!'

I felt my inner thoughts battling against the words I uttered.

The little man on the paper seemed to grin at me, and I suddenly felt physically sick. I turned to stop Arnold, but he had already left the room, even as I opened my mouth to speak to him. I heard the clang of the front door as he slammed it. I regretted my insistence. I hated myself for having persuaded Arnold to fetch Ian, and, obeying a sudden impulse, I seized the papers and prepared to throw them into the smouldering fire. The little man's eyes on the paper followed mine as I moved, as though daring me to carry out my intention. I stopped and stared at the grinning face... and I replaced the sheets on the music stand, with a thrill of unpleasant fear running down my spine.

Arnold was away some time. When he came back, he had brought Ian with him and between them they carried the latter's cello – a very beautiful instrument in a fine leather case. Ian, compared to both of us, was a mere child: he was barely twenty-eight, with a gentle, effeminate face and a weak body that was greatly at a disadvantage beside Arnold's towering strength and healthy vitality. But he was a fine fellow for all his physical deficiencies, and in spite of the difference in our ages, we were all three the best of friends, brought together by our common interest in music. Ian played in various concerts and was an excellent cellist.

I greeted him warmly, for I was very fond of him, and before showing him the music, made him feel quite at home. But Arnold had probably put him on his mettle, for almost at once, he asked me what this blessed trio was about, and why we were so eager to play it, and why we made such mysteries about it?

'Arnold told me it was beautiful and awful all at the same time, and quite a difficult piece even from my point of view, which I presume must be taken as a compliment. I don't mind admitting I'm keen to play it.'

Arnold grunted his disapproval from behind the thick clay pipe he always smoked, and I felt a guilty qualm in my mind that for some reason made me hesitate. As Ian looked a little surprised, I overcame my reluctance and, taking up the old manuscript, handed it to him. He looked at it carefully for several minutes without uttering a word, then he handed back the piano and violin parts, keeping the cello part, and remarked, 'It ought to be deuced good, you know. Yes, that is quite a find you've made there, Greville, quite a find. But what an unpleasant little picture that is at the top. It is quite out of keeping with the music, I've a feeling.'

'I don't know about that,' Arnold murmured. 'I can't say I agree.'

Ian looked up in some surprise, and I, sensing some embarrassing question concerning the music, rose to my feet and said, 'Well, since we are all ready, there's no sense in wasting time talking. Let's get to work.'

There was little time wasted in preparing our instruments. Ian was eager and in some excitement; I was, for some strange reason, peculiarly nervous; Arnold, I noticed with a little irritation, was moody, and placed himself at the piano with a good deal of ill grace. Why did he accept to play his part so grudgingly, I wondered as I tuned my fiddle. After all, this was just a piece of music like any other. In fact, it was more beautiful than many I had heard and played. Surely his musician's enthusiasm would be fired at being given such scope to express itself! For this trio, in its way, was a masterpiece.

I ran a scale and looked at the little man; the name Paymon in that neat, precise hand danced before my eyes and made me blink. I would have to stop my eyes wandering to the picture if I wanted to play my part properly. But wherever I looked, the man on his dromedary seemed to follow me and leer at my futile efforts to evade him. I glanced at Ian and noticed that he was looking a little annoyed.

'This damn little picture is blurring my eyes,' he complained rather crossly. 'It seems to be everywhere!'

'I noticed that myself,' I admitted.

'I can't get it out of the way: the best thing to do is to cover it up.'

I gave them a small sheet of paper each and we all three pinned the sheets down upon our respective pictures. I felt a certain amount of relief at not seeing that ugly face and, tapping my stand with my fiddle bow, said, 'Are you fellows ready?'

Two silent nods, and we began.

And now, how can I describe what happened, or how it happened? It is fixed in my mind and yet I cannot find words suitable to impart to you the horror of our experience. I think the music was the worst part of it all. As we played, I could hardly believe that this... this hellish sound was really being created by our own fingers. Hellish. Demonic. Those are the only words for it, and yet in itself, it was none of those things. But there was something about it that conveyed that ghastly impression, as though the author had composed it with the wish to convey profane emotions to its executants. I confess that I was frightened – really and truly afraid – possessed of such fear as I have never experienced before or since: fear of something awful and all-powerful which I did not understand. I played on, struggling to drop my fiddle and stop, but compelled by some force to continue.

And then, when we were half-way through, a strangled cry from Ian broke the horrible spell. 'Oh God, stop it, stop it! This is awful!'

I seemed to wake as from a dream. I lowered my violin and looked at the young man. He was white and trembling, with dilated eyes staring at the music before him. He looked, with his thin face and yellow hair, like a corpse.

I murmured hoarsely, 'Ian, what is the matter?'

He did not answer me. With one hand, he still held his cello; with the other – the right one – he made a sign of the cross and murmured, 'Christ – oh, Christ, have mercy on us!' and sank in a dead faint onto the carpet.

In two seconds, galvanised into action, we were beside him and, Arnold supporting his head and shoulders, I administered what aid I could to him, though my intense excitement made me of little use. He was very far gone, and it took us nearly twenty minutes to revive him. When he opened his eyes, he looked at us both, a prey to abject terror, then, clutching at my coat in fear, he murmured, 'The music… the music… it's possessed. You must destroy it at once!'

We exchanged glances, Arnold and I. Arnold seemed to say 'I told you so' and I accepted the rebuke. But I obeyed. This music was evil and had to be destroyed. I rose to my feet and went to the music stand. Then I suddenly felt the blood draining from my face and leaving my lips dry. For the music lay on the carpet – clawed to pieces. Only the grinning man on his dromedary was intact…

It was some weeks later, when we had somewhat recovered from our experience, that I ventured to open the book I had recently bought and which had been the cause of so much trouble. I had the name Paymon on the brain, and quite by chance, I opened the Infernal Dictionary at the letter P. I had no intention of looking for the name Paymon. I did not, of course, think it existed in any dictionary. I merely turned the pages over and looked at the illustrations. At the sixth or seventh page of that letter, my attention was attracted by the only picture in the column – that of a hideous little man, seated on the back of a dromedary. The name Paymon was written beneath it, along with a small article, concerning the illustration.

I read avidly. *'Paymon: one of the gods of Hell. Appears to exorcists in the shape of a man seated on the back of a dromedary. May be summoned by libations or human sacrifices. Is very partial to music.'*

LOVE AND DEATH

Reggie Oliver

"There was something fascinating in this son of Love and Death."
— *The Picture of Dorian Gray* Chapter III

"Mr Isaacs, I want you to find *Love and Death* for me."

I reminded Sir Joseph that I was not a detective.

"I know that, but you were close to the man who painted it, and you are an artist yourself. Besides, I trust you. You will be well paid for your pains. Would I be correct in thinking that you might be in need of funds just at present?"

He passed a quick appraising glance over my frayed cuffs and threadbare suit. In other men that look might have constituted an insult, but Sir Joseph Behrens was that treasurable rarity, a rich man with a heart and a conscience. He did not despise my poverty, nor did he pity it, he merely noted it as a friend might do. Sir Joseph, moreover, is a man of taste: he has been known to buy my paintings; more to the point, he had bought *Love and Death* for five thousand pounds and he wanted the painting back.

When, some minutes later, I was shown out of Sir Joseph's town house in Upper Brook Street, I knew the comforting sensations of one who has twenty gold sovereigns in his pocket, but I was also a prey to apprehension. How could I of all people unravel a mystery that had been baffling the police for months?

Love and Death had been the sensation of the Royal Academy Summer Exhibition of 1885 and Sir Joseph had bought it at the Private View. Shortly after the close of the Exhibition both it and its creator, the artist Basil Hallward, disappeared. Now all that remains of the painting, as far as the public is concerned, is a rather muddy reproduction of it in the Royal

19

Academy catalogue. Like many others, I saw it at the exhibition and remember it well.

They say that George Frederick Watts painted his much lauded version of the same subject shortly afterwards to compete with Hallward's masterpiece, to eclipse it if possible, but it is nothing like. Indeed, the two images are in some ways diametrical opposites, and, even though the Watts still exists to be seen, it is to my mind at least, a pale, paltry thing by comparison with Hallward's *Love and Death*.

In the Watts painting Death is a towering figure, looming over Love who cowers in his shadow. In Hallward's work, as seen at the Royal Academy, Love is a naked man in the muscular pride of his youth. He stands in the foreground in the midst of a wild landscape beyond which the sun sets in glory, but he is chained by the left wrist to another figure, shrouded and of indeterminate sex who crouches on the ground to Love's right and slightly behind him. Love casts a glance at the cowled figure of Death, and the expression on his face is – or should I say *was?* – one of the marvels of this work. It is agonised and yet somehow accepting, such an expression as you might have seen on the crucified Christ by one of the masters of the Mannerist period, except that Love is beardless and his hair a riot of bronze curls.

I, Martin Isaacs, had been a pupil of Basil Hallward in my young days and used to mix colours in his studio for a while, and sometimes paint in the backgrounds for his portraits. After I had left to fend for myself we had stayed friends, though in later years he became more reclusive. However he still retained his position as one of the most fashionable portrait painters of his day. His other work, mostly landscape and "genre" scenes, sold well, but I noticed that a certain dullness had entered into his canvases. They remained as accomplished as ever, but they generally lacked that spark of something which is to be found in his earlier work. You might call it "genius", but I hesitate to employ that overused term by which critics pretend to explain the inexplicable.

Basil once admitted to me that his art had lost its way, but when I pressed him for a reason for it he was silent. In anyone else, I would have said that a woman was at the bottom of it all, but Basil always gave the impression of being immune to strong emotional attachments, dedicated only to his art. In society he was faultlessly urbane, and his reputation was spotless, but there was something impenetrable about him, even to those, like myself, who were privileged to call ourselves his friends.

One night a little over a year before his sudden and mysterious vanishing I was working late at my Chelsea studio. Whenever I can I prefer not to paint by artificial light, but I had for once a lucrative commission for a series of panels, depicting mythological subjects, to decorate a room of a well-known writer who lived in Tite Street. I was being well-paid for my work which would be much noticed and praised, but I had an exacting deadline to fulfil.

As I was executing a delicate series of ripples on the water in a panel depicting *Echo and Narcissus* I heard a knocking on my door. Few people called on me this late; few people in all conscience called on me at all as I have something of Basil Hallward's dedicated reticence in my nature. Putting down palette, brushes and mahl stick I went to the door. It was Basil. He wore a Homburg hat and a heavy greatcoat with an Astrakhan collar, and looked for all the world like a prosperous theatrical impresario. His face was flushed and he seemed to be in a state of high excitement.

"My dear Martin," he said. "You must come with me at once. I have a cab waiting outside."

"But Basil," I said, noting that he wore evening clothes under his greatcoat, "I will have to change. I can't accompany you like this," and I indicated my paint-stained smock.

"Just take off your smock and put on an overcoat, Martin. We are not going anywhere respectable."

I had become used to Basil's peremptory ways. In society he was all suavity, but with his closest friends – as close as any could be – he tended to be brusque. It was a kind of compliment to be so treated. When I had joined him in the cab he tapped on the roof with his stick and commanded the driver to take us to the Shoreditch Empire.

"As you may know, I have a taste for low theatrical experiences." he said. "Some time ago a former friend introduced me to them." Then he was silent. I knew better than to pierce the veil of his self-absorption with any further enquiry, but recalled that some years back he had caused a sensation with a series of paintings portraying the life of music halls and other such haunts. One in particular, entitled "The Juliet of a Night" had excited a denunciation from the pulpit by no less a figure than the Dean of St Paul's. Basil, with his usual mixture of impudence and canny discretion, had merely withdrawn the painting from exhibition without apology, sold it privately to a patron of his work, and moved on to a series of canvases depicting fashionable young ladies listening to sermons in fashionable churches. Whether there was any satirical intent in this move no one knew, and Basil Hallward was characteristically tight-lipped on the subject.

As the cab clattered eastwards, our surroundings became dingier and more oppressive, the gas lighting less frequent. At length we drew up in front of that palace of pleasure known as the Shoreditch Empire. It has since been rebuilt by Matcham in his inimitable style, but in those days it was a wild, noisy place, full of hissing gas jets and bevelled mirrors, smelling of sweat, stale beer and orange peel.

An obsequious usher who evidently knew Basil showed us to what he was pleased to call a "box" on the prompt side of the stage and some six feet above its level. It contained two rickety gilded "fauteuils" and had a heavy damask curtain which could be drawn across the front of the box to create an illusion of privacy. Basil dismissed the attendant with a sovereign and a request for champagne.

I could not understand why Basil had dragged me there. The orchestra was vile, the audience (if that is the right word for the rabble in attendance) was raucous, malodorous and half drunk, and the turns were as witless and vulgar as any in London. As we arrived a statuesque woman of magnificent *embonpoint* in a sequinned gown was bawling out a number whose refrain was: "And he gets me behind with the rent!" This was echoed by the congregation with loud cheers at each interminable repetition. When the champagne arrived it was corked, so Basil sent it back, but the replacement bottle was scarcely an improvement.

The large lady was succeeded by a pair of painfully thin adagio dancers whose woeful act was almost immediately greeted with a chorus of whistles and catcalls from the pit. They were not so much given "the bird", as a whole flock of them. The Chairman mounted the stage and hurried the dancers from the scene before announcing that "all the way from Italy, at Enormous Expense –" here, Basil gripped my arm – "the mighty Roman Hercules, Signor Torrigiano, will demonstrate for your especial delight and edification his astonishing feats of strength."

There was a flourish from the orchestra and the curtain parted to reveal a backcloth intended, I presumed, to depict classical antiquity. On the stage were displayed a number of pieces of equipment which usually accompany a "strong man" act. Then, onto the scene stepped "the Roman Hercules" himself.

"Is this what we came to see?" I asked. Basil merely nodded, his eyes fixed on the stage. I could sense excitement and tension in every muscle of his body.

Torrigiano was indeed a fine specimen. He was, at a guess, in his mid-twenties and at the very peak of his physical prowess. His musculature was well toned but not excessive and he moved about the stage with a natural cat-like grace. He was tall and well proportioned while the features of his face, though they did not bespeak, I thought, high intelligence, were ruggedly handsome and topped by a mass of highly oiled bronze curls. He wore a loincloth over which was draped a leopard skin suspended from one shoulder.

The act he performed was little different from the ones I had seen at circuses in my childhood, but Torrigiano's physical perfection and the fluidity of his movements gave the "turn" some distinction. I was mildly impressed but did not share Basil's rapture. The audience was mainly quiet until the performer's final *tour de force* which was to hold up above his head a long pole at either end of which were balanced two children – girl twins, I suspected – of about four. They wore white tights and spangled tunics. Their hair was curled and the same bronze colour as Torrigiano's. With their big dark eyes, delicate features and golden complexion they looked like Raphael angels. The audience greeted this finale with considerable enthusiasm, and Basil was one with them, a look of childish delight on his face. Torrigiano bowed gracefully to the ovation, holding each child by the hand on either side of him and, as he lifted his head, I saw him cast a glance in our direction. It was an apprehensive, almost a furtive look. When he saw Basil's vigorous applause and flushed face, he seemed relieved.

He left the stage and was replaced by a comic with a red-nose and huge painted eyebrows who darted about the stage singing in a scratchy voice:

"My hat's a brown 'un, A brown 'un, A brown 'un,

My hat's a brown 'un – And don't I look a toff!"

During these inane proceedings Basil turned to me with shining eyes.

"Well, what do you think?"

"Of Young Hercules, you mean?"

"But of course! Who else?" The absurd song about the brown hat seemed to be wildly popular with the public below. Basil cast a look of furious scorn upon them and turned back to me.

"A fine looking fellow certainly," I said.

"But more than that. There is a spiritual quality, don't you think? Something rough-hewn, utterly unaffected, but deep. He will bring my painting back to life. Martin, you don't know how tired I am of these simpering society women with their weak chins and witless attitudes. And as for the men...! I feel I have found true beauty again! He must pose for me!"

"Have you asked him?"

"Not yet! Not yet!"

"He seemed to know you."

"I have been coming here every night since Thursday. Yesterday he was off but I was assured he would be here tonight. We must go back stage now."

"Do you really need me to be with you while you ask him to model for you?"

"Martin, I am right, am I not? This fellow has something remarkable. We could make beautiful art from him, could we not?"

"*We?*"

"I mean I, but you could use him well too, couldn't you? I will lend him to you. Come, there is no time to waste!"

We hurried from the box while the song about the brown hat was still delighting the house. Basil took me to a pass door which led back stage and we descended a flight of rickety stairs. Below us was a seething melée of stage hands and artists. A troupe of performing dogs was being assembled in the wings to follow the comedian of the brown hat.

Several people looked up at Basil as we descended, as he was evidently a "swell" and a man of consequence. The Chairman, a large sweating man with a heavy moustache, and a watch chain substantial enough to choke a bull mastiff, approached us and asked if he could be of assistance.

"I would be obliged to you if I could make the acquaintance of Signor Torrigiano."

"Certainly, sir. With pleasure, sir. And might I trouble you for your name?"

"I am Basil Hallward." The Chairman looked blank. "The artist."

"An artiste? Indeed, sir? In what capacity? And where might I have seen you on the halls?"

"I am a painter!"

"Ah, yes, sir. Indeed, sir. This way, sir." Evidently the borders of Basil's fame did not extend as far as Shoreditch.

He led us out of the stage area to a wooden corridor where, leaning against one of the doors was a woman. The two Raphael angels, now clad in spotless white pinafores were clinging to her skirts. She was large, though not fat, jet-haired, handsome but heavy-featured. She eyed us with suspicion.

"A gentleman to see your husband, my dear," said the Chairman.

"He change," said the woman. She almost spat the words out at the Chairman whom she clearly despised.

"This is Mr Hallward, the artist. A painter, my dear."

The woman transferred her haughty glance to Basil, and began to look him up and down.

"Why he wish to see my Franco?"

Basil smiled, inclined his head and, indicating the children, said: "Your daughters, madam?"

In response the woman merely drew the two girls closer in to her skirts. Just then the door opened and Franco Torrigiano emerged. He wore nothing but trousers held up by braces and a singlet and he was drying his hair with a cloth.

It was this vision of him that impressed me more than his rather stilted incarnation as Hercules. He was like some superb animal, serenely unconscious of his beauty: innocent even. He looked at us with mild curiosity and made Basil a little bow. His wife approached him and, in a harsh whisper, addressed him rapidly in their native tongue. Torrigiano listened, his head cocked to one side serenely taking in her agitated diatribe. Then, laying one hand on her shoulder and the other on the head of one of his daughters, he seemed to stem the tide of her discourse. Having done so he beckoned to Basil.

"Signor, we talk?"

Basil nodded and the pair of them walked up the corridor away from us while we remained behind. His wife looked at me and said: "You a painter also?"

I nodded, surprised at her perspicacity. She seemed to divine my thoughts, for she gave a little contemptuous nod in the direction of my right hand on which I noticed there were still traces of the chrome yellow I had been using. For a moment her teeth were bared in a mocking smile and she almost laughed. Then one of her daughters asked her a question in Italian and she busied herself with her offspring. It was as if I no longer existed.

When Basil and Torrigiano returned from their *tête-à-tête* they shook hands formally and Basil, with the curtest possible nod to the Chairman and a little gesture to me that I should follow, took his leave. When we were in the cab going West I asked if he and the Italian had come to an agreement.

"He will come to me in the mornings to model for me, and has named his price," said Basil. He gave a short laugh. "He clearly knows his own value – or rather that witch of a wife does." After that he wrapped himself in silence till we were safely back in Chelsea.

I heard nothing from Basil for almost a fortnight. Finally, one afternoon, I decided to call on him. Knowing his moods, I was quite prepared to be told by his servant Latimer that he was "not at home"; however when I arrived I was shown into his studio almost immediately.

Basil greeted me warmly and expressed surprise that I had not called on him sooner. I had rarely seen him so animated; he seemed twenty years younger. I was reminded of the Basil I first knew when I came to his studio as an eager young acolyte.

Around the walls of his studio were displayed a multitude of drawings, some charcoal, some in sanguine chalk, and a few vivid oil sketches on canvas. They all depicted the same subject, and one that I recognised immediately: Franco Torrigiano "the Roman Hercules". Every one of his sketches pulsated with life. They looked as if they had been dashed off in an exultant frenzy, but their precision and perfect accuracy of proportion were astonishing. The sanguine drawings, mostly of Torrigiano's head, were sensitive and delicate without being in any way effete; the charcoal sketches of his torso and lower body were powerful without crudity, and in his oil studies he had shown the man entire: golden and godlike in form, but also utterly human. They were a wonder to behold.

My pleasure at seeing him so rejuvenated, so restored to his true artistic self, was slightly mitigated by the fact that he had another visitor. Reclining on the divan of Persian saddle bags in the corner of the studio and wreathed in the smoke of the Balkan cigarettes that he habitually smoked was a long lean man with a saturnine expression, his dark hair and beard just beginning to be flecked with grey. I had met him once or twice before at Basil's studio and at one of his exhibitions. I doubt however that he knew me by name, but I knew his: it was Lord Henry Wotton.

A friend of mine had once described him as "Mephistopheles in a frock coat." I do not subscribe to that kind of colourful language: I only knew that I was nothing to him and it was better that way. I had barely expressed my admiration for Basil's new work when Lord Henry broke in:

"My dear Basil, you have recovered your – I was going to say your youth, but that would have been to commit the sin of a *double entendre,* and I am a creature of paradox rather than puns. A paradox is a way of creating a new truth; a pun merely desecrates an old one. One should always strive to be original, and you have regained your originality by becoming a second Michelangelo. In you the *Renaissance* has been reborn. Ah, there I go again with a play upon words. It must be the effect of that dreadful Gilbert and Sullivan operetta which my wife insisted that I drag her to last night."

"But these are just sketches, Harry," said Basil. "They are only the beginning. I cannot yet say where they will lead, but they must lead somewhere."

"On the contrary, my dear Basil, you must lead and they will follow.

But tell me, where did you find this miraculous model? Is he a horny-handed son of toil whom you plucked blooming from a nearby midden, or is he some innocent tennis-playing creature from the Arcadian Vales of Croydon or Peckham?"

"Do you really think I would tell *you*, Harry?" A look passed between them which I could not fathom.

"Perhaps not. I will enquire no further. You artists who bare your souls in public are so intensely private: you like to think we know nothing about you when in fact we know nearly everything, and what we don't is not worth knowing. This new man of yours is a creature of myth. He may come from the gutter but he belongs among the stars – Orion the Hunter, the Great Bear, and the Weeping Pleiades. You must not bring him down to Earth, at least not *this* Earth. He was born to tell us mighty truths, or, better still, beautiful untruths. Keats alas was too young to know that truth is *not* beauty, nor beauty truth. Beauty is only beauty: that is why we reach for it; because it is beyond our grasp."

"Harry, you know, sometimes I think you almost tell the truth yourself."

"Oh, I hope not. That would put me quite beyond the pale in society. The Duchess of Berwick's doors would be closed to me for ever."

"The Duchess of Berwick is neither here nor there."

"Quite possibly, my dear Basil, but she does have a house in Belgrave Square which most people agree is better than either here *or* there. Well, since you are unable or unwilling to satisfy my curiosity, I must go and *un*satisfy someone else's. I have an important engagement to miss on the other side of town and I must not be too late." He rose and without so much as a nod in my direction went over to Basil and taking both his hands said: "Basil, whatever has happened between us in the past, I am sincerely glad that you have rediscovered your genius. *Au revoir.*"

After he had gone I said: "Lord Henry was right. You have found something new."

"I do not need him to tell me that, Martin. Lord Henry is not really a bad man, just a bad influence. That sounds like one of his idiotic paradoxes, but it happens to be true. As a matter of fact I have started on something which may be... You will know why I couldn't show it to Lord Henry. You can't show unfinished work to someone who is not an artist, however much of a connoisseur they may be. They will never understand that it is a journey not an arrival, and that the destination has not quite been decided upon."

He went to a portfolio stand and drew out an octavo sheet of paper.

On it he had created a composition in watercolour. It was meticulous and exquisite like all his best work and would have looked to the untutored eye completely finished, except that he had "squared off" the painting in pencil so as to transfer the design to a large canvas.

It showed a scene in most particulars identical to the *Love and Death* which I describe as having been shown at the Royal Academy, but there were a few significant differences.

In the first place Love was not chained to Death. He stood where he did at the Academy and looked towards Death. But Death, robed and cowled was seated at a greater distance from Love than subsequently, among some rocks in the middle distance. Beside him on the rocks was placed an hourglass whose sands were only just beginning to trickle into its lower chamber. The expression on the face of Love had been left blank. Even at this inchoate stage, the composition and its concept struck me as immensely potent. I told Basil that he had the beginnings of a masterpiece on his hands. Basil gave me a wistful look as if he took little pleasure in my endorsement.

"I am not sure I am very lucky in my masterpieces," he murmured. He had returned to his former remoteness, but we parted on good terms.

As Latimer was showing me out of the front door I glanced across the street. There standing with her back to the park railings opposite was a woman wrapped against the rain in a red shawl. She was looking fixedly in the direction of Basil's house, but her eyes registered no recognition or interest when she saw me. I glanced back at Latimer who gave a grimace of disgust and re-entered the house slamming the door behind him. I knew those heavily handsome features, those burning Southern eyes; they belonged to Signora Torrigiano. Her presence excited a momentary curiosity, no more; I had my own griefs and concerns to attend to.

I next saw Basil about a month later at the Private View of the Summer Exhibition at the Royal Academy. Unlike Basil I was not, of course, an Academician but I happened to have had a work accepted that year. (Entitled *The Blessed Damozel*, it fell victim to philanthropy, having been bought by a prominent soap manufacturer who put it on display in his art gallery for the edification of the workers who toiled at his toiletries.)

I encountered Basil in Gallery III where the prime canvases of the Summer Exhibition are usually displayed. It was where *Love and Death* had been hung, flanked on one side by a Millais, on the other by a Leighton, and outshining them both. He was walking arm in arm with a man who might have been described as well dressed had the colour of his necktie not been such a virulent shade of red. It was some while before I identified his companion as Signor Torrigiano. Basil's expression was serene and happy but Torrigiano, for all his finery, looked extremely ill at ease. They paused before *Love and Death* where an admiring crowd had already gathered.

I saw a number of fashionable men and women approach Basil to express their appreciation. I drew closer to observe, though I could not hear what was said above the general murmur of the hall. The ladies and gentlemen addressed Basil with eager deference, and he responded by introducing his companion. A few awkward words were exchanged between Torrigiano and the ladies and gentlemen who smiled faintly, then drifted away. Their disdain for the Italian was undisguised. This scene was repeated, almost identically, several times. Both Basil and his model embarrassed, and finally infuriated by these encounters, moved away from their painting in my direction.

I could not pretend I had not seen them so I came forward to greet them. Basil seemed relieved.

I said rather formally: "I congratulate both you Basil and you Signor Torrigiano on *Love and Death*. It is unquestionably the star of the show."

Torrigiano looked at Basil enquiringly.

"This is Martin Isaacs, the painter," said Basil. "And my friend. You will remember, Franco, he came with me to the Shoreditch Empire that night."

Torrigiano smiled warmly and took my hand in both of his. Despite the gentleness of his handshake I was conscious of the immense strength behind it.

Basil said: "Franco and I cannot stand another minute of this fashionable bear-pit. We are going to the Café Royal. Would you care to join us, Martin?"

I said I would be glad to. As we descended the steps into the courtyard of Burlington House, Torrigiano suddenly stopped dead. I followed his gaze and saw across the courtyard not far from the entrance to the Society of Antiquaries, a large woman in a red shawl. Her dark eyes were fixed on us.

Torrigiano looked at Basil sheepishly. "You excuse me, Basil?" Basil sighed and nodded. Then to me. "You excuse, signor?" I bowed; he bowed back, then hurried towards his wife. Basil turned to me: "The Café Royal?"

I knew at once that any discussion of events that had just occurred was out of bounds, but Basil needed company. He began to talk rapidly as we turned into Piccadilly and made our way towards Regent Street and The Café Royal.

"Do you know someone has already bought *Love and Death*? I deliberately put an absurdly high price on it so that nobody would buy it, but they have. Now I am in a quandary."

"You can always paint another."

"Can I? Can I? Perhaps Rubens could, or even Raphael, but to me a painting is not simply a piece of work, it is an event. It happens and is gone and a fragment of yourself goes with it. Sometimes too much."

"But haven't the wise men down the ages taught that what you give of yourself is always restored to you in some way."

"I used to believe that. Come, we shall drink to my success. I have become a rich man thanks to *Love and Death*."

We entered the gilded halls of The Café Royal which, for all the lavish taste of its decoration, reminded me irresistibly of the Empire Shoreditch. A waiter who evidently knew Basil bowed obsequiously and was ushering us to a table when my friend stiffened.

"I am afraid, my dear Martin," he said in a frozen voice, "that I have suddenly remembered an urgent appointment. Will you forgive me? Another time, I promise you." And with that, he darted out of The Café Royal, leaving me and the waiter staring at each other in bewilderment.

He had seen someone, or something, of that I am sure. I scanned the room and my eyes lighted on a group of young fashionably dressed men seated at a table where, I noticed, several bottles of champagne had been consumed. It was these gentlemen, I am sure, who had caught Basil's eye. The men looked to be mostly in their early twenties, but there was one, scarcely older than they, but somehow more poised and mature, to whom they deferred. He was strikingly, magnetically handsome with that male beauty which, though in reality transient, seems ageless because you see it in the faces of Greek Gods and quattrocento Christs, and in every land and culture where a male divinity is worshipped. I was sure I had seen him before, but could not place him. He said something at which all the others laughed and, as they paid homage to his witticism, he looked up wearily. He saw me staring at him across the room, and something about the glance he returned made me leave the Café as precipitately as Basil had done. It was not so much the hatred as the emptiness in those eyes that pierced me.

The following day I received a note of abject apology from Basil together with several boxes of blooms from the most expensive florist in London, a less than appropriate peace offering for a struggling and starving artist. Basil's note also stated that he would be heavily occupied until the Summer Exhibition was over, a clear indication that a visit would not be welcomed. My own irritation with him made me content to take the hint.

It was three days after the close of the exhibition when I received an urgent telegram from Basil to call on him at once. I went without hesitation. When I arrived at his door, his servant Latimer showed me in and ushered me through to the studio without a word.

"Ah, there you are," said Basil, as if I were late for an appointment, then, turning to Latimer – "You may go now and finish packing my things."

Basil was distracted and hollow eyed. I had never seen him so restless and out of sorts. He beckoned me: "Come," he said. "Come to the window. Look!"

Across the street in the very same position that I had seen her before and wearing her red shawl was Signora Torrigiano.

"Sometimes she stands there for hours on end staring at this window," said Basil. "Sometimes she goes away for a few days and I imagine I am rid of her, but she always returns. It has become unbearable."

"What does she want?"

"I have gone over and spoken to her many times, but Maddalena – that is her name – always says the same thing. Her husband cannot come. He is sick. I have made him sick. He is wasting away and it is I who have destroyed him. She says I have taken his vital spirit and put it in the painting, and that I must either give her the painting or the money which bought it. Only that can restore her husband. It is madness. I have tried reasoning with her, but she holds to her primitive peasant superstition for dear life. What can I do? I am leaving tonight for Paris by the midnight train. I can work there on a painting I have in my head, a great work, I believe. If I succeed I shall return and all will be well. If I fail I shall send word to my servant Latimer and he will give you a letter from me. You are to obey the instructions in that letter. It is nothing criminal, but it may be distasteful to you. You are the only person I can trust. Will you do this for me?"

I could do nothing else but agree. I asked if he had yet delivered *Love and Death* to its buyer.

"I am loath to let it go," he said. "I cannot help feeling that its perfection is yet to come."

"Perfection in art is a Chimera."

"Perhaps, but it is one we must still cultivate. Would you like to see it?"

He drew aside a dust sheet which had been draped over the canvas. I gazed once more in wonder at Basil's work. It was a marvel still, even more marvellous to look at out of its frame and the heavy, formal surroundings of the Academy, yet something troubled me. The painting had been subtly altered. The figure of Love was as before, but Death had moved. It was no longer, as at the Academy, in a crouched position on the ground; it had turned and was about to rise up and, if I was not mistaken, advance with menace on Love. I glanced at Basil enquiringly, but his look was far away and I dared not suggest something which may only have been my imagination. Soon he was covering the canvas again as if only a brief exposure to it were tolerable.

He went to the window once more and looked out. Maddalena had gone, and for a brief while he became his old self again. We talked of harmless inconsequential things. He praised my *Blessed Damozel* and congratulated me on the soap magnate. I am glad that my last memory of him was of laughter. We embraced warmly at parting and I never saw him again.

Personal concerns and ambitions drove him from my mind until I read in the papers of his disappearance. Then I felt paralysed: what was I to do? I would have liked to join in the search for him but I had no resources with which to do so. It was only when I was asked by Sir Joseph to find *Love and Death* that I could address the issue. I felt I should do my best to resolve the mystery both for Sir Joseph and Basil.

Sir Joseph's influence enabled me to have access to the police files on the case which were meagre enough in all conscience. Latimer had been interviewed, as he had first reported the possible disappearance when Basil had failed to wire him from Paris as he had promised to. But he gave the barest of details. Having despatched his principal luggage to Waterloo Station to await collection Latimer had seen Basil off in a handsome at about a quarter to nine. Basil, wearing an ulster cape and carrying a Gladstone bag, was evidently planning to go somewhere before boarding his train, but Latimer had not heard the address he had given to the driver. It had been a foggy night and, despite appeals by the police, no cab driver came forward to say where Basil had gone. He had not arrived at Waterloo to board the midnight train.

That, to all intents and purposes, was the sum total of information to be gleaned from the police enquiry, but I was sure that Latimer had more information to give. He must, after all, still be in possession of the letter that Basil had written to me. But Latimer had also disappeared from the scene, leaving no forwarding address. After several unsuccessful attempts to find him, I finally put a notice in the personal column of *The Times*, sensing perhaps that the man's venal instincts might be appealed to.

If Mr Latimer, formerly servant to Mr Basil Hallward R.A will contact this box number he will hear something to his advantage.

Within a few days I had a response. Latimer was working at a gentleman's club in Piccadilly, a somewhat disreputable establishment by all accounts. Thither I went to interview him.

I had perhaps given a vague suggestion in our brief exchange of letters that a legacy from the (presumed) late Mr Hallward was a possibility, so it was a disappointment to Mr Latimer when he was apprised of my real mission. However, having mentioned that he would be generously rewarded by Sir Joseph if any useful information was forthcoming he became more communicative, if to little effect. He vouchsafed me only one item of possible interest.

One night, a few days after Basil Hallward had been reported missing, his house had been broken into. Latimer was on the premises and could give no satisfactory explanation as to why he had not heard the event and raised the alarm sooner. However, the way he consumed tumblers of gin and water in my presence and at my expense may go some way to solve the mystery. The police were alerted the following morning, but nothing of value would appear to have been removed. It was only when Sir Joseph's man had called round to collect *Love and Death* that Latimer noticed that it was missing from the studio. To forestall further embarrassing enquiries, and because he was receiving no payment for his caretaking activities at Basil's house, he left it to find gainful employment elsewhere.

When I asked Latimer who could have taken *Love and Death* he opined that "them *Eye-Talians* was at the bottom of it all," and that he had seen "the woman" – Maddalena – lurking about in the street on several occasions after Basil had gone.

Finally, I asked Latimer about the letter that had been left for me. At this Latimer looked rather shame-faced. He said that he remembered that there had been a letter but could not say whether it was still in his possession or not. When I mentioned that a sum of money would be available to him on its discovery, he said he would endeavour to find it. I gave him my card and left.

It was clear to me that my next task was to find the Torrigianos. I will not describe the long and tedious process by which I finally tracked them down to a miserable room in a Limehouse tenement. The stairs I climbed to get to them were treacherous and threatened to give way under me at every step; the bare brick walls were slicked with damp. The winter was on us and a moist chilliness seeped from every pore of the building.

I stopped on the landing in front of their door which, before I could knock, was opened by Maddalena. She had aged since I last saw her, she had become gaunt and haggard, and her clothes were near to rags.

"You!" she said. "Mr Painter. You have money?"

I nodded and she let me in. As I took in the scene I began to feel ashamed at my pretensions to poverty, for this was abject, on a totally different scale to my own. The room was virtually bare but for a few rickety sticks of furniture. Maddalena's two daughters sat silent and hollow-eyed at a table. They were gnawing on pieces of bread cut from a quartern loaf which they eyed jealously. There was a window half covered with a piece of sacking and, leaning against one wall was what looked like a canvas shrouded in a sheet.

Maddalena followed my glance scornfully. "So, you come for that?"

I nodded.

"You care nothing that it make him dying?" She pointed to a corner of the room around which a rough screen of blankets had been erected. The next moment she had torn down the blankets to reveal a squalid pallet on which lay the barely living body of Franco Torrigiano. I knew him – just – from the lank, bronze curls, now silvered, that clung to his forehead. He was the colour of a bleached bone and his once magnificent frame was almost skeletal. The eyes, deeply sunk, stared vacantly at the ceiling, and his hands fumbled convulsively with the threadbare blanket that covered him.

"Why Maestro Hallward not come?" Maddalena asked. "Why he send *you*, Mr Nothing Painter?"

"Don't you know? Hallward has gone. Vanished. He cannot be found."

Maddalena laughed harshly: "So! The painting kill him too! *Bene!*"

"What are you talking about? What nonsense is this?"

"You think nonsense! I show you! I show you what nonsense!" She darted over to the other side of the room and with a flourish that would have done justice to a fairground barker tore away the sheet to reveal *Love and Death*.

I was struck dumb. The figure of Death now dominated the entire painting, obliterating the landscape with the tattered grey folds of its shroud. Only a few golden splinters of the setting sun could be seen through the mouldering cerements of Death which now loomed over Love and seemed about to engulf him. The thing's head was still half shadowed by a cowl – mercifully! – but what could be seen was fixed into a mirthless rictus of triumph. Love still maintained the same pose as before, but the expression on his face had subtly changed. The look of agonised resignation had been replaced by one of blank despair. *Eloi! Eloi! Lama Sabachthani!*

"You see?" said Maddalena, almost exultantly. "It has taken his body and his soul! It is cursed!" Suddenly she picked up a knife from the table and hurled herself at it. Before I could restrain her she had carved a great ragged rent across the canvas. She was lifting the knife to strike again when a great howl of agony came from the bed in the corner. At once she dropped the knife and ran to her husband. Her two daughters looked on steadily, silently, with clear, haunted eyes.

Maddalena cradled her husband in her arms muttering soothing noises, then she looked up at me fiercely.

"Go! Take it. And be damned to Hell with you!"

While she continued to minister to her sick husband I put as much money as I could spare on the table and took the canvas. Then I left that wretched place of misery and wandered the wet streets with *Love and Death* until I found a cab which conveyed both of us to Sir Joseph Behrens' house in Upper Brook Street. Sir Joseph was in the country, but his butler Lane who knew of me and my commission, received the painting for him.

Two days later a rather grimy envelope was dropped through my letter box. Inside it was a cleaner envelope with my name and address written on it in Basil's familiar Italic hand. This envelope had been opened, doubtless to extract the bank notes it had once contained: a conjecture, but I knew Latimer of old. The letter within was intact.

My dear Martin,

If you receive this letter it will mean that I have not succeeded in my endeavour in Paris and have gone beyond all assistance. It would take too long to recount all the incidents that have brought me to this, but I must, with some reluctance, give you my conclusions.

Since my earliest years I have been in pursuit of one thing and one thing only: Beauty. It was the lodestar of my life and all things were subordinate to it. Not that I did not value what Keats has sublimely called "the holiness of the heart's affections", but I believed that "all these things would be added unto me" if only I truly and purely pursued my ideal. Twice I believed I had found that fulfilment; twice I was betrayed. I now know that beauty is only a mask, and that the corruption it covers is the reality. I know that Love does not endure, that it is threatened and ultimately conquered by Death; I know that if we pursue Beauty, we pursue not a noble ideal but a phantom that leads us ultimately to the Gates of Hell. That is why if you receive this letter it means I have decided that the canvas entitled Love and Death *is to be destroyed and that you must do this thing for me. I once told you that I was unlucky in my masterpieces. This was far from being an exaggeration. I have been destroyed by my masterpieces; worse still, I have destroyed others by them and this must stop.*

My aim in Paris will have been one last attempt to create a work of pure beauty that has no taint of corruption in it. Your receipt of this letter is proof that I have not succeeded.

I have no claim over you except that of friendship and these few notes for your pains. You have not been my only or my dearest friend, but you have been the only one who has never betrayed me; do not do so now,

Yours with affection,
Basil

That day in the post I also received a cheque from Sir Joseph for thirty guineas, as full and final payment for my work in finding *Love and Death*. To me at that moment it might as well have been thirty pieces of silver. I had returned his work of art, but tainted and mutilated. I had no further answers to offer, only a deeper and more impenetrable mystery. Unwittingly I had also betrayed my friend Basil Hallward.

Some weeks later, at his request, I paid a call on Sir Joseph Behrens. I was shown into his drawing room and, to my relief and surprise, he greeted me warmly. He was standing by the window which was open and looked down upon the garden. A light summer wind that was stirring among the trees brought into the room the heavy scent of lilac, and the more delicate perfume of the pink-flowering thorn.

"My dear Martin," said Sir Joseph, addressing me for the first time with unexpected familiarity, "I am most grateful for your efforts on my behalf. I have had the canvas restored, but I will not have it on show. I have placed it in an attic room and covered it with the Burne-Jones tapestry I no longer like, depicting *The Expulsion from Paradise*. The room will be locked, but I may sometimes visit it. *Love and Death* is too great to be destroyed and too terrible to be displayed." Sir Joseph stared out of the window for a moment, lost in thought, then he said: "You and I, Martin, must be content with our own mediocrity. It is what keeps us alive."

The silence that followed oppressed us both.

"But surely," I said at last, "Love *is* stronger than Death?"

"We must believe so, Martin, even when it appears to be untrue."

IN THE LIGHT OF ST IVES

Ray Cluley

As Emily walks the darkness, flashing her torchlight into each vacant room, she realises that, yes, a house can be haunted. Not just the old, neglected buildings, the ones with overgrown gardens and broken windows, but also neat, well-maintained, detached holiday homes like this one. She'd never given it much thought before. Now, sneaking around in the dark, she can't *stop* thinking about it. She feels like a child again, a child on a dare, though she's gone further than creep up to touch the front door: she's let herself inside. Not so much a child on a dare, then, but a burglar, making her way around the house by torchlight, treading carefully as if the neighbours are right in the next room. Not that she'll take anything, she's just looking. And not that she'd broken in. Not technically. The door was already broken.

In the living room, cast over the sofa, is the tatty throw her sister has owned since university. A patchwork of primary colours stitched with felt animals, bright silhouettes of camels, elephants, lizards. On the coffee table, a scattering of open books and the candle holder Claire made years ago when sculpture was her thing. Lumpy lines of dribbled wax have hardened, running down to smooth puddles set as sickly yellow circles. On the walls, prints Claire has possessed since her teens. The Lady of Shalott drifting away from the quiet Nighthawks diner towards Dali's long-legged beasts in the desert. Familiar favourites. There are newer pictures too, of course, just as there are ornaments and cushions and hanging displays Emily hasn't seen before, but the room is certainly Claire's. She can feel her presence as if she'd only left moments ago, a trace of her left lingering like perfume.

From the living room, into the kitchen. Again, signs of Claire in a brass plate clock, a comedy coffee mug, an array of crystals arranged at the window. By day the crystals would probably catch and cast the light around in bright sparkles but now the window is a large rectangle of night's darkness. A sweep of the torch shows Emily her own reflection there, ghostlike itself in the room, a non-presence quickly gone as she directs the beam at other things. A row of empty wine bottles by the recycling, but nothing excessive. An ashtray that needs emptying but isn't overflowing. Dishes waiting to be washed.

"At least you're eating properly," Emily says to what there is of Claire in the room. "That's good."

A brief gust of wind rattles the window in its frame. Emily can hear the faint hush of the sea below as it sweeps ashore, retreats, and repeats the process. There's no traffic noise. She doubts there's much even at a more conventional hour. And none of the drunken ruckus Emily associates with two o'clock in the morning, either. Little wonder Claire liked it here. Nevermind the wonderful light, the peace and quiet must've been a tremendously welcome relief. Artists need that as much as light, don't they?

Emily's phone buzzes in her pocket, startling her in the quiet she'd been appreciating. She'd left her bag at the hotel but the phone went everywhere with her, even late night trespassing.

It's a message from Tom. U still awake?

She tucks the torch into her armpit and thumbs back a reply. Yeah, went to Claire's.

How is it?

Haunted, she wants to say, but types: It's fine. After a moment's thought she adds: It's nice.

She had texted Tom earlier, unable to sleep. She misses him and their comfortable bed and their comfortable life, even the humdrum noise of the city. He'd been awake as well, and after some messages back and forth about Claire they'd exchanged a few dirty texts but Emily couldn't focus and so they'd said their goodnights again. And now here she is, sneaking around Claire's place at two in the morning and wondering where it all went wrong for her little sister.

Another buzz: Badly damaged?

Nothing so far, she taps back, but most of the damage is upstairs I think. I can smell the petrol though.

There's been a tinge of it in the air since she'd first come in but now, heading away from the kitchen towards the conservatory extension, the smell has become more potent. Sharp, but not unpleasant. Until you consider why it's there.

The conservatory was one of the reasons Claire had taken the house in the first place. The conservatory and the bedroom upstairs, because they both caught so much of the famous St Ives light. "The house floods with it," Claire had written in one of her letters (never a text or even an email, oh no, Claire didn't do technology), "and those two rooms become bright suntraps for endless hours. I should have moved here years ago."

Years ago you weren't interested in painting. It was acting, or poetry, or learning some faraway foreign language. Or all of the above, all at the same time.

Her phone buzzes and flashes to show Tom asking, Is it safe?

Yes, don't worry.

She tells him she loves him and sends a kiss as well. Sincere, but also an indication she's done texting for now. Tom understands. He loves her too, kiss kiss.

Emily opens the door onto the conservatory and the overpowering smell of petrol wafts into the kitchen. The windows had been left open in here, just the small ones at the top of each pane, but a lot of the smell has still been contained. It'll be quite a while before it goes away, Emily thinks, though she's no expert. She covers her nose and mouth with one hand and steps inside.

A folding table has been collapsed and it leans against one of the walls, draped with a paint-stained sheet that doesn't quite cover it. Rows of tabletop flowerbeds have been covered with boards to make temporary shelves for pots and jars and canvases. The wood has absorbed much of the petrol. They'll probably need replacing, Emily thinks, wondering if they're still dangerously flammable – the conservatory no doubt gets very warm in the day. The floor is stone, but right now it looks as though the beach has invaded, a carpet of sand covering most of the slabs. Soaking up petrol puddles, she supposes.

This was where Claire had been seen by the neighbours, "acting peculiar". Although the house is detached it still presses close to the neighbouring properties. Mr or Mrs Neighbour had already called for help by then. They were also the ones to call the fire service, which was about as much as Emily had been told over the phone.

She looks at a few of the canvases to see if any can be saved but each is a mess of solvent-washed colours running in ruined lines. Unless they're *meant* to look that way. One looks like it had been a person once, maybe two figures entwined and blurring together, but now it twists and melts, slipping down the canvas in streaks of yellow and green.

"Claire, honey," Emily says to the empty room. "What happened?"

Emily had arrived in St Ives in the late afternoon, the light bright but beginning to fade. Her first impression was that it was prettier than many seaside towns but she wasn't as impressed by its beauty as others had been over the years. She suspected her reason for being there had sullied the view. Plus her journey down had been an ordeal. Four beaches and an oceanic climate made St Ives a very popular town in the summer and it seemed all of its visitors were using the same roads as Emily to get there. Finding a place to stay had been difficult, too. Using Claire's house was out of the question and all of the quaint places in St Ives were fully booked, so after a drive of nearly seven hours, most of that on the M4, Emily checked into a bland chain hotel just off the A30. She stayed long enough to dump her bag and splash her face then headed into town, wanting to see the place that had drawn Claire so many miles from home.

She walked the narrow streets, all shops and galleries, and then each of the beaches where St Ives was dazzling blue sky, bright sands, and a sparkling clean green sea. Cornwall, almost entirely surrounded by coastline, belonged more to the sea than it did the rest of the country. Britain's tentative foot dipping its toe towards the North Atlantic. Perhaps *that* was what had had drawn Claire, ever the rolling stone. The idea of escape. Breaking free from whatever binds you. Maybe that was what she liked about painting.

Emily had arrived late but still she saw many artists at work around the town. St Ives was an international cultural centre and even had its own Tate but she wouldn't have time to visit. It would have seemed too much like a holiday anyway if she'd done that, though she did treat herself to fish and chips. She ate her early dinner leaning against the rails at the lifeboat slipway, paper warm in her hands as she looked at the lighthouse on the end of Smeaton's Pier. She wondered if it was a working lighthouse or simply one of history's leftovers. Claire would know. She'd have looked it up in the local library, visited the museum, all of that. She'd have swum in the sea and strolled the beaches and walked each and every one of the coastal paths by now, storing the views away to paint later in some abstract fashion of hers, all of which was very well, good for her, until six months or so later when she gave it all up to move somewhere new, *do* something new, follow her latest artistic passion.

Fifteen. Emily had counted *fifteen* artists on her walk around town, sketching in pads or sitting at easels near or on the beach. They recreated that beach and the bay and the boats, everything, over and over again with sweeping strokes of their pastels or brushes, sketching bright lines or spreading vibrant water colours. It was a pretty place, of course it was, but so was all of Cornwall, wasn't it? Weren't most coastal places? She didn't understand why Claire needed to come all this way, to this particular town. But then when was the last time she'd really understood her little sister?

One time, when they were children, they had been playing on one of the broken swings in the park. The rubber seat had been split, both halves dangling from the chains, so they'd pretended to be lady-Tarzans, jungle-calling to and fro. Claire, though, at the highest point of one of her swings, decided to let go. For a moment she had been a beautiful gliding figure, hair streaming, body straight, and then she'd landed with a crack that broke her leg. Later, after the cast had been put on, Emily had asked why she'd done it. Why she'd let go. Claire had shrugged and said, "Seemed like a good idea at the time." Their parents had blamed Emily because Emily was the oldest and was supposed to look after her little sister. Claire had got away with a lot back then. Got a lot of attention, too, and with a cast on her leg she'd got even more. Emily hated that cast more than Claire did.

There were too many chips for Emily to finish so she wrapped what was left and pushed the paper deep into a nearby bin so the gulls couldn't get at them. Claire would have fed the birds, probably. Would have ignored the sign that urged otherwise and thrown chips at her feet, laughing at the feathered chaos.

With the smell of the sea in her hair and clothes, the sharp tang of salt and vinegar on her lips and fingers, Emily checked her watch and saw there was still an hour to go before visiting hours. She spent all of it waiting on the pier as a woman nearby sketched seagulls spiralling the lighthouse opposite. The light was bright on the glass. The birds looked like wind-blown ash rising from a high fire.

If the house is haunted it's not just by Claire. Her presence is everywhere, but there are also traces of the owners, or perhaps previous tenants. The kitchen units, for example, would never have been Claire's choice and no amount of handle-hung bells or crystals or animal chimes was about to change that. The wallpaper coming up the stairs is definitely not Claire either, though a large picture of scattered flowers certainly has a Claire-esque feel to it. Maybe because she's strung fairy lights around the frame. There are photographs too, but they're local landscapes and too generic to be anything Claire might have taken or bought herself. A beached boat, leaning in the sand. The smashed-splash of waves against weed-strewn rocks. The lighthouse on the pier, a stone perch for seagulls. 'Holiday birds' Claire used to call them. Family holidays had often been to the seaside because Claire loved the sea and the sand and the holiday birds.

Seems she can even haunt the things that aren't hers.

Emily's torchlight bounces back from a mirror on the small landing where the stairs turn right. Again she's a ghostly figure, face shadowed, but this time it startles her because there, in the gloomy night glass, someone stands behind her. She turns, torch in both hands slashing a beam of light through the darkness. A human lighthouse sweeping the monsters away. But there's nothing behind her. Only the stairs back down.

"Of course."

At the top of the stairs is a short hallway with three doors. Or rather two, and a doorway where one used to be. The smell of smoke is much stronger here. The upstairs of the house wears the odour like a stain, haunted by the fire that had almost consumed it.

She opens the first door onto what was supposed to be a spare room, though from the look of the bed sheets and the clothes strewn everywhere (Claire had always been more 'floordrobe' than wardrobe) it's being used as the main bedroom. It's positioned at the front of the house whereas the main bedroom at the back faces the wonderful sea views and all that magical St Ives light. Claire would be using that one as a studio.

Emily isn't sure what she's looking for, only that she'll know it when she sees it. She draws the curtains closed so she can risk the main light but nothing happens when she flicks the switch. She directs her torch at the ceiling. There's a colourful glass bead lampshade, very Claire, but the bulb has been removed.

On the wall are a couple of prints. One of them Emily knows well because Claire's owned it since childhood. Two sisters holding each other in a picture for the poem *Goblin Market*. There are canvases, too, stacks of them, all piled against a chest of drawers. Emily might not really understand art, but she usually recognised her sister's style. Claire tended to use stark, striking colours, rendering objects and scenery down to the most simple of shapes. Even people would be little more than smears of fleshy colour, expressionless and yet somehow expressive. There are few like that here, though. One of them shows a crowd of shapes, upright yellow-flesh tones seeming to emerge from a background of black, one figure standing separate, arms to the sky. Another canvas is aswirl with blacks and greens and yellows, a universe in birth or some bleak horrific whirlpool, and Emily wonders why Claire needs the famous light of St Ives so much if she's only going to paint the dark.

But there are others. Brighter, more colourful. Hard to make out in the torchlight though, unless they really are just panels of colour. Yellow again, and green. Some are bisected, half and half, while others use the entire canvas to transition gradually from one colour to the other. Some are entirely green, dark shades shifting into pale, others are shining gold fading to the lightest tones of something sepia.

Claire trying something new. For a change.

And there she is now, smiling from the bedside table. Beaded necklaces have been draped over one corner of the photo frame but Emily can see enough of the picture to recognise it. Both of them as children, clutched together in a smiling hug at some beach or another. Emily's struck by how fierce their embrace seems, bodies pulled tight, one to the other, faces touching as they grin at the camera. Claire grips Emily with both arms. Emily returns the hug with one, her other arm up so she can shield her face from sunlight making her squint.

"Looking good, sis," Emily tells the picture.

This time it's true.

Emily had greeted her sister the usual way at the hospital but the truth was Claire didn't look good at all. She was only in for observation now that her burns had been treated but to Emily she looked seriously ill. Her long blonde hair, usually so beautifully cared for, was lank and oily. Her skin was sallow. Shadows around her eyes spoke of little sleep. There was a black crust at the corners of her eyes.

"Looking good? Think you might need glasses, Em." Her voice was husky.

Emily filled a cup with water from a nearby jug but Claire shook her head. "Hug first."

Emily hooked one arm around her sister and held the water away to avoid a spill while Claire squeezed her briefly with both arms. She took the drink with, "Don't suppose you have anything stronger?"

Emily smiled. "Drank it all on the drive down."

"Selfish. How about a cigarette?"

"Not allowed to give you anything flammable."

Claire coughed up some of the water when she laughed. She wiped her mouth and said, "Bitch."

Emily glanced around the room but no one seemed offended. Two old women sat up in bed, one reading, the other watching a soundless TV.

"I saw your new friend outside," Emily said. She was referring to the policeman sitting in the corridor. "Seriously, Claire-bear, what the hell?"

Claire shrugged. Emily thought of the time when they were children at the park. Claire flying, Claire landing, a good idea at the time.

Claire coughed again, this time without humour. "Smoke inhalation's a bitch, too."

Ray Cluley

"Gives you a sexy voice," Emily said. "You could do one of those call-in things. Phone sex."

"Yeah, baby."

"Yeah, like that."

Emily sat in a bedside chair but found she was too low and too far away so she stood again and took her sister's hand. They both stared at their hands instead of each other. One of Claire's wrists was bandaged, wrapping her arm as far as her elbow. The other was wrapped in something like cling film, the skin bright pink beneath. Claire picked at an exposed fingertip and Emily was horrified to see tiny flakes of black stripped away. Paint, she realised. Not skin, not fingernail. Paint.

"You're lucky to be alive."

"Yeah. I've always thought that."

"Seriously. You're lucky all you got was those splashes on your arms."

"I know."

"What happened?"

That shrug again.

"Your neighbours said you -"

"They're going to commit me," Claire said.

"Hey, no. They can't. Not just like that."

Claire squeezed Emily's hand and said, "They probably *should* commit me."

"Come on," Emily said, "Who hasn't tried to burn down a house?"

Claire tried to smile.

"We've all done it," Emily said, smiling back.

The smile Claire had struggled with dropped away, replaced by sudden tears. "All done it," she repeated.

Before Emily could ask what was wrong, Claire said, "Anyway, it wasn't the house. It was the stupid paintings."

"The paintings? *Your* paintings?"

Claire nodded and wiped her eyes, smudging lines of black from each corner. Soot, Emily supposed. "They couldn't have been *that* bad," she said.

"The light was wrong."

"Okay."

"I tried to fix it."

"Hmm. Didn't exactly think that through."

Claire was crying again. Maybe she hadn't quite stopped.

"Hey, honey, no." Emily stroked her sister's upper arm and shoulder. When Claire leaned to Emily's body she stroked her hair and said quiet things to calm her until, "You've got paint in your hair," drew a muffled response from Claire.

"What was that?"

Claire leaned away and wiped her eyes. "Naples yellow?" she said. "Or misty grey green?"

"I don't -"

"*Fucking yellow or green?*"

Emily was quick to try hushing her. The other patients were looking over and Emily tried to smile them away.

"They seep into *every*thing, Em, *everything*. Seeping colours. Fucking *seeping* colours, *everywhere!*"

"Claire -"

Claire began clawing at the coverings on her arms and a bandage around her chest. "Look!"

By this time a nurse was in the room, either alerted by Claire's outburst or summoned by one of the others. He hurried to Claire, taking Emily's side of the bed. The police officer came in as well. Emily had to step back to free some space.

"Now Claire, we need you to stay calm, remember?" the nurse said. "We talked about this."

Emily watched as Claire fought against even gentle restraint. "What's wrong with her?"

The nurse only glanced at her, a brief turn of the head, before returning his attention to Claire.

"What's *wrong* with her?"

The policeman said, "Come on," and placed a hand on Emily's back to guide her from the room but she shrugged herself away. Claire was crying.

"They seep," she said. "They *seep*." She held eye contact with her sister. "Naples yellow," she said. "Misty grey green."

Another nurse had arrived and the police officer again urged Emily to wait outside, steering her more firmly this time.

"You'll see," Claire said. "Yellow and – Emily? *Emily?*"

"I'm here."

"Yellow and green. *Seeping*."

The main bedroom is black with smoke damage. Colourless. An absence in the house like a cavity. The carpet, where any remains, is the sodden black of trampled ash. Beneath, blackened boards. Emily wonders if it's safe. The walls wear permanent shadows. Blackened paper peels away from them in scabby curls or rises in blistered lumps yet to split. The window is a glassless opening taped over with a sheet of plastic that flutters at one corner where it's come unstuck. Whatever curtains or blinds had been there are gone. The ceiling is a single night-cloud of soot except where a light fitting droops in a malformed melted shape. The bed had been stood upon its side to allow more room for canvases and a vague shape of it remains, though the wooden slats are charred stumps and the mattress has slumped away from them, a collapsed heap little more than fused and twisted springs. Easels have been reduced to charcoal. Canvases are blackened square frames, if that. Emily's torch only seems to emphasise all the darkness in trying to sweep it away. The room is a black box, recording what had been done to it and speaking it back in a language of ash.

"Shit, Claire. Good job."

Where had Claire stood? Did she watch from the doorway as smoke fattened and rolled in the room? Did she stand in the middle of it all, flames licking the walls around her? Would there have been a blast, like in the movies, throwing her out into the hall? She'd been found unconscious but surely she would have had more serious injuries if that were the case. And besides, she'd only used a bottle of white spirit to get the fire started, only downstairs got the full petrol treatment. Emily imagines her sister standing with her arms open, proud of her latest work, fire burning, bathing her with its heat and colour. Flickering reds, oranges, yellows. Naples yellow? Emily imagines her glistening with sweat and reflected light, arms afire from where she'd splashed herself from the bottle, shadows dancing over her body as the flames flickered and licked everything it was to devour. What was that term for light and shadow in art? Chiaroscuro? Claire would have been a Chiaroscuro sculpture of flesh, watching her conflagration as it destroyed everything else she had made.

Emily bends and picks up an angle of wooden frame, intending… she doesn't know what. To tidy? She drops the charred wood and dusts the ash from her fingers, wiping them on her jeans.

Did all artists go mad? Was that like an occupational hazard, the price paid for creativity? Or was the crazy artist thing just a cliché?

Emily doesn't have a fucking clue.

"Oh, Claire-bear."

Her voice is little more than a sigh. Her sister had always been a bit crazy but not *crazy* crazy. Emily decides she'll talk to Tom about letting Claire stay with them again for a while. If the doctors say she can, and if the police allow it. Emily will take care of her little sister. It's what Mum and Dad would have wanted.

A sudden gust of wind tears against the plastic at the window, a loud abrupt sound and then a series of them, like a flock of startled birds flying away in haste. Emily makes her way carefully to where the window used to be. Patches of carpet squelch underfoot, still wet from the efforts of the fire brigade. She holds the thrumming plastic, stills it, and looks out from a torn corner at the night coast. She thinks of the sand down in the conservatory, spread across the stone floor, and the way the ashy carpet here puddles under her feet. The seaside of St Ives expanding into the house. She stands in a burnt dark sea over a petrol-soaked shore.

Emily returns to the spare room. She picks up the photo of her and Claire, wanting it for when she goes back to the hospital. Her fingers are black, and her palm. Soot, she realises. Ash. Not paint. But she's thinking of what the doctor told her when she wipes it off her hand.

"Self portrait," she says, shaking her head.

While the nurse calmed Claire, one of the doctors spoke to Emily in the visitor's room. This is the room where they break the bad news, she thought, and waited for it.

"As I said on the phone, her burns aren't *too* serious. She'll have scars, but we can do something about minimising those."

Emily nodded, waiting for him to get to it, and here it was, the awkward pause. The "but". And then...

"Considering the *reason* for her burns, and some of her *behaviour* since, I'm recommending a psychiatric assessment." He raised his hands against a protest that didn't come. "Just to see where we stand. To decide the next steps in whatever *treatment* your sister needs to get *better.*"

Emily nodded. This was okay. She could deal with this. "I understand she was quite distressed when she was admitted?"

Ah, the formal tones of her coping mechanisms.

The doctor seemed to relax a little hearing it, Emily noticed. The gulf between her and Claire widened just a little bit more, but in this situation it was useful.

"Well there were the burns. She would have been in quite some pain. And the duress of a house fire," the doctor explained. "But I believe there may have been some concerns *prior* to this. *Leading* to this, in fact."

"I see."

"When Claire was admitted to us, she... When she first came in, her... Some of the staff thought her burns were far worse than they really were. It was quite a shock to them. She was almost entirely black, you see."

"I don't understand."

He nodded.

"Before she came to us, before the fire, your sister painted herself."

"What, like a self portrait?"

"No. I mean, she'd painted her body. Black paint, all over herself from head to toe. Her skin, but not her clothes. Her hair as well."

Emily nodded. She didn't know what to say, so she nodded. Like it was a perfectly acceptable thing for the doctor to say. Painted herself? Must have been for a creative project or something, some new expressive art.

"When can I go back in to see her?"

"She's just being moved to a more private room. For her comfort."

"And so she won't disturb the other patients."

The doctor gave her a tight-lipped smile and stood. Emily copied him so he wouldn't be standing over her. "She's been sedated but you can see her for a few minutes."

Sedated, definitely, Emily thought, seeing how Claire fumbled with a pillow. She was slowly plumping it into a more comfortable shape, or trying to. When she saw Emily she said, "*Heyyy*," long and drawn out, then slurred three syllables into two with, "Em*ly.*"

"Looking good, sis." She smiled and said, "The room, I mean. Nice upgrade. No other patients to cough their germs all over you. Even got a picture on the wall. What is that, Picasso?"

"Van Gogh."

"Yeah, Van Gogh. Picasso did that weird woman one, didn't he? Weeping into her hanky with both eyes on one side of her face."

Claire's eyes were trying to close but she kept blinking them and opening them extra wide in her struggle to stay awake.

"What's this one called, I wonder?" Emily said, trying sarcasm to draw her sister out from whatever drugs she struggled in.

Claire smiled a loose smile. "*Sun*flowers."

"Original."

"*No...*" Claire dismissed the picture with an exaggerated sweep of her bandaged hand. "Just a print."

The joke surprised Emily into laughter. "Yeah," she said. "You're getting better already." She stood beside her and stroked her hair. Claire said something but it was too low, too slurred. "What was that, hun? You want a nurse?"

Claire shook her head. "Feel... worse."

"Free drugs, honey."

"Jealous?"

Emily stroked Claire's hair, trying not to see the paint in it. She stroked until Claire slept and gave her sister's question

Jealous?

more thought than she was probably meant to.

Emily wakes to a slice of light streaming between almost-drawn curtains. She's still holding the framed photo of her and Claire as children, had fallen asleep with it clutched to her chest. A corner has pressed an angle into the skin of her left breast to form an arrowhead pointing heartward. Emily rubs at it, rubs at her sleep-crusted eyes, and realises with sudden surprise that she's still in Claire's rented house. She sits up in panic and fumbles for her phone to check the time, relieved to see it's probably too early for anyone official to discover her trespassing. She doesn't know if the police or fire specialists still have to investigate the scene but she doesn't want to be around if they do.

In the bright light of day she sees the room differently.

"Oh Claire."

In the bright sunshine, Emily sees the room is a hideous shade of yellow. A sickly hue has been painted directly over the patterned wallpaper – she can still see some of the floral designs beneath, flowering buds and dark lines of vine held as shadows under slap-dashed strokes of paint. Claire hadn't moved the furniture to do it, either. Paint stains the quilt, the sheets, and the pillows in blood-splatter patterns to show where Claire had simply painted around the bed. Emily pulls the mattress away from the wall to reveal a large clean area of paper.

"Missed a bit."

The canvases stored against the wall are more striking in the natural light as well. Panel after panel, more than she'd thought, of misty grey-greens lean with a matching number of yellows. Sometimes the colours are together on one canvas, mixing

seeping

into each other, but mostly they're separate.

Emily retrieves her torch and casts a final look around to check she hasn't left anything behind. The bright colour of the room reflects on the glass of the photo frame to give Claire's skin a jaundiced tinge. It makes her toothy smile seem like a grimace of pain. Emily tucks it under her arm on her way to the burnt bedroom. She's left nothing there, either. It would be easy to spot amongst the black. The brightening sunshine of early morning makes the room even more ghastly, makes the room its own shadow despite the light streaming in at the plastic window. A coastal breeze stirs the covering but any fresh salty tang it may carry is lost beneath the lingering smell of smoke.

She goes to the window frame, treading squelches from a carpet of sodden-cinders. On the beach, even at this hour, an array of artists have already set up to work. Before them, the dazzling sand and sun-dappled sea.

The first time Claire ran away Emily had gone with her. Their intention was to get to the seaside, any seaside. They'd stuffed a backpack with a change of underwear each and two bananas and fled from some petty or imagined slight they blamed their parents for. Waiting at a bus stop, they'd counted their collected coppers to find they only had enough for a single ticket. Rather than address who should go they'd decided to eat, only to fight over whose banana was whose because one was a ripe yellow, barely spotted, and the other was still pale green.

Yellow and green, Emily thinks, wondering if that's why the memory has resurfaced. Colours seeping from the present into the past, or from the past into the present.

She pauses on the stairs, thinking she hears something. Someone. Moving in the house. She stands silent and turns her head to listen. She even holds her breath.

Their parents hadn't even considered Emily missing that time they'd run away. Hadn't worried about her at all. When she'd returned home, all the concern was for Claire. They'd assumed Emily was out looking for her.

In the mirror, her reflection is held in open-mouthed pause. There's a green tint to her skin.

Jealous?

It was the wrong word, but to have corrected her, to have said *envious*, would have been to admit it was true. For all her fickleness, Claire was always living her life while Emily only managed hers, and if it all went wrong – *when* it all went wrong – someone was always there to pick up the pieces. To traipse around burnt buildings and sit around in hospitals...

Emily touches her skin, wipes at her eyes, but the green remains. The pasty grey green of somebody dead.

"It's the light."

Claire's voice startles her. She sees her in the mirror, her reflection's twin standing at the bottom of the stairs, and suddenly she's afraid to turn around. In case she's not really there.

"The light's different here," Claire says. "Cleaner. Purer. Shows you everything for what it really is."

"What are you doing here, Claire?"

"I came because of the light."

"I mean, here. At the house."

Emily turns around to look at her properly. She's changed from her hospital gown into clothes black with old fire and paint, her bandage stark white in contrast. On her wrist she still wears the hospital band with her name on. She's run away, Emily realises. Again.

"I have to see," Claire says. She squats to pick up two cans at her feet and for a horrible moment Emily thinks she's come back with more petrol, that she's here to finish what she's started (for a change), but the cans are just paint cans.

"It's going to take more than a coat of paint to get your deposit back, sis."

Claire shakes her head but instead of whatever she was going to say, asks, "How is it?"

"Medium to well done. If you mean the main room. *Yours* is a lovely bright yellow, if a bit slap-dash."

"What?"

"Not like your paintings. Which are good, by the way. Same colour, some of them, but with way better control in the brushstrokes. Abstracty, but in a commercial way. You could easily sell them. Back in London."

"What are you talking about, Em?"

"If you come home –"

"No, I mean, the paintings. I painted over those."

"Well, not all of them."

Claire's movement up the stairs is so sudden and so fast that Emily is startled back against the mirror. She moves aside as her sister hurries past, "I *know* I did," and glances at herself in the glass. The green tinge has gone, if it was ever really there. Just a trick of the light.

Claire's cry from the bedroom is so mournful that Emily covers her own mouth to stop from joining her. Then she cries again, this time a sharper, frustrated sound, and Emily hears the noise of things being thrown.

"Claire!"

Emily rushes to the room to see it already strewn with canvases.

"I painted over them," Claire says, throwing one after the other aside. "I painted them black. All of them, black. And the fucking wall." She throws one of the paintings at the wall. The wooden frame splits but the canvas holds it together in a broken shape and Claire slumps to the floor. She sobs in a sea of yellows and greens.

Emily sits beside her and holds her, careful to avoid Claire's injuries. "I'm here, Claire. What is it? Hmm? What's wrong?"

Claire leans into her. "The colours," she says.

Emily pulls her closer. "Hey, honey." Holds her with both arms. "Hey."

"They've come back."

"Who, Claire-bear? Who's come back?"

"The *colours*." She pulls away from Emily and grips her arms. She holds her so fiercely that it hurts, and Emily wonders how Claire can bear it herself. The sensitive skin of her burnt arms must be tight with pain.

"Will you help me?"

Emily remembers again the time they'd run away. Why had it not crossed their minds to stick together? Why did they need to decide who got the bus fare when they could've just walked, *together*? *Share* the fucking bananas?

Emily nods. "Yes," she says. "Yes, of course I'll help you."

Claire sweeps aside canvases, flips them over, until she finds what she's looking for. Some sort of pallet knife of paint spreader tool. She sets one of the cans upright and levers its lid. Emily picks up the other can and stands it beside her sister's. Both are large cans from a DIY shop. Black emulsion. Well, whatever. If it helps Claire she'll happily take up a brush, paint the whole house. Paint herself as well if she has to, slap on coat after coat of the stuff. Do like The Rolling Stones said and paint it black, paint it all black, if that's what she wants.

"With you here it'll be better," Claire says. "You're *sensible* and -"

The lid pops free from the first can.

"Oh no."

"What is it?"

Claire leans over it to reach the other one.

"What's wrong, sis?"

Claire gets the other lid off as well – "*No!*"- and slaps the can away. It falls before Emily's able to catch it and spills its contents over the floor. Not black, but yellow. *Naples* yellow, Emily assumes. The paint is thick and slow to spill so Emily reaches to turn the can upright but Claire strikes her hands away from it and knocks the other one over as well, grey-green paint glooping free to mix with the yellow.

They watch the spreading puddle of colours seep into the carpet. Seep into their clothes.

Seep into everything.

THE BOOK OF DREEMS

Georgina Bruce

In the Book of Dreems, a dog is a friend.

Fraser told Kate the dog was in her head. You imagined it, he said. The mind can play all sorts of funny tricks. But Kate was sure about the dog. It was the only thing she remembered: the little dog running around and through her feet as she tripped, stumbled, whirled in the darkness. A long vague slow sick wrestle with wet branches and thorny bushes, and the little dog tumbling at her feet, whining and yelping. After that – nothing. A lacuna, a drop of darkness in her mind. As if someone had reached in with thumb and forefinger and pinched out a little of her brain. An absence felt in the centre of her head, a something missing.

Fraser said, the doctor said, everyone said – there was no dog. If there'd been a dog, it must have run away. The doctor told her, strange things happen to brains when they black out. She explained it all in a calm voice. There's no damage, she said. It's common to not remember a traumatic event, the brain's way of protecting you. It's a good thing. You don't have to worry.

Yet there was an absence. A dark matter. A black hole with its chaotic corona, an event horizon over which tumbled thoughts and memories and intentions, if they drifted too close, got caught in its gravitational pull. When Kate tried to think about the accident, to imagine, to edge her thoughts towards that black lake, she lost herself horribly. She forgot. She sensed her self dissolving into the thick inky void, and was afraid.

While she was in hospital, the apartment changed shape. It moved through itself like a Necker cube, an optical illusion, turned itself inside out, doubled itself in rooms and hallways. Maybe it was a sleight of hand. Or maybe it was the twist in a Mobius loop, a different dimension on the same plane. Or maybe it was just broken. Kate tripped over its fracture lines. She walked into walls. She banged her knees on the table, trapped her fingers in

53

the cupboard door, called Fraser to help her with the window that wouldn't come unstuck. She didn't know what to do with herself.

"Bed," said Fraser. He put an arm around her and walked her to the bedroom, pulled back the bedcovers for her, tucked her in like a child. It made him seem somehow fatherly, a thought that hadn't occurred to Kate before, despite their age difference, his forty-seven years against her twenty-two. But then, she hadn't known her father, so how could she compare? Fraser was so certain, so sure of himself and his place in the world. She was grateful for that, for everything he did for her. She wanted to be reassured by him, by his calm presence and the touch of his hand. But his fingers felt hard and cold, strangely repulsive. She thought they'd argued, before the accident. Had they? She remembered anger darkening Fraser's face, and something dark and wet slithering from his mouth, some black fluid leaking from his eyes and nose – but that couldn't be right, that was her broken brain talking. She drew his hand to her lips, forced herself to kiss his palm, though it felt waxy and stiff. Everything was a little strange, it was normal for things to be strange, when you'd been concussed. That's all it was, she told herself. She put his hand down on the bed, carefully, like it was a valuable object.

"What did we fight about? Before the accident, I mean. I can't remember."

"We didn't fight," Fraser said. "We never fight."

"Was it something to do with the program? Something to do with… those things?"

"The Dreemy Peeple?"

Kate hated them, those dolls or robots or whatever they were. She never told him that outright, but she did. She hated them. They frightened her.

Fraser smiled. That smile of his. "Sweetie, we didn't argue. Actually, we talked about going to the moon."

"Oh. But – I don't *think* I want to go to the moon…" She had to be so careful, when she disagreed, not to hurt his feelings. He was a very sensitive man. And he'd been under so much pressure lately, she didn't want to upset him.

"I know, my love. I know that now." He smiled sweetly. "I'll be a while, okay? Some emails I need to send. Sort out some glitches. Hate those glitches." He leaned down to kiss her. She kissed him back, tried to draw him into the kiss. But his lips were cold and rubbery, she didn't know how to kiss his lips when they felt so lifeless and numb. And he broke away. "You need your sleep."

"I'm not tired."

"I won't be long."

"Fraser?"

"What?" He stood in the doorway, waiting for her to speak, his hand on the light switch.

"What happened? I can't remember anything."

"Nothing happened. Go to sleep." He left the room, turning out the light and closing the door behind him. The darkness felt heavy, pressing down on her. What did he mean, *nothing happened*? Why wouldn't he tell her anything? How could he just leave her in the dark? It wasn't like him, she thought. Or maybe it was like him. She tried to remember Fraser, what he was like. She knew she was being strange. He was right there, in the other room, working. But it was strange, it felt like he'd gone. Oh, but she was being ridiculous. Fraser was Fraser. It was Kate who was wrong. Of course. Even before the accident, she had a terrible habit of being wrong.

When she woke in the early hours, Fraser had come to bed. He was sleeping, lying straight and neat as a pin. Distant, almost alien in his composure. His eyes were closed but Kate suspected he was awake deep down. Awake somewhere inside himself. Maybe she could speak to him in the middle of the night. The real Fraser. Her love. She thought about loving him. Her body flooding with love for him. A stomach lurch, an electric jolt, a shiver when she thought of him. The real Fraser, not the strange one who brought her home today, who slept here like an empty doll of himself. Where was he? Could she wake him? Bring him back? She stroked the inside of his elbow, glanced her lips over his shoulder. Whispered. *Wake up. Kiss me. Touch me.* But he was gone. His breathing was regular, so harsh and monotonous it sounded machine-like. He lay completely still, his wanting self hidden away somewhere, inside another dream. Kate sighed and rolled away from him onto her back. She closed her eyes. *I want you to touch me. Not you. I want the real Fraser.* Why wouldn't he wake up? Where was he? It was as though he'd vanished, disappeared so completely she thought she must have imagined him, he had never been real in the first place. And still she couldn't bear it – the absence of his mouth, his hands, his hair in her hands, his tongue around her tongue – she couldn't bear the absence of him – and she didn't understand. He hadn't gone anywhere. He was there, right there beside her. But untouchable. As cold and distant as the moon.

Fraser left for the moon the next morning. He put the apartment keys on the bedside table, next to Kate's head. "I don't want you to dream anymore," he said. "While I'm gone, I want you to learn to stop dreaming. I hate it when you dream. It's so loud. It keeps me awake, and I need my sleep. I need to be on top of my game. You understand? No more dreams from now on." He kissed her cheek. "I'll call you from the moon."

It was a plane to Florida and then a shuttle to the Moon Unit Hotel and Resort. A long, long journey. Kate went back to sleep after he left, woke up in the early afternoon, in a panic, knowing she had defied him and dreamed something, not knowing what the dream was, but something she shouldn't have dreamed, something illegal. He wouldn't know, it would be okay, he couldn't possibly know. She was worried, though. She didn't know how to stop her dreams. They just came, or not, regardless of what Anna wanted. He must have been joking, she thought. He must know you can't stop dreams. He had a strange sense of humour at times.

She wandered around the apartment, Fraser's keys in her dressing gown pocket, swinging against her thigh as she walked. The apartment was definitely different from how she remembered. It was the weirdest feeling. Brain damage. That inky black lake in the centre of her head, sucking at her memories. It had taken them, taken the other rooms, the staircases and hallways. She didn't even know what the apartment was supposed to look like. It was as though she'd never been there before. Rooms upon rooms, and rooms within rooms. Some of the doors were locked. But there was a key for every door on Fraser's key ring, and she opened them all, one by one, to see what was inside. They were just ordinary rooms. Bedrooms, bathrooms, sitting rooms. A library. She spent some time in there, trying to read a book that kept all its secrets from her. She could barely even read the words, they were so faint on the page, broken whispers from another story. It was unsettling and she put the book away, and left the library. She came back to the living room, curled up on the sofa in front of the television. She didn't want to go to bed in case Fraser called – he'd been travelling all day and night, it would be awful of her not to be awake when he found a moment to call. She sat upright on the sofa, biting the inside of her cheek to stop herself from sleeping.

When Fraser called, she answered on the first ring. She needn't have worried. He was in one of his tender moods, tired and tender, and she wondered why he couldn't always be this way with her. He said he missed her. He wished she had come to the moon with him. She promised him she would, one day. Next time. But she was lying – she was afraid of going to the moon, afraid of the shuttle, afraid the oxygen shields would fail, afraid of the Dreemy Peeple that wandered the hotel, served drinks in the bar, made the beds, waited tables. They were everywhere. In Fraser's room.

She could see one behind him, a Dreemy Peep slumped over his bed, wires spilling out of its back. Broken. Its arms were dislocated and hanging from its shoulders. Its legs popped out at the hips. A strange misshapen thing. Its head was turned towards the screen and when Fraser moved aside, Kate got a glimpse of its face, a dented and torn raggedy hole in the plastic at its temple. It reminded her of someone, but she couldn't think who.

"I should have stayed," Fraser said. His image crackled over the screen. "You could be up to anything. Plotting, scheming, planning my downfall."

"Oh that's all I do, all day long." Kate smiled.

"Don't laugh at me."

"I'm not. I'm sorry. It was just a silly joke."

"Yes it's so funny. Your husband far from home, you think you can do anything you want. Don't be like those other bitches, Anna. Don't be a typical bitch girl. You're better than that."

There was the sound of popping plastic and synthetic voices from Fraser's room. The Dreemy Peep slumped over the bed was twitching and twisting, speaking in a strangulated blur of static. Kate tried to hear what it was saying, but it was too faint, too weirdly spoken, stuttering out of its wires and speakers. She thought she saw a glaze of despair in its eyes as they shuttered forward in its head. She must have imagined it. But Fraser had turned and seen the Dreemy Peep too.

"Glitches!" He screamed. "Hate these fucking glitches. I better go. Sleep time for you. And no more dreaming, don't forget." He signed off before she could ask if he was joking.

Kate turned the television on again. That stupid advertisement for Doctor's Rain's Travel Gum. With the cartoon dog that ran around farting rainbows and singing.

When you're lonely and in pain
Make a call to Doctor Rain!
Chewchewchew! No longer blue!
Doctor Rain is here for yoooooooooou!

Kate couldn't figure out what the dog had to do with the jingle or even with the gum. Dogs like to chew things, she guessed. And they're happy. Or was the dog supposed to be Doctor Rain? It didn't make any sense. But there was something she quite liked about that little dog. The sweet way it bounced around, a silver key dangling from its collar. The way it winked at her, at the end of the advert. Its stupid, cute little face.

The advert ended and the screen went black, then gradually broke into a buzzing static blur. Rain, torrential rain. A little copse of trees and bushes, a deep wet green, water dripping from the branches and tips of the leaves. And under one of the bushes, a woman, naked, curled up in the wet soil. Blood poured from a cut on her head. Kate put a hand to her temple, felt the tender wound tied up with wiry stitches. On the screen, a boot swung towards the woman's face, smashed into her cheekbone. A caption flashed up: THROUGH THE NIGHT DOOR. Kate grabbed the remote control and turned the television off. She felt sick. She didn't like to see that kind of thing. But she was fine. She was fine. Maybe she was dreaming. It was so late. She should go to bed. Bed was the best place for her now. Sleep. No dreaming.

But in the hallway, she lost her bearings. Somehow, impossibly, she walked the wrong way from the living room to the bedroom. She turned herself around in circles, not knowing which way to go next. The long, doorless hallway kept taking her around corners, tighter and smaller corners, until she found herself at the foot of a little wooden staircase that led up to a hatch in the ceiling which led... she had no idea where it led. She'd never been in this part of the apartment before. Not that she could remember. It was cramped and close at the foot of the stair, claustrophobically trapped by the angle of the corners that spiralled around it. So she went up. Up the little wooden stairs. Through the hatch. She climbed out into a kitchen, crawled out from underneath a table in the middle of the room. The only light came through the window over the sink. Kate could see it was twilight and raining. It was strange, so strange. She had a memory of this place. Like she'd been here before. All so familiar – the cheap wooden table, the photographs stuck to the fridge. Kate knew those people, the people in the photographs. But she couldn't place them, couldn't think of their names. Friends? Family? Was that... someone she knew? But the longer she looked at them, the stranger they began to seem to her. Their skin, their faces – they looked wrong, too smooth, too shiny and stiff. Looking at them made her anxious. She wanted to open the back door, to let some air into the room. She reached up above the door frame and felt around until she put her fingers on the key she knew would be there.

The door opened into an overgrown garden. A sea of green, swaying and dipping in the rain. The water pummelled against her, soaking her through to the skin. Cold, shivery... and something not quite right. There was something out there with her. Something that crawled and mewled piteously under the bushes. A bloodied, moonstruck thing. Smashed in and broken. She was terrified of it, terrified and ashamed. She turned back to the door, but the door was gone, the house was gone. The light in the garden was failing, the rain coming down harder than before, and the moon drifted out from behind trees. A white eye staring down at Kate, transfixing her, pinning her to the spot. She wanted to move, to turn and run, but the next thing she felt was her knees buckling as she was hit from behind, a mud-caked black boot travelling towards her head.

The moon opened Kate. Traversed her. Translated her. Broke and rewrote her. Her face stretched out, the bones snapped and splintered, a sensation of her whole self being pulled forward, through her mouth. Her hands shrivelled, fingers melted together. The moon churned through her, a hundred new smells, her milk-sweet mother running in the grass between trees, in night's glamour, fresh cold rain dripping from leaves. The moon roared, it sawed through her, turned her inside out and silver bright. She tried to beg forgiveness but she'd forgotten the moon's language. It was a prising apart of dimensions, it was two knives scraping each other to death. It was a whispering rustling creature in the leaves. She spoke but her words came out stripped of meaning, in strings of saliva and bile, she spat and retched words into the dirt, and they crawled away like blind white maggots, and burrowed into the soil. She forgot the language of her own self, and when she cried, it was the whimper of a beaten dog.

Alone, alone, she was a creature hiding in the woods, in the cold rain, in the sharp grass and velvet-soft moss, not knowing herself at all. Lost in the dark spaces between things. But a voice spoke in her ear, spoke without meaning, and he was there, he was with her. And she was glad, she wanted him there. More than anything. Yes. She clung to him, wild panic let loose. Come back, he ordered her. Stop dreeming. He made the world for her again, pulled shapes from the darkness and built walls for her to live in. He covered her body with his own, held her down, crammed her into a person shape, pushing and moulding her body until it made sense again. He traced words against her skin, speaking in tongues, sharp tooth, soft lip, a fluid language that flowed inside her. He pressed his fingers to her, where she was tangled and wet, slipped and stroked inside. It was an entanglement of mouths, tongues, lips, it was a summoning, a gathering spell, bringing her into her self. She clung to his neck, breathing in the smell of his skin, his realness. (But how was he there? How had he returned from the moon so quickly? No, no, never mind that. Don't doubt him. Don't fear.) Yes, he was so real. And the bed was real, the room was real, everything was real and really there. It had never gone away. She had never gone away. Only... maybe, maybe she had slipped, wandered a little too near that black lake of forgetting, the dark lacuna in the centre of her mind. She was afraid, but Fraser loved her, was loving her, holding her in the world with his own hands.

Yet his tenderness was a passing thing. He unpeeled her arms from around his neck. "Turn over," he said. He gripped her wrists and pinned her out across the bed, her face pressed into the pillows. "Do as I tell you," he whispered. "I have to fix this one little glitch."

She couldn't move if she wanted to. She was frozen in place, as passive and inert as one of those terrible Dreemy Peeple dolls. And yet he was making her feel so real. So much more real than she was in that other place, with the rain and the dirt. The hallucination or whatever it was, the way her body had changed, turned inside out. That wasn't real. But this was. This felt so real. Painfully real. So real it hurt. He levered her open at the seam, pierced her with stiff fingers.

"You've been dreeming, Kate. What did I tell you about dreeming?"

She whispered, "I'm sorry. I'm so sorry."

"How can I trust you now? You're just like all the others, aren't you? Admit it."

No, no. Sorry. Please. How could he doubt her, after everything? But all his softness had leached away, into the darkness, into some other realm of himself. He was rigid and furious. He stabbed at something inside her, popped something in her back. She felt her wiring spilling out, pulled out in Fraser's hands. He wrenched her arms and legs from their sockets, made her a strange broken shape.

"No more dreeming. Swear to me."

She couldn't speak. She couldn't even move her head, let him see her eyes, to make him know how sorry she was. So sorry.

"Glitches. Fucking glitches. Don't think you can use them against me."

No. She wouldn't. Couldn't. Didn't even know what that meant. Just please, please stop now.

"Don't break my heart." He spat the words out, forcing her head down into the pillow, tearing her hair from the tender wound. "Don't be like all the others."

He went away again the next day, leaving Kate a long list of rules to keep to. He would know, he said. He'd know if she broke any, if she even thought about breaking any. *No dreeming, no listening to the moon, no screaming, no touching yourself, no opening the door, no running away.*

But Kate couldn't help breaking rules. And she couldn't help the moon from whispering its broken language into her ears. A fractured, jumbled language, words cracked open and drained of blood, bleached bone-white.

It was wrong, it was terrible, of course it wasn't real. No. But she didn't know how to stop it. She couldn't silence the moon, so she silenced herself. She closed her mouth and stitched it shut. She knew she would never, could never tell Fraser. Not about the moon. Not about the strange television, or the dreeming dolls, or the night doors, or any of the other thousand tiny secrets she was keeping from him. He mustn't know anything. He mustn't know that she knew. That was the only way she might survive him. Keep everything secret and hidden away.

She was a closed case, her skin zipped tightly around a million unspoken words, a whole alphabet of herself, crazed little letters she had to keep still and quiet and contained within her body. They moved around inside her, spelling out blackbirds and spiders, ghosts and books and rotten apples, dead leaves and murdered girls and wrong music and long falls in the darkness. She felt chaotic inside, under her skin, stuffed tight and swarming with dirt. She couldn't stand it. She wanted to explode out of her body, unspool out of herself, unravel the tangled mess until she was nothing but one long thin strand stretched out across the universe.

But no. She would never be free. There would always be this pain, this bone-crushing pain in her head. She took a handful of painkillers, too many, she couldn't help it. Needed the pain to stop, couldn't take any more, couldn't stand the sawing at her bones. She screamed, knowing she was breaking his rules, not caring. The scream burst up from somewhere deep inside her, calling up some ancient vision of herself, her throat raw with the rush of air, emptying her lungs. She screamed and felt something break inside her head, a snapping of some connection. Then there was a brief loose emptiness, and she felt something warm and wet on her cheek. Something dark, spreading over the pillow. Blood. She was bleeding. Shaking, she got out of bed and stumbled to the bathroom. In the mirror she saw dark stains over her face and hands, streams of liquid running from both ears, dripping down her neck, her back, her breasts, everywhere. But it wasn't red. It wasn't blood. She wiped her fingers over the mirror. Black smears across her reflection. Black ink, leaking from inside her head.

Dreeming. I'm dreeming, and he'll know. He'll know. He'll come back and fix me, fix my glitches. He'll fix me and I'll be good again, I'll be his Kate again.

But she knew she wouldn't be good again. She knew this time, he wouldn't forgive her, that in fact he was impatient for her to break his rules. Excited. He couldn't wait. And she knew that she was no good to him now, now that she'd broken the spell he'd cast over her. He would see it and be bored right away. He'd kill her. He'd turn her into a Dreemy Peep. Even if he couldn't tell by looking at her face, he'd see the ink all over the bathroom floor. All over the mirror. Smudged over her face and pooling at her collar bone. No, no. He was on the moon. He couldn't see her. He couldn't, could he?

She stumbled out of the bathroom and down the hallway towards the front door, trailing black droplets behind her. He was in the apartment somewhere, she could sense him. Coming after her with his tools and his hands, ready to fix her glitches, rewire her. Make her good again. Again? How many times? What even was she now – just a thing made of plastic and wires and spare parts? But it wasn't true. No, no. That's just what he wanted her to think.

The door was locked, of course. Kate went through Fraser's keys frantically, looking for one that would open it. But she knew she knew she knew – there was one key he would never give her. The key to her escape. The keys failed, one after another, until she had tried them all. And yet – there was something. A little something, dancing around her feet. When she looked, there was nothing there. But she remembered a little dog. A little dog with a key hanging off its collar. That had stayed with her. Stayed in her head.

Kate scratched at the bandage over her wound, pulled it away. She dug at the stitches, picked them apart with impatient fingers. Blood spilled over her hands, making it harder to grip the wiry threads and pull them out. When the wound was open she stabbed inside it with her thumb and forefinger shaped like a beak, digging around in the broken skull, pulling out a bloodied silver key.

The door opened into Fraser's room on the moon. She knew it would, it must do. She was there already, too, broken and slumped over the bed, her back panel open and wires tumbling out. And Fraser standing over her yelling, "Fucking glitches! You're just like the others, full of disgusting glitches. Stop dreeming! Stop it!"

Kate came closer and he saw her and turned on her, grabbing her by the shoulders, slipping because of all the blood and the black liquid on her skin.

"What the fuck? What's this?"

He slammed her down onto the floor, but couldn't get a purchase on her. The floor was slippery now and she was soaked. In the confusion, she managed to climb on top on him, press herself over him and hold him down for a moment. It was pouring from her now, the black ink rushed out of her, like blood from a severed artery, covering them both. It was a lake of ink, flooding out of her and into him. That black lake inside her head, that black lake of forgetting. It spilled out and out of her, and as it drained away, she remembered. Remembered how he had dragged her outside in the night. Dragged her by her hair. How he had kicked her, stamped down on her head with his big black boot. How she had screamed and begged for help, for someone to help, for the moon to fall down and rescue her. She remembered it all, and everything that had come before that, the slow silencing, the friends she had dropped, the job she'd given up. She wanted it all back now. She wanted her life. Her self. She would take it all back.

Black lake water flooded over Fraser, into his mouth and his eyes. It made him stutter and twitch uncontrollably. She saw blue sparks fizzing over his skin, heard the crackling of his insides, the liquid sloshing in his hollows. She slumped back on the floor, and watched as he struggled to sit up. Still in his clothes, his smart leather shoes, his legs splayed straight out before him. His mouth stuttered open and closed, his eyes rolled back in his head. He was broken. If not, she would smash him to pieces. His smooth skin and his perfect hair, all sticky with blood and ink. And his moving parts, clogged up now and stuck. His mouthpiece twitched. A blue filament arced through his eye, leaving it black and empty. No. His eyes had always been empty. She saw her own self reflected in the glossy dead orbs. That was all she'd ever seen in him, after all: her own love, her own strength. She was the one who'd been real. Kate, and the others, the bitches with glitches. They were the real ones, humming with so much reality that Fraser couldn't bear it, would do anything to deny it, kill it. But it was undeniable. She felt it in herself now, in her aching, beaten body. She felt it thrumming inside her veins, thundering to her heart.

THE AFFAIR

James Everington

Neil hadn't meant to begin an affair that night, but thinking back his intentions had seemed to have little to do with it. He certainly wouldn't have said he was unhappy when he left the house–or rather, he'd have said that he had a realistic view about the ratio of happiness to unhappiness marriage and fatherhood might provide. As a younger man certain song lyrics and lines from movies had suggested more, but those echoes had long since faded. But he would have admitted to a certain feeling of release as he left Lynda and little Charlie (mercifully asleep); he called out to Lynda that he loved her and wouldn't be late back, meaning the first more than the second. He didn't get many opportunities for a night out anymore.

He always met Peter in the same place, despite the fact it had changed out of all recognition over the years. It had once been an independent, old-fashioned pub split between bar and lounge, with worn leather seats, low wooden beams and snug alcoves where you could sit alone. It was now part of a chain, more deserving of the term bar than pub. The wood had been stripped away, the alcoves removed, the two rooms merged to make one large, high-ceilinged space where everyone could see everyone else. The kind of place Neil would never normally enter, nowadays, save it was where they'd always met. He supposed the refurbishment must had been sudden, like his first grey hair appearing, but in his memory it had been a gradual change, unnoticed until too late. He still saw hints of how it had been, memories in the corner of his vision that fluttered away if he looked them head on.

He'd first met Lynda here, too.

When he arrived that night he took out his phone and saw that Peter wasn't coming.

Damn, Neil thought, without really taking in his friend's excuse. They only met twice a year, nowadays – already it was possible to work out roughly how many such nights they had left before one of them made their excuses permanently. But he wasn't going to just head back home; Neil bought a pint at the bar and, feeling self-conscious, fiddled with his phone in a manner he hoped suggested he was waiting for someone. It was very noisy in the bar, with people shouting over music that seemed comprised of samples of the music of his own era, fragmented and repetitious. He had a dizzy and déjà-vu like moment where every young voice echoing in the bar seemed to be one from his past.

He sipped his bitter; without anyone's presence to distract him he wondered for the first time in years whether he actually liked the taste. Stop over-thinking your pleasures, he thought, aware at that moment someone was approaching his table but not looking up because it must be their mistake.

"Is this seat taken?" a familiar voice said.

He looked up in surprise. Lynda? What was *she* doing here? She was standing with one hand on the free chair, looking at him quizzically. He didn't recognise the dress she was wearing, or the vivid pink of her fingernails, or the expression on her face. But the last wasn't quite true; he *did* remember that look, along with decades old songs, physical photographs, the feeling that life was there for the taking.

The dim light in the bar made everything look wrong and for a brief moment he was unsure if this really was his wife – didn't she look too young? – but there was no one else it could be.

She was still waiting for an answer to her question.

"Uh, sure," he said, gesturing to the chair. "Go ahead." As if talking to someone he didn't yet know.

She sat opposite him and he couldn't help but notice how short her dress was as she did so. But he had no reason to feel guilty for looking; it was his wife. Nonetheless, he blushed. She placed her drink on the table, a glass of rosé – but Lynda *hates* rosé, Neil thought. But then it had been over ten years since he'd *asked* her what she wanted to drink, on their rare nights out, rather than just buying her usual white wine spritzer.

"So, you've been stood up?" she said, as if he were someone who still could be, and he felt a nervousness he hadn't felt around a woman for years. Her voice, although husky, seemed to rise into the high ceiling of the bar as she spoke to him; she kept eye contact for a heartbeat longer than a stranger normally would and Lynda normally did. She didn't pull down her skirt even as she saw him looking. She didn't call him by name or mention hers. At first Neil didn't know what to say.

But going to the bar to get more drinks gave him chance to think, and he figured it out.

This was something Lynda and Peter had set up. A treat, for him, to have Lynda turn up and pretend to seduce him, flirt with him as if they were strangers – hadn't he read, somewhere, of couples doing that when they had bedroom troubles? He wondered how Lynda had got ready so quickly, and when she had arranged the babysitter. He wondered how much she had told Peter…

But he was overthinking things again.

Returning, he tried to just go with it, to pretend this wasn't Lynda, or was *another* Lynda at least. Like someone dancing after a gap of years he tried to remember how to hold his body when flirting with someone; for brief moments he overcame his clumsiness, his nervousness, as if forgetting who he was. But self-consciousness wasn't something he could throw from himself for long; he began to stutter and blush, felt the ache in his lower back from leaning towards her.

She was a natural and never broke character once.

"I'll call you," she said, standing up, leaving him with half a pint still to drink. When she took out her mobile he didn't recognise that either. How much had she spent on this? he thought as he recited his number, both of them pretending she didn't know it.

Then she kissed him goodbye and the sweet taste of rosé on her lips made him momentarily stop thinking like that; stop thinking at all. The lust he felt for her was like something else he couldn't think about too much or it would fade. But she was leaving anyway and he sat back down shakily, finished his beer. With the taste of wine still on his lips, the bitter lived up to its name.

You cunning bastard! How long have you been planning this? he messaged Peter (he was of the age to compose his text messages like written sentences), but his friend's reply made little sense. Looking back, he saw Peter's original reason for not coming out had been because his father had been taken into hospital. He'd assumed Peter had to have been involved to make the plan work, but then why would he have used such a crass excuse as that?

When Neil got home twenty minutes later, the house was dark and Lynda was in bed asleep, as if she had gone to bed as soon as he'd gone out (her usual habit). There was no sign of any babysitter. In his haste to get into bed, Neil forwent his normal listen at Charlie's door for his son's soft breathing. Lynda seemed surprised and sleepy when Neil rolled her over, but what had she expected the effect on him to be? As they made love Neil wondered how his wife had so quickly erased the signs of the woman she'd pretended to be. And that was when it almost went wrong, *again* (more over-thinking), but he quickly closed his eyes and thought of the other woman, the other Lynda at the bar, and he was able to avoid the usual anti-climax. Afterwards, Lynda kissed him, pleased, her mouth dry and tasteless.

The next morning Lynda asked him how his night with Peter had been, just like she always did. The ordinariness of the question allowed Neil to mask his confusion, and give his usual non-committal answer.

The following Friday afternoon, he got two text messages almost simultaneously. One from Peter, informing him that his father had died. The other from the number Lynda – the other Lynda – had used in the bar that night. *Are you free after work for a drink?* No name at the end, just Xs. Was he free? He remembered the taste of rosé wine sweet on her lips as he replied that he was.

And it was in the spirit of playing along, rather than attempting to cover something up, that he texted Lynda on her usual number to say he'd be late back from the office.

They met at the same bar, he sat alone again before she approached. He hadn't seen her when he'd arrived (although he had looked) but already she had a glass of rosé in her hand. He had one in front of him too, its lightness and sweetness in comparison to what he normally drank as intoxicating as the alcohol.

She sat down without needing to be invited this time; she was wearing another new dress, if anything even shorter. She was already smiling at something he'd said; she touched his forearm as she spoke, sipped at her wine and smiled at him with lips he imagined wet and sweet-tasting. Did she really look younger, Neil wondered, or was it just the roving lights of the bar and his own dim eyes that made her seem so? Maybe she was just acting younger, like the Lynda he'd used to know, before Charlie, before, well, everything. He felt younger too, his movements as he leant towards her laughter feeling like memories of how he'd used to move: looser, lighter, less clogged and tired. When he spoke it was like he was speaking words from years before; as if those words, and those years, were somehow present, free and bird-like in the high-ceilinged bar and he just had to ignore any doubting thoughts and reach up and hug them back to himself…

Or as if his words were being voiced behind him by someone else in this bar, another him, a heartbeat before he spoke.

"Your wife will be waiting," Lynda said, confusing him, unmooring him. "But maybe before…" Her words trailed behind her as she rose and moved towards the back of the bar. Following in her trail, sneaking into the Ladies, it was again as if memories of his past guided his movements now; but surely he and Lynda had never done anything as daring as this?

Afterwards, Lynda snuck out the cubicle first and when Neil did so a few minutes later, still grinning and legs atremble, she was nowhere to be seen.

When he got home Lynda was just taking a lasagne out of the oven. "Because you had to work late," she said, as if she didn't know. "I put Charlie to bed without you," she continued. "It was getting on." She looked harried and tired in the hot, cramped kitchen; a yawn split her face and echoed on his. Lynda looked nothing like the woman he'd been sat with less than an hour before: no makeup, baggy jeans, mussed up hair. Neil couldn't believe it was the same person.

Couldn't believe it could be, at all.

And so it went on. If Lynda noticed he was working late more often, meeting Peter more often, she didn't say anything – in order to keep up the pretence, the thrill of it, Neil thought of it in those terms. As if it weren't his wife, really, who sent him those text messages each time. As if she didn't know exactly what happened: always meeting in the same bar for drinks, sometimes followed by food, sometimes simply by eager and thoughtless sex in toilet cubicles or alleyways or anonymous hotels. Lynda never once mentioned it, any of it, when she was back home (always before him) and he found her watching TV, or on her laptop, or just asleep with her back to him. And Neil's pretence at secrecy and deception became routine even as it became more elaborate. Became instinctive, so that he barely thought of the woman he was seeing as Lynda at all.

He had no rational reason to feel guilty but he did, a sweet guilt like something else from his past remembered, another sensation he'd forgotten the intoxication of.

The guilt was perhaps why he didn't notice at first that *Lynda* was going out more, as well. With her friend Jenny, she said, which was plausible for Jenny was her friend despite the fact that they only met occasionally. Maybe the first few times Lynda *had* met Jenny, because it wasn't until the third that she came back home and tried to rouse Neil from his sleep with keen and fluttering hands. He almost pretended she hadn't woken him, fearing another no-show, but the fruity, fermented taste on her breath was like a reminder of the *other* Lynda, an echo that roused him.

The next morning he asked her now her night had been and her reply was vague. While she showered, he checked her mobile and found that the invitation she'd had for the previous night had come from a phone number she didn't have in her contacts. Which didn't mean it wasn't from Jenny, although Neil couldn't help but think that the text read like it had been written by a man; read in fact like he might have invited Lynda out, had texting been a thing when they were courting. Read like something sent by a younger him, only here in the...

But Charlie was awake and crying, and the thought slipped from him into the air.

He showered after Lynda and when he came out he found her going through his clothes in the wardrobe. She stepped back quickly as though startled out of doing something she was nervous about.

"Oh," she said. "I just wondered if you'd bought any new shirts because..." She trailed off, as if momentarily doubting what she was saying. "A cornflower blue one or... any new shirts?"

Neil shook his head. Lynda bought all his clothes, nowadays.

"Maybe I should get you one," she said brightly, quickly shutting the wardrobe. "It would suit you, I think."

The babysitter, Neil realised, must have been in on it too, for when he called her she claimed she hadn't babysat for Charlie for months.

As ever, the bar was noisy, music and people's voices amplified by its open space. This time, not going to meet Lynda, the *other* Lynda, Neil noticed the young faces of the clientele more, physically felt his age, like a heavy coat he couldn't shrug from his shoulders. The hubbub of voices and laughter around him seemed to rise to the high domed ceiling above. And there seemed something naggingly *familiar* about the echoing speech, but the associations fluttered free from his thoughts like things lost from his grasp before he could place them.

Neil sipped his drink – on his own it seemed overbearingly fruity, sickly – and looked around the bar for Lynda and Jenny.

When he saw her, his wife, the person she was with obviously wasn't Jenny. He felt no surprise as he watched this other person; he could see the easy way they moved, hear the way his throaty laughter harmonised with the echoing acoustics of the bar. He fitted in, he looked right, he wore a neat cornflower blue shirt. Neil watched his wife raise her pink-hued glass to her lips but pause in the act, laughing at something the man opposite her had said. Neil was too far away to hear Lynda's laugher, but knew what it must sound like: laughter remembered, from this very building.

Even from behind he knew the man who had just made her laugh so hard looked like him. Another Neil; Lynda was seeing another Neil.

Starting to feel tipsy from drinking on an empty stomach, he looked back to Lynda as she finally took a sip from her glass. She was wearing none of the new and exciting clothes he'd seen the *other* Lynda wear, but a somewhat faded, conservative dress that he remembered from their last significant anniversary. Makeup applied in a rushed hand in the brief gap between Charlie going down and her taxi arriving. The smile she gave to the man sitting opposite – him!–had a franticness to it, as if she were an actor unsure if she could still remember her lines. Her attempts at flirtatiousness similarly faltering, something once effortless weighed down.

Neil wondered if he looked like that, when he met the other Lynda.

And of course, the *other* fucking Neil moved with none of that sense of effort, of years, of weight. Nothing held *him* back as he attempted to seduce Neil's wife.

A desire for aggression, for confrontation arose in Neil's mind like something briefly airborne, but then he thought how futile it would be. He drank the feeling down with the last of his overly sweet wine. Neil turned away, walked stooped beneath the high ceiling, which echoed with laugher, young voices, and one false note.

The babysitter was surprised he was back so early; he paid her for the whole evening and quickly hustled her out the house.

He listened outside Charlie's door, but his thoughts were too distracted for him to remember if he'd heard his son's breathing or not. He wondered if the man Lynda was with, the other Neil, was merely a younger version or someone who *he* could still be. Somehow. If he shed off everything ponderous, everything that slowed and tired him...

But when Lynda returned a few hours later, he pretended to be asleep, thoughts fluttering in his head which he couldn't pin down.

He didn't know why he felt the need to act, just that he had had reach out and grasp whatever was happening rather than let it slide by uninfluenced. So:

He booked the babysitter.

He told Lynda, his Lynda, that he was taking her out. Looked for a flicker of guilt in her eyes when he named the bar but couldn't tell if what he saw there was an echo of his own reaction.

He messaged the *other* Lynda to meet him at the same place and time.

And he messaged the *other* Neil from Lynda's phone while she was bathing Charlie. The same message.

Two replies agreeing.

He bought a cornflower blue shirt and hid it at his office.

He told Lynda, *both* Lyndas, that he'd have to work late the night of their date so he'd meet them straight at the bar,

Two replies agreeing.

In the toilets at work he put on the new shirt, feeling its tightness around his gut. It was years since he'd bought his own clothes, maybe he'd gone up a size and not even realised. After some deliberation, he left the collar button undone.

Maybe he had overthought things again?

The dim lights of the bar made people's movements seem to flutter in and out of his focus as he approached the woman sitting alone at a table. Which Lynda had got here first?

"Is this seat taken?' he said. Repeated. He couldn't tell which it was who looked up, but as her eyes widened with reflected cornflower he almost didn't care. Did she realise which Neil he was, as she gestured towards the empty seat beside her, as her hand touched his arm as if the colour of his shirt was something tangible she could run her fingertips through? Neil felt oddly uncertain just who he was himself; when he spoke his words felt untethered, rising into unpredictable currents of air.

He went to the bar and bought two large glasses of rosé; when he went back to her his thoughts threatened to tumble down and silence him, for what was he to say? All their conversations seemed to be about Charlie nowadays. But that wasn't how he was with the other Lynda was it, a middle-aged and tongue-tied cliché? The pressure he felt to perform seemed an echo of that he felt in the bedroom. Neil took a sip of the wine to give himself chance to get his act together (and an act was what it was); still unclear just who he was talking to he tried to make his words light, easy things that never settled on anything definitive but were airily suggestive.

He slowed as he thought he heard the echo of his speech a beat behind him, in this cavern of a bar. Heard words and laughter slipping past him before he could grasp their source or meaning.

The more he thought about what to say, the less he was able to speak.

And Lynda, now, spoke too loudly as well, as if she too were trying to speak over the noise of another's words. But maybe it was just because of the loud music? Her eyes looked to Neil then behind him to the crowded bar for inspiration; they were both trying to talk as if they didn't know each other, as if they still had lives not pulled down by each other's. He saw now the lines around her eyes, the tiredness not fully concealed. How had he ever been in doubt which Lynda she was, or which Neil sat with her? He desperately kept talking.

In the echo-chamber of the bar an alternative version of their conversation seemed to play out – a second behind or a score of years, he wasn't sure. Because *they* were here, weren't they? He had invited them and they'd both said they'd come. And naturally, they'd found each other. He tried to emulate the rhythm and cadence of those words he could only faintly hear, only faintly remember, but his efforts merely made him sound like he was babbling to hide how little he had to say.

Neil shifted in his seat, looked round; he couldn't see them. Nonetheless he was sure they were there, in some *other* version of this bar, having the time of their lives – his life! – just out of reach and earshot.

Both he and Lynda had fallen silent and every thought in his head seemed unspeakable through triteness, through having been said before. The silence between them created space for the echoes and it was like his head was ringing. He downed his drink and it felt sickly and sweet inside him.

"Another?" he said desperately; Lynda nodded gratefully.

Stop over-thinking it he thought as he pushed towards the bar, aware of the space and noise of the high ceiling above, assailed by the swooping flutter of gull-like laughter and raucous, uninhibited words. Stop over-thinking it, he's *you*, he's got nothing that you can't recapture… But was that really true? Had he ever been so relaxed and artless and young?

He was carrying both of their empties back to the bar. No one else did it anymore but he stubbornly stuck to the habit; it was something he'd done since first coming here with Peter and Lynda. As he pushed through the crowd of young faces the music being played seemed to step up a gear, increase in volume – he'd not liked or recognised what had been playing before but now it was worse, an almost incomprehensible noise as if his taste had receded even further into history in just a few seconds. Everyone else reacted with shared recognition, shifted their bodies naturally to this new beat, changed their stance, flung out their arms. If he could just move with this new beat…

One of the empty wine glasses Neil was carrying slipped from his hand and smashed on the floor, seemingly audible over the hubbub of the bar.

He had the sensation of things sunlit and dappled scattering overheard, vanishing at the sharp noise, leaving a silence that persisted behind the thud of background noise. The bar seemed emptier than a split second before. As a young-faced barmaid rushed to sweep up the shattered glass, ignoring Neil himself, his embarrassment as he walked away was another dull and clod-footed thing.

He was straining his ears, looked all around, but could sense nothing behind the gaudy chrome and wood of this bar he was too old for, could hear nothing over the echoless repetition of music he no longer understood. He looked upwards to the high ceiling and the feeling of empty, merciless space gave him vertigo.

Somewhere, he thought, somewhere they held hands – *we* held hands! – and left together after the first drink. Somewhere they had done that, for he knew: the others were no longer here.

He reached the front of the bar, looked back to see Lynda, who gave him a little wave. She looked small and nervous sitting on her own, surrounded by people half her age, and his urge to make her feel less so was laced with the resignation that he felt the same.

He wondered if the babysitter would think to call him if something woke Charlie; he checked his vacant phone for messages.

The barman looked implausibly and voraciously young; he asked Neil what he wanted. Neil looked to the high, empty, echoless chamber above him one last time.

He hadn't even asked her.

He felt sick.

His shirt was too tight.

"Uh, white wine with ice and a pint of bitter," he said, so quietly the barman had to ask him to repeat himself over the surging sound of a love-song that echoed somewhere, but no longer around him.

FRAGMENTS OF A BROKEN DOLL

Cate Gardner

Razor wire pinged. Howls echoed both without and within the city, shaking in the hollow of her belly. Trill pulled the tatty rag-doll to her chest, dragging at its limbs to dislodge grey and black and green stitching, her fingers working at the stuffing. The room was dark. It was always dark because she wasn't allowed a candle and the electrics didn't work, but her eyes had adjusted and she could see outside; find what was causing the razor wire to scream.

The house backed onto the prison, rents were cheap and either they lived here with a leaking roof, dodgy plumbing and the smell of death or in a cardboard box in a doorway. Harry had forbade her from working. She was too frail, or too young, or too old, or mentally incompetent. Always a different reason. Floodlights revealed most of the prison yard but the wall surrounding the prison was dark: a dull and pitted concrete topped with razor wire. Wood creaked as Trill opened the window. The doll's belly burst, throwing a ball of cotton stuffing into the wind that dropped onto the bleeding hand of an escaping man.

They regarded each other. Trill held her breath until it seemed her throat would explode. Harry told her the prisoners were locked up because they'd murdered children and women and girls, always girls, and Trill knew she was both of those things, or was, or would be. Harry kept her safe. Harry and his uniform. Trill released her breath to spit on the floor. Now she couldn't find the man. He'd dropped from both wire and wall, probably onto the nest of old mattresses that the dossers slept on. If he'd landed on cobbles he'd have smashed a bone.

Good.

Trill crept down the stairs, which were determined to betray her. Harry didn't like her having the highest room in the house because she'd tumbled down stairs when she was very little. Age four or five or maybe sixty-two. He allowed her the attic because she screamed if all she could see from the window was wall. Snores echoed from the ground floor. Harry didn't like heights.

The keys hung on a hook beside the front door. Trill grabbed them, although she didn't want to open that door, but if Harry found them gone, he'd check the street and not the back yard. In the kitchen, rusted bolts left orange welts on her hands. If the prisoner were still in the alleyway he'd hear the scrape and he'd run. He'd hear the scrape and wait to murder her.

For a moment, the back yard seemed darker than her bedroom and her foot found the shovel she'd left out to trip Harry when he went for a smoke. She didn't like him smoking. Father smoked. She recalled puffs of orange hair and tar stained fingers, the strike of his belt, and the cough that echoed in the courtroom where mother pinched Trill's arm and then pulled her sleeve down to hide the bruises.

Trill is clumsy.

Something clattered in the back alley. The escaped prisoner was still there. The murderer. This had to be one of the silliest things she'd done and that included stitching her skirt to her knee when fixing her rag doll and telling her school friend that bleach tasted like apple juice. The latter proving the only time father was proud of her.

Daddy's girl.

Trill pressed her ear to the door out to the alley and then her eye to the gaps in the slats, but she couldn't see and she couldn't hear anything. Her breaths came in jerks and she wasn't certain if it was due to exertion or laughter. Oh, she wanted to laugh so loud and so hard. People always laugh when they're nervous. She'd laughed when Katy screamed that her throat was burning, when Katy knocked the apple-juice-bleach onto her school skirt and a pale wash grew across the fabric. The back gate proved a struggle. Her fingers refused to work this evening, perhaps they were tired and needed to rest while the rest of her wanted to dance and whoop and catch a killer. A siren awoke within the prison. Its shrillness galvanised her hands and she pulled the door open. The wood splintered. The door hit her in the face and caused her to fall back. The killer pushed through the door and undid her hard work by bolting it. Now *his* breaths came in jerks.

The thing that worried Trill most was her nightdress. It was floral and ugly and she was certain it twisted above her Tweety Pie knickers. Her back hurt. The edge of the shovel dug into her shoulder; if it drew blood, she'd need another Tetanus injection. The killer did something unexpected. He helped her up.

"A little lady like you shouldn't be lying on damp cobblestones."

He sounded like he'd stepped from an old movie, the kind with steam trains and black and white streets, and where everyone wore hats. Blood dripped from his hand.

"They'll smell your blood," she said. "The dogs."

She pulled at the lace that cuffed her sleeve and wound it around his hand.

"Thank you for your kindness."

Then she whipped the lace off causing him to wince. She'd hurt someone who had sliced and throttled and stabbed women and children and girls. She'd kick him in the balls too but her knee didn't reach that high.

She showed him her fists. "So I can persuade the dogs to hunt elsewhere. Don't make me fight that back gate again."

She'd disarmed him, just as she had Daddy when she'd dragged her doll to the police station and for the price of an orange lollipop had given up the bodies in the chest freezer, including Katy.

"You can lock the gate."

She had the keys.

Wheels scraped along tarmac, sirens blared as the prison gates opened fast enough to rattle the bones from her skin. Dogs barked. Trill had traced the blood cloth against the outer prison wall, along the alley and out onto the main street. They wouldn't find the killer in her kitchen or buried under her bed. It's tiring when you need to move faster than cars and men and dogs, especially when you should have been tucked in bed hours ago. She should have warned the killer about Harry and his uniform.

Harry took care of her. Harry would take care of them both if the killer didn't throttle him. She kept to the side roads, like the killer would. Ideally she'd run along the alleys but they'd put gates up and she hadn't the skill or the time to climb over them. She'd get as far as she could and hope it enough distance.

Goosebumps peppered her arms and, despite the chill, tiredness caused her to close her eyes so that she moved as if sleepwalking. She wandered onto the High Street. Chaos woke her. The sirens couldn't compete with the noise erupting from the pubs, the drunks spilling out to join the taxi lines, the shouts, the hollers. She pressed her hands to her ears and screamed but no one heard and whether she was young or old no one came to her aid. If Harry would let her have a mobile phone she'd ring him to come and get her, she'd ring him and get him out the house before the murderer ate his liver.

There are Coco Pops and Chocolate Mini Rolls in the cupboard and surely anyone would eat them before a man's liver.

Trill dropped the bloodied lace in the collection tin of a man sleeping in the doorway of an abandoned shoe shop. She wanted to curl up next to him and sleep, but resisted. If the police found her wandering they'd take her home and find Harry's innards hanging from the lampshade.

There were cars parked outside the prison gates and chaos almost equal to the High Street. Trill passed in the shadows, her nightgown dirty at the hem and sleeves, but still white enough that they should have noticed her passing. They probably supposed a killer wouldn't wear flannelette.

Despite the reverberating shake of Harry's snores, the killer sat in the kitchen nursing a mug of tea and nibbling stale toast.

"You can't hide in the attic 'cos I hide there. Goodnight then. Oh, and please don't eat my Harry's heart."

Trill slept soundly.

The killer slept on the floor beside her bed. He clutched the tattered remains of the rag doll. She stepped on him as she climbed from the bed. Well it was a silly place to lie.

He awoke with a start and grabbed her ankle. If he snapped the thin bone, he'd trap her in the attic forever or until it healed. This didn't worry her. Outside the window, the prison remained alight and awake is if they still expected to find him lurking beneath a bench or camouflaged against the wall. She waved.

"What the fuck?" the killer said. "Get down."

"If I were harbouring a killer why would I wave at the guards, silly?"

"You look like you're signalling for help."

"Oops!"

She waved again.

He dragged at her nightdress, wrenching her away from the window and pressing his hand to her mouth. He tasted of blood and cigarettes. He shook her off.

"Did you just lick my hand?" He wiped it on his shirt. "Should have run last night, shouldn't have hid."

The killer paced the room. He'd attract Harry's attention, Harry would put on his uniform and blow his whistle, and they'd both hang from a noose. *They don't hang people these days.* Daddy had hung by the neck, tongue hanging from his mouth, a wet patch at his crotch. She hadn't seen it, of course. You weren't allowed to watch the dead swing no matter how much you loved or hated them. Mummy died in prison when her breasts rotted and no one cared, no one cared.

"Would you like a cup of tea?"

He paused.

She continued, "Before you murder me."

"I'm…" He crumbled then. Fell to his knees and sobbed so loud the dogs in the prison kennels would catch it.

"You don't like tea?" *Am I four or forty-five? Am I nine or ninety?* "Coffee then."

"I don't know why I… What came over me? Is it too late to go back?"

"It's always too late to go back."

She should go downstairs before Harry came upstairs and paraded his starched uniform and polished buckles. If the killer let her leave. If she were the killer then she wouldn't trust a child to keep a secret or an adult not to scream of murder.

Harry climbed the stairs. With each step discovery, with each step a twitch of the killer's limbs as if she had injected a poison into his veins and he was about to slip into a fit.

A long breath to the window and Trill began to write HELP in the steam. Well Harry would have to think her kidnapped. Although, didn't Harry know her better than that?

"What sort of name is Trill?" the killer said, his pleasantness evaporating, nerves taking control. "You sound like bird food."

"Dad kept parrots that used to scream of murder until Dad froze them and served them to the neighbours as turkey sandwiches. Mum wore their feathers to the party. I remember laughing 'cos the neighbour's wife was a Polly and the husband wore an eye patch."

"You couldn't make it up," he said, pulling the door ajar and peering down the dark staircase. "Who's Harry?"

Who's Harry? "Harry is my" – *brother, son, uncle, grandfather* – "family. Harry will blow his whistle and the roof will fall down on all of us. You should hide in the wardrobe or under the bed or throttle my scrawny neck before I tell on you."

The killer had no time to consider this and chose an alternative solution. He hid behind the door. Harry was dressed and his hair slicked back with oil.

"There's been trouble at the prison. Keep the doors locked and if the police call, pretend you're not home. Stay away from the windows."

He glanced towards the window then but her breath had faded. In a moment he would turn and leave and either see the killer and cause a murder or leave her with the killer.

"You hear me, Trill?"

"Bring, bring, there's a voice on the line but the static is interfering with its message."

"I've no time for this."

A floorboard creaked. A heartbeat dragged out waiting to discover the outcome of the killer's movement. He had no weapon, no tie with which to strangle Harry. He had surprise but that only went so far. A swift turn to Harry's heels and the game was set.

Harry held his arms out to his sides and tried to keep Trill behind him. His mind would be whirring and the more it whirred the more the steam would fog until all conclusions ended in disaster.

"Let me call from the window," Harry said. "It's best for all if I alert the authorities to your location. You won't get away. You won't leave this house and see your family again. You don't want to stay here. Even we don't want to stay."

With no weapons between them, the men were evenly matched, although Harry had the hindrance of trying to keep Trill behind him. She giggled.

"I just need space to breathe," the killer said. "I'm innocent. Miscarriage of justice."

Trill spat at the word *justice*. Her spittle landed on Harry's shoulder. He didn't notice. Trill waved her hands at the killer who seemed to want to ignore her. *Pfft!* After she'd mislead the police and their vans and their dogs. She'd wave her nightie from the window and invite the dogs in for supper. *Yum, yum, killer's bum.* Harry pressed his elbow against her chest, urging her back, caging her in. She stomped her foot in the manner of a three-year-old and felt the pain of a seventy-year-old shoot up her leg.

With Harry distracted by Trill's strop, the killer punched him in the side of the head and Harry fell down.

"Oh!" Trill said. "Well that was rather naughty."

"I didn't mean. I just… I can't go back. I don't belong there. Have I killed him?"

"Possibly." She stepped over Harry's prone body. *No blood.* "Would you like some apple juice?"

"I just… I just… I just…" He played like a broken record.

Trill understood why Katy had drunk her apple-juice-bleach, she was little and stupid and trusting. This man, though, this supposed killer. He lay slumped across the kitchen table. Harry picked up the killer's arm and allowed it to flop to his side. Then he sobbed. Trill sobbed too for it seemed the thing to do. Then she gathered the torn bits of her doll onto her knee and began to sew it together, this time careful not to thread the needle through the paper-thin skin at her knee.

THE LIES WE TELL

Charlotte Bond

Cathy opens up her daughter's schoolbag and finds a letter stuffed down in the back pocket. She opens it, narrowing her eyes as she reads, then strides into the kitchen, clasping it in front of her. She shoves the letter between her daughter's face and the cereal bowl.

"Isabelle, what's this?"

Isabelle looks up. Cathy sees both calculation and fear in her wide blue eyes.

"A letter?"

"It says we've got a parents' evening next week. When were you planning on telling me this?"

"We only got it yesterday," Isabelle says, her voice small.

"Really? It's dated last week." Isabelle looks down at her cereal and Cathy feels anger prickling her skin. "What have I told you about telling lies?"

"That I mustn't," Isabelle says, her voice even smaller.

"That's right. We don't tell lies in this house. You know what will happen if you do…"

Isabelle doesn't reply but shrinks lower in her chair.

Ethan, Cathy's son and Isabelle's older brother, snorts into his tea. "Yeah, right," he says, matching his mother's glare. "Everybody tells lies. Even you."

"No I don't."

Click

She glances at the radiator. *Shit. That's all I need. Don't break on me now.*

Cathy turns her attention back to her daughter. "I'm going to fill in this form and give it to you. If I find out that you've not handed it in, there'll be trouble. Understand?"

"Yes, Mum." Isabelle's voice is practically a whisper.

Cathy nods. "Good. Now get ready for school. I've got a showing at nine and I can't be late."

Click

Cathy scowls at the boiler then marches to the bottom of the stairs. "Vikram!" she calls. "The bloody heating is playing up again. It must be air in the pipes. Get it fixed, will you?"

Her husband appears at the top of the stairs. As he descends, he does up his tie. "I'm backed up at work, Cathy. I've got staff appraisals to do. Can't you take an afternoon off?"

"No, I can't. It's much easier for you to take time off."

Click click

She points at the radiator in the hall. "There it is again! Did you hear it?" Vikram hesitates. She can see by his frown that he didn't. "Fine. I'll sort it. Just like I sort everything else around here."

Click

She glances at her husband, to see if he's heard it this time. It's louder out here in the hall for some reason. But he has turned his back on her, using the hall mirror to straighten his collar. She glares at the back of his head. His lustrous black hair, which she'd fallen in love with, is thinning and streaked with grey. In his reflection she can see the lines around his eyes: dark crinkled skin showing his age.

What did I ever see in him? she thinks as she climbs the stairs. *Whatever it was, it isn't there now.*

Cathy pulls up outside the property at nine o'clock sharp. The viewing is booked for nine-thirty, but she likes to arrive half an hour early. It gives her a bit of time before the rush of the day engulfs her. She has no qualms about the lie she'd told her daughter.

Cathy opens the door, pushing back against the accumulated mail. She scoops the envelopes up and dumps them in the bin. Then she does a walk round of the property, checking everything is in order – although this semi has been empty for about six months so it's unlikely anything has changed. Virtually no one is interested in this place after they've looked around and done a bit of research. The area is a dive, the place is riddled with damp, and although the owners have tried to impress with a brand new en-suite, the plumbing is shoddy and water leaks everywhere whenever you turn on a tap. She finds a dead fly on an upstairs windowsill and disposes of that in the bin as well.

When she is satisfied everything is as it should be, Cathy sits down in one of the few remaining chairs and digs out her phone. She glances at her watch: 09:16. A good amount of time to herself. She opens up the patience app and starts a new game. In a drunken row once, Vikram had told her it was ironic how she loved that game so much given how little patience she had with everyone else in real life. Cathy had retorted with a home truth of her own. She forgets what it was she herself said, but she still remembers his words every time she opens the app.

The viewing couple arrive five minutes early, which annoys Cathy. But she plasters on her best estate agent smile and ushers them into the property. They exchange formalities, information and small talk before Cathy says, "Shall we get started? This really is a lovely property."

Click

The sound makes her jump. It's coming from behind the couple. She tries to peer round them.

That's odd. The radiator's behind me, not them. Maybe there are some water pipes in the walls.

"Really? How so?" asks the man, leaning to his left slightly to insert himself into her field of vision.

Cathy recovers herself, focusses on him and begins the sales patter. "It's near local schools, if you're thinking of starting a family –"

"No." The woman says it brusquely, indicating there is a history.

Cathy doesn't miss a beat and her smile doesn't slip. "It's only a short walk to the shops and many of the pubs and restaurants around here are excellent."

Click

"In fact, my husband took me for an anniversary dinner in a lovely place just around the corner from here. I can highly recommend it."

Click

She grits her teeth but the couple are staring around as she talks. They look interested in the property and Cathy doesn't want to lose that, especially if they haven't noticed the annoying clicks. She forces her smile wider. "Shall we start in the kitchen?"

They do a tour of the kitchen, Cathy standing with her shoe over the cigarette burn in the linoleum. Then the lounge, the dining room and finally back to the hallway.

"Shall we venture upstairs? The bedrooms really are the best bit."

Click

Cathy gives a nervous laugh. "I'm sorry about that noise. Must be air in the pipes. We have the same thing at home."

The couple exchange a glance then the man says "Sorry? I didn't hear anything."

"That's good then. Must just be my ears attuned to it. It'll be sorted before you move in."

Click

"Shall we? There's a beautiful view from the window of the guest bedroom, and the master bedroom has an en-suite, relatively new, all in good working order."

Click

It's okay. They can't hear it. It's not spoiling anything.

When the upstairs has been inspected, Cathy leaves them alone to discuss their options. She takes herself into the kitchen, firing up her app again and losing herself in the methodical game. It soothes her nerves, on edge from the constant clicking of the heating.

Halfway through her third game, the man pops his head around the door. "Do you think there's any leeway on the asking price?"

Her fake smile widens.

By the end of the day, Cathy has secured two offers: the couple from this morning have made an offer on the house, and another pair have made an offer on a flat that she showed them round yesterday. She works late, sorting through the paperwork and pinging off emails. She texts Vikram, telling him to pick up the kids, then ignores his replies. She knows he'll do it if she doesn't answer.

The office is empty when she finally shuts down her computer. She is grinning, and feels like she's floating on air as she takes the lift down to the underground car park. There are no people but plenty of cars; the air heavy and smelling slightly of petrol.

Her heels give off staccato beats on the tarmac. She pulls out her phone and checks her messages. There are six texts from Vikram, each of them piling on more and more anger until he's writing in capitals with an abundance of exclamation marks, telling Cathy how he's had to call in his sister and that Cathy is a terrible wife and mother.

She smirks as she puts her phone away. "Yeah, yeah, Vikram, but you'd be lost without me."

Click

Cathy's feet stutter to a stop. She stares around. There are thick pipes running along the walls, but somehow she knows the noise didn't come from them. Some primal instinct, buried deep inside, tells her that she's not alone in this subterranean room.

"Hello?" she calls out. She clenches her fist, ensuring the stones of her engagement ring are uppermost, ready to gouge a potential attacker's face should she be forced to hit out into self-defence. "Hello?"

There's a rasping noise that takes her a moment to identify: it's the sound of something being dragged over the floor. The noise seems to surround her so that she can't tell where it's coming from.

What the hell is that?

Oh god. What if it's a killer and he's dragging the body of his last victim to his car? The idea seizes hold of her mind and she suddenly knows that this is exactly what is going on.

There's a killer in here, and he's coming for me.

"I'm going to call the police!" she calls out.

The dragging noise ceases immediately and the quiet is somehow worse. Her pulse races and her stomach churns. She glances towards her car. It's about twenty feet away. *Can I make it? Is that enough of a head start if he comes after me, wherever he is?*

The silence stretches out as Cathy considers her options, then the dragging sound starts again and it's too much for her. She pelts towards her car, every second expecting a hand to grab her collar, yanking her backwards.

She presses the key to open the doors; the lights flash. She is running so fast she practically slams into the driver's door. As she pulls it open, she risks a glance behind her. The car park is empty. She climbs inside, shuts the door and locks it. Her breath forms fog on the window as she pants heavily. Shaking, she looks in the mirrors, trying to spot her potential assailant. She thinks she sees him in every shadow.

Cathy slides the key in the ignition and, with a screech of tyres, she is flying towards the exit. She presses the button to make the barriers rise and they do so with the awful slowness of a nightmare. She's going so fast she fears she might crash into them, but she doesn't want to slow. As she speeds underneath them, there's a sharp metallic twang as the car's aerial clips the barriers.

Then she is on the main road and driving away, her knuckles tense and white on the steering wheel.

By the time Cathy reaches home, she's just about calmed her nerves. She's poured her fear into road rage, leaving her drained but more mentally balanced.

She parks up and gets out. As she reaches the front door, it is pulled open. Vikram stands there, his face contorted with fury. But then he takes in her appearance and his eyes widen.

"Cathy, what's happened? You look dreadful."

Realising that here is a smooth way to avoid an argument about the kids, Cathy allows her shoulders to slump. She pushes past him, sighing as she drops her keys on the hall table. "I worked late and there was someone in the car park. I'm pretty sure he was going to attack me. He stalked me and he was dragging something. It scared me shitless." She gives a nervous little laugh that isn't feigned.

"Oh hon," Vikram says, pulling her into an embrace. She tolerates it because it's preferable to the row that had been brewing.

"Thanks. I just want to get in and forget about it. What's for dinner?"

"Just some ready meals I picked up on the way home." Vikram's face hardens as his mind clearly circles back to his anger. "I didn't have much time, what with you texting at four o'clock to say you couldn't pick the kids up from their clubs."

"Sorry, work was terrible. I just couldn't get away." She reaches out, cupping his cheek the way she did when they were young lovers. His stubble prickles her skin. "You're such a sweetheart. I love you."

Click

She snaps her hand back as if electrocuted. "Did you hear that?"

Vikram cocks his head. "No."

"It's the bloody heating again."

He puts a hand on her shoulder and smiles gently. "Well, that's a job for tomorrow. Let's just get some dinner, okay?"

Vikram goes into the kitchen as she hangs up her coat. She glances at the post piled up on the hall table. There's a folded piece of yellow paper with her name handwritten on it. Frowning, she unfolds it. The paper is thick, more like vellum than paper. Inside is written a number.

999,887

The ink is smudged and there's an unpleasant, greasy feel to the paper. Her frown deepens. The hairs on the back of her neck prickle as if someone is behind her, so close their breath chills her skin. She turns, but the hallway is empty.

Exhaustion sweeps through her then. She goes into the kitchen, puts the letter in the bin and pours herself a large glass of wine.

Two days later, Cathy pulls up outside Ethan's school, tyres screeching as she slams on the brakes. The fury is like a white-hot rod running through her core. She can't decide who she's most angry at: Ethan, for being ill when she was waiting for an important call; Vikram, for not being free to pick up their son; his sister, for not being free either; or herself, for being a shitty mother and putting work before her children. Although she's pretty sure it's not the last one.

"Bloody kids," she mutters as she grabs her bag and climbs out of the car. "Sometimes I really wish I hadn't had them."

She walks to the school office, her back straight, her stride even. She ensures her expression makes it clear just how busy she is and how annoyed she is at having to be here. The receptionist is unfazed.

"Just sign in please, then I'll take you to Nurse Wilkinson." Cathy scrawls her name and details, taking a small amount of pleasure in making her writing so atrocious that it's practically unreadable. The receptionist doesn't seem to care. She signs the book herself then pushes a buzzer that opens the door.

Cathy follows the woman down the corridor, eyeing each watermark or piece of peeling plaster with disdain.

What's happened to all the bloody taxes I pay? Aren't they supposed to keep the school looking decent?

The receptionist pushes open the door to the nurse's room. Cathy stares around. It's empty. "What's this?"

A woman in a white top and black leggings steps out from behind a screen and smiles broadly. "Ah, Mrs Chaudhary?"

Cathy nods. "Yes. I'm here to collect my son. Where is he? This had better not be a waste of my time."

The nurse's expression hardens. She glances past Cathy to the receptionist hovering beyond. "I've got this, Rachel. You can go." As the door behind Cathy closes, the nurse smiles reassuringly. "I promise it's not a waste of your time, Mrs Chaudhary. Ethan is indeed unwell, and is currently in the men's toilets."

Cathy wrinkles her nose. "Which end of him is it?"

The nurse gives her a sympathetic look. "Both ends, I'm afraid."

Cathy rolls her eyes. "Bloody brilliant. Just as well I keep some grocery bags in the car. How long will he be?"

The nurse glances at the clock and her forehead creases in concern. "He has been in there a while. We'd best go and check on him."

The nurse leads Cathy to the staff toilets. "We use these for the poorly children. It helps keep them separate from the rest of the school and control infections." She gives Cathy a knowing look. "I don't need to tell you that adults are much better at washing their hands than children, so the risk of bugs spreading is much lower putting them in here."

"Can I just go in and get him?" Cathy asks impatiently.

"Sure. I'll head back to the infirmary. Come find me if there's a problem, but otherwise you can just take him." She smiles again and heads back down the corridor. Cathy glares at her retreating back.

My, you're quick to dump and run, aren't you?

She pushes open the door. The sickly-sweet smell of urine wafts over her, but there's also something below that. It's just a hint, but it smells like meat gone bad.

God, just what has he been throwing up?

"Ethan?"

There is silence. She can see all the cubicle doors are closed, but only the one next to the wall has a red bar on the lock indicating it's occupied.

She steps inside. "Ethan, it's Mum. I've come to take you home, at great expense to my day, I might add."

"Mum?" The voice is quiet and edged with fear.

"Yes. Who else would it be? Now hurry up. Unless you're throwing up, in which case get it all out of your system. I've just had the car cleaned and I don't want you vomiting in it."

"Mum... there's something in here with me."

"Yes. Me."

"No, Mum. Next to me. In the cubicle. It smells horrible. I can hear it breathing."

Cathy's eyes flick to the cubicle next to her son's. Another waft of that rotten smell assails her nostrils and nausea flutters in her stomach.

"Don't be ridiculous. There's nothing there."

Click

"What was that?" Ethan asks, panic clear in his voice.

Cathy can't answer. Her mouth is dry. The sound definitely came from the cubicle, not from the pipes or the radiator this time. Her gaze drifts to the gaps beneath the cubicle doors. She can see her son's feet in one, but the one next to him appears empty.

"Please, Mum. Check. Please." The pleading, frightened tone speaks to Cathy's mothering instincts, buried as they are, and she's walking forward before she even realises she's moving. She halts in front of the door, trapped by indecision: to fling it open hard and fast, or push it open gently?

She reaches out a shaking hand and pushes the door gently. She is convinced she'll see some hulking monster with oversized jaws that click and clack when it moves them. But the cubicle is deserted. Something has been there, however – there's a bloody handprint on the pristine white toilet seat.

Cathy reels backwards, sickened and appalled. She sees a bead of blood trickle to the edge of the seat, forming a droplet, before the door closes on the rebound.

Something is scrabbling at the back of her mind, a memory trying to force its way out. Blood. Bloody... She can't quite grasp it.

"Mum?"

Cathy's tongue feels thick in her mouth. "Can you move?"

"Yes."

"Then let's get the hell out of here."

The red bar turns green and Ethan's pale face peeks out. "What was it? Did you see anything?"

"There's nothing there." Cathy pauses, unconsciously waiting a beat to hear that click, but it doesn't come. "Hurry up. I want to go home."

They walk down the corridor at speed. Cathy grips Ethan's shoulder tightly, although whether she wants to keep him close for his safety or hers, she cannot fathom. She just knows she needs to get outside and let the fresh air wash the stink from her nostrils. She ignores the receptionist calling after her and waving the signing in book. When they finally step outside, Cathy takes three deep, gulping breaths before she feels strong enough to walk to the car.

Ethan retches three times on the way home, but nothing comes out of him except saliva, which is caught by the plastic bag she's given him. By the time they pull into the drive, he's squirming and making the most appalling smells. Cathy undoes the front door as quickly as possible, then Ethan is pushing past her and racing up the stairs, one hand clamped on his backside.

Cathy scowls after him. *There goes my nice clean bathroom.*

His hasty footsteps have scattered the morning's post all over the hallway. Cathy bends down to pick it up. Her hand hovers over a folded sheet of paper. Her fingertips tingle at the memory of the greasy feel of the last piece. She picks it up, opens it and stares at the number written inside.

999,901

She crumples the paper, goes to the bin and throws it inside. "Bloody kids. What kind of stupid prank is this?" Her hands are shaking as she goes to put the kettle on.

"Cathy?" Vikram's voice penetrates her dreams. She opens her eyes blearily to see her husband standing over her. "It's nine o'clock. I've let you sleep as long as I can, but you need to get up now. We promised Isabelle we'd take her to the zoo today."

Cathy moans and rolls over. "Can't you do it? You don't need me."

"No." There is steel in Vikram's voice; it's not his normal, placating tone nor the frosty tone he uses when they argue. She twists to look at him. His arms are crossed. His normally soft brown eyes glitter like dark gems. "It's a family day, Cathy. You promised her we could go after she got that reading award. It's her treat and, believe it or not, she loves her mother and wants to spend time with her."

"Fine," Cathy says, flinging off the duvet. "I'm up. Satisfied?"

Vikram just walks out of the room.

Cathy takes her time showering and getting dressed. *I'm the breadwinner around here. It's my weekend too. I deserve some time off. They'll just have to wait.*

When she gets downstairs, she finds Vikram and the children standing by the door, coats on. Isabelle holds up a box. "We made you some toast, Mummy. I put lemon curd on it, just like you like."

Cathy takes the box and stares at it. Then she looks up accusingly at Vikram. "What about coffee? You know I need my coffee."

"We're stopping at the petrol station. I'll get you some there. Come on." He pulls her coat down from the peg and hands it to her. Her skin feels hot and tight as anger courses through her.

"No. I'm going to have breakfast and —"

But Vikram has already turned away and opened the door.

"Come on, kids," he says, and they head outside, leaving Cathy standing dumbstruck, coat in one hand, box of toast in the other.

"You bastards," she mutters under her breath. "You don't care about me at all, do you?"

Click

Cathy jumps so much she almost drops the box. The sound definitely came from down the hall, nowhere near the radiator. Slowly, she walks up the hallway, scanning the carpet and the walls for anything which might give a hint as to where this noise is coming from. Halfway down she stumbles back as a familiar, rotten stench engulfs her. She drops her coat, her hand covering her mouth. Her watering eyes are drawn to the understairs cupboard. She remembers a time in her childhood when their pet cat brought in a dead rabbit and left it the broom cupboard where it stank the place out during the heat of a summer day. This smell is similar, only more potent and more putrid.

Oh god, what if there's a family of dead rats in there or something?

She opens the cupboard and bends down to see inside. It's too gloomy to make out much. She recognises the tall, thin silhouette of the vacuum and the cluttered shadows of the cleaning shelves. But there's something at the back, a shadow that is completely out of place. It looks like a figure sitting atop a pile of something.

"Cathy!" Vikram's voice is so unexpected and loud that she screams.

She turns to him, her heart pounding in her chest, her breathing rapid. He frowns. "What the hell are you doing?"

"There was this noise. Then this smell. And…" She tails off, remembering the strange shape. Vikram's presence bolsters her courage and she reaches into the cupboard to turn on the light. The hunched figure turns out to be a large dust sheet that's fallen over a bucket.

Vikram peers into the cupboard beside her. She steps away. "Sort that, will you? It stinks in there and I need to put on my shoes."

As she walks away, she hears him mutter, "I can't smell a thing."

Then you're lucky, she thinks. It takes a good blast of fresh air to clear away the stench from her nostrils.

The cold air nips at every patch of exposed skin. Cathy digs her hands deep in her pockets and tries to stifle a yawn. This is the same zoo that her mother brought her to as a child and it holds little more excitement now than it did then.

But I did promise Isabelle, I suppose, she tells herself as she stamps her numb feet.

Besides, she is glad to be out of the house. She hasn't been sleeping well; her dreams are filled with jaws that go clickety-clack and bills from utility companies that have numbers so high she can't comprehend them. The bills come on pieces of paper which bleed onto her fingertips.

She stares at two rhinos that look utterly bored. She tries to push down the dreadful knowledge that is creeping through her mind: she knows where the noise is coming from now. It's coming from under the stairs. She feels it with a certainty that clutches at her bowels whenever she thinks of that dark cupboard.

The fuses are in there. And the old electricity meter. Maybe one of them is malfunctioning. I'll get Vikram to look at them when we get home.

The thought calms her and she has enough energy to engage with Isabelle, who is desperate to go and see the octopus in the zoo aquarium. Cathy allows herself to be led in that direction. They step inside and tropical heat washes over Cathy. She lets out a contented sigh, relishing the warmth.

Click

Cathy's head snaps round looking for the source of the noise.

Click click

It's coming from the darkness of the doorway.

Click click click

Cathy backs away, nearly knocking Ethan off his feet. "Hey! Mum!

Watch out."

Vikram grips her arm, hissing in her ear, "Cathy, what's wrong with you?"

Cathy stares at the zoo employee who is standing in an alcove by the door. The girl stares back, surprised and wary of this attention, then the door opens again and the girl looks at the newcomers. Her thumb moves, pressing the button on the small tally counter hidden in her hand.

Four people enter.

Click click click click

The door opens and a couple come in.

Click click

The girl's eyes stray back to Cathy; she gives a slightly nervous smile. "It's for fire regulations," she says. "I count them on the way in, and Mick counts them on the way out. We have to do it when we've got a big exhibition on like the shipwreck one."

"Yeah, sure, not a problem," says Vikram. He tugs Cathy away, demanding in a low voice. "What *is* up with you today?" Cathy doesn't answer; she doesn't know.

By the time they get home from the zoo, the sky is darkening and Cathy is exhausted. It's a struggle just to get out of the car. She staggers to the front door, leaving Vikram to deal with the kids.

As the door swings open, she sees the post on the floor. Sure enough there's a folded piece of yellow paper. She opens it.

999,992

The numbers blur as her hand shakes. "Who the fuck is doing this?"

"Cathy! Don't swear in front of the kids," Vikram snaps. The three of them are standing behind her, waiting to come in. Vikram is glaring, Ethan is smirking and Isabelle looks confused.

Cathy's fear morphs into anger and she shakes the letter at Vikram. "Some idiot's harassing me."

Vikram frowns. He ushers the kids into the living room and takes the paper. He studies it for some minutes then looks at her.

"I don't think this is paper, Cathy." He brings the note to his nose, sniffs it. He swaps hands, rubbing together the fingers that were just touching it and she knows he too can feel the grease. "I think it's animal skin."

It feels as if her stomach has dropped to her feet. Her fingertips burn and she rubs them on her jeans. "Animal skin? Ugh. That's sick."

Vikram tries to hand the note back, but she refuses to take it, hiding her hands behind her like a child. He rolls his eyes and places it on the hall table. "Keep this one. If you get any more, take them to the police." Then he walks into the kitchen, as if that settles the matter. Cathy stares at the note, feeling utterly alone in a house full of people.

She starts down the hall, intending to get a very large glass of wine, but her eyes stray to the door of the cupboard. It looks innocuous, but she imagines it opening up, a hand reaching out for her as she passes. A shudder shakes through her and she turns away, walking into the living room.

Cathy spends the rest of the evening in a daze. Vikram has to nudge her whenever the kids ask her questions. When Isabelle asks what's for dinner, Cathy looks at her blankly. Vikram grits his teeth then calls for pizza. Isabelle is delighted; Ethan is smug.

The television is on while they eat, but Cathy can't process what they're watching. There's an idea trying to burrow its way up from the depths of her brain. Something from her childhood is being tugged towards her consciousness every time she thinks of that clicker at the zoo, of that bloody handprint on the toilet.

Bloody...

She can't stop staring at the hallway. It's like the cupboard has become sentient, that it sits there like a hulking animal, biding its time.

"Goodnight, Mummy," Isabelle says, throwing her arms around Cathy's neck. Startled from her thoughts, Cathy hugs her back and sees that Isabelle is already in her pyjamas. She glances at Ethan who is also in pyjamas and reading a comic. She looks to Vikram who is staring at her sternly. "I thought it best if I handled bedtime tonight," he says.

The house is quiet while Vikram is upstairs settling Isabelle and Ethan. Cathy closes her eyes, trying to force some calm into her mind.

What is wrong with me?

It's lack of sleep, that's all.

And the bloody heating. That's driving me nuts.

She holds her breath, listening for the clicking of the air in the pipes, but there's nothing. She exhales and tries to let her mind drift, to find some peace from her raging thoughts. It must work because suddenly she's snapping her head forward, going from sleeping to awake in an instant.

It takes her a moment to take in her surroundings. Vikram is sitting on the sofa opposite, watching her. She gets the feeling he's been there for a while. There's an unfamiliar expression on his face. It looks like fury.

"What's the time?" she asks.

He stands. "It's bedtime. For me, anyway. You can sleep down here, you slut."

Cathy's mind is so anaesthetised the insult causes her no shock or anger, only confusion. "Slut?"

His hands ball into fists. "I was looking for that picture from summer, of all of us by the pool. I knew that my mother sent it to you by text so I went through your phone just now and I found all the text messages from Steve," a glob of spit springs from his mouth as he says the name, "about the two of you, about your meetings, about your..." he pauses, clearly working up to the word 'affair.'

Cathy stands, her legs feeling like water. So many thoughts run through her head but she finds herself inanely saying, "But I have a security code on my phone."

"Yes. And now I know why. If you want to hide a sordid affair, Cathy, I'd recommend having a code that isn't our eldest child's birthday." Vikram's eyes are alive with a dark fire she's never seen before. He takes a step towards her and Cathy takes a step back, almost tumbling back into the chair.

"But that was months ago, Vikram. I haven't –"

Vikram cuts her off, his voice low but somehow more threatening than if he was shouting at her. "I'm going to bed. Alone. While I'm upstairs, thinking about whether I can trust you or even bear to touch you again, I want you to lie down here and think about what the hell you're going to do to make this up to me and the kids, or where you're going to stay if I decide to kick you out."

He stalks towards the door. Cathy calls out after him. "But it meant nothing."

Click

"I didn't start it. It was him."

Click click

"Damn it, Vikram! Can't you hear that?" She rushes to the door, but can't bring herself to step out into the hallway.

Vikram, one foot on the stairs, shakes his head incredulously. "After everything I just told you, you're more concerned about the bloody pipes? You're a piece of work, Cathy." His normally placid face twists into a sneer.

Cathy watches as he climbs the stairs. She hears the bedroom door open and close. The world seems to tilt around her. She shakes her head, trying to dislodge the feeling that everything's going horribly wrong.

She is desperate to find something that she can control. Her eyes alight on the letterbox and her heart leaps.

"Yes," she murmurs, "that I can do something about."

Click

She glares at the radiator in the room behind her. "Just shut the fuck up, okay? I'm not in the mood." She storms into the kitchen, driven by anger and purpose. She roots through the drawer where they keep all the odds and ends. She finds the duct tape and brandishes it with a grin. Then she marches to the front door and kneels down. She tears off strip after strip, plastering them across the letterbox. When a thick mass of grey covers every section of it, she smiles and stands up.

"There. That'll stop you little bastards from pestering me."

Click

She spins round. It's dark behind her. The kitchen is dark, the living room too, but she doesn't remember switching off the lights when she left either of them. There's another click, the sound of a door being unlatched. With a gentle creak, the door to the under-stairs cupboard swings open. A sickly yellow light spills from it. The smell of rotting meat quickly fills the hallway.

Cathy is repulsed. She doesn't want to go towards that light, but her feet are already moving that way. The answer to what has been plaguing her is in there, she knows it. Part of her wants to see it, to confront it; the rest of her wants to flee screaming. It feels like she's in a nightmare, and she convinces herself that seeing this through to the end is the only way to make herself wake up.

The boards creak as she walks down the hallway, drawn towards that light.

She places her hand on the cupboard door to steady herself and peers inside. The vacuum cleaner is hidden by a pile of bones. Some are yellow, some are warped, some are a perfect gleaming white and some of them still have shreds of flesh attached to them.

Cathy's gaze travels up the pile of bones to the creature sitting at the top. The creature has the shape of a man, but he's as small as a child, and his skin is wrinkled like a crone. He clearly once wore clothes, but they've rotted away and now only shreds of filthy fabric cling to his wizened body, mimicking the decaying meat that clings to some of the bones. The creature meets her gaze and grins at her, showing a mouth filled with yellow, jagged teeth. Bits of slimy black flesh are caught between them.

"Ah, Catherine. I'm so glad you came. My belly is fair empty." She stares at him and he cocks his head. "You *do* know who I am, don't you?"

Cathy's mouth is dry but the words come out as a croak. "Bloody Bones."

The creature's grin widens. "So, you were listening to your mother. I hope you've told Isabelle and that she listened well. I hope you warned her about how I come in the night to take away naughty children who tell lies.

"Of course, it's not only small children I take," he adds, "but most people ignore that part of the story."

He holds up a piece of yellow paper, like the paper she's been receiving. This sheet is ragged and bleeding around the edges. There is a mole in the bottom corner. But what draws Cathy's gaze is the number scrawled in the middle.

999,997

She shakes her head. "This is a nightmare. You're not real."

Bloody Bones lifts a hand. Between his gnarled fingers is a tally counter, just like the one from the zoo. But this one is battered and filthy, clearly very old. His thumb depresses.

Click

"You're just a story."

Click

"Stop doing that!"

"I'm just keeping track," he says with a casualness that infuriates her.

"This is just a nightmare, it has to be."

He cocks his head, a pitying look in his eyes.

She glares at him and snarls, "You don't scare me."

"Ah! There we are."

He holds the clicker up for her to see, his thumb poised above it. The counter reads *999,999*. He presses down.

Click

The numbers flick round to zero.

Goosebumps rise over Cathy's skin and she starts to tremble. "What does it mean? What did you do?"

"Don't blame me. *I* didn't do anything," he says, reaching down for his bag. "It was all you, Catherine, all your lies. Big ones, little ones, I just kept count."

He tugs at the cord around the neck of the bag and it falls open – and keeps opening, becoming impossibly wide. The world tilts again and Cathy feels herself falling forward. Her arms pinwheel, her fingers reach for anything that can arrest her progress. But she's not falling towards a bag; what she sees below her is more like a tunnel. There are figures clustered around the walls and they look up at her. Their own personal misery is momentarily forgotten as they raise half-chewed arms in greeting. Those who have skin left on their faces smile as they welcome a new member to their pitiable ranks and Cathy falls inexorably towards them, her screams mingling with theirs.

TING-A-LING-A-LING

Daniel McGachey

The Bells of Hell go ting-a-ling-a-ling
For you but not for me:
For me the angels sing-a-ling-a-ling,
They've got the goods for me.
Oh! Death, where is thy sting-a-ling-a-ling
Oh! Grave, thy Victory?
The Bells of Hell go ting-a-ling-a-ling
For you but not for me.

It surely wasn't the singing of the troops that caused Dr Lawrence's companion to blanch so startlingly? On home shores for a leave that was supposed to have come permanently two Christmases before, their song was a blend of music hall jauntiness, psalm, and that gallows humour so vital now the gallows' shadow loomed across the map of Europe. For Lawrence, it was a painful reminder of the dwindling of the youth that had so recently packed the playing fields and lecture halls of the university he had long thought of as home; this soldiers' choir might have been a gathering of those lads after a rugby match or race meeting. Many would never return to complete their studies, and Lawrence wondered if there would ever be room again for such boisterous but innocent merriment now that the world had proven itself quite mad.

"I'm sorry, I..." They spoke at the same instant, each suddenly aware that they were not alone with their thoughts. The embarrassed shrug from the fellow seated opposite and Lawrence's own self-conscious smile would have told any observer that these weren't close friends sharing a convivial Yuletide dram. Not that anyone was observing, those thronging the public house too immersed in their own efforts to be of high spirits to pay heed to the sombre pair at the corner table.

97

"Perhaps somewhere quieter? My study's not so far..."

Lawrence's companion waved away the suggestion. "It's rather refreshing to be amidst such bustle, and – well, yes – life."

"Of course," agreed the doctor, raising a toast. "To life – to be celebrated when lived fully, and commemorated when lost valiantly."

"To life," repeated the other, touching his glass to Lawrence's.

"I can only reiterate how deeply sorry I was when the news reached us about Jonathan," said Lawrence, regretting how facile the words sounded even as they passed his lips.

Jonathan Hinchcliffe had been the type of bright lad who left an impression, and, although it had taken Dr Lawrence a moment to recognise the fellow who'd hailed him as he stepped from the tramcar not half an hour previously, at the mention of his brother's name a nagging sense of familiarity had crystallised. He was considerably older than his brother – his thin hair greying where Jonathan's had grown thickly dark, his face sallow where his brother's had been tanned and ruddy, but there was still a startling resemblance in those green eyes, sparkling with that same curious intellect. "I apologise for startling you," Reginald Hinchcliffe had said. "A near stranger accosting you in the street, how awful; but we did meet when I visited Johnny last Spring term. Just that one time, but of all his tutors, you were the one who made the greatest mark."

"Very kind of you to say so," murmured Lawrence. "Your brother was a promising student, and an exceptionally popular young man around the college." Indeed he was both these things, a fiercely intelligent fellow, yet never smug or superior about his abilities; a fact that added enormously to that popularity. And one which made it harder to accept that he had died a grim and bloody death in some French field. "If you've come to retrieve any of Jonathan's effects, I believe he took his belongings when he enlisted, but the porter's staff..."

"It was you I came to see, Dr Lawrence. My chancing to encounter you here simply saves me the trouble of enquiring at the college." Then, with meaning, Reginald Hinchcliffe added, "Jonathan really did speak of you often – more particularly of your, how to put it...? Your particular area of expertise?"

"Ah," breathed Lawrence with a familiar sense of dismay. "Mr Hinchcliffe, I'm afraid my rather unusual field of study was closed off some time ago. It was attracting a degree of," he sought a palatable explanation, finally settling on, "unwelcome interest. Reputations, particularly eccentric ones, persist in closed environments, but whatever Jonathan may have heard no longer applies and was, in any case, hugely exaggerated."

"Which is precisely what I told him, Doctor. Naturally a scholar of folklore encounters ghostly tales, and who could blame him for taking an interest in such yarns? I well know that much of what is found in antiquity is as commonplace as the trivialities we take for granted nowadays. Any additional colour is welcome. But to believe you'd actually encountered the genuine article in the flesh – or lack of flesh, should I say? These things categorically cannot be. Well... that is what I thought."

"But," prompted Lawrence, albeit reluctantly, "you no longer think so?"

"Do you?" asked Reginald Hinchcliffe, fixing him steadily with his dead brother's eyes.

"Let's get out of the cold, then we can see what is to be believed or not."

Which was how Dr Lawrence had found himself in that crowded ale-house with his late student's elder brother, both men studiously avoiding the subject that had brought them there in the first place.

Lawrence, reaching back to that single prior encounter and grasping at the first strand of memory to float his way, ventured, "Jonathan mentioned that you worked in a museum. But not locally, or I certainly would have met you more than once."

"You have a good memory, sir. Though when it has to encompass the days of, let's say, Pliny and Horace, one shouldn't be surprised. I don't wonder that our paths never crossed as, after an only marginally satisfying apprenticeship at one of our metropolitan institutes, I took to seeking out the obscurer treasures to be discovered in our smaller rural collections."

Lawrence smiled. "Then I find it stranger yet that we avoided one another so completely, for such places were my familiar haunts." He might have then spoken of those peculiar legends often found in such outlying institutes, whose basis in awful fact would shock all but those who knew what they truly sought. But his resolve not to dwell on such dark matters remained firm, despite his suspicion that this resolution would shortly be rendered infinitely more difficult to uphold. "Yet you no longer lead this nomadic lifestyle?" was what he instead enquired.

Reginald Hinchcliffe shook his head. "My last post as curator was of a tiny establishment in an equally tiny northern hamlet, where I zealously rooted out what still remained of the locale's *objets d'intérêt*. I would have been content, no, happy, but for the regular frustration of locating the precise piece to form the highlight of an exhibition, only to see it slip from my grasp due to the meagre funds at my disposal. Sponsors, benefactors,

Good Samaritans; I have sent what can only be described as begging letters, hoping to find one or all of these."

"And with no luck?"

"Oh, I found my sponsor," shrugged Hinchcliffe. "For one of my charitable appeals arrived on the desk of Mr Rupert Fosdyke."

"The business magnate? Wasn't there some fuss a year or two back, when he tried to buy some masterpiece or other from the National Gallery?"

"A Landseer, yes, and a few minor Flemish works. And it might tell you something of Fosdyke's wealth, and of his determination, that, after the summary dismissal of two decidedly substantial offers, on the third attempt he raised his bid so dramatically that only the prospect of potential scandal prevented its success.

"Rupert Fosdyke wrote, in highly flattering terms, of what I had achieved on slender means. A surprise to me, as I'd no notion he'd ever visited my little museum. What, he wondered, might be the upshot of combining my skills with his purse? By his invitation, I met with him at his home, Everfayre Manor. Now, on first view you would think it a finely restored Tudor hall, whereas it has stood less than forty years, built to Fosdyke's instructions. And in every room his reputation as a devotee of the arts was vividly confirmed. Paintings, sculptures, furnishings and ornamentation all spoke of the collector's mania, and here lay my sole reservation."

"Your desire to share the relics of the past sat at odds with the notions of private collections, accessible only to a privileged few?"

"You're as intuitive as Johnny always insisted, Doctor. That was the very concern I raised. But, as Rupert Fosdyke explained, 'You may see me as selfish in keeping these wonders for my solitary pleasure. But, in their lengthy lifetime, what is the relatively short span in which they are mine to enjoy? I am naught but a temporary custodian, and when I am no longer here to treasure them, then such museums and galleries as are fit to take them – a matter on which a man like yourself would be well placed to decide – will be welcome to them.'"

Was that a whistle Lawrence let out? If so, he felt it justified, remarking, "A difficult offer to resist".

"Impossible," conceded Hinchcliffe. "Thus I became adviser, procurer, and curator of the museum that is Everfayre Manor, charged with seeking artifacts at risk – collections due to be split by auction or private sale, or those housed in inadequate conditions, their futures far from assured. By this route I came upon that object whose... hidden properties prompted me to recall my brother's vivid accounts of your less orthodox pursuits."

Dr Lawrence has, more than once, had dealings with objects that boasted 'hidden properties'. One has only to think of the quill pen whose ownership was traced back to a debauched medieval bishop whose practices were far from saintly, and which inexorably guided the hand of a more recent owner until the final words it put down were in the form of a suicide note. Or to recall those bewitched face masks, through whose eyeholes could be glimpsed... but, no; Dr Lawrence chose not to recall the masks. Yet, even having long foresworn such matters, deference to his late student led him to sigh only briefly before saying, "I think I'd better order us a fresh round of drinks, and then you may give me the full account".

My occupation (*began Reginald Hinchcliffe*) should have sent me roving between the fabulous art houses of the continent in pursuit of acquisitions. Such is now, alas, an impossibility, and who can say whether anything worthwhile might survive the dismal carnage? Oh, an unworthy concern, petty in the face of the loss of young men's lives, but decades spent preserving the efforts of our forebears have left me acutely sensitive to the needless loss of works that have survived the centuries.

Yet still I found myself, on a night in February of this year, at an unpromising address on the upper floor of a tenement slum that nevertheless housed what appeared to be the Limehouse District Store Room for the *Palais du Louvre*. Here, there, all around, crates lay open to display riches beyond my most fervent hopes. Here were paintings whose mere frames, let alone the canvasses, would fetch a king's ransom! Elegant and delicate figurines which had survived the destructive orgies of the Revolution were housed alongside silver candlesticks that might once have illuminated grand fetes attended by Louis the XIVth and his courtiers.

"But, how?" was as close to a sensible question as I could form when I found my voice.

Said my hostess, "I gave account of my situation in my letter to your Mr Fosdyke."

"You mentioned reading about my employer's collection in *The London Times*, and spoke of certain items you believed may interest him. You are... rather, you were... housekeeper to a nobleman in the Marne region?"

Madame Sophia Lousalle nodded. "My master, the Duc de Vorache, in the days leading to the overrun of our lands by the Germans, gathered what had been bequeathed him by his ancestors, and charged his household to flee while still we could, with as much as we could transport.

Had we dared travel together, our burden would have excited curiosity, so one by one we left our lives and our home behind us. Had I delayed by a single day, I would have been lost, my cargo looted, my life..." A shrug. "The Channel appeared the one barrier which might hold our enemies back. Almost two years have I waited, guarding my lot. Until now. For now I must accept that my friends, my master, be they alive or dead, failed in their escape."

"Madame," said I, my eyes straying around that remarkable room, "I doubt even my employer could instantly lay his hands on the true value of this collection."

"I do not ask its true value. Only that it *is* valued. My needs are few, but such funds the Duc granted me to meet these are now depleted. As I have guarded these things, they have made me their prisoner. I ask only sufficient that I might seek life beyond these walls. I am a country-born woman, Mr Hinchcliffe. The city holds no comfort for me."

Was she a lunatic? If she had any idea of this treasure's worth – and I firmly believe she had every idea – could she simply give it away in this manner? And could I, in all good conscience, accept? "I will strongly advise my employer to be generous in his offer." Mad or not, she deserved a just repayment.

She seemed content with my assurance and, when I begged leave to examine the pieces more closely, her bland gesture to do so suggested she'd already mentally surrendered any stewardship of them. So, like a child on Christmas morn, I dropped to root amidst the straw and sackcloth that had protected these rarities during their conveyance across land and wave. And it was while I was gingerly striving to unveil a bronze statuette of some promethean figure that my hand brushed against a shrouded object, and I first heard it...

Ting-a-ling-a-ling...

Prometheus was cast aside, still bound in his wrappings, as I drew this mystery prize to me. And even muffled in sacking, with each inch I dragged it, it emitted that same compellingly melodic *Ting-a-ling-a-ling-a-ling*...

Ah, here we had it now, uncrated and unwrapped! A clock! A clock like none I had ever seen. More than a clock! Not merely a wonderfully intricate sculpture in brass, but a work of mechanical artistry. What it depicted was a town in miniature, with twin rows of buildings – here the church, with its spire and its churchyard; there the schoolhouse, with its rooftop bell; in one street the houses, in the other shops and workplaces, a stable and an inn. These dwellings and places of trade were presided over by what I can only describe as a citadel – an edifice of spires and turrets and lofty windows atop a high central hill. And the clock face itself was set into the tallest of these towers, a cyclopean watcher at the heart of the township.

The architecture might have derived from any number of places across Europe – perhaps designed to portray any town, anywhere – and may have originated at any point in the last two centuries. I could have searched for hours amongst the elaborately detailed surfaces for a maker's mark, but I grew more preoccupied yet with my realisation that far more than the manufacturer's identity was concealed from me. The buildings, you see, all bore shutters in the windows, their interiors hidden, and I now saw that each shutter, each door too, was affixed by tiny hinges. If they were attached in this manner, surely they must open? And if they opened, surely there must be something more to be revealed.

Sliding a thumbnail into the hairline gap between the arched church doors, I succeeded only in bending the nail painfully back on itself. There was no yield, and I feared any attempt with a more substantial implement might damage those slender hinges. My thumb in my mouth, I said, "The clock's workings must power this remarkable piece of automata. May I have the winding key?"

A shake of the head.

I could have damned her for insolence, for here, amidst these uncommonly rare works, was one article that went beyond uncommon and may even have been utterly unique. Such was sure to appeal to Rupert Fosdyke, but more-so even than this was his particular passion for clocks, watches, timepieces in general. Among his earliest concerns as a young man with a growing fortune was a watchmaker's workshop, which he had swiftly expanded into a manufactory. Since this success, he'd always regarded clocks as a symbol of good fortune. Already his collection numbered a Huygens pendulum clock dating from 1658 – the second oldest known to exist, certainly the oldest outside of the Netherlands – and one of only four extant precision clocks devised by John and James Harrison. Were I to present him with this piece, I would certainly secure the sum the lady deserved for her loyalty to her lost master. Yet she seemed determined to thwart me. "Why won't you give me the key?"

"If it is not with the clock, it is not here."

"Then where in damnation...?" Then I remembered her lost friends, and my apologics began. "In the duke's haste, there must have been items put astray," I sadly concluded.

But, no. "The Duc de Vorache prized greatly *l'horloge de l'éveil* – the

Awakening Clock, I think you might say? It was the first of his treasures to be safely packaged. He perhaps dispatched the key under separate protection, to prevent hostile hands from seizing both. A clock without a key has as little use as a key without a clock."

With that, and with one last, long look in which I attempted to memorise every detail in order to accurately describe it on my return to Everfayre, I ran a hand over the clock – eliciting a final pleasing *ting-a-ling* – and took my leave of Mme Lousalle. It was only at the door that I thought to ask, "Did you ever see this 'Awakening Clock' in motion?"

"Monsieur, I did not." And then I was out on the landing with the sound of a door closing and chains snapping to behind me.

On the train, I had time to consider Mme Lousalle's curious claim that, despite its prized status, she had never seen the clock working. Logically, with an elderly, delicate mechanism, the duke would have been wary of damage through overuse. Having dismissed this minor puzzle, I was left with the problem of how to persuade my employer to purchase an extremely decorative, yet ultimately useless timepiece. As it transpired, I didn't have to.

"Shorehouse," declared Rupert Fosdyke when I had described the dilemma of the missing key. And, when I'd begged his pardon, he continued, "Eric Shorehouse, at the Maidstone works."

"Ah, indeed," said I, the penny dropping; Maidstone being the clock factory's location.

"He's the supervisor. Well, that's the title on his wage slip. What he is, really, is a craftsman, practically as skilled as his old father, who was there when I bought the place – the main reason I did buy it, truth be told, skills like his being worth the investment. Now, if Eric Senior was still with us..." He lowered himself slowly behind his desk, reaching for the telephone. "If anyone can fashion a key for any clock you'd care to put in front of him, it's Eric Shorehouse. I'll tell him to get himself round here for dinner tomorrow, before he takes a look. That should give us ample time to get to London, conclude our business, and bring back the spoils, eh, Hinchcliffe?"

And so, for the second time in as many days, I made the journey from Everfayre to Limehouse, this time by private car, and with my employer by my side. We followed swiftly in the trail of a telegram advising Mme Lousalle of our impending arrival, and were followed in turn by a van, commandeered from one of Mr Fosdyke's local concerns to carry back the bulk of his impending purchase, rather than trust them to the mercies of the railways.

Rupert Fosdyke was always at his most impatient when anticipating a fresh addition to his collection. Even so, it was rare for him to venture far from his treasure house in order to make the purchase in person. Yet plainly this unusual artifact fascinated him; he was practically quivering in his seat, and frequently exhorted his chauffeur to make haste.

The old man drew a considerable sum from his bank in London, before we proceeded deep into that warren of wretched streets. The elegant automobile looked entirely incongruous idling outside that dreary building – like an ocean liner in a forest clearing. Leaving the chauffeur and the press-ganged van crew to guard the vehicles, Mr Fosdyke and I went within to finalise the transaction with the Frenchwoman. And, leaving her with an empty front room and a well-filled purse, we parted company with Mme Sophia Lousalle.

The return journey was less comfortable, a significant portion of the motorcar's back seat taken up with the clock, still wrapped in its sacking. It also took considerably longer, as Fosdyke was now given to urging his chauffeur to slow down, to avoid rattling the precious cargo over uneven roads. I was massively relieved, you can be sure, when the high chimneys of Everfayre were glimpsed at last over the treetops.

But my work wasn't over. My employer supervised as two footmen and the chauffeur carefully ported the clock from the vehicle to his study, leaving me to instruct the workers on where to deposit the crates, before tending to their unpacking. So I barely offered more than a cursory nod to the dark young fellow with lively, intelligent eyes, who limped from the manor to join in overseeing the transportation of Rupert Fosdyke's most prized purchase. It wasn't until the paintings and sculptures had been arrayed around the walls of the long gallery to await inspection that I had my first proper meeting with Eric Shorehouse.

"A pleasure, Mr Hinchcliffe," said he, moving stiffly forward and shaking my hand warmly, quickly confirming my impression of a clever mind at play behind those dark eyes and that searching expression. Those eyes, though, were not long affixed on me, as we were all drawn to the gleaming timepiece taking up much of Mr Fosdyke's desk. One could only imagine the scale of the fireplace above which it must once have sat – elaborately sculpted in its own right with, at its heart, a blazing fire large enough to warm some vast, palatial chamber.

"And this arrived from France?" queried the horologist, all the while circling the desk with short, hobbling steps. "It's not French; that I can say with certainty. The face and hands, lovely though they may be, have none of those romantic elaborations I would expect."

With slow, deliberate care, he ran a finger along the miniature street that wound its way between the buildings. "Yes, clearly there is some mechanical action supposed to take place. There are these little slots and grooves, you see, like tracks. Without the key we will see nothing, but maybe luck will be with us," and from his jacket he produced a ring, around which hung winding keys of various sizes. Squinting at the opening in the rear of the varnished wooden base, he selected a narrow cylinder from the jangling bunch and attempted, with much delicacy of movement, to press it home. A near inaudible *tut-tut* and another almost identical key was chosen, this procedure repeated a dozen times, sometimes accompanied by the murmur of some indistinct oath – certainly more indistinct than Rupert Fosdyke's rising grumble. With a final sigh and a rueful shrug, Shorehouse returned the ring to his pocket. But his words offered hope yet. "It struck me that as individual a design as you described would have an equally individual key. So I brought my work case with me – my old father's bag of tricks, with a few of my own thrown in. It'll take a little longer, naturally, but this nut will be cracked."

He excused himself momentarily, returning with a battered old Gladstone, which he opened up almost reverently. By use of melted wax, carefully poured, he could create a precise impression of the winding mechanism, from which he would then manufacture a replacement key. From Mr Fosdyke's grin of anticipation, he evidently felt he'd made exactly the right decision in summoning the young fellow.

In the few minutes required for the wax to harden once more, Shorehouse marvelled, "I thought I knew all the great clockmakers, but the like of this I've never seen. If I could only open her up and take a look at her workings... Oh, not that I intend any such thing, sir, there's no call for apoplexy. Merely thinking aloud. A life, since boyhood, spent amongst the inner mechanics of clocks and watches makes you naturally curious on viewing a new piece. But, now, I think we're set, yes, so if I just ease the string out..." A look of puzzlement replaced that of satisfaction on his dark features as he examined the plug of wax.

"Did it work?" prompted Fosdyke. "Can you make me a key?"

"I think so, yes," murmured Shorehouse, distractedly. "But, you see? Mostly I find keys that fit a square or hexagonal slot, but this..."

"It's a star," said I, peering at the angular furrows in the waxen cylinder.

"A pentacle," Shorehouse corrected me mildly. "Most unusual."

"But still workable?"

"I'm quite sure, yes." And he placed the impression snugly into a small tin, returning it and his other paraphernalia to his bag. "I'll need to take it back to Maidstone, of course."

"Tomorrow," insisted Mr Fosdyke, as he led us through to dinner.

"Tomorrow," agreed Shorehouse, with a decisive nod. However, and I don't think this is mere hindsight, I detected a less than decisive tone to his voice.

The following days passed, as far as I was concerned, in cataloguing the remainder of the purchase. Most items were easily dated, but several required a degree of research. I kept my employer apprised of each development, yet he appeared distracted. I'd no difficulty in deducing what it was that preoccupied him, as I frequently caught his gaze wandering to the side table where the as-yet-unawakened Awakening Clock temporarily rested.

Frequent telephone calls were made to Maidstone, despite my attempts to subtly suggest that his increasingly impatient interruptions would hardly aid the watchmaker's progress. The apologies and excuses – the metal was too brittle and had cracked, an urgent order for the army had to take priority – did little to mollify Fosdyke. I was startled once to walk in on him bellowing into the receiver at such a ferocious volume that he left himself breathless and had to be assisted to bed. It was then that I realised all was not well with my employer's health, and though he stubbornly resisted the idea, the doctor insisted upon rest.

During this period – in which a nurse had to practically stand guard over Fosdyke to prevent his return to his work – I spoke again to Eric Shorehouse. It was he who telephoned, in fact, having grown worried after not receiving his customary insistent call in several days. Knowing that his lack of progress was a cause of undue stress to my ailing sponsor, I enquired if Shorehouse had any inkling when the key might be ready.

"It's ready now." Even across the distorted line I could tell there was no triumph in his achievement.

"But?" I supplied, filling the silence on the line.

"Mr Hinchcliffe, I will come today, though I have my concerns about bringing what I believe is an object born out of bad designs to a bad place. I think that you and I should talk before I say anything to our mutual employer."

Mystified, I agreed to a private meeting, and some hours later we sat in the drawing room where I prompted him to share what was on his mind.

He did so hesitantly, yet soon abandoned his diffidence to display a natural story-teller's skill. And as he spoke, my mind was irresistibly drawn to my brother's many tales of his antiquities tutor and his rumoured exploits in the realms of phantoms and shadows. It wouldn't be too long after this that I would find myself wishing I'd listened to that inner voice's promptings and called upon you there and then, Dr Lawrence.

Reginald Hinchcliffe looked up from his glass. "You realised the significance of that unusual design on the key; I saw as much in your change of expression."

Lawrence needed to consult no textbook before declaring, "The pentacle can be interpreted in many ways, and has appeared in the practices and beliefs of numerous peoples – from the Celts, who associated the five-pointed star with Morrigan, or the Hebrew belief that it represents the first of the Seven Seals, to a symbol of Christian protection. But in more recent times, the last of these has been inverted to serve occult ends, such as the *'Sigil of Baphomet'*, the Black Goat, representing the absorption of forbidden knowledge. Your young watchmaker believed there to be some cabbalistic meaning to the design?"

"Oh, I thought it nonsensical," laughed Hinchcliffe bitterly. "But I heard him out. And what he told me of his suspicions, despite my disbelief, made me shudder..."

"My notions must seem ridiculously fanciful to a learned gentleman," said Shorehouse wryly. "To me they might also, had I not been raised with such tales from my cradle. Clockwork and stories, the two things – after love and respect for others – my father bequeathed me. And I think the stories I heard at his knee were very different from those told in any English nursery.

"One of the many things Erich Shoenhauer left behind in his own country was his name. Upon his arrival on English soil, he was Eric Shorehouse. He was all too aware that a foreign name can prompt hostility, a foreign Jewish name all the more so. And now that madness has befallen the world, I retain my English name, not to conceal that I'm a Jew, but to avoid being seen as an enemy amongst my friends purely for being, by descent, German. You see, it's more than my being lame that prevents me enlisting with others of my age."

"A man cannot be answerable to his ancestry," said I, aware in the back of my mind that my own brother could well be fighting against this young man's kin.

He smiled sadly. "I don't think the mobs that put bricks through the windows of folk they once viewed as neighbours, or put light to shops owned by German immigrants, feel the same. The fact that I never have once visited the land of my father's birth would matter little with them.

"But even never having been there, I feel I know Germany through the stories my father told me. The myths and the fables – the child-protecting *Weisse Frauen*, the *Lorelei* and her fatal song, *Holda*, and the *Golem* – these were my childhood companions. Stories he surrounded me with, and clockwork. And, on one night which I never will forget, these two combined terrifyingly into one."

My young visitor paced stiffly before the fire, as if chilled. "My father was at his work table, carefully piecing together a gentleman's watch that cost more than he earned in three months. I was at his elbow – I must have been seven or eight – working my way through the guts of an old mantel clock I'd taken apart and reassembled a dozen times. As I watched Father's skilful hands engaged in the task I thought God had surely designed them for, I laughed, 'My father, you have the hands of a magician. For if you can repair time itself, what else could those hands do?'

"It was meant as a compliment, but he looked at me sternly, and bade me put aside my task. 'My son,' said he, 'such vain ambitions are not for us to consider, and I shall tell you why. It is a story my father told me and his father told him. He, my grandfather, knew the man it concerns – the finest craftsman in the west of Germany, in all of Europe perhaps. Let me tell you what I was told of *jahr ohne sommer...*'

"And my father told me of 'the year without a summer', when all of northern Europe was awash with storms. My great grandfather was, like his descendants to come, a clockmaker, and a skilled one too by all accounts. But there was another, even more ingenious! Friedrich Valkenburg was an artist and he, in words I had innocently echoed, had been praised as having a magician's touch, so precise and beautiful were his creations. Precision pieces, minute in their every detail. Toys with the movement of life in miniature. Just like that clock of yours! Yet not all saw beauty there, and some would insist that he genuinely practised some unspeakable magic rituals whilst alone in his workshop. Superstition? Perhaps. Friedrich was a scientist, a man ahead of his day, and one who believed that mechanics and physics held the key to every mystery, be they in life or in death. This would have been all well and good if it had remained purely a theory. But Friedrich put his theories into practice!"

I could only suggest that this artisan was clearly versed in the theories of Galvani and his followers, but Shorehouse pressed on. "He was unbalanced in his mind, all reason overturned. There had been an awful tragedy, you see. His only son, Heinrich, a mere lad of some fourteen summers, was killed, his cart lost on a mountain road eaten away by the rains. He was found, broken and lifeless, at the foot of the hill. Friedrich locked himself away from the world, his workshop shuttered and barred for weeks. In this time he was seen only once, when he crept out at night to nail a declaration to the church doors. *'Place no faith in those who falsely promise eternal life,'* it proclaimed, urging the villagers to forego the next day's service and to gather at his workshop to witness his finest work to date.

"Even the priest obeyed the summons – he would have preached to an empty church otherwise – and young and old, my great grandfather amongst them, convened in the yard outside Friedrich's home. Here Friedrich – looking like no skilled craftsman, more a crazed spectre, pale and bearded, eyes reddened through lack of rest – appalled and alarmed them with his claims that he had defied 'the Creator and Taker of life'. And so saying, he wheeled out before them the product of days and nights in his workshop, his filthy creation – the homunculus – Heinrich!

"His own son, stolen from his early grave, was unveiled in front of that fearful audience, who shrieked their horror. The priest fell to his knees and was sick in the dirt. It wasn't merely the spectacle of the corpse, propped up, naked and putrefying before them that caused their terror. It was what had been done to it in the name of Valkenburg's blasphemous science!

"Friedrich believed the human form to be nothing but a sophisticated machine, and there was no more sophisticated mechanic than he. So he had opened up the shell of his boy and simply replaced the components which no longer functioned. He had rebuilt him – a clockwork man within the skin of his son. And where the skin couldn't accommodate its new contents, he had remoulded it, 'improving' upon the design, so that what he had wrought was both more than and far less than human. Cogs and gears were now primed where internal organs had once worked. Pistons and rods emerged and receded again into the flesh of the arms and legs, and a leather pump could be seen between the exposed ribs, where the heart should have been. A hollow tube connected the gaping mouth and the stitched together lungs, in order that the creature might breathe. While the eyes, having shrivelled and dried in death, had been plucked out to make way for lenses of ground glass and mirrored prisms.

"Those who hadn't fled at the mere sight of this abomination watched as the grief-maddened creator freed his nightmare child from his restraints, calling the name he had been given while alive, beckoning for him to come to him. To come to his father's arms.

"Poor Valkenburg. His madness had blinded him to the impossibility of his undertaking. His son lay still and motionless, as dead as when they'd found him at the bottom of the mountain. The realisation struck hard, and it spread through the crowd, waking them from their daze of horror. They seized rocks, branches, whatever came to hand, and laid waste, smashing and burning all that Friedrich had spent his life in creating. Clocks and astronomical instruments and toys were wrenched apart, their pieces scattered and trampled. And when they entered the workshop and saw the debris of Friedrich Valkenburg's final task – the defective and broken *parts* that had been removed to make way for the newer, stronger workings – they put the whole place to the torch."

"And Valkenburg?" I asked, so drawn in by his retelling that I momentarily forgot it was nothing but a story told to frighten a child.

"In his shame, and in the confusion of the destructive chaos, he fled. To where, none could say, yet most believed his only escape would be over the border and into Switzerland."

"And from Switzerland then to France?" I prompted, striving to keep my incredulity in check. "That's what you suggest? That your clockwork monster-maker is also responsible for the Awakening Clock? Even if this were so, what can there be in a one-hundred-year-old story to concern us now? By your account, Friedrich made a poor showing as, what's the term...? A necromancer? Ah, but there's more to the story?"

Shorehouse's voice dropped to a conspiratorial level. "Friedrich's shame was thought to have been the futile madness of his actions, and the obvious fact that they could never have succeeded. But my father's grandfather and the others who witnessed it knew that his real shame, his real horror, was that it had worked! The homunculus had responded to its father's voice, and it had walked!"

"And you think that Valkenburg might have continued in his experiments?"

"That I do not know," conceded Shorehouse.

"Nor do you know for certain that he, if he ever existed, is the manufacturer of the clock which sits not a hundred feet away. I cannot think this crazed ghoul you describe could have been responsible for so complex and intricate a work. Besides, it's simply a clock, a machine to mark the passage of time, not some mechanised cadaver. What can be the harm in it?" Had I only known! But on I went, relentless in my scepticism. "However, I genuinely believe that the reactivation of that clock will restore life, in a way. For I can think of nothing else that might revive Mr Fosdyke's spirits, can you?"

My dogged ebullience in the face of his childhood horror story seemed to lift Erich Schoenhauer Junior from his sombre fears and, with a ghost of a smile, he picked up the key. "Of course, Mr Hinchcliffe. Let us put away childish things, eh? And, I confess, despite my misgivings, I'm curious indeed to see the clock in motion."

As foreseen, Rupert Fosdyke's delight in his unexpected guest's delivery of the key had the effect of a rare tonic. He brushed aside his nurse's stern admonitions and, flinging on a dressing gown, led the small procession downstairs to his study. Here the watchmaker checked his own pocket hunter, before opening the glass pane in the citadel tower, and adjusted the hands to the correct time. He then, with a touch of ceremony, handed the winding key to the old man and observed closely as it was inserted and turned.

With the faintest of *whirrs*, the clock came alive, a ponderous, echoing *thock* speeding into a soft, regular *tick-tick-tick*. We watched, spellbound, as a minute passed, then another. Only a further sixty seconds remained before the minute hand would reach its apex. Six o'clock. For that full minute none of us, I think, dared breathe.

Then the chimes – *ding-dong-ding-dong-ding-dong* – quite distinct from those tinkling notes I had first heard, but a pleasing peal nevertheless, emanated from the vibrating bell in the spire of the church. With a further *whirr*, and a metallic *clink*, the arched doors of that building sprang apart, while yet more *clinks* and *clanks* denoted the opening of doors along the street of houses. Fosdyke's fingers found my arm, his grip strong despite his infirmity, his free hand pointing elatedly as people, inch high people of beaten brass, emerged from their doorways to glide down the curve of the street, through churchyard gates that swung lightly apart, and into the sacred building itself, the vaulted doors *chink*-ing closed behind the last of the clockwork congregation.

Another minute or two ticked past before any of us broke our gaze and our silence, Shorehouse saying simply, "Evensong?"

My employer roared with laughter and clapped the young man on the back. "You're as brilliant as your father, lad. Come now, this calls for drinks, and we've fifty-five minutes to enjoy them, before we return for the next show."

There was, indeed, a next show when, at seven o'clock, the church bells pealed once more, and those same townsfolk, now about-faced, left their devotions and returned home. And supper was interrupted as we again trooped through at eight to watch as the beautifully realised coach and horses emerged from their stables, coach bells jangling throughout their circuit of the town, and then stabled themselves once more.

It was at this time the nurse began making dire threats if her patient didn't return to his sickbed. His look, the pout of a crestfallen child whose toys had been confiscated, was swiftly overtaken by a bright smile, as he opened up the clock-face and carefully rotated the hands until the clock showed nine. Thus, in quick succession, we witnessed the inn doors open to reveal the landlord, clanking his bell with a spring-loaded arm to rid himself of his miniature patrons; the night watchman who strode the streets by the late hours and chimed *'all's well'*; the early rise of the baker, seen through his shop window clanging the doors of his oven open and shut six times; the heavy, thudding gongs of the blacksmith's hammer; and the morning, lunch, and home-time bells of the schoolhouse, bringing half-inch children back and forth between home and study. For every hour there was a variation, as if we were giants watching over a living township going through its daily routine. In all, we observed this ritual three times over, before the nurse finally won through and my employer departed, leaving Shorehouse to once more set the hands to the right hour. This done, he extracted the winding key, advising me, "If it's lost I cannot promise to make another, as I had great trouble in manufacturing that one."

When he had gone – reluctant to stay overnight, away from his young family, he insisted – I considered his words and, deciding that the safest place for the key was with the clock, I reinserted it. It would only be later that I'd have cause to wonder if Shorehouse's exact words weren't closer to 'I was greatly troubled'. Such uncomfortable thoughts were yet to beset me, but, as I prepared to retire that night, one thing did strike me. Throughout our rapid tour of the many sights and sounds of the clock, I had at no point heard a chime remotely approaching the pleasing *ting-a-ling* that had first drawn me to the piece.

By the next morning my employer looked to have rallied yet further. Still forbidden from returning to his full duties, he was allowed, following much haggling with the nurse, to place a number of telephone calls to those with whom he'd entrusted his concerns, and to sign a few urgent papers before being ushered back to his recuperation. As ever, he protested. "I thought we agreed a few hours were acceptable?"

"You've had your few hours, Mr Fosdyke."

"Rot," he cried, marching to the side-table. "The clock hasn't chimed... Oh! Stopped. Sometime after twelve. Tell me I haven't paid a fortune, Hinchcliffe, for a broken clock."

"The rapid turning of the hands may have wound it down," I reassured him, twisting the key and hearing the *whirr* and *tick* in response.

"It must be kept wound at all times," said he, adjusting the hands. "I'll attend to that. Have the servants bring it to my room. At least I'll have something to keep me entertained during my hours of imprisonment."

This last was directed at the nurse, who patiently retorted, "And you shouldn't have many more of them, which'll be a relief to both of us."

Sadly this cheering prognosis was not to be borne out quite in the manner intended. That very night, I found myself in my darkened bedroom, relieved to have been awakened from a peculiarly unsettling dream. A short-lived relief, though, for a commotion of slamming doors and running footsteps snapped me fully awake. As I thrust my head into the passage, I saw two of the footmen and a teary-eyed maid, all in their night attire, rushing about aimlessly, while the ashen-faced nurse attempted to create order. Seeing me, she cried, "Call the doctor, sir. Mr Fosdyke has been taken gravely ill."

I raced downstairs and placed the call. The doctor was none-too-happy at being roused – unsurprising as, from the office clock, I saw that it was several minutes after one. It was only on hearing the name of his wealthy patient invoked that he agreed to make all haste. I then returned to the scene of the tragedy, attempting to shoo the staff back to their own quarters. Exasperated, I demanded to know why the nurse had summoned them all. She had no time to plead her innocence before the damp-eyed maid said, "We all heard it, sir. A cry. No, a scream! It came so sudden, and at full pitch. We heard it through the house. And then a great crash." Had that been what had wakened me, a shrill of fear rising out of nowhere?

I found my employer in his bed, a pale, miniscule figure, fragile as china or porcelain, boxed in by the elaborate bedposts at each corner. But from the toppled table and the shattered remains of the water jug, it was clear that he'd been up and awake when his attack had occurred. The nurse confirmed that when his cry had brought her running, he'd been sprawled on the carpet, as if attempting to crawl from the bed and from the room.

He was conscious, but barely so, and he shrank back across the mattress as I approached. At last a spark of recognition flared in his wide eyes, and he attempted speech, his lips rapidly moving but only the hoarsest of breaths escaping. I made out only a single whispered word – one whose meaning was lost on me. And as the doctor arrived and made his examination, I heard the soft chiming of the clock on the cabinet by the door, the tiny night-watchman setting out on his rounds, as though declaring, *Two o'clock, and all's well*.

But with Rupert Fosdyke, all was not well.

He lasted two more days and nights, throughout which he spoke not one intelligible word. The doctor put his decline down to the effects of a sudden shock, though no source for such an upset could be found. But he was, after all, of a considerable age. Even his bull-like tenacity must have had its limits, and these, it seemed, had been reached. And with his passing, it was clear that I would never understand the meaning of that final word he had uttered with such urgency to me: "Thirteen..."

There was much to be arranged after the funeral, the majority of it concerned with the disposal of Rupert Fosdyke's estate and possessions. He'd neither married nor produced an heir, and had outlived any siblings. Some distant cousins and a middle-aged spinster niece received generous endowments, while the servants were left with sufficient funds to last them into a comfortable retirement, and his many businesses passed into the control of their various boards of directors. This left the house, which would eventually be sold, and those works he had so devotedly spent his life in acquiring. Here his will showed him true to his word on that initial interview. I was to select fitting beneficiaries amongst the nation's museums and galleries. This would be no easy or rushed task. There were lists to make, visits to arrange, merits to judge, and decisions to agonise over. Only after several months had passed – during which time my late sponsor's private chamber was respectfully closed up, the pieces he'd kept aside for his own pleasure added to those on display throughout the house – did the process of packing the first of the works up for removal commence. It was then that the incidents also commenced.

On entering the long gallery on an autumn morning, I was irked to find that several portraits earmarked for an Edinburgh gallery had not, as I'd clearly instructed, been taken down and securely crated up. My mood was already sour, as my sleep had been uneasy – concern over this first shipment, I'd thought – so to see those paintings still hanging, their crates discarded carelessly below them, left me furious. I rang for the footmen, who had been retained until the house could be stripped of its treasures, and when I'd said my piece, they exchanged glances and shakes of their heads. "I'm sorry, sir," said one, "but I think maybe someone's playing some silly joke on us." His look suggested that I wasn't entirely ruled out of the list of suspects. "You see, these pictures were packed away, like you'd requested, sir."

"Joke or not," growled I, my patience worn thin, "I want what I asked done immediately." The rhythmic gong of the tiny blacksmith at his smiddy rang out from above the gallery fireplace, the clock having been placed there and wound only the night before. Ten o'clock, which left only an hour to pack – or repack – the canvases before their transport was due to arrive.

In the days that followed, there were more of these 'jokes'. I could no longer put them down to simple excuses for a failure to complete tasks, as

items that I, myself, had packed – some Grecian pottery, a rare book of
Goya's etchings – were found the next day in the places they'd long sat.
No one amongst the staff would admit to being the culprit so, decreeing it
a job best left in expert hands anyway, I gave them notice to quit. Harsh?
Perhaps, but there was more than mere obstructiveness at play. Whatever
nocturnal activity was taking place at Everfayre had developed into
something destructive. A window was found smashed in the drawing
room. Someone had scored deep marks in the panelling of the hallway, the
old wood slashed and splintered. Food was stolen from the kitchen, the
torn remains of chicken carcasses and other bones discovered scattered in
halls and corridors. And then there was the smell – such a dank and
stagnant stench that lingered long into each morning.

I soon realised I'd underestimated what my now solitary assignment
would entail. On my first night as Everfayre's sole occupant, I found
myself still deep in my work, harassed and distracted, until night had long
fallen. In part, I was glad of the long, heavy toil, as it might have led to a
sleep untroubled by dreams. Even still, I found myself grumbling at the
lateness of the hour when the clock whirred into life to strike twelve –
Ting-a-ling-a-ling-a-ling-a... five, six, I counted, eight, nine... but, wait, I had
surely heard the chiming of midnight already that night... *a-ling...* eleven...
and this was definitely not the sound of the night-watchman's bell...
twelve... *a-ling...* Thirteen?

Tiredness making me miscount, I told myself. But would overwork
have brought so vividly to my eyes this new and unknown motion of the
clock? The hands were still – no, not entirely still, but hovering, vibrating
to the tiniest degree, a fraction of a sliver away from the numeral one.
While, below, a more definite movement gathered momentum. A
movement centred around the churchyard. I hadn't noticed until that
second that each and every grave slab and mausoleum entrance was – as
with the doors and shutters – fixed on a hinge. Why should I have noticed?
I hadn't looked, for who would have expected the need for such things?
But as I grew aware of this detail, those slabs swung slowly aside, and the
crypt doors creaked open wide. And, as the awful forms within began
more fully to emerge, so too emerged the full memory of that dream which
had haunted my nights.

I am a stranger in the dream, at the very least a man walking in streets
that are unknown to him – unknown, but is there not something familiar in
these houses and stores? Those people I encounter seem not to know me,
nor even to see me. They simply glide past unheeding as I approach. I have
no home here, and the shops and inn – those places where even an

unfamiliar traveller should be granted a welcome – are closed and barred to me. I think I must be seeking sanctuary or rest – the night is darkening, and a full and watchful moon looms above and behind me – for I am drawn to the church. Even here I am denied entrance, for the gates are closed, the church unlit. Then a chime rings out that forces the breath from my body, drowns my yell of fright, and shakes the earth below my feet. And when I look back, the moon is not the moon at all, but the monstrous face of a vast clock atop a stark, black tower. And as its unseen bell tolls, I hear those tremors split the ground in the churchyard. The gates are shaken wide open, and I see what is flung up out of the deep ground there, and there, and there, that do not lie still, but beckon me to join them, even as they move swiftly to join me.

That dream came clearly to me as I stood looking down on that selfsame town my dreaming self had wandered, watching as those final, terrible seconds were replayed in miniature – misshapen figures in shroud-tatters, or of little more than bone, springing free of their tombs, gliding out through the gates and into the streets, the doors of each house opening before them, allowing them to enter unchecked while the inhabitants slept. And the final fragmented memory of that nightmare came to me only then – the sound of screams that rang out like distant bells in the night.

These screams resounded only in my own head. But the sound that drew my helpless eyes from this macabre tableau was real, and it was close by. A low, appreciative sigh. My head turned, against my every conscious desire, as if it too was governed by some internal, unstoppable clockwork. And when I saw the form that stood in the shadows, looking not at me but at the painting before it, I sobbed aloud and fled for the safety of my room.

It was Rupert Fosdyke, dead for months, yet there, in the flesh before me!

I woke, cramped and fatigued, curled up in the chair I had thrust against my chamber door – as if so flimsy a barricade could hold out what I had seen! What I *believed* I had seen, my rational mind urged in a bid to reassert itself. Had that vision not been the real dream? When I braved the dawn-lit gallery it seemed so. Perhaps the entirety of the preceding night had taken place purely in my mind, for all of that long night's work, those artworks wrapped and packaged, had been undone.

My reaction to this may surprise you. It certainly did me. I laughed. A laughter tinged with hysteria, probably, but that vast room echoed with my roar. "A promise is a promise," I told the four walls. "You can't hold onto them forever. You have to let them go, so you can go yourself! Do you hear me, Rupert Fosdyke?"

Had I gone mad, shrieking ultimatums to an empty room? Actually, I felt certain of the logic of my conviction. Fosdyke, who I had seen only hours before in a pose I knew very well, would never peacefully surrender his prizes if he still had power to walk these halls. It was he who had come back, night after night, to restore the pieces to where he rightfully felt they belonged. I did not believe in ghosts, and yet to argue against them would be to disbelieve the evidence of my own eyes. There had to be a reason for this phenomenon. "What is it that keeps you here?" My only answer came in the steady tick of the clock above the fireplace.

"Thirteen," I muttered to myself as I turned the hands and put the town rapidly through its daily and nightly rituals. "Thirteen!" I left the hour hand poised, beyond midnight, on the cusp of one o'clock, and I waited, the sound of gears spinning and springs tightening almost lost beneath the thudding of my heart. And it was my dismayed groan that drowned out the single clang of the watchman's bell, as the hand moved into place over the one. Whatever strange property this machine possessed, it was not to be tricked. I would be patient, and await the appointed hour.

That hour came round, finally, but I had much to occupy myself with in the interim. Opening windows throughout the property to banish that unpleasant smell was the first priority. The next was summoning a plumber, who – despite his frequent exclamations, as if he'd made some startling discovery – could find no cause amidst the pipes for the foul air. Then there were the rats, not living, but left in the parlour like an offering from some house-proud tomcat after he'd had his own cruel fun. There was no cat in or near the house. If a larger, more ferocious rat had struck, might that explain the scratches on the walls and doors? But a rat, no matter how large, could surely not have beheaded the figure of Aphrodite in the upper hall, nor caused those stains, like scorch marks, that blemished the canvases in that same corridor? An angry and petty act by one of the dismissed staff? I knew them all to be respectable, respectful souls, yet I clung to this reasoning, as the only solution remaining was a supernatural one, and this I quickly dismissed. The ghost of the old man may have walked abroad, but he was the last person – living or otherwise – to cause such wanton damage.

I was only a shade less adamant in my views as I sat in the gallery, fire ablaze, all lamps lit, as midnight came and went, the minutes passing at a crawl. I had nothing at all to fear from the spectre of my former employer. In life, he'd been a generous and affable individual, and I'd no reason to think that death should have fundamentally changed him. So, when the thirteenth chime sounded, I felt only a thrill of excitement as an indistinct outline, a mere sketch of a form, came into being. Had my surroundings inspired my feeling that, as it swiftly resolved itself, the hand of an unseen artist was rapidly applying accumulating layers to give the outline solidity and the appearance of life? Even then there remained a greyness about it, as if the pigments had been diluted, the true, vital colours lost.

I called his name, softly at first, as unwilling to distract him from his appreciation of the gallery's contents as I had been while he lived. "Mr Fosdyke?" I repeated, approaching him – not too close, as the idea that he might pass straight through me was still a repulsive one. I think he heard, for a puzzled frown creased his brow and he looked, finally, away from the paintings. I addressed him a third time, waving my arms vigorously, as though to a friend spotted in the distance. A slow smile spread across his face, and his eyes fixed on me at last.

"This is wondrous," I yelled. "Incredible! Yet here you are! Oh, but I have so many questions." I whooped and I laughed, but the smile had turned rigid on his pale face, becoming a look of incomprehension and... was that actual fear? Fear on the face of a ghost? He spoke, but the words were as unintelligible as those he had attempted on the night of his attack. I sensed a questioning tone, but he might have been calling from another room, so distant and distorted were the sounds. And when he saw that his meaning was not reaching me, he raised his hand, extending it cautiously toward me, as if fearing that I was some intangible visitant.

I don't know what I would have done if that grey hand had touched me, but it never did make contact. From somewhere in the house came a resounding crash. This din was heard by what had once been Rupert Fosdyke, for he looked warily to the door at the western end of the gallery. A second crash boomed out, and from above I heard the pound of footsteps.

"What is this?" I cried, but the phantom merely moved to stand gazing at the clock with a look of helpless horror. I strode to the west door, determined to once and for all face whatever was at the root of this mischief – my determination faltering as the doorway loomed closer and those noises of unseen destruction grew louder. I am not a brave man, I don't think, and to venture out into the dark was an unnerving prospect. But it was what I saw when I turned back that sent me plunging through that door, racing through shadow-filled corridors, until I was once more safely – I hoped safely – sealed in my own room.

The eastern gallery door had been closed when my vigil began. Yet as I now looked back, the doorway stood empty. No, the door wasn't merely open. It was no longer there! Even so, what I should have seen through the opening was the oak panelling of the hallway. It should not have been a long and narrow corridor, stretching away apparently for miles – a featureless passageway lit up in flickering bursts by what seemed the sparks and flashes of some unthinkable infernal machinery! And in these sudden, intense brightnesses, I glimpsed the figure of what might once have been a man. It was only a silhouette, a black shape in the far distance, but in those moments of darkness between the crackling flares it drew ever closer, and with it was carried the smell of damp and dirt, and something sharply metallic. It slouched stiffly, like its form didn't fit comfortably, yet on it remorselessly stepped. I could hear its footsteps – a regular, too regular, rhythmic pounding – and I heard its breathing – hollow, rasping, each sucking gasp drawn through a twisting tube. Even though it was still a far way off down that impossible corridor, I saw, before I fled, the hollow discs of glass where the eyes should have been, reflecting back those pulsing explosions of hellish light.

I paced in my room, listening to intermittent noises echoing through the house, straining for the sound of a regular, mechanical tread approaching my hiding place. I fumbled with my watch, anxious to see how long I'd been locked in. It had stopped, the hand stilled on the hour. My bedside clock told the same tale, as no doubt every clock throughout the house did. It was only as I grew conscious that I'd heard no other sound for some period of time that I glanced once more at my watch. The hands were moving, the minute approaching half past one, time flowing once more at its natural pace, not held in limbo for a frozen hour, during which the dead walked.

I know I must sound like a man woken suddenly from a doze, thinking an hour has passed in a second of dreaming, but this was no dream. It strikes me too as astonishing, the rapidity with which I accepted concepts that should otherwise have appeared ridiculous to me. But accept them I did, and as I knew that nothing would roam until that accursed clock once again reached the hidden hour, I fell into a grateful sleep that lasted long into the afternoon.

I'd intended telephoning Eric Shorehouse that day, but what was I to tell him? That the clock seemed indeed the product of Friedrich Valkenburg's insane science? That the clockmaker had succeeded in his unholy experiments? And that his device had summoned that original, flawed experiment from its unknown grave? I'd sound just as mad as those villagers had thought Valkenburg. And, if I did confide in the young watchmaker, what would he be able to advise? That I destroy the clock? And lose the chance to fathom the secret recesses of its mechanism? I did not make that telephone call.

My evening was spent in clearing away the debris of that late night rampage by the thing summoned by the clock. Priceless china crushed to powder under the tread of artificially powered feet, tapestries torn and smeared with stains I dared not examine. My anger was tempered by the knowledge that these were not deliberate acts. How could a machine, scarcely governed by a decayed brain, know or care about artistry and beauty? And what else could have caused this damage? There could be no other ghosts in this house of false antiquity, could there?

Oh! What kind of historian was I? I could accurately date a shard of pottery reclaimed from beneath foreign sands, yet I had never once thought to investigate the history of the spot I now inhabited. Hours were spent in the library, searching what shelves hadn't already been picked clean for volumes focussing upon the town and its surroundings. Of Everfayre Manor there was naturally no mention. But of what had once stood where the grand house now presided, there was much to be said, and none of it easy reading.

The preceding centuries were grim times to be convicted as a criminal. To suffer from any form of mental abnormality in those unenlightened days was equally unmerciful. And here, both lawbreakers accused of 'moral insanity' and these more innocent 'unfortunates' faced but a single fate – imprisonment and, inevitably, death in what was locally known as the "Neverfair Asylum". Early in the nineteenth century, relatives of one 'unfortunate' presented a petition in the House of Lords against the warders' treatment of their charges. The asylum was closed amidst public outrage, but not before countless inmates had died in wretched straits, hanged in the asylum grounds, or left to rot in filthy wards. Several on the staff were themselves imprisoned for their brutalisation of those in their supposed care, and the whole edifice was torn down. And its dead? They still lay in the earth of their unmarked graves. They still lay, but did they lay still?

Two phrases returned to mind. Shorehouse's talk of bringing "an object born out of bad designs to a bad place" was the more recent memory, but there was another. A description Mr Fosdyke had employed when describing his joy in supervising his home's construction, watching it rising, "like a flower slowly blooming where once even weeds had withered".

I knew then what had brought Fosdyke screaming to the brink of death. The inhabitants of those body pits, the vicious ones and those whose mental anguish had been turned vicious by their confinement. If they had been awakened, and had come prowling and gibbering out of the darkest corners of his chamber... such a thing would have put paid to a younger, healthier man, would it not? I was of no mind to wait to find out! I had time, just, before those thirteen chimes were due. I would remove myself from the house for an hour, until I was certain that what stalked within was at rest again.

Yet as I raced down the driveway, keen to put a safe distance between myself and Everfayre, a thought formed, so dreadful that it paralysed me. I could wait my hour, certainly, but what if the Awakening Clock was to stop – if the mechanism was to wind down during that uncanny hour? Would the house and its surroundings remain trapped within this time of the dead? How far did its influence stretch, and were its perimeters secure? Might it seep out, spreading like a corruption throughout the land? Surely our shores would prove no barrier.

My God! How long before it touched the continent, emptying the war graves almost as quickly as the generals could fill them? How long until the phantoms held dominance across the world and the living were merely spectres? Again, I am not a brave man, but I ran back to the house, praying for each extra second, ready to wind the clock and ensure that this hour would also pass.

Ting-a-ling-a-ling... Too late to complete my mission and escape again, still I ran for the fireplace. The crypt doors were open... I reached behind the clock, grasping for the key. The dead were out of their graves... My fingers fumbled, the key fell loose. The cemetery gates stood wide, the smell of rising decay growing strong... Still I groped for the key in the shadows. The doors to the homes of those unsuspecting townsfolk were opening. They creaked like heavy oak on iron hinges. A chill draught caressed the back of my neck, and I knew that it *had* been the creak of a real door. The western door yawned wide, as something large and grey lurched out of the gloom. Several other large, grey things followed, some walking or running, others crawling on all fours, reduced to little more than animals.

They were men, or had been, turned the colour of the clay under which they had been buried, their human features as indistinct as a faded photograph, their forms rudimentary, as if they too had forgotten what they once had been. Their jabbering voices were the echoes of someone shouting down a tunnel, as they frantically swarmed and staggered. This room was unfamiliar to them, and they pawed at the paintings and clawed at the draperies. Then another voice rang out, and they fell as still as grey statues. However vague and unformed the words were to my ears, I knew their tone – Rupert Fosdyke imperiously demanding to know by what right his home had been invaded.

Those statues turned, moving with alarming speed as they fell upon him. Arms flailed, fingers clawing, and teeth snapped as they tore into the old man. And even though my late employer's apparition had appeared muted and washed out, I saw that his blood was still a vivid, vital red.

I hadn't been aware that I had found the key until it dropped from my numb fingers. The sound as it struck the stone hearth was as distinct as any bell. They heard it, those grey, crimson-spattered fiends, for they turned. There was the echo of a whimper, of a snarl of confusion, as they regarded me. I wasn't of their kind, and there was dread there. Dread, but also savagery, and a hunger long-endured that would never be sated. With slow but intent purpose, they began their approach.

I sought my escape route. Through the door by which they had entered? It was the only way, for the other door was once more lost, and that surging corridor was there in its place. Its monstrous inhabitant – a creature whose rigid face was, at best, a parody of a human visage, at worst a demon – had almost attained entrance to the gallery, and still it marched on in its unwavering, mechanical stride.

I snatched up the key. I couldn't leave it to these dead things. A clammy, lumpen hand seized my wrist. It may have been centuries dead, but still it had strength, and there was definite triumph in those slurred features. I kicked, I howled, and I dragged myself away from the brute. Something else bit into my arm, and above those blackened teeth, between which I glimpsed scraps of meat and fur, feral eyes glinted with dull malice. I lashed out, sending both my attacker and the key flying. Malformed heads swivelled, following the gleaming progress, not knowing what it was, yet understanding that it was in some way valuable.

I had no strength to fight my way past, and they scrambled, squabbling ferociously amongst themselves over this tiny sliver of metal. Then came the explosion, a reverberating, crashing thud, and one of their number dropped suddenly, a red puddle spreading below it. The creature was in the room, that vast, unfathomable corridor vanished, leaving only the solid door at its back. It raised its long – too long – arm once more, the hand a fused mass of blood and bone and metal. Light flared from that hand, I clasped my hands over my ears, and another ghost fell, taking only part of its head with it.

I must have been screaming, even over their howls and shrieks, for they all turned to look on me with the curious gaze animals must see daily through the bars at the zoo. Even the creature, with its eyes of glass, and that hideous snout that tapered down to what hung between the exposed ribs, tilted its head almost inquisitively. Then the frozen scene blurred into motion, as those mad spirits threw themselves at the being, rending, thrashing, and falling one by one as fire spat from a metallic finger. I watched, my eyes fixed upon the battle, unaware of the threat closer to where I crouched until too late, as a cold paw gripped my throat, and I was dragged to my feet.

I could smell the dank soil on the futile, purposeless breaths of the giant that held me. Amidst the grey I saw lingering traces of purple, where the noose had bitten into its wide neck. It called something, some challenge, to the creature, whose only response was a wet rattle in that dangling tube, before its arm fell to its side, and something heavy fell clattering from its hand. I thought this was to be the last sight I would ever see, my vision hazing as the breath was throttled from me. But even as my eyes closed, I heard the rapid approach of pounding feet, the echo of a grunt, and I was violently shaken from the giant's grasp to drop oblivious to the floor.

It was the touch of something cold that woke me. I was propped up in a chair, almost as if I'd dozed off and experienced a frightful dream. But the evidence as I opened my eyes was against that. Lifeless, colourless forms littered the floor, amongst them that of the giant, his neck fearfully contorted, the noose's job finally accomplished.

A figure stood before the fire, its posture held awkwardly, as if the insides no longer fitted its skin. It stared at the clock, as if waiting. At the gasp from my swollen, tender throat, the figure turned to me. There were no cogs or springs between the ribs showing through the torn and muddied uniform, just the purple-grey, bulging mass held in place by stiff arm, the retrieved gun – that metal finger grown cold again after expelling its deadly fire – clamped hard against the soft expanse. The grotesque face had been torn by those flying claws, and from the slivers of flesh exposed beneath I saw that it was naught but a mask, one whose protection was no longer necessary. And when I looked beyond the lenses, the eyes that looked back at me were so familiar that they might well have been a reflection of my own.

And then I knew.

A bloodied hand raised itself into a salute, just as one o'clock chimed, and before the vibrations of that bell were stilled, I was alone, with only the ticking of the clock for accompaniment, and only the cold key in my hand to grip as I wept.

Reginald Hinchcliffe's voice was a whisper. "It's older brothers who are supposed to protect their younger brothers from harm, isn't it?"

"Johnny," said the scholar sympathetically. "When was this?"

"Two months ago. I received the telegram two days later. *Lieutenant Jonathan Hinchcliffe was killed in action 12th October 1916*'. He had been dead almost two weeks that last time I saw him. It had been a long, slow march home for him."

"The Jonathan Hinchcliffe I had the privilege of knowing would have always made that effort gladly," said Lawrence.

Reginald Hinchcliffe grimaced. "And I ran from him! I'd thought him Friedrich Valkenburg's monster. A clockwork hobgoblin come marching out of an old folk tale. If such a thing ever existed, it's long gone by now."

Dr Lawrence, though, was inclined to think that the clockmaker's offspring had indeed lived on, after a fashion. 'The year without a summer' – 1816 – had been the year when a poet and his young lover, along with their artfully decadent friends, had holidayed on Lake Geneva. It was here that a nightmare experienced by that girl had become a story which had lost none of its horrid fascination after a century. Was this nightmare, he now considered, inspired by something she had heard during her Swiss sojourn? Or was it, perhaps, born out of something she had seen with her own eyes?

Lawrence said nothing of these musings, instead enquiring, "And how do you wish me to help? You seem to have pieced together the explanation – what we can hope for in that line – by yourself."

"What I wish is for you to have something, Dr Lawrence," said the other, taking a small, metal object from his pocket and placing it in the scholar's palm.

"And the Awakening Clock, itself?" asked Lawrence, warily examining the complex design on the winding key.

"I have it still," admitted Hinchcliffe, "though it has remained wound down ever since that night. Everfayre Manor is gone, stripped of its treasures and sold on. Only that one piece remains for, naturally, I could never sell it, and any museum that accepted it would, quite properly, attempt to set it in motion again. I couldn't run the risk of them succeeding, so I look after it."

"Is that wise?" said the doctor, mildly.

"I could have smashed it to pieces, indeed, very nearly did. But that destructive urge isn't in me. There's too much of that in this world as it is. But can I trust myself? That's what troubles me. With the device I could restore my brother to my side, for one more hour, every night. My brother, my parents, all those I've known and lost... And that is a power no man should have. Take the key, Doctor. It's the only one, and the one fellow I know who is capable of making another never will. He already knows the story, you see."

Lawrence weighed the key in his palm, a light thing to carry such a heavy burden. "My brother trusted you, Dr Lawrence," said his companion. "So shall I. I owe him that."

Without a word, Lawrence pocketed this most peculiar Christmas present. He opted not to ponder on the possibility that the brilliant Valkenburg had continued his experiments, and that the item in Hinchcliffe's safe-keeping might not have been the sole result of his toils. Instead, he chose to consider the testimony that he'd just heard, which indicated that love and honour truly survived, and that there might yet be bright things to be found in dark places.

And, as these two fellows finished their drinks, those assembled troops – snatching an opportunity for joy before returning to horrors worse yet than those encountered during even the darkest of Lawrence's researches – had commenced a more traditional song.

"God rest ye merry gentlemen", they sang, and it was a sentiment with which those two companions could only wholeheartedly concur.

TOOLS OF THE TRADE

Paul Finch

One thing that always irritated Adam was conspiratorial behaviour by his informants.

Okay, quite often they were whistle-blowers, guys who were breaking rank to pass quiet confidences which, if they stood up sufficiently to make it into print, would definitely mean trouble for someone. But there was trouble and then there was trouble. This was a small town by Lancashire standards, a nameless smudge on most people's maps, so even exposing shenanigans at the highest level of the local authority wouldn't make too many waves. Woodstein and Deep Throat it wasn't. And yet, when Adam arrived at the railway station forecourt that unseasonably mild November lunchtime, Dick Wetherby was sitting in one of the bus shelters, his overcoat fully buttoned, its collar turned up to conceal half his face, the rest of it hidden behind an outspread copy of *The Times*. The one or two other commuters present ignored him, but they'd doubtless spared him at least a glance or two, wondering what he was up to.

"You realise it's ten degrees?" Adam said, slumping onto the bench alongside him. "And yet you look like someone who's about to go polar trekking. It's a bit of a give-away."

"My job could be on the line with this one," Wetherby replied tightly.

Given to nervousness, he often said things like that. Wetherby was aged in his late forties, and was a tall, gangling beanpole with a mop of limp yellow hair, watery eyes and a pair of steel-rimmed glasses perched on a protruding woodpecker nose. Adam was a similar age, but by contrast shorter and stockier, with a shaved head and a reddish moustache and goatee. It was a slightly thuggish look even in a jacket and tie, as now, though that misrepresented the truth. Adam Croaker *could* be a bruiser, but only in intellectual terms. Not that he felt peacefully inclined towards Wetherby at present.

"Dick… because you're insisting on keeping this thing quiet, I've had

127

to come here during my lunch-break. Everyone at the office thinks I nipped home because I forgot my butties. Please tell me this is going to be worth so much trouble."

"It's about *that*." Wetherby nodded across the main road. Adam glanced over there, puzzled.

Tunbridge Railway Station wasn't situated in the most salubrious corner of town. Oh, on paper it was a hotspot: officially part of the town centre and located on Tunbridge Hall Road, a key thoroughfare; and it wasn't as if the station itself serviced an unimportant railway – the elevated line traversing the town's rooftops and chimneys, and in fact passing over an arched bridge not one hundred yards to the left of where they now sat, was part of the West Coast Mainline, the most direct route between London and Glasgow. Directly behind the railway sat the bus station, which was never less than heaving. If nothing else, this district was always busy. But transport hubs rarely attract the more upmarket standard of boutique, on top of which the Recession hadn't been kind to Tunbridge anyway, so much of what passed as retail property in this always rather functional zone having suffered considerably. A lot of it was now 'to let', while what remained would have been unappealing at the best of times. The row of shops indicated by Wetherby was a case in point: cycle repairs, a tattoo parlour, a scruffy takeaway and a thrift store, all their signage decayed, all their windows filmed with layers of dust.

"Which unit am I looking at?" Adam asked irritably.

Wetherby tutted. "Not the shops, you prat… though God knows, they add to the bloody eyesore. The Great Northern. Or what's left of it."

Slowly, the penny dropped. Sandwiched between the tattoo parlour and the takeaway, a padlocked grille blocked off a broad, rectangular recess with a grimy brick arch over the top. The grille itself was old, caked in rust and hung with scraps of waste-paper – but not as old as the recessed entry it denied access to. This was so dark you'd never know that six yards into it stood a heavy oaken door, also locked, and that on the other side of that a flight of stairs led up to what had once been the reception area to a very elegant hotel. Adam's gaze roamed up and across the dilapidated façade of the once fine Victorian building.

A relic from the age of railway hotels, the Great Northern's baroque-style terracotta frontage had once been the first sight to greet weary travellers when they emerged from the railway station opposite, its handsome bay windows ablaze with warm and welcoming lamplight. Now, those same windows were either broken and boarded, or covered by drab interior hangings. The fact they still boasted fanlights and balustrades added to their air of faded grandeur. Pale shadows of the ornate painted lettering that had once adorned the structure – GREAT NORTHERN HOTEL – had been visible up until a few years ago, but now the damp, the soot and the general dinginess that crept over everything in the heart of a post-industrial town like Tunbridge had accounted even for those.

"Okay," Adam said, his interest pricked a little – the Great Northern had been a bone of contention at Council meetings for as long as he could remember. It was listed, so it couldn't just be demolished, but no one ever seemed to want to buy it and spruce it up, and if they did, it soon ended up back on the market. "Tell me more."

"You know we had a vigil there last week?" Wetherby replied. "Well... something happened that ought to be of interest to you."

"You had a *what* last week?"

"A vigil. You know, we sit in all night, set our equipment, take readings, see if we can make any kind of contact..."

"Just a bloody minute!" Adam was well aware that Dick Wetherby, though a serious-minded person in his professional life, was also very keen on his hobby, which was paranormal investigation. "Are you saying you've brought me here in your capacity as ghost-hunter rather than officer of the Council?"

"The Council don't know anything about this." Wetherby lowered his voice further. "And they must never know. They're quite close to Degley & Sons, who own the damn place. If word gets to old man Degley, he'll move in and take all the credit, not to mention the profit."

"What's this about, Dick?" Adam glanced at his watch. "Because I'm telling you, I've got a stack of stories to write today, most of them piece-of-crap press releases that came in this morning. I don't particularly want to do it, but as you know, we haven't got half the news team we used to, so someone has to..."

"This is your way out of that," Wetherby interrupted. "We're not just talking a front-page lead here, Adam. This'll be something you can sell to the nationals... but that would be a waste, in my opinion. If I were you, I'd be looking to write a book. I assure you, this is hot stuff."

"Ghosts are ten-a-penny, Dick." Adam stood up. "Especially if you haven't got any proof. Even if you *have* got proof, it's going to need be better than a few midges masquerading as orbs, or the odd creaky floorboard which suddenly becomes 'electronic voice phenomena'..."

"It *is* better than that."

"There are haunted houses everywhere. It wouldn't surprise anyone in Tunbridge if the Great Northern had one or two spooks. Nor would it particularly bother them…"

"Jack the Ripper."

"I mean… what?"

Wetherby peered up at him with po-faced sincerity. He even had the good grace to look a little unnerved by the information he was imparting. "Jack the Ripper, Adam… that's what we're talking about here."

"Jack the Ripper?"

"Are you denying that's the one murder case the whole world still talks about? The one that everyone on the planet would love to see solved? How would you feel about being the man who achieved that?"

"On the say-so of a ghost? That'd boost my credibility."

"On the say-so of DNA. Yeah… that's right, Adam. Modern forensics. No one'll be able to argue with that, will they?"

Adam pondered this, refusing to allow himself even a tingle of excitement. "Let's get a coffee," he finally said. "I feel more than a little conspicuous standing arguing with you in this bus shelter, and I've got to get something inside me… at present I'm running on fumes."

"Are you telling me that building has been empty since 1889?" Adam asked, incredulous.

"No, course not." Wetherby stirred his latte. "It's been used for other things since then… British Restaurant during World War Two, stand-in Council Chamber when the Town Hall was being refurbished in the 1960s. There was even a flea-market there in the '70s."

"Think I remember that." Now it was mentioned, Adam had some vague recollection of going upstairs into the building as a kid, seeing collapsible stalls set up amid shabbiness and dereliction, selling second-hand records, paperbacks and other bric-a-brac.

"But it ceased to operate as a hotel in the summer of 1889," Wetherby added. "No reason was ever really given except that guests stopped staying there. We can only surmise, I suppose."

"You mean because it was haunted?" Adam did his best not to sound too scornful.

"The Victorians were very superstitious about suicide. As far as they were concerned, if anything was likely to cause ghostly activity, it was that."

Adam glanced again at the bits of paperwork Wetherby had pushed across the coffee shop table. Ironically, most of them were printouts from 1888 editions of the *Tunbridge Gazette*, his own newspaper, and related to the "dreadful self-destruction of a London Jew" in an upper room at the Great Northern Hotel on November 9th that year. It seemed that one

Julius Baczkowski, who had arrived in Tunbridge that evening having ridden north on the all-day train from London, had cut his own throat with a razor blade – not once, but twice – and subsequently died on his hotel bed amid gouts of blood.

"Have you noted the date?" Wetherby asked.

Adam shrugged. "November 9th. What's special about it?"

Wetherby sipped from his cup. "November 9th 1888 was the day on which Jack the Ripper's last victim, Mary Jane Kelly, was killed. Her mutilated corpse was discovered at 10.45 that morning, the foul deed having been committed during the early hours. More than enough time for Baczkowski to catch an early morning train from London Euston and head north."

Adam eyed him sceptically. "I hope you've got a bit more for me than this."

"I've got a lot more if you'll hear me out." Wetherby sipped again, noisily. "When we first went into the Great Northern last week, on November 9th..."

"The same date on which Baczkowski died?"

"Of course. It was his ghost we were trying to contact. Bear in mind, all we knew about him at the time was that he'd committed suicide in his room in the Great Northern. We didn't know he was a Ripper suspect... in fact no one did. He was never officially named as such, though I looked into his past afterwards and it wasn't too hard to find some suspicious details. To start with, he was a Polish Jew. Remember, at the time the police were strongly convinced the Ripper was of Polish/Jewish descent. In addition, Baczkowski was a boot-mender. You must have heard all that stuff about Leather Apron?"

Adam nodded, but still wasn't finding any of this persuasive.

"Baczkowski lived in Southwark," Wetherby said. "Which is across the Thames from Whitechapel. That may have explained why he was never fingered for the crimes – the coppers were convinced the Ripper was a local man who knew his way around, but apparently Baczkowski's ex-wife lived in Whitechapel, and he regularly used to turn up there drunk and causing trouble. He probably got to know the neighbourhood pretty well..."

"Just tell me what happened at the hotel the night you went in," Adam interrupted.

"Well... it's a bit of a dump, as you can imagine. The building's doors last closed in 1983 and it's been empty ever since. But we finally found the room where Baczkowski took his own life, and held a séance in it."

"I thought you paranormal investigators were all supposed to be scientists."

"We take a scientific approach... we *always* do." Briefly, Wetherby looked affronted by the implied slight. "We set up all our usual kit, temperature gauges, tape recorders, the lot. But if you're trying to contact spirits of the dead, there are some tried and tested methods."

"And did they work?"

"At first we got nothing. I mean it's a rickety old building, there were creaks, taps... all the usual things that TV mediums get so excited about when it should be plain to anyone with half a brain that town centre structures are constantly on the move. We heard all that stuff, but nothing particularly unusual. Until just before midnight – about quarter-to in fact, which was the estimated time of Julius Baczkowski's death – when there was a scratching sound. Really loud. From all around us." He paused, awaiting a response.

Adam gazed at him blankly. "Dick... I'd be more surprised if the Great Northern did *not* have its own rat population."

"Bollocks, Adam! These *weren't* rats. I worked in the Planning Department for eight years. I've been in more than my fair share of condemned buildings. I know the sounds rats make. This was nothing like that. What we were listening to were human fingernails, or something very similar, being drawn over a rough surface in long, slow movements. And it just went on and on, getting louder and louder..."

"Human fingernails?"

"For sure. Like I say, all around us... but with no visible sign of the cause."

"Someone was hiding. Someone who'd got there ahead of you and was trying to scare you."

"We considered that possibility, though it seemed unlikely. Degley's firm had provided us with the keys to go in. They knew what we were doing, but they weren't particularly interested. They're not even based in Tunbridge, they own dozens of similar buildings across the Northwest. As far as they're concerned..."

"Could anyone else have known? Someone at the Council maybe?"

"No one I told," Wetherby said. "I don't make a big deal of this sort of thing... not at work, anyway. People might think it a bit weird."

"I wonder why?" Adam replied.

"Hey, do you want this information or not. I mean, you're not the only journalist."

"Go on... there was a scratching sound."

"Yeah. We couldn't trace it, but we really searched. Like I say, the place is mouldering to its foundations and crammed with rubbish, but we checked everywhere. All the adjoining rooms and passages. There was nobody hiding. Anyway, then it stopped – bang on midnight. After that there was nothing, no more phenomena of any sort… and we were in till seven the next morning. But the really spooky thing is what happened the next day, when I went back there."

"You went back?"

"Yeah. Alone." Wetherby finished his coffee. "I was supposed to return the keys that afternoon. After the vigil, I'd obviously gone straight home and tried to get some shut-eye, but I couldn't sleep. I kept thinking about what we'd heard, trying to work out what it might have been, and then something occurred to me. The one place we hadn't looked when we were hearing those terrible sounds… under the floorboards."

Despite his innate doubts, Adam found himself listening with increasing interest.

"I intended to return the keys to Degley's agent in the afternoon, as planned," Wetherby said. "So I went back to the hotel just before lunch. It was still a scary old place, even at midday, especially with what I thought I knew about it – namely that someone had been concealed under the floorboards in that room."

"Perhaps going up there alone wasn't too smart a plan, Dick."

"On the contrary. Going up there alone has worked out perfectly for both of us. Or it will."

"How so?"

Wetherby leaned forward, intense of expression. "Because of what was lying under those floorboards when I lifted them."

"You actually lifted them?"

"Not all of them. Most were solid, but I found a few loose ones in the corner of the room where the bed would once have been. What I found under there, Adam, is what sent me scurrying off to look a lot more deeply into this Julius Baczkowski character…"

"Don't tease me, just tell me."

"It was a pair of knives."

The few diminutive bristles of hair remaining on Adam's scalp began to stiffen.

Wetherby sat back again. "Vicious looking things, they were… I'm not talking penknives, if you know what I mean. But both were very old and caked in rust."

For the first time that day, Adam couldn't form words, either scathing or otherwise.

Wetherby regarded him unblinkingly. "That's right, Adam. I found Jack the Ripper's knives."

Adam didn't get much work done that afternoon. At least, none that he was supposed to be engaged in. As official chief-reporter, he tended to be given a lot more leeway at the *Gazette* than would normally be the case. For example, he was more senior both in age and experience than the news editor, while the overall editor was a distant, omnipotent force responsible for several other titles at the same time, whom he rarely saw – so when, instead of transforming the usual raft of ho-hum press releases into reams of compelling column inches, as was his usual duty, he immersed himself in the known facts of the 1888 Jack the Ripper investigation, no one actually noticed, or if they did, they didn't comment.

As Dick Wetherby had said, nowhere in any of the suspect lists did Julius Baczkowski's name appear. Which was perhaps surprising given how many suspects there'd been, though it was noticeable that a large number of these had been fingered for reasons verging on the ludicrous.

For example, Richard Mansfield, the eminent actor, was connected to the crimes because of his hypnotic portrayal of Mr Hyde in the West End that summer. Similarly incomprehensibly to modern eyes, the wife-murderer Frederick Bailey Deeming was the subject of much speculation, even though it was known he was in South Africa at the time of the Whitechapel slayings. In addition, there were the usual conspiracy theorist suspects whom everyone already knew about: Prince Albert Victor, the Duke of Clarence; Sir William Gull, private physician to Queen Victoria; and even children's author, Lewis Carroll – in none of whose cases was there a shred of even circumstantial evidence. Perhaps more serious were the accusations levelled at the likes of Serewyn Klosowski and John Pizer. These had been persons of genuine interest to the police at the time, and for pretty good reason. Klosowski was a Polish immigrant to Whitechapel, a barber by trade, and had a violent antipathy towards women – he was later hanged for three different murders. Polish Jew John Pizer was another Whitechapel resident with a history of violence against the fairer sex; he'd previously been convicted of slashing prostitutes with knives. Present-day researchers had done their bit too, tossing a few other viable names into the hat: Aaron Cohen was believed to have contracted syphilis from a Whitechapel prostitute, and his subsequent violent behaviour led him to be incarcerated in Colney Hatch lunatic asylum – at which point the murders mysteriously ceased; Alexander Pedachenko was a Russian-born medical man and Czarist secret agent, who for a brief time was thought to have been at large in London on a mission to embarrass Scotland Yard. Neither of those suspects impressed the modern-day 'Ripperologist' community – but both involved that Eastern European and/or Jewish factor again. Apparently, this stemmed from the alleged anatomical skills demonstrated by the murderer. Though the notion that he might have medical knowledge was jettisoned at an early stage of the enquiry, it was felt that he might be a butcher, slaughterman or furrier, skilled professions which in Whitechapel during the 1880s tended to be monopolised by immigrants.

But no matter how determinedly Adam perused the lists of names, there was no trace of a Julius Baczkowski.

Was that good or bad?

He simply wasn't sure. No one had been prosecuted at the time. Even now, one hundred and twenty-nine years on, the case was still officially open, which meant that the police's preferred suspects must have had solid alibis. One footnote appended by a famous criminologist to an investigators' forum caught Adam's attention:

The problem with the roll-call of Ripper suspects is that it reads like a Who's Who of 1880s London society. The reality is almost certainly that Jack the Ripper was nobody; that he was utterly faceless to the wider public. A street-sweeper maybe, a dustcart driver, a bricklayer or ditch-digger; a working class person of no fame whatsoever, who could move easily and anonymously through the teeming multitudes of Whitechapel, who could drink in the local pubs without causing a stir, and maybe even mix on familiar terms with the street-women. The sheer ordinariness of this person would have been his greatest shield. That is why he wasn't apprehended at the time, and why he has never been named and shamed since.

Until now perhaps, Adam thought, sitting back from his computer.

Briefly, he allowed his mind to wander.

Was it possible? Could it actually be…?

One thing Dick Wetherby had said was definitely true. If those were the Ripper's knives, and they'd been concealed under those floorboards on the same day Mary Kelly died, possibly there'd be DNA traces on the blades. According to Wetherby, Mary Kelly's grave was still visible in St. Patrick's Roman Catholic cemetery in Leytonstone. How difficult could it be to get a court order for an exhumation under these circumstances? It didn't help of course that Adam wasn't a police detective attempting to close a case. He was a journalist on the make, but it wasn't like there wouldn't be widespread interest. There could certainly be a book in this, and potentially a very lucrative one. Wetherby had mentioned the 1992 publication, *The Diary of Jack the Ripper*, which had controversially named Liverpool cotton merchant James Maybrick as the killer. The theory had been debunked since, but the book had still gone on to sell a million copies. Of course, in that case the author had been able to protect his position because all he'd needed to do was present a diary he'd claimed to have found and yet withhold it from public view until he'd struck a deal with a publisher. There'd been no necessity to dig up a dead body, no suggestion that he was in possession of a murder weapon the police might still have an interest in.

Of course, before Adam and Wetherby could work out any strategy, they had to retrieve the knives, which for some bewildering reason the council clerk had left in situ. In explanation, he'd muttered something vague about not wanting to leave his fingerprints on the weapons and trying to avoid interfering with something that might be classified as a crime scene – not without first consulting a 'professional' like Adam.

"If nothing else, I have to look at them," Adam had told him. "They're still under the floorboards in that upper room, yeah?"

"Right at the top of the building," Wetherby had replied. "I can find my way back to it easily enough. The only problem is, we'll have to go tonight... after dark."

"Why would that be?"

"Because we've no longer got permission to be in there. I've had to return the keys, like I said."

"So how do we get inside?"

"I made a copy of the keys first."

Adam had only just managed to keep a lid on his exasperation. "Well... if we weren't on the verge of committing illegal acts before, Dick, we almost certainly will be now."

"So do we just leave it? The find of the century?"

"No, we bloody don't. We'll go after dark. Where do you want to meet?"

"Same place as earlier."

"Not conspicuous at all, then?"

"It's a bus stop, Adam. There're loads of people coming and going there."

"Okay... what time?"

"How does eight suit?"

"Eight's fine."

Adam glanced at his watch. It was now nearly five. His shift was almost over. He had plenty time to go home, have a shower, get some tea, fabricate some not entirely untrue story to Angie that he was chasing an interesting lead, and then maybe sit on his bed for half an hour, agonising over whether this was a sensible course of action. To boost his courage, he leaned forward and tapped on his keyboard, calling up again the webpage concerning *The Diary of Jack the Ripper.*

That figure hit him again, right between the eyes.

One million copies sold…
One million copies…

And that find hadn't even solved the case, whereas this one might. He snorted with laughter. It was truly an amazing concept – that studious, bespectacled, ever-cautious and methodical Dick Wetherby might have made both their fortunes with some crazy ghost-watching stunt. But stranger things had happened.

The ghostly aspect of all this was another problem, Adam told himself as he walked from the car park to the railway station, pulling on a pair of leather gloves. It was ten to eight now, dark, dank and noticeably colder. A stiff breeze had picked up, whipping dead leaves along the pavement. Rush hour had ended and, it being a weekday, there was almost nobody around.

Mention ghosts and people would automatically snigger. It wasn't as if there couldn't be other more rational explanations for scratching sounds under the floor. Most folk would jump to the same conclusion he had – rats. Perhaps that was the story they should adopt: that Wetherby had been drawn to the corner where the floorboards were loose by local wildlife? No one would particularly question that, except they might find it a tad convenient he'd then found these amazing artefacts. That said, claiming that supernatural forces had been at work might add some colour to the story. Okay, the usual sceptics would scoff, but it was curiously logical in a Gothic, romantic kind of way. The Great Northern itself would garnish the tale with hints of the esoteric.

Tunbridge boasted lots of town centre buildings that harked back to a more opulent era: towering edifices of industrial brick, but handsome too, decked in the mock-classical style with Italianate cornicing and traceried stonework. Even those now converted into office blocks or carpet warehouses, or simply standing empty and desolate, hinted at venerability. But none quite matched the Great Northern in terms of lost glory. It was no architectural gem – not by big city standards. But it had overlooked Tunbridge throughout the rise and fall of the 'muck and brass' empire and ever since, slowly gathering grime, its extravagant rooms filling with dust and decay. The thought that it had been partly used as a flea-market while the rest of it stood gutted and silent was shudder-inducing. Could the original architect ever have envisaged *that*?

Now, of course, it wasn't even a flea-market. Just a hulking outline in the Lancashire night. The dim lights from the one shop still open on its ground floor, the takeaway, failed to conceal the scabrous façade rising overhead. For the first time it struck Adam that they were heading inside there, that they were actually going to wander – or more likely *blunder* – through that warren of abandoned rooms, passages and stairwells with nothing but torches.

Wetherby was waiting at the bus stop, as promised. He was even in the same seat and had the same rolled-up copy of *The Times* jutting from his raincoat pocket.

Adam sat down alongside him. "Why did you decide to hold a vigil in *there*?" he asked.

"The shopkeepers downstairs had been complaining," Wetherby replied. "About noises from the supposedly empty floors overhead. Substantial noises… as if people were moving around."

"Why didn't the police go in?"

"They did. Not enthusiastically, I have to say. I mean, what was the worst they could find? Squatters? A bunch of kids looking to vandalise a property that had already rotted beyond recognition because its absentee owners couldn't be bothered looking after it? It was hardly a priority for them."

"And?"

"They found nothing. There was no sign anyone had been up there in decades."

"How thoroughly did they check the place out?"

"So thoroughly that when further complaints were made, they didn't bother going back."

Again, Adam's eyes roved the high, barren frontage. "You remember where the room is? I mean *exactly* where it is? So we won't be inside any longer than necessary."

"I remember." Wetherby glanced sideways at Adam, his thin mouth crooked into a half-smile. "Not scared, are we? The man who reports fearlessly on police and local authority cock-ups, on establishment corruption, on frauds and embezzlers and child-abusers?"

"Let's just say that none of that will help if you and me get caught breaking into this place. Quite the opposite."

"Well…" Wetherby stood up. He didn't seem half as nervous as he had done that lunchtime. "That's why I said meet me here at eight. It's a bit quieter now."

And that was true. Aside from people arriving at and departing from the railway station, there wasn't a great deal to attract anyone to this part of town with business hours over. Beyond the railway bridge lay the Hexley ward. That had always been rough. Row after row of crumbling terraced houses originally built to accommodate the population of Tunbridge's mills and coalmines, but, like those ancient industrial structures, the terraces and their occupants were long gone now, leaving empty lots and the odd derelict shell. The only folk to be found over there these days were dealers and good time girls.

Wetherby set off across the road. Adam pulled up the hood of his anorak before following. He didn't think there'd be any surveillance cameras trained on the entrance to the Great Northern, but you never knew. They stopped on the far pavement, in front of the grilled entrance. The only person in view from here was the young Asian guy in the takeaway next door. He leaned on the counter, his uniform baseball cap worn at a jaunty angle, but his face disconsolate. He gave no indication that he'd noticed them, and they were quickly able to step out of his line of vision.

Satisfied, Wetherby produced a key-ring with two keys on it and attacked the padlock. Even though he'd opened this same padlock earlier that week, only after much grunting and twisting did the thing spring apart. The grille opened outward with a dull groan. Wetherby stepped through, Adam bustling after him, eager to be away from prying eyes. The recess on the other side would normally be littered several inches deep with chip wrappers, curry cartons and the like, but Wetherby having been in here twice recently, all that had been cleared aside. Faded black-and-white tiling was just about visible in the exposed floor-space.

While Wetherby re-locked the grille behind them, Adam pressed forward, hands extended, until he'd reached the hotel's main door. It was made from heavy oak and had once been painted black, but said paint was now peeling off in scales, and where the great brass knocker had hung, only the corroded nubs of screws protruded through clots of oily dust.

Adam's eyes gradually attuned as Wetherby pushed up alongside him, prodding around the lock and attempting to accommodate the larger of the two keys in the finger-sized hole he finally located. Surprisingly, given that this lock was much older than the first, and therefore presumably much rustier, it opened quickly and easily, but with a dull *clunk,* which Adam fancied would echo through the entire building. The door pushed inward stiffly. After about three feet, it jammed, but that was sufficient for Wetherby to slide his gangling body through. Thanks to his stockier build, Adam had a little more trouble, but no sooner was he inside than Wetherby pushed the door closed again. There was another shuddering *clunk* as its catch reconnected, a sound that echoed and re-echoed through the empty rooms and passages above. Adam fumbled his torch from his coat pocket, but before he could switch it on a man spoke to them.

Or whispered. Semi-incoherently.

It was no more than three or four words, possibly "serve thine master". But it was delivered directly into Adam's right ear, as if whoever the fellow was he'd been waiting just inside the door. Adam reacted violently, swinging around, half shouting as he lashed out with the torch rather than actually switching it on.

"What're you playing at?" Wetherby hissed. He apparently hadn't heard anything, but now hit the button on his own torch.

It flooded their immediate area with light. The space was tight: enclosing walls turned scabrous and damp, the stairs that rose into blackness in front made from stained, uncarpeted wood. There wasn't room for anyone else to be standing there.

"I heard something," Adam said. "Right in my ear."

Wetherby pondered this, but didn't seem unduly surprised. "This place'll play lots of tricks on you. The main thing is… when we go upstairs, go quietly. We don't want that bloke in the kebab shop calling the police again."

To Adam's mind, the police turning up no longer seemed quite so ominous. But he understood the need for caution.

"You're sure there isn't already someone up here?" he asked as they stealthily ascended. "You know… dropouts, druggies?"

"We've just come in through the only entrance," Wetherby replied. "And we gave the place a thorough going-over the last time we were here. There's no one… apart from that spirit. Assuming that's what it was."

Yeah, Adam told himself. *The spirit of Jack the Ripper. Hooray.*

The stairway was steep, the darkness at the top so intense that it might have been a black lid firmly closed. However, on the hotel's first floor there was more light than they'd expected. Here, they were back in the realm of windows, and though many of these were covered with dingy sheets or slanted boarding, the sodium glow of the streetlights outside managed to filter through, creating a brownish, almost sub-aqua gloom.

Adam had half expected to find the remnants of a once-fine carpet, perhaps an old reception desk with a bell at one end, maybe a chandelier suspended overhead, dangling cobwebs so thick with dust they were more like rotted drapery. But of course, all the hotel fixtures in this place had been removed long ago, as had any relics of its days as a restaurant and/or stand-in Council chamber. Again, he recollected how as a small child he'd come in here with his father when it was doubling as a flea-market. But there was no sign of the temporary stands and stalls that had been erected on that occasion either. All he saw now was a cavernous space that ran perhaps thirty yards to his left and thirty to his right. In the wall directly facing him there was a tall, arched window with fragments of stained glass remaining, though its former image was no longer recognisable.

The beams from their torches speared left and right as they pivoted at the top of the entry-stair, but did little to penetrate the dimness, exposing only sticks of broken furniture, scraps of fallen plaster and more dust-heavy floorboards. Adam sniffed. The air wasn't as foul as he'd expected; tainted by decay, naturally, but fresh breezes blowing through various apertures brought relief from this. Then his torch winked out. Only momentarily; but he had to shake and fiddle with it before it came on again.

"That thing not working?" Wetherby asked, keeping his voice low.

"Who's got a torch that works properly?" Adam replied, still fiddling with the device, as if the mere act of twisting it more tightly together would compensate for it being old and worn-out. "There's one under every sink in every house, but how often do they have bulbs or batteries? It'll be all right. Loose connection or something. Just goes on and off from time to time."

"Use the light on your phone maybe?"

"This'll be fine." Adam tried to keep the snap from his voice, but it wasn't easy given how irritated he was with himself for not having brought a better torch. So much for the investigative reporter. "Anyway, where to?"

Wetherby gave this some thought; it took several seconds longer than it perhaps ought to have. Adam shone his torch up into the council officer's face, which seemed curiously pensive.

"You're not telling me you've forgotten already?"

"I've not forgotten," Wetherby replied. "The thing is, Adam… we're *really* going to rewrite criminal history here. Have you considered that?"

Adam was briefly puzzled as to why Wetherby was bringing this up now. But then the truth struck him. "What you actually mean is how are we going to split the profits... yeah? Even though I'll be writing the book, you want an equal share, maybe more. And unless I provide you with some kind of confirmation of this, you're not going to show me the evidence. Is that right?"

Wetherby shrugged. "I obviously can't make you sign a contract or anything that's legally binding. Not at this stage. But it would be good to know your thinking on this."

"Look, Dick... we wouldn't be here at all if you hadn't found this stuff." Adam understood the guy's need to protect his interest, but nonetheless was frustrated that here was someone else expecting to make a fortune out of a book when they couldn't string two words together themselves. "But ultimately, you can't write the damn thing... and if you don't mind me saying, that's going to involve a lot more work than you and your mates spending one night in here as part of a vigil."

Though they conversed quietly, their voices echoed, reverberating through the shadows. It was vaguely distracting in that it made it difficult to imagine that someone wasn't lurking nearby, eavesdropping.

"All that said," Adam added, "I can't do this thing alone either. We've got to convince people – agents, publishers, newspapers and the like – that what we've got here is real. And that's going to involve us making a very professional case."

"I can definitely help with that," Wetherby said. "I mean okay, I'm just a civil servant... but in the ghost-hunting community I'm widely respected."

"*Whoooaaa*, wait up! If we go big on the ghost-hunting stuff, people are *not* gonna buy it. It's the criminologists we want to appeal to. The obsessives who spend every waking moment trying to work out who Jack the Ripper was. For that, we need to be factual, we need to use science."

"All right, but we keep this a two-man deal, yeah?" Wetherby said.

"I'm *not* going to cut you out of this," Adam replied. "I couldn't even if I wanted to. Suppose these knives are what you say they are. Suppose there's visible blood on the blades that can be traced back to the Ripper's victims? Even then we'll have lots of hoops to jump through. Interviews to give, phone-calls to field, articles to write. It's going to take at least two of us to handle all that crap."

Wetherby nodded glumly, as if this reassurance was the best he could realistically hope for. He offered his gloved hand. "Let's at least shake on it... a two-man deal."

Adam shook. "A two-man deal."

Wetherby strolled on, heading left. Adam followed, stabbing his torchlight every which way. They entered a passage, which, without windows, was virtually black. At the end of it, they turned right and commenced climbing a wooden stair so narrow they could only ascend in single-file. From the top of this, rather than find themselves in another corridor, they had to progress through a trio of odious little rooms that had been stacked almost to head-height with furniture and other hefty oddments, many of these draped in mouldy sheets. Adam shook his head as they sidled their way around and between. Despite all he knew about civic matters and the hard-headed characters involved, it still amazed him that certain money-men would resist spending their cash to spruce up a premises like this and get some new companies into it, because that wouldn't alter its long-term value, which stemmed mostly from the mere fact it was a town centre property. To avoid risking a minor loss, they'd prefer to be owners of a crumbling ruin filled only with grot.

Then his breath caught in his throat – so sharply that it hurt.

They'd just entered the third room, and his gaze locked onto its far corner, where a figure clad in dingy white and wearing a tatty old clown mask was seated on a stool.

For half a second, Adam was frozen with shock.

Wetherby chuckled, an unusual sound for him. "Sorry, Adam… should have warned you." He grinned broadly, which was equally unusual, and perhaps with good reason, as it revealed an unsightly row of longish yellow teeth, all browning at the root.

"Christ almighty…" Adam stuttered, staring at the corner.

Wetherby edged his way over there, pushing junk aside. "This is probably a leftover from that flea-market you remember."

Clearly it was a mannequin, life-size and dressed in some kind of ancient Pierrot costume. Adam could even make out the pompoms down the front of it. But the really weird thing was that it seemed familiar. He wasn't sure whether it was possible to remember detail from so long ago – what would he have been, six years old? – but suddenly he was sure that he'd seen this thing before.

"Here you go." Wetherby pinched the clown's face by its nose, and lifted what was evidently a very old rubber mask with a mop of greenish, moth-eaten fur on top to serve as hair. Underneath it lay a featureless polystyrene head.

Adam still couldn't speak. He was now certain that he remembered the object, or at least the costume. He'd come in here with his father one Saturday morning. Well… not *here*, as in this crammed upper room, but downstairs, in the main lobby, where the flea-market had been set up. One of the stalls had been selling off old circus props or pantomime gear, or something like that. The woman behind the counter was a gypsy type with long grey hair and dangly earrings, wearing a big, multi-coloured poncho. But there'd been someone else with her too, standing alongside the counter rather than behind it – wearing this very same Pierrot outfit. Of course, it had been in good condition then, whereas now the clothing was dirty and threadbare, the mask yellow where it should be white, orange-lipped where it should be red.

At least the eye-holes were empty now, unlike that day back in the 1970s, when…

Adam shivered.

"Nothing to worry about, m'dear," the gypsy lady said when he tried to hide behind his father. "All trickery. All façade."

The figure wearing the mask stared down at him, the white-gloved fingers meshed together across its belly. And those eyes glinting like pinpoints of fire…

"When we first saw it, it was covered by a sheet," Wetherby said, letting the mask drop back into place, where it hung slightly askew, seemingly turned in Adam's direction. "We recognised its human outline though. Scared the crap out of us. Course, we had to uncover it to see what was underneath. There're a few other bits like this in here."

He turned to a smaller object on his right, positioned on what looked like an old office bureau. The featureless cloth draped over the top of it resembled a hangman's hood, especially when Wetherby whipped it away to reveal another polystyrene head underneath, this one still smeared with fragments of garish make-up, creating the impression of a face that had distorted in agony.

"You all right?" he suddenly asked, seeing how pale Adam had turned. "It's just bits of rubbish. Stuff no one wants."

"Let's… let's get on, eh?" Adam said.

"Yeah, sure. We're almost there."

Wetherby sidled back through the junk, setting an old rocking chair creaking noisily, before reaching the next doorway and stepping through it. Adam backtracked in pursuit of him, but halted before the doorway, hovering there, peering with fear and fascination at the costumed form, in particular at its shadow-filled eye sockets, which still looked to be fixed on him. He wondered what he would do if he glanced away for a second and when he looked back found the mask's upward-curved smile curved downward into a frown. Of course none of that happened, though it must have been a trick of the light that the shape of the mannequin appeared to

144

have adjusted slightly, as if it had shifted its whole body to look at him more clearly.

Adam reached out to still the rocking chair, then turned and passed through the door, jabbing his torchlight in front of him. It revealed a junction of three passageways lined with closed rooms and floored with mildewed planks, all leading off into darkness. But no sign of Wetherby.

He listened, expecting to hear the Council officer's receding footsteps as he plodded off into the distance. But there was no sound at all. At first. Then... abruptly, there came a faint rustling of aged cloth, as if something was stirring to life in the room behind him.

It was the perfect time for his torch to wink out, plunging him into Stygian blackness.

Adam almost shouted, though in truth he hardly dared. He listened, horrified, to what sounded distinctly like movement across the room he had just vacated, as if something was lurching its way through the jumble.

He jerked his way forward blindly, groping in every direction, cursing aloud as he dropped his torch and heard it roll away from him – and heard something else at the same time: the arthritic creak of the rocking chair again: once, twice, three times as something forced its way past.

"Wetherby!" he choked as he stumbled on, arms outstretched but hands finding nothing he recognised. "For Christ's sake!"

Behind, he could now hear clear sounds of pursuit. Whatever it was, it had come out into the passage. With shuffling footfalls, it blundered along in his wake.

"*Wetherby!*" he all but shrieked.

If anything, that rustling tread behind came on with greater firmness.

Adam knew he was proceeding down an open corridor, and so drove himself forward recklessly, on the verge of running, sweat beading his eyebrows. At any second he would connect with something, even if it was the facing wall of a T-junction. But where would he go from there, left or right? As he deliberated, the stumbling, lifeless form at his rear sounded closer. Surely it would reach out for him now and latch a dirty-gloved paw onto the back collar of his coat? He'd been in the process of digging through his pockets for his phone. Now, by instinct, he gave up on this and dodged sideways, moving no more than a couple of feet before caroming backward from a heavily fastened door, toppling and landing with a *crash*.

Despite a darkness so dark it blotted out all vision, he sensed a tall, thin figure totter to a halt directly to his left. It towered over him, stationary yet within touching distance. Adam struggled to breathe, the air rasping through his chest, which had tightened like a vice. And then… a searingly bright light glared to life on his right.

It filled the immediate area of passage, revealing – nothing.

"Had a fall?" Wetherby enquired, emerging around the next corner.

"Jesus wept!" Adam jumped to his feet. He gazed back along the corridor towards the doorway connecting with the junk-room. It was bare of life; there was nothing there. "Dick by name, dick by nature! What the bloody hell do you think you're doing, scooting off when you know my torch is on the blink?"

"Sorry, mate… thought you were right behind me."

Wetherby sounded genuinely contrite, but Adam wondered if there wasn't some veiled amusement in his tone. He glanced back along the passage. His own torch lay close to that dark doorway. Only vague, indistinguishable shapes were visible beyond that – none of them moving, but he knew he hadn't imagined those sounds of pursuit.

"Which direction have you just come from?" he demanded.

"From round that corner," Wetherby said. "I was only a couple of dozen yards away. I heard you take a tumble."

"I could have… shit, I could've sworn there was someone behind me!"

"I told you, this place plays…"

"No, this was no trick. There was someone there. I *heard* them. They came out of that room."

"Adam, there's no one else here, I assure you."

"I know that… That's the problem."

Adam's eyes remained fixed on the doorway as he walked back down there and bent over to retrieve his torch – he only realised that a diminutive grey-furred form had darted past him, vanishing into the room, when it brushed his arm with its whipping tail.

"Good Christ!" he yelped, jumping backward again. But Wetherby only chuckled, something he seemed to be doing regularly now, even though Adam had heard never him do it previously.

"There you go," Wetherby said. "That's your problem. A rat."

"A bloody rat…" Adam twisted his torch, and immediately its wavering beam was restored, the effect of which was to plunge what little he could see of the junk-room into deeper darkness. However, he knew he couldn't press on from here without at least checking. He ventured back to the doorframe and glanced through, torch held in front of him like a weapon. Nothing met his eyes except the sheet-covered heaps of lumber and the made-up dummy head and clown mannequin in the far corner, the latter still perched where he'd left it, mask hanging askew. Dust motes fluttered around it in the glow of the beam, but they fluttered everywhere in this place merely from the passage of air.

"A rat," he said again, under his breath. Listen though he may, no scuttling or scampering sounds came to his ears. No rustling of old rancid cloth.

They turned and pushed on, Adam urging Wetherby forward, telling him he didn't want to spend any longer in this decaying heap of brick than he had to. Round the next corner, they came to a broader stairway than the previous one. It had balustrades on either side, though again was made from bare wood, so it was impossible to prevent their feet from clumping as they ascended. Twice Adam spun around, spearing his light down behind him, convinced the echoes of their footfalls were someone following. On the first occasion his light revealed nothing, just the bare boarding at the foot of the stairs. But the second time there was a rat there; a horrible twisted little thing, sitting upright on its haunches, peering after them. In the glare of the torch, its tiny eyes glinted like points of flame.

Adam continued to watch it as he climbed – until he half tripped.

"Careful," Wetherby said from in front. "You're an accident waiting to happen tonight."

When Adam looked back again, the rat was nowhere to be seen.

"This place is a shithole," he asserted.

"Make a good opening for the book, won't it? The terrors we braved sniffing out the tools of the Ripper's trade."

Adam didn't laugh.

At the top of the stair, they joined another corridor. This, having not been involved in any of the temporary uses to which the Great Northern Hotel had later been put, was vaguely plusher. It possessed a carpet, though it slid beneath their feet and was green with rot. The tarnished relics of brass lamp fittings hung at head-height every ten yards or so. There was much dripping of water up here. It stained the doors and walls, while the plaster ceiling had entirely collapsed, exposing sodden, skeletal lathes.

"Cost millions to fix this place up," Adam said. "No wonder no one's ever tried."

"It'll get a new lease of life when *we're* finished," Wetherby replied, halting. They'd come to the last door on the corridor. "Anyway, this is it."

Adam watched while his guide turned the handle. The door swung inward, and a foul blackness – fouler and blacker than it had any right to be, even in this place – exhaled outward. Adam had some fleeting vision of a vast but decayed presidential suite: tattered hangings on every wall, the immense Gothic skeleton of a four-poster bed, a colossal hearth deep in stone-cold ashes. But in fact, it was nothing more than a poky little room stripped of any ornament: damp, plaster-strewn floorboards; peeling walls; yet more exposed rafters.

A few lumps of half-melted candle were all that remained of the séance Wetherby and his cronies had held here. Behind the single narrow window, which still contained grubby glass, the brick buttress of a protruding left-hand wall afforded only the narrowest of gaps, beyond which lay the opaqueness of night, though even in daylight you'd have seen no more from here than the desolate waste of the Hexley ward. Oddly, it struck Adam that it wouldn't have been much better back in 1888: parallel lines of rain-wet roofs stretching to a distant horizon where a row of factory chimneys belched smoke and soot, the sky beyond them red with the hellfire of foundry and furnace. If Julius Baczkowski was the Ripper, he'd have fled one Whitechapel only to arrive at another, or at least a near-exact replica.

"So what do you think?" Wetherby asked.

"What do you expect me to say, Dick? Yeah, it's horrible."

"You could write an entire chapter on this room alone, eh?"

"Let's get real,' Adam retorted. 'It's just a gutted bedroom… probably not even safe to enter. The sooner we find these knives – or whatever they are – and get out of here, the happier I'll be."

Wetherby pointed to the farthest corner. Adam strode over there and hunkered down. When he prodded at the floorboards, they were indeed loose. Hefting the torch in one hand, he reached with his other and, one by one, lifted them, half expecting another rat to emerge – right in his face, maybe an entire pack of them.

Instead, he exposed an underfloor cavity and inside this a wad of dust-web so thick that it was more like a cushion, though as Wetherby had said, this had already been thoroughly rummaged. What had been retrieved from it now lay on top: two items side by side. A shadow flickered across the room – a fleeting ripple effect, nothing more, yet surely unnatural in electric torchlight. But this only distracted Adam for a fleeting millisecond. He gazed down at the knives. There was nothing exotic or ornate about them; they clearly weren't museum pieces. But they weren't toys either. If anything, they looked like basic butchers' knives; curved, heavy-bladed, bone-hilted, and more than capable of slicing open a human body. In keeping with this ugly thought, they were both spattered with age-old reddish/brown stains.

Adam's scalp prickled. Could it be? Was it actually possible after all these years?

"I can't believe it," he said slowly. "I cannot bloody believe it."

"I told you," Wetherby replied. He sounded strained with excitement.

"But, wait... these are in such good nick. They look sharp enough to cut even now. How could they have been preserved so well?"

Wetherby shrugged. "If they were down there all that time, undisturbed..."

"That's not good enough, Dick. People will say they look too good to be of nineteenth century manufacture. They'll accuse us of creating a hoax."

"I'm sure there's some test we can have done to prove it."

Adam hadn't yet touched either of the two weapons. He was long in the habit of doubting good fortune when it showed up – mainly because the occasion was so rare. But Wetherby spoke the truth. They didn't need to go public with this until they'd found some lab guys to back them up. Warily, he reached down, nudging the hilt of the first knife with his gloved thumb. He wasn't quite sure what he'd expected to happen when he did this. No raddled, bloody claw burst up from underneath to snatch his wrist. The knife didn't crumble to dust. In fact, when he caressed it properly with his fingers it felt solid: the blade didn't drop out of the hilt; its edge was indeed razor sharp. Eventually he took hold of it properly. It was heavy in the hand, but well-balanced. For all its length – the blade was maybe ten inches – he fancied it would be easy to manoeuvre at close-quarter.

It was only when Adam stood up that he went dizzy.

The floor of the bedroom tilted, the walls cavorting around him. He thrust an arm out to try and steady himself, but tottered against the window, face pressed on the grimy glass, seeing again those parallel rows of dingy Victorian terraces, jumbled chimneys, rain, mist. Briefly he could even smell it: the dank stink of winding brick alleys, of smoke, sulphur, urine, the foulness of diseased breath, of ragged clothes mouldering on emaciated frames.

"Christ!" he said, shaking his head as he forcibly jerked himself out of it.

Wetherby chuckled. "This place, I'm telling you."

Adam was startled to see that he'd jammed the knife into the wall. It had penetrated several inches into the rotted plaster. "Shit... look what I've done!"

"It'll be fine."

Adam tugged on it, waggled it, tugged on it again. He gripped the hilt tightly, fiercely... and with a dull grating of metal, the blade slid free, apparently undamaged.

"Good quality knives, these," Wetherby commented, approving.

The gash Adam had inflicted on the wall looked gruesome. A deep cleft; a trickle of greenish moisture ran freely down from it. He probed at it, even took his glove off to fully assess the smooth wetness of the incision.

"There's life in this old building yet," he observed, sniffing his fingertip.

Wetherby approached, bent down and scooped up the other knife. He adjusted it in his palm, as though he too appreciated its weight and balance. "Here's to the future, Adam. Our two-man show still on, or what?"

Adam didn't bother to answer, not even as they headed downstairs – just pulled his glove back on as he descended from floor to floor with quick, sure steps.

The stench of the place no longer bothered him. They saw no more rats. Even if they had, it wouldn't have mattered. That was the way of it. These vermin-ridden places, these blots on the landscape; they were loaded with foulness but also with memory. They were anchors to the past, which, grim and sordid as it often was, was the tale that underwrote all their lives. Speaking of which, they dallied in the junk-room no longer than they needed to. Adam was amused by the scare he'd had earlier. The unknown, frightening though it seemed at the time, should never be as daunting as the actual known. Because though he *knew* they had good times ahead, it would still involve an awesome challenge. When they left the building, Adam waited in the shadows while Wetherby closed the grille and fastened the padlock. It was late evening now, cars still passed and occasional figures could be spotted on the railway station forecourt, but what did that matter? Most likely they wouldn't notice anything. People didn't. That had been proved hundreds of times.

Once the building was secure, they set off walking.

"Keep that blade safe," Adam said.

There'd been an unspoken agreement between them to take one knife each. If nothing else, it would ensure that neither could gain an advantage over the other.

"Don't worry." Wetherby dug into his coat pocket. "Wrapped it in this." He drew out the bundle of cloth that had served as the hangman's hood in the junk-room. By accident, the knifepoint had torn two rents through a single fold so that when he opened it out, they resembled eye-holes.

Adam nodded as they passed under the railway bridge.

He'd been very careful stowing his own blade, wadding it in a handkerchief and placing it in a different pocket from the clown mask. The mask was neatly folded, but would need a new string. But that was no problem. An old shoelace would do. Anything they could find before they reached the Hexley ward, where all these years later the street-girls still plied their lonesome, night-time trade.

DEPARTURES

A.K. Benedict

She has no idea where she is but, judging from the lager farts rising from the fabric under her forehead, she'd say she was face down on a pub banquette. Someone must've called her out last night for a quick one and the quick one turned, as they do, into a lengthy ten. Maybe she lucked out at a lock-in. Maybe she was held, if only for a moment.

She sits up slowly and opens her eyes. The world lurches. Yup – she's in the corner of a pub, an empty bottle of gin on the table in front of her. Her head, though, doesn't feel like a piñata under attack. And there's no burst of guilt, shame or screaming nerve endings. If she's lucky, her eyeliner is still in place and not smeared across her, or someone else's, face.

Something's wrong, though. She knows that as surely as her name. Something is off-kilter, like the illusion of a straw kinked in a cocktail glass. She doesn't know what. She can't even be sure if she's been in here before. The generic pubness – Christmas tree slouched in the corner; decorations that look like they've seen better days but probably haven't; punters muttering; barmen buffing; cigarette smoke filling the room – means it could be any number of bars in Dublin.

Two men turn from the bar. The nearest, a scowl of a man in a barrel of a body, looks her up and down, then sneers. She sinks back into the seat. The other man is tall and gaunt with a very long neck. He moves slowly towards her, like an ambulant Nebuchadnezzar of Champagne.

'You're a weak man, Henrik. Can't you mind your own fucking business for once?' the sneering man says.

'Leave it, Carny,' Henrik says. He has difficulty walking, as if he's moving one frame at a time. 'You're awake, then,' he says when he reaches her. He sits down. 'Don't mind Carny. He's always been at war with the world.' He grins, making his face look like a crumpled hankie. 'You'll be feeling pretty rough, I should think.'

'Could be worse. You were here last night, then?' she asks.

153

'I'm always here.'

'You're the landlord? Tell me if I've broken anything, will you? You know, tables, chairs, laws, hearts? I've no idea how I got here.'

'No one does.' He crosses his legs infuriatingly slowly, like a skeletal Sharon Stone in slo-mo.

The coffee machine fumes behind the bar. 'I need coffee,' she says. At some point, memories are going to surface and she needs to be in a fit state to apologise/call the police/run.

'It won't do you any good, I'm afraid,' he says. 'You know that, deep down.' His hand moves haltingly across the table to hers.

She tries to yank her hand away but it's stuck in place. This is one weird hangover. 'Do I know you?' she asks. She attempts to cross her fingers, hoping that they hadn't crossed a line last night. Her forefinger twitches but otherwise won't budge. And she has never been this cold. This is more than too many shots of Jagermeister.

'No, but I hope we'll be friends. I'm Henrik. I'm the welcoming committee.'

'Isn't there usually more than one person in a committee?'

'Our numbers have dwindled lately. Maybe you'd like to come on board?'

'I'm not much of a joiner.'

He looks at her, head on one side. 'You really don't remember what happened, love?'

'Could you just tell me what I've done, who I've offended and what the fuck I drank last night and then I can go home or have my stomach pumped?' She's no one's love.

'Do you know where your home is?' he asks.

'I wasn't that drunk, thanks. Soon as I know where I am, then I can make my way back. I can't be that far out.'

'You're at the airport. The pub in Departures.'

Okay, maybe she can be that far out. 'Then I'll get a cab.'

'I'll call them from the bar. What's your address?' he asks.

'It's...' But the words don't come.

'Which side of the river?'

She should know this. She knows she knows this but she can't even picture her front room.

'And who shall I say the taxi's for, Miss?'

Again, she opens her mouth to tell him but the noun that represents her has gone. She can't find her first name, or her second. She doesn't even know if she has a middle name or what her job is, or if she has one. It's like searching for something in her handbag that she's sure is there but there are only old mints, ticket stubs to a film she doesn't remember and Tippex. And now someone's tipping the Tippex over everything she knows. Even facts and trivia are whiting out. She doesn't even know which Monkee's mum invented Tippex. Or was it Post-its? At least she knows that she doesn't have a partner. That one she knows deep inside her, where the yearning lurks.

'Not so easy, is it?' Henrik says.

'Someone must have given me something,' she says, panic rising. She can't remember her own fucking name, what else is she blotting out? 'I need to go to the, what's it called? Building with off-white corridors, smells of disinfectant?'

'The hospital.'

'That's it. Tell the taxi to take me to hospital.'

'I think it's a bit late for that, sweetheart.'

She tries to stand but nothing happens. 'Was it you? Did you do this?' She's shouting but her voice sounds far away.

'Ssh,' Henrik says, 'take things slowly. No one here did anything to you. Take a good look around. You'll get it soon enough.'

'Can you just fuck off?'

He doesn't just fuck off. 'Notice anything odd about the smoke?'

There *is* a lot of smoke in the room, more than she'd expect for a pub the morning after a lock-in. So she still knows her pub etiquette. Trust that to be the last thing to go. Also, the smoke isn't hanging in ribbons; it courses round the room as if it has a destination in mind. The room doesn't smell of smoke: it smells of bleach, coffee, greasy chips and beer. And if no one's smoking, the doors are open and the fire isn't lit, then there shouldn't be smoke at all.

'You're almost there,' he says. He looks sad. His tone is tissue soft. 'Look closer.'

She gazes into a streak of smoke as it passes the table and feels as if her heart has been placed in the ice bucket. There are faces in the smoke. Noses, mouths, eyes that do not see and limbs that move quick as a flick-book. See-through and swift, there are people, almost people, moving en masse like mist.

Or ghosts.

She tries to get up but her legs won't move. 'What are they?' she says.

'Don't worry, they can't harm you.'

'That's not what I asked.'

'What do you think they are?'

'Don't give me this Socratic shit, you know what I think they are.'

'Tell your little friend to shut up,' Carny shouts over without even looking at them. 'Or I'll shut her up.'

'Nice place you've got here,' she says. 'Arseholes at the bar and ghosts taking up valuable drinking space.' She watches two spectral faces turn her way as if they can almost hear, then they're gone. 'What do they want, anyway?'

'A drink before their flight, a drink after their flight, a break from working on security, a few minutes not to talk, a burger and chips before their sister arrives... They're all here for different reasons, just like us.'

'Us?'

'They're the ones with busy lives. We're here to watch them.'

The air around her feels thickened, as if it has skin. She reaches for her glass, able to move now but it takes a huge effort, as if pushing back something she can't see. She needs just one drink to steady her nerves. Her fingertips reach the glass, and pass straight through.

'What's going on?' she asks.

'You'll remember soon enough,' Henrik says. His eyes are the soft amber of a cloudy pint.

'Remember what?'

'How you died.'

'What're you talking about now? I haven't died, they're the ones who are –' She breaks off. One of the spirit people, a man, leans over to grab the glass. His arm brushes through hers, making her feel colder than ever before. He looks straight at her, blinks and shudders, then whisks back into smoke. And then she knows. It's the way he looks at her: she is the ghost.

Three days have passed, three days in which she's pushed Henrik away; tried to leave but couldn't move from her booth; wrestled with death and being yet dead, denying it, crying over it; tried to remember something, anything. You'd think she'd recall, wouldn't you, how she died, at the very least? But no: she just sat here, staring into the table as if it'd open into a brown pool where she could tickle out memories as if they were trout. But nothing surfaced. All the while the giggling river of the living flowed past, eddying, flitting, living. At least she thinks it's been three days, it's hard to tell, minutes go so quickly: hours pass across the face of the clock over the bar like micro-expressions. Clocks should have days and years on them. They should hold onto time more tightly.

She should've held onto life more tightly. This wallowing has got to stop. She's all for spending your life in a pub, but what's the point if you can't drink?

'Henrik,' she calls out.

Henrik looks up from trying to soothe an exchange between Carny and another customer.

'It won't make a difference, you know,' Carny says, his mouth contorting, as Henrik walks over to her. 'You can help as many people as you like but you still failed her. You're weak. You're water to her whiskey, you always were. You'll give in, down the line.'

Henrik closes his eyes as he sits down next to her.

'What was all that about?' Sian asks.

'There's something he wants to know and I won't tell him. Never mind that. You're looking a little brighter,' he says. 'I was worried about you. We all were.'

'Apart from Carny.'

'Carny only cares about himself.'

'What is this place?' she asks. Her voice comes out stronger. 'Hell? Limbo? Valhalla?'

'You didn't say heaven,' Henrik says.

'We may be in a pub but this isn't heaven. I'd be feeling more guilty if this were heaven.'

'It's none of those, as far as we know, although limbo is nearest. We've no real idea, though. There's no authority figure to tell us what's happening, only guidance passed on by, and to, the passed on.'

'"The passed on". So life looked at me and said, "I'll pass on her having her thirty-third birthday".'

Henrik clapped his hands together. The sound was empty. 'That's a good start, you know how old you are.'

'Maybe it's all coming back.'

'Give it time. Anyway, sometimes it's the other way round. People pass on life for their own reasons.'

'I'd never pass on life,' she says.

'Good for you,' Henrik says. 'As far as what this place is, we think it's a literal last chance saloon.'

'What's the last chance?'

'The chance to do it again, to relive a section of our life and make decisions that will lead to us not dying, not so soon anyway.'

She feels hope flow. 'What do I need to do?'

'That's the tricky bit,' Henrik says. 'You're going to have to remember who you are.'

'And then what?'

'The people you see moving around you are, in a way, ghosts – they're in the past. Each one is in their own timeline running up to their death. At some point in your past, you came here. Your job is to wait and then find yourself among the millions.'

'Then what?'

'Then grab hold of you, fold your future spirit into your past body and persuade it not to die.'

'Piece of piss, then,' she says, clinging to sarcasm like splintered driftwood at sea. 'Seeing as I've no idea what I look like, what my name is or how to move in this weird space/time fuck up.'

'We'd better get you moving, then,' Henrik says.

An hour, a day or a year later, she has managed to cross halfway across the pub. Somehow, knowing that she is on a different plane to the febrile world of the living helps her move through it. A year, a day or an hour later, she's standing in the Departures hall. Streams of the living weave in and out like DNA strands. They twist round her, flinching as one if they accidentally touch her.

Spectres gather. Lots of them. They stand by departures boards, check-in desks and cafes. Heads slowly turning, they scry for themselves in the smoke. Henrik says that the dead are found in places where large numbers pass through – museums, concert halls, terminals. She'd never liked airports, found them too crowded and frantic, but maybe she knew, deep down, that the dead were waiting, that it was far more busy than the living imagine.

She wanders slowly through security and into the perfumes hall, the mist of sprayed fragrances feels heavy on her spectral body, as if walking into doorway beads. What had she been thinking about? A man. She'd been talking to a man. In a pub. Memories of him are disappearing like flights from the departures board. Henrik. That's it.

Mistrals of people pass, leering at each other as if in masks, mouths stretched wide. So many of them; as overwhelming as the intersecting smells of alcohol and aldehydes. And she has to recognise herself among them. It's impossible. She'll never get out of here. She sinks to the floor and curls up as the feet of the fleshed flow past.

'Didn't I say, "Don't go too far on your first trip"?' Henrik says when she comes round. She's back in the pub.

'I did, but then I didn't remember.' All she wants is to lie down on her banquette and sleep.

'That's why you shouldn't go too far. The pub keeps our memories, don't ask me how. It's like they're pickled in alcohol. Staying conscious helps, if you can.'

She concentrates on the poster by the bar. It's a traditional Irish prayer that appears on tea towels, magnets and beer mats. You've probably seen it on a mug at your auntie's house – it starts with the words, 'May the road rise up to meet you', and ends with the blessing, 'May God hold you in the hollow of his hand'. In this poster, though, the last three words have been eroded, either by time or sun or adjacent packets of pork scratchings.

Henrik follows her line of sight. 'It's why we call this place the Hollow.' He crosses himself then says, 'May God hold us in the Hollow.'

'I thought the aim was to leave,' she says.

'We've been given the opportunity to redo parts of our pasts, I don't know if everyone is as lucky. As far as we know, some people go straight to the next stage, if there is one. Or go nowhere at all. Being held in the Hollow is an opportunity, a blessing.'

'Tell him that,' she says, watching Carny stalk the smoke in the room. The living move away from him as if he were bellows. She feels their panic. It changes the taste in the air, adds iron, like a mouth filling with blood. The ghosts stay away too.

'What's his problem?' she asks.

'He was killed,' Henrik says. 'Don't ask me the whys and wherefores, and definitely don't ask him, but that's what drives him – finding his murderer and killing him.'

'But he's a ghost. I saw him struggle to smash a pint glass. He wouldn't be able to kill anyone.'

'Well, that's the other side of the blessing,' Henrik says.

'Isn't the other side of a blessing a curse?' she asks.

'You could say that, although the curse is on both us and the living: if, for example, you think you've found your past self and embrace her but get the wrong person, then you've marked that human for death.'

'Shit.'

'Yes, they may die straight away, in weeks or years, but before their time. And *you'd* fade away instead of living again. We only get one choice. One chance.'

'This is what I'm here for? Who made up this game?'

Henrik shrugs. 'Don't know. But those are the rules.'

In the smoke, a family passes, pulling suitcases, then two women, hand in hand, kissing: happy people off on blink-quick holidays.

'Fuck you,' Carny shouts into the smoke, nostrils flared, hands in fists.

A.K. Benedict

She knows how he feels.

After that, she only goes into the airport on short sorties before circling back to the Hollow. Atoms of memory reattach themselves. She knows now that she lived in Dun Laoghaire and that Shirley Bassey recorded three James Bond theme songs.

And she's remembered her name. *Sian.*

That evening, or another, she sits with Henrik in the Hollow, staring into the flickering people stream as if it were a fire.

'What do I look like?' she asks.

'Well,' he says, squinting at her. 'You've got dark brown eyes, like stout. Got as much in them as stout as well.'

Sian laughs.

'Your hair is brown with blonde bits in, like my wife used to have. And cheekbones that could crack open a can of Batchelors.'

'You don't talk about your wife much.'

'No. Well,' Henrik says, looking away. 'I don't like to. She's my angel's share.'

Moaning comes from the booth next door, as if someone were writhing in pain.

'That's my cue,' Henrik says. He gets up, then turns to Sian. 'Do you want to help?'

She shrugs. It's something to do.

A newly made ghost is on the neighbouring banquette, arms looped about her knees, rocking. She whimpers. She's young, in her mid-twenties.

'It's all right, everything's all right,' Henrik says.

Sian stops herself saying that it really isn't.

The young woman looks up at Henrik; then, on turning to Sian, her eyes widen, her pupils slowly eclipse the blue. It's as if she knows Sian. Has known her. She shakes and Sian wishes she had the ability to hug her. Her eyes close.

'We're here when you need us, just say,' Henrik says, softly, and leads Sian away.

The next day, the young woman is more alert, looking around the pub. When she sees Sian, she almost smiles. Sian moves over from the bar and sits down next to her while Henrik begins his slow, kind unveiling of the Hollow, the airport and the search that goes on inside. The words drift past Sian as she takes in everything about the woman: her name, Marta; her age, twenty-six; her job, lab assistant; her clothes, tight jeans, Flaming Lips T-shirt two sizes too big; her hair, shaved at the sides and a rumpled quiff.

'Have you got any words of wisdom, Sian?'

'What?' Sian says.

'Any sage advice for Marta, here? You've been through this recently.'

'I don't think I'm the one to ask. I've only just worked out what my name is.'

Marta looks down at her lap as if disappointed.

'I can tell you one thing,' Sian says, quickly. 'The living look scary but they're frightened of us, for some reason. We're not out to hurt them.' She looks across at Carny. 'Not all of us, anyway.'

'But we can hurt them. Get it wrong and we condemn them to an early death. They know that by instinct. The living haunt the dead and the dead the living; that's the way it's always been,' Henrik says.

'Well, that's a cheery thought to wake up dead to,' Marta says. Her voice is quiet. Her sarcasm is as refreshing as the first pint at the end of the day.

'I'll leave you to it,' Henrik says, then walks slowly over to the corner where Carny has the ghost of a guitar player backed against the wall. Carny holds out a warning hand to Henrik; Henrik backs away.

'Who's that man?' Marta says. She's staring at Carny, her hands making claws and trying to grab the edge of the seat.

'That's Carny. Not a happy man. There are plenty of good people in here, though. It's got that waiting room spirit thing going on. If we were alive we'd be passing around sweets. All we've got to share are stories and I haven't got many of those.'

'Why not?' she says. As she looks at Sian, a current of past and future runs between them.

'I don't know how I lived or how I died. Henrik says memory loss can happen in death, during trauma. So I think we can say I didn't die well.'

'Who does?' Marta asks.

'Joan Crawford. Apparently her housekeeper prayed for her and Joan shouted: "Damn it! Don't you dare ask God to help me!". Don't ask me how I know that. I didn't know I did.'

'The last words Bogey said to Bacall were, "Goodbye kid, hurry back."'

'Wouldn't it be great to know someone as well as they did, to have them know you?'

'It would,' Marta says.

They go everywhere together: they walk through departures, even into arrivals; sit in silence watching the ghosts of the living; talk for whole turns of the clock as thin films of memory return: Sian's stray cat, Patricia

Wentworth; a holiday in the Highlands with her first girlfriend; the clothes left in the airing cupboard. Sometimes they go looking for themselves, or to watch others find themselves, like a reunion show on TV. One afternoon, they're sitting on a bench near check-in when a ghost cries out in joy and moves towards a passenger, holding out her arms. The passenger turns. It's not the same person. Sian calls out but the ghost has already descended on the living person like dusk. They both stagger back, sharing a scream and nothing else, till the woman grabs her left arm and falls onto the ground, dead.

They sit in silence. It's too big a risk. They can't leave each other for that. Anyway, having found each other, the importance of finding themselves is receding. Marta turns to her and moves forward. Their lips do not touch, as they never can, but they miss each other in the same space and that's almost nearly good enough for now.

There's a lot of almost kissing after that. They're nearly kissing in Sian's booth when Carny kicks off.

'He's here. The cunt's here,' Carny says, pointing into the smoke. His face is a red knot.

'Who's he talking about?' Marta whispers.

'The man who killed him, I think,' Sian says, standing up.

Carny strides around, herding the billow of smoke. The adrenaline tang in the room soars. Sian moves towards him.

'Let it go, Carny,' Henrik says, gently. 'You tell me to mind your own business, how about you do the same?'

'He murdered me. He placed his hands round my neck and strangled me into this place. This *is* my fucking business.' Carny says, staring at the large man he's isolated from the flitting living. The man runs towards the door but Carny is there. Wherever the man goes, Carny is there. Carny reaches for his throat.

'Maybe you're part of it, have you thought about that?' Sian says. She doesn't know how she's doing it but she's moving quicker.

'Fuck off back to your girlfriend,' Carny says, turning on her.

'Maybe you're here so that you can go back and make it right. Just by going back and altering one thing, the timeline will have shifted. You have one chance and you're wasting it on him.' Out of the corner of her eye, she sees the man move away, fear stretching his face into a scream.

'He *killed* me. Would you let someone get away with that?'

'If I had the chance to live again, yes,' Sian says. 'I'd replay it, change the ending.'

'I *will* replay it,' Carny snarls. 'I'll replay that cunt killer's death, over and over as I die.'

'I'm afraid you won't,' Henrik says, over Sian's shoulder.

Carny looks around. His intended victim has gone. 'You cost me my chance,' he says to Sian, his face twisting. 'And you'll pay.'

'A ghost can't kill another ghost, can it?' Sian asks.

Henrik says nothing.

They, along with Marta, are walking round the airport in the early hours. Shops and check-ins are shut and the only noises are from the living snoring on beds made from suitcases. They'll jump up soon and run to fidget in line as the place comes alive, but for now, there is calm across the airport.

'I mean, I don't have to worry about him unless I find my living self?'

'Not necessarily. I think the best thing to do is to find your living self as quickly as possible,' he says. 'And then stay away from this airport.'

'So there *is* a way,' Marta says. 'But how, if we can't even touch?'

'Few of the dead know about it. I don't even know if it's real. Don't think I'm going to tell you, either, or anyone else, even though they beg me,' Henrik says. 'I'm not having that as well on my conscience.' His voice is all pain and edges.

They walk on, not talking, past a family slumped over a bench. Their sped up snoring sounds like pigs talking.

'Is there a way, though,' Marta says, her little finger an ache of an inch from mine, 'that we *can* touch?'

We both look at him. He sighs. 'Over time, just as you adjust to moving in a different dimension and affecting the living, you become stronger in this one. It's not touching as you remember, but it's as good.' He screws his face up and closes his eyes, as if pushing back a memory.

'You said that you didn't want "that as well" on your conscience,' Sian says. 'Is that something to do with your wife? Your angel's share?'

'What's the angel's share?' Marta asks.

'It's the small percentage of alcohol that evaporates from the casks,' Henrik says.

'And you call your wife that because...?' Sian says.

'Because she got away. Because I wasn't brave enough to follow. Now, please,' Henrik says. His eyes ghost with tears. 'I've tried to help you. Leave me be. Stay away from Carny; get away from here. Anger is the only thing fuelling him and you've removed his method of revenge. He'll be looking for another one. And I don't know if I can hold him off.' He walks off, as quick as Sian's seen him walk.

163

'I shouldn't have pushed him,' she says.
'We both did,' Marta replies.

Whenever they're there, Carny taunts them. He stands close. Watching. His jaw works backwards and forwards as if chewing gum. 'Enjoy yourselves while you can,' he says. 'I'll always be here.'

Henrik sidles over. He can't look them in the eyes. He seems paler, even less substantial. 'He knows,' he said. 'He knows the method. He's building up the strength but you must find your bodies.'

They avoid the Hollow after that, only going back to refresh memories. The more they know about themselves, the more likely they can find their living bodies as they roam slowly round the concourse, Carny following. They hear him whistling even when they can't see him; can smell the cologne of beer, stale smoke and semen that follows him even in death.

Moving through the crowds, they search the faces of thousands of women, Marta looking for Sian and Sian Marta, as they know each other's faces better than their own. And then, one day, Marta turns to Sian with a face of fighting micro-expressions.

'What is it?' Sian asks

'You're over there,' Marta says, pointing to Accessorize where a woman is buying a white woolly scarf.

'That's me?' Sian says. She can't connect with that woman but the memory of the scarf loops round her. It was warm and slightly scratchy, like fingernails at her neck.

'Go. Quickly,' Marta says, pushing her away. 'And don't come back.'

Sian walks up to the woman with brown hair and stout eyes. The woman opens her mouth and there is a moment of recognition and sadness before Sian opens her arms and walks into her own.

It takes time to find room inside Sian. Her ghost tries to snake into her thoughts but they're taken up with her job of writing questions for TV quizzes and factoids for crackers, and her evenings are taken up with booze and near lovers. It's hard to hold onto the Hollow and what happened there. The ghost in the living can feel it leave her, bit by bit. She tries to get herself to write the words 'Marta' and 'Henrik' and 'Carny' but they only appear in dreams. Soon, there isn't much room between future and past Sian, only a thin space where a memory might be.

Sian carries certain things around with her, though. She has a fondness out of nowhere for a certain Irish blessing, a fear of being followed and an aversion to flying. It's trains, buses and boats or she's not going anywhere.

Her friends don't know why this change has taken place and neither does she, only that she's going nowhere near departures and there's a hollow in her heart.

A day, a week, a year later, Sian's sister, Yvonne, is flying back from New York for Christmas. 'Pick me up, would you?' Yvonne said when she called. 'It'll cost a fortune in a taxi.'

'Are you joking? With the dollar as it is? And it's not as if you're not making money.'

'You sound like Dad.'

'Ouch.'

So she was picking her sister up at the airport. She couldn't find a good enough reason why she shouldn't, not even to convince herself. And it wasn't as if she was going to departures.

Sian sits, scarf on to counteract the draft of the automatic doors, hands round a huge coffee. She went for the gingerbread latte. It's Christmas, after all. She looks up, and a man is staring at her. He isn't tall but he's got broad shoulders. A chill that has nothing to do with the draft flows down her spine as if she's being unzipped. She pulls the scarf tighter around her.

He moves slowly closer. The cup slips between her fingers, sending hot coffee everywhere as she realises – she can see through him. Other people move around him without seeing or acknowledging him but he is coming for her. She knows that. She doesn't know how she knows, but she does.

She scrambles up, kicking the chair away and stumbles out of the café, looking back to see where he was, but he's closer. And there's something familiar about him. About his sneer.

She runs up to the information desk, out of breath. 'Help me, please, I'm being followed. I think I'm in danger.'

'Slow down there, Madam,' the smooth-skinned, groomed woman behind the desk says. 'Who is it that is chasing you?'

Sian points to the man walking slowly towards her.

The woman, whose name badge says Rhiannon, smiles at her, eyes Liffey cold. 'There's no one there, Madam.' Her pencilled eyebrows flick reverse Vs.

Sian turns away. The man is there, inches from her. She can smell him – a blend of whiskey, tobacco and decay. 'I told Henrik he was weak and I told you you'd pay,' he says. His hands reach for her.

'No,' says another voice.

A young woman is standing behind him. Her hands are on his neck, her sinews straining, her eyes closed. She squeezes, pulling him back, away from Sian.

'How are you doing this?' he spits out, each word a struggle.

'Henrik,' the girl says. 'Said he had to do something to make up for it all.'

Sian's heart contracts and expands as if breathing. 'I know you,' she says.

'You do,' says Marta. 'And I know you.'

The man, Carny, collapses to the floor, holding his throat. He is pulsing, like a faulty light bulb.

'We don't have much time.' Marta's pulsing too.

Sian walks towards her.

'No, we can't,' Marta says, backing away but Sian is quicker. Their fingers touch and their lips kiss and for one moment she is held.

'Hurry back,' Marta says.

Sian opens her eyes. Marta and Carny have gone and she is in the middle of a stream of people, alive and dead, and she is totally alone.

As soon as she gets home, Sian writes it down. All of it. Not on a computer, on paper she can hold to her and read when the memories fade, and when the ink fades she writes it out again. She writes facts for crackers and quizzes for idiots but knows she knows little. Sometimes she sits in the Hollow, watching the terminally slow Styx of the dead, waiting for what is stalking her. She doesn't know how long she's got. Maybe Marta will be there in some way. Maybe she's here already. May she hold her in the Hollow. May she hold her in the hollow of her hand.

THE TASTE OF HER

Mark West

"So, how does my wife taste?"

Startled, Ian Burgess looked at Keith March, who was piloting the Cessna aircraft they were in. The plane banked right, high over Gaffney. "What?"

Keith turned to face him, his smile tight. "I asked if you liked the taste of my wife."

Turbulence hit the little plane and Ian hoped it covered the guilty panic that he knew must be showing in his face. "I don't know what you mean."

"Yes you do you fucking liar. I know everything."

Ian had played poker with Keith a few times and knew he was a good bluffer. But was he bluffing now?

"Ian, you've fucked Julie and ruined my life." He dipped the nose of the aircraft and checked a couple of gauges. "So, for both our sakes, don't make it any worse by lying now."

The two men had known one another for more than ten years, having met at the squash club one evening when both had been let down by their partners. That first game led to a weekly match, which quickly moved to drinking sessions, trips to a restaurant and then evenings out with Keith's wife Julie and Ian's succession of girlfriends.

Keith March was a successful businessman, who'd used his wits to build up an empire and then some inside information from his bank manager to survive the worst of the credit crunch. Before, his primary holdings had been in property and a couple of Ford dealerships, but now he owned a good chunk of prime retail space in the town centre. Ian Burgess was a born salesman, good at his job but poor with money, always getting out of scrapes by the skin of his teeth and the cut of his Armani.

This disparity drew them closer – they disagreed on most things but enjoyed the arguments and, to a degree, envied the other's lifestyle. Keith enjoyed his rewards and his third and younger wife but he would have preferred a more devil-may-care approach to life. Ian, on the other hand, didn't crave the funds or stability but he was in love with Julie and would have given the world to be with her.

Ian cleared his throat. "Keith, there's got to be some mistake."

"Bollocks." The word sounded hard and clipped.

Ian could hear the panic that was starting to creep into his voice, making the lies sound hollower each time he uttered them. "You've got it all wrong."

But Keith hadn't and so here Ian was, two thousand feet in the air with a man whose wife he'd been sleeping with for the past two years, terrified out of his wits. He didn't like flying, never had, and this Cessna was little more than a toy plane. Keith had insisted he sit in the front with him but there was hardly any room as he didn't want to lean against the flimsy door and daren't jog Keith's arm. He couldn't stretch out his legs for fear of pressing the pedals there and every time he looked out of the window, the wings seemed to be bowing.

It was noisy, too, almost too loud to hear himself think. It wasn't like on commercial planes, where the drone of the engine could be quickly and easily ignored. No, the Cessna was loud enough to necessitate them wearing headphones and talking through mikes. He looked at Gaffney, spread out below him like a child's playset and felt bile rise in his throat.

Keith glared at Ian. "Shut up, Ian, you make me sick."

And with that, he pulled back hard and the plane lurched in the air. Ian groaned and only just managed to swallow back a mouthful of vomit.

Although Keith and Julie had been married for twelve years, Ian always considered her to be a trophy wife. She was tall and slim, her hair a deep auburn that cascaded around her shoulders in softly curled waves. She had a thin, friendly face and lips that he longed to kiss from the moment he met her. Her eyes were almost turquoise and he dreamed of the day that he could do nothing other than stare into them, losing himself in her.

She began to flirt with him just after they met and Keith, if anything, had found it amusing. Julie would put her arm around Ian, indicate that when Keith wasn't looking they could steal away somewhere and each Christmas and birthday she gave him a kiss that got more intense as the years went by. She seemed to enjoy it and so did Ian, but it was killing him inside. For eight years, he denied himself the fact that he loved her when all he wanted was to take her away from her husband who apparently couldn't care less.

It was a quiet Sunday lunchtime when he went to Keith's to pick him up for their weekly squash match. The air was hazy, the sun bright and hot. He parked on the driveway and before he'd reached the front door, Julie had opened it. She was wearing a white vest and white shorts, which accentuated the deep tan she'd picked up on a recent fortnights holiday in the Algarve. Her nipples were hard and clearly defined against the cotton of her vest and her legs were brown and smooth. He wondered, for the thousandth time, what it would feel like to have them wrapped around him.

"Hi, Ian," she said, smiling brightly.

"Hi, Julie, how's life?"

"Oh," she said and rested her bare left foot against her right shin, "can't complain. Do you want to come in?"

"Sure." Anything to be able to look at her. "Is Keith about?"

She shook her head slightly. "No, he got called out about ten minutes ago. He tried to ring your mobile but…"

"I turned it off," he said and thought of his phone, sitting in the glove compartment.

She smiled. "So we gathered. He told me to bring you in, make you feel at home and that he'd get back as soon as he could."

"How long will that be?" he said, hoping that it would be some time.

"He reckoned at least a couple of hours." She stepped to one side and indicated towards the lounge. "Come in, do you want a beer?"

"Please," he said and went to sit on one of the overstuffed sofas. Their house was immaculate, minimalist but exuding expense. Julie came through with a can of Stella and a glass of white wine and sat next to him. She passed him the can and leaned back, blowing a stray hair from her forehead.

"Thanks," he said.

She smiled. "So how are you, Ian?" Leaning back, her breasts moved freely under the vest. She moved her legs, the muscles stretching. He couldn't look away and hoped his erection wasn't obvious in his shorts.

"I'm well."

"How's the love life?"

She often asked him that, a smile playing at her lips but today, it sent a shiver up his spine. "Not good. Sophie and I split up a couple of weeks ago so I'm currently on my tod."

"Celibate then, eh?"

"Maybe."

"Join the club," she said quietly. She was staring out of the patio windows at the far end of the lounge, rubbing her left knee with delicate fingertips. "Listen," she said and turned her attention to him. "Could you do me a favour?"

"Of course," he said, without thinking. "Whatever you want."

She sighed. "I'm not sure I should ask but my feet are killing me.

Would you mind giving them a rub?"

He smiled at this unexpected turn-up for the books. A foot massage would be good. "No."

"Thank you. Keith hates feet and I do so love having mine touched and teased."

He looked at her quickly and she smiled, dipping her head to peer at him through her eyelashes. Could this be it, could he have been so blind before that she liked him too? "For what it's worth, I think you have lovely feet, Julie, Keith's missing out there."

"Thanks." She turned sideways, resting her back against the arm and put her feet gently in his lap. He put his can down and lifted her right foot, his left hand under her heel. He stroked the soft skin of her sole, which made her toes flex. He pressed his right thumb into the pad of skin below her big toe and she let out the lightest of moans.

He continued this for a couple of minutes, rubbing, kneading and massaging as best he could and looked at Julie. Her eyes were closed and her right hand was resting lightly at her throat. He ran his thumb down her sole and up to her ankle and a soft groan escaped her. He reached further, his fingers tracing a line up the toned, smooth skin of her calf. She angled her left foot, her toes brushing against his erection. He moved further, beyond her knee. His erection felt like it was going to explode. Julie pulled her feet away and reached for him. She held his cheeks and kissed him hard, her tongue darting into his mouth.

That first time was everything he'd hoped it would be and more besides. The next time was amazing, the time after that even better and within the week they'd made love more times than he had in the past few months. Her body enthralled him, teased him and delighted him and he loved to stroke her soft skin, running his fingers and lips all over her, making her moan and moisten. She did things to him that he'd never experienced before, taking him to levels of pleasure he'd barely even dreamed of in the past. They fitted together, they were the perfect match. Apart from her husband.

Ian hated going behind Keith's back and, a couple of times as they chatted in the pub or played a game of squash, he had to fight an urge to come clean. He also hated the fact that he and Julie couldn't be together all the time and it drove him nuts that each night, Keith lay down with her and ignored her beautiful body, whilst Ian lay alone.

"I know everything, Ian," said Keith, levelling the plane, "so don't try and bullshit me."

"Keith, I'm telling you…"

Keith grunted and turned the plane sharply to the right, throwing Ian against the door. He swallowed back more vomit and held his stomach.

"Don't fucking lie to me." He threw the plane to the left and then back to the right again, tossing Ian in his chair like a small boat lost on a raging ocean.

"Okay," Ian said, "no more, please."

"Just tell me why, why did you do it?"

Ian looked down at his lap, watching his fingers twitch with nervousness. "Because she's beautiful and I couldn't resist. But neither of us wanted to hurt you, you have to believe that."

"Yeah, right. Ten years we've known one another and this is how you treat me? We were friends, Ian, didn't that mean anything to you at all?"

"Keith, I'm sorry, really."

"Sorry?" The rage in Keith's voice almost whited out the headphones. Ian saw his knuckles were white on the yoke. He was staring ahead, his mouth a tight line. "Julie was all that mattered in my life and now I have nothing, thanks to you. Nothing at all."

Keith tilted the nose down. The engine note changed and the windscreen was now not just showing sky. Ian, pushed forward in his seat, held onto the dash. "What are you doing?"

"There's nothing left, Ian, so I'm finishing it off."

Keith got his private pilot's licence three years ago and had been trying to get Ian up in the air ever since and this was the first flight he'd given in to. Keith was late turning up, complaining about a customer who reckoned they'd got a bad deal. He quickly carried out the flight checks and they were off, Keith confident behind the controls. Ian was even starting to enjoy himself, though he still couldn't bear to look down at the ant-sized people below, going about their business.

"Did you know that air travel is the safest form of transport? More people die from falling out of windows than they do from plane crashes, unless a jumbo goes down of course. But these little beauties…" Keith tapped the dash. "They take a hell of a lot to down them. Even if you stall them, they'll glide." He looked at Ian. "So keeping this in a dive is quite hard work."

Ian looked into his friend's eyes and saw nothing there, no feeling or emotion and real panic gripped him. "Jesus, Keith, what are you trying to do?"

"Don't you get it, you miserable fucker? I'm going to take away from you and Julie what you and Julie have taken away from me."

Ian's mouth dried up. "For God's sake, man."

Keith pushed the yoke forward harder and the plane pitched down. The ground now filled three quarters of the windscreen and Ian was pushed hard into his seat restraints. The engine protested, screaming.

"Keith," yelled Ian, "for Christ's sake, pull the plane up, pull it up!"

"Tell me how she tastes, you bastard." Keith's voice was almost raw and spittle was flying out of his mouth to patter against the windscreen.

The ground was coming towards them at an alarming rate and Ian closed his eyes. Would losing Julie – or the thought that she was with someone else, his friend or not – really push Keith over the edge like this? Would it be enough for him to kill himself? Ian saw Keith's dead-eye stare and the sweat beading on his forehead and realised that, yes, he would.

Keith flicked a switch and the engine cut out. All that could be heard now was the loud whistling of the wind.

Ian screamed and felt his bladder go. A dark stain appeared at the crotch of his trousers.

"Tell me if you liked her taste."

Ian felt vomit rise in his throat but couldn't stop it this time. It came out in one retch, hitting his trousers and the dash and the floor.

"Yes," yelled Ian, spitting to clear his mouth, "I did, I do, I love the taste of her, I love the feel of her. Is that what you wanted to hear, you sick fucker, are you satisfied now?"

Keith smiled and pulled back on the yoke, straightening the plane gradually. He flicked the switch and the engine kicked back into life. The plane levelled out at seven hundred and fifty feet and Keith banked left, heading back for the airfield.

"You know what, Ian? That does make me feel better."

Ian looked from Keith to his lap, at the pool of vomit and the urine stain cold against his leg. Tears welled in his eyes and all he wanted to do was get back on terra firma because he was terrified of what Keith would do next.

They arrived at the airfield without incident, though Ian's heart didn't stop beating too fast until the engine was off and the plane had stopped moving. Keith got out and went into the main building to settle his account and Ian took the opportunity to get away. He hurried to the car park but saw, to his dismay, that Keith had blocked him in.

"Shit." He got some wipes out of the car and tried to clear the mess from his lap. A couple of minutes later, he heard someone come up behind him and lean in close.

"I don't want you to come anywhere near me or my wife in future, have you got that?" Keith's voice was a harsh whisper in his ear. "If I ever catch you so much as sniffing around Julie again, I will kill you – I will tear you limb from limb. Do you understand?"

Ian felt short of breath, his heart hammering in his chest again. "Yes," he said, "yes I do."

"This never happened, none of it. You're not on the manifest, you were never here. Fuck off out of my sight now."

"I will." Ian was aware of his hands, shaking uncontrollably against his leg. He was nothing, had nothing, Keith had taken away everything, including Julie with this plane stunt. Dimly, he knew he should warn her but guessed she already knew – Keith must have got the information from her.

Keith got into his car and drove away quickly, kicking up a spume of gravel that peppered Ian's legs and dug chips out of the paintwork on his boot. Ian leaned on his car, took deep breaths for long enough to stop his hands shaking and his heart to slow down, then drove home.

As soon as he was inside, carefully checking that Keith hadn't parked nearby, he went upstairs to get a shower.

The first speckles of blood were on the last riser. As he reached the landing, he saw a trail that led into the bedroom. He groaned, feeling bile rise again.

He gingerly pushed open the bedroom door. It was empty but two streaks of blood had soaked into the carpet, leading from where he stood to the en-suite door. A laptop, not his, was set up on the dresser. He tapped the mousepad as he walked by and the screen faded from black onto a Twitter feed. Onto Julie's Twitter feed.

I can't take it anymore, all this furtiveness, makes me feel dirty, read the first entry.

Have told my lover that I want it to end, he's not happy.

There was a gap of several minutes before the next entry. Ian read it with tears gathering in his eyes. *Lover is very angry, swearing & punching the walls. Scared now.*

Lover has hit me, told me that if he can't have me, no one can. Wish I'd never got involved.

There was one more entry and Ian had the horrible feeling that he knew what it'd say before he even read it. *Lover has gone berserk, very scared now, please call the police.*

His address was listed. Shaking his head, tears now running down his cheeks, Ian pushed open the door to the en-suite.

There was blood everywhere – the floor, the walls, the sink and the toilet seat – and a heavy metallic smell hung in the air. He looked at the mirror and saw something written on it, in blood. The upper words had run into the lower ones, but Ian could still read, 'Help me'.

His stomach rolled and he dry retched. The shower curtain was drawn and he could see a shape through it. He pulled it back and fell to his knees, whimpering, all strength gone.

Julie March was hanging from a hook that someone had screwed into the ceiling above the bath. One of his belts was around her neck, dug deeply into the flesh. Her lips and face were blue, her eyes bulging grotesquely. There was blood around her mouth and the end of her tongue, poking through her broken front teeth, looked blunt as if she'd bitten the tip off. Both of her forearms were criss-crossed with deep wounds that were tacky with blood.

He heard a car skid to a stop outside and the sound of heavy footsteps.

Sobbing, Ian stood on the edge of the bath and unhooked Julie. He didn't have a chance of holding her up and her dead-weight pulled them both down, to land in the shallow pool of blood that had collected. He whimpered and buried his face in her neck, her blood against his lips.

There was a loud knocking at the door, someone shouted his name.

"My baby," Ian said and kissed Julie's ruined mouth, savouring the taste of her for the last time.

SUN DOGS

Laura Mauro

It hadn't rained in close to seven weeks the night I met you. The rain-barrels were down to the last silty dregs, the skies stubborn in their pale blue clarity. I wasn't even certain the car would start; it chugged to life on the third attempt, emitting a choked gurgle like a throat full of sand. My sole back-up plan: an ageing Chevy Cavalier, tyres balding, paintwork leprous, a quarter-tank of gas which might not even get me the whole way to Wildrose.

My parents had been preppers; I should've known better. Boxes of ammo next to the bread in the pantry, towering crates of bottled water in the basement. Rucksacks in the hall closet piled with emergency supplies – should the End Days catch us unawares – and a framed cross-stitch on the wall: "Failure to Prepare Is Preparing to Fail." Pastel colours, delicate bluebell border; a portent of doom, handcrafted with love.

I left at dusk. The sky was a cut mouth bleeding out onto the western mountains. It seemed there was not a single soul out on the highway that night except for me. If the Chevy broke down, I'd be screwed; cellphone reception was null this far out into the desert, and hadn't that been the entire point in the first place? Going solo on the edge of civilisation: the complete amputation of my former life, gangrenous with regrets.

I had a foil blanket in the trunk, a protein bar in the glovebox. Half a bottle of water in the footwell. Not good enough. I kept an eye on the fuel gauge as I drove, foot light on the gas. There was a gas station at Wildrose, a general store and a gift shop. A campsite out back full of shiny-white RVs, gleaming despite the dust. Desert adventure for kindergartners. A thought came to me in my mother's voice, criticism from beyond the grave: at least they have water.

The way station was just visible on the horizon, a halo of light lingering over the scrub and above it, a fat, pale moon. Not the blood-red moon of my childhood terrors, heralding the arrival of the End Days – peeling back the curtains, peering up at the sky through parted fingers,

175

because you could never tell when it might happen, and you would have to be Ready when it did.

The asphalt gleamed black in the headlights. Something ducked out of the road, into the sparse cover of the scrub. I saw it in the rear-view mirror; bright eyes sparked momentarily, the shadow of some slender creature crouched just off the roadside. Kit fox, maybe, or bobcat. I turned back to the road.

A man stepped out in front of the car.

I hit the brakes hard. The car arced wildly; my hands were tight on the wheel, my eyes squeezed shut, awaiting the impact, the crunch of bone against metal. When I opened them, the car was still, and the man was intact, staring at me with wide-eyed surprise in the middle of the road. I unbuckled the seatbelt with trembling fingers, aware now of how sore my sternum felt, how fast my heart was beating. Slowly, I stepped out of the car.

The man took a step forward. Clutched tight in his hands was a hunting rifle. .204 Ruger, walnut stock. Approach with caution. He had a canteen of water at his hip, heavy-duty boots, scuffed and well-worn. He scanned me. "Are you hurt?"

My ribs ached with each exhalation, muscles contracting over bruised bone. "I'm fine," I said. His shoulders were loose, his fingers slack on the gun. No obvious signs of hostility, but I was a lone female on an empty highway, and I was unarmed. I could almost hear my daddy rolling in his grave. "You ought to take care if you're coming out here in the dark. I could've killed you." I swallowed hard, tasting sour adrenaline. "I could've killed us both."

The seashore hiss of cicadas filled the momentary silence. "I'm sorry," he said, after a time. He wasn't looking at me. His eyes were focused on some point beyond the car, out towards the darkened scrub, dust-pale in the moonlight. I wondered what he was looking for. "Are you alone?" Eyes locked on mine now, a bright, lunatic urgency. I looked quickly over my shoulder, judging the distance to the car. "It's not safe to be alone out here," he said, "especially at night. There're some vicious creatures around. You got a gun?"

"Yes."

"Keep it loaded. Carry it with you." Staring back out at the roadside now, finger inching closer to the safety catch. His paranoia made my skin itch, as though it were contagious. "A kid got killed up at the campsite yesterday. Some kind of animal got him. You'd best take care."

"I've lived out here for some time now," I said, mindful of how he held the rifle, how intently he scanned the horizon. My muscles were tight, my breathing a little too quick. "I can handle animals just fine."

He snorted. "They're getting bolder. People feed them like they're pets. Try to get pictures with them, if you can believe it. They've forgotten to be afraid of humans and they ain't keeping their distance like they used to." He stepped off the road, into the sand. I flexed my fingers, loosening too-taut ligaments. I thought about asking what he was doing here, alone on the highway; what he was looking for out in the scrub. I caught the sudden glint of his rifle scope as he turned, the muscular heft of him illuminated in the headlights, and I thought better of questioning him.

The car had come to rest at an angle, bisecting the highway. I slipped into the driver's seat and locked the door behind me. The man was a little way off the road and moving further, cautious steps like a hunter flushing out a deer, gun raised and ready.

This time, the engine started on the first try. I hit reverse, pulled the car around; wheels ground on gravel. I peered over my shoulder as the car reversed.

And then I saw you, cowering in the back seat; skin and bone and blood, torn blue jeans and a man's leather jacket; I bit back a cry of surprise, staring in rapt horror at the bright blood pooling on the seat beneath you, fingersmeared over your face like warpaint. You looked up at me, eyes wide, finger pressed urgently to your lips, and I could sense your terror so acutely I could almost feel it; a shot of panicked adrenaline straight to the heart.

I had no water and precious little fuel, but I swung the car round. He couldn't fail to notice the change in direction, but I paid him no mind as I hit the gas. If I drove fast enough, he'd never know where I'd taken you. If the fuel held out, we might even get there in one piece.

"It's going to be okay," I told you, though I had no idea if it really would. You pressed your face into the worn fabric of the back seat, exhausted; your limbs were slack, your eyes closed. It looked as though you were dying. The thought terrified me, not because I cared about you, but because, although I could shoot and skin and gut a deer without so much as flinching, I had never in my life watched a human being die.

The wheels ate up the distance. Above, the night gathered like a bruise. I wondered what had happened to you. How you came to be out there, all alone in the desert, and whether it was you the man had been chasing in the dark.

The car ran dry a quarter mile from home. I had to carry you the rest of the way, first on my back, then in my arms when you at last fell unconscious. My bruised ribs ached with the weight of you. Your skin was hot, as though you'd baked a while in the sun; you felt empty in my arms, exsanguinated, breathing shallow. Helpless. I thought about leaving you there. Taking you a way off the road, out into the dunes, so that when death came for you – inevitably, I thought, cradling your bird-hollow bones – the coyotes and hawks might pick your remains clean. But home was close, and your heart still beat, and I thought we've come this far. Only a little further now.

Home was a brick and timber shack built on land that had once been my father's. He in turn had bought the land for next to nothing from a man who'd run a campsite there in the early 90s. It was where my dad had always intended to 'bug out' to when the End Days came. As it turned out, heart failure came first. He hadn't prepared for that eventuality.

I didn't want you in my home. You have to understand that. Those last hundred metres to the house were beset with doubt. I couldn't have left you bleeding by the roadside, entirely at the mercy of an armed stranger; I knew the ways men could hurt women, how inclined they were towards it when the power balance shifted in their favour. I could've taken you to Wildrose, made you someone else's problem, but if he had been chasing you – and my instincts were screaming that he had – then he would surely think to look for you there. I can't honestly say why I took you with me except that in all my years, I had never seen anyone look quite so afraid as you had in that moment.

You stirred when I laid you out on the couch, mumbling something unintelligible. I peeled off your jacket, pulling limp arms through worn sleeves. Your limbs were slender but your muscles were tight as cord beneath the skin, the lean physique of a long-distance runner. I wondered when you'd eaten last. Adjacent to your right shoulder was a puckered hole, a glistening crater of flesh and bloody, matted shirt.

I cradled your head against my chest as I lifted you up, hoping to find an exit wound. Whoever had shot you had done so from a high angle, standing above you; the exit wound was lower down, suggesting a diagonal trajectory. Clean margins. One hand cupped the back of your skull as I traced the radius. I pried at the shredded edges of your shirt, peeling it gently away from the wound. Your muscles tensed; if you weren't so weak you might have fought me.

"It's okay," I murmured absently. Your dark hair was thick beneath my fingers, the matted pelt of a wild thing. "You're safe now."

Slowly, you relaxed, allowing me to peel away the fabric. There was blood on the couch, a faint scrim of dirt. Your lips moved against my skin, barely a whisper. It sounded like 'thank you'.

You slept while I cleaned your wound and stitched the edges together – not a beautiful job, but good enough. I washed my hands, aware that I had only half a bottle of water left, no fuel, no way back to Wildrose. My nearest neighbours were two miles away. I didn't want to leave you alone, but that half bottle wasn't going to stretch much further. I didn't know when you'd last eaten or drank. You'd need water far more than I would when you woke.

I sat on the porch and lit a cigarette; I blew smoke into the breeze, watching it dissipate. It was long past midnight and my bones felt heavy beneath the skin, my eyes weary; I hated the idea of sleeping only yards away from a stranger. I'd lived alone for years, long before I even considered relocating to the desert. I'd never been close to my brother as a child; my school reports bluntly stated that I did not play well with others.

The lunatic cry of a coyote cut through the night. The sky was starless, the moon obscured behind a thin veil of cloud. I'd smoked almost down to my fingers. When the sun rose, I would set out with my hat in my hands and ask the Burnetts for water. They'd be quietly scornful, but I could swallow that, and they wouldn't deny me.

I stubbed the cigarette out on the step and came back inside. You watched me approach, and I saw how you cringed away from me – the simultaneous drawing inward of all your muscles, humble as a beaten dog. I hated you for that; I hated that pang of sympathy, that sharp, sudden ache in my heart.

"I'm not gonna hurt you," I said. I sat down opposite. The foldout chair creaked under my weight. You flinched. "I promise you that. But you can't stop here for long."

Your eyes were wary beneath your sweat-tangled hair. You knotted your hands in the blanket, thick with dirt beneath the nails, black crescents on bony fingers. "I don't want to," you replied, curt. Your voice was water on gravel.

"Is there anyone you want me to call? I don't have a phone here, but there's a family nearby who do."

You shook your head and looked away, staring sullenly at the curtains. It occurred to me then that you might be as unaccustomed to the company of other people as I was.

"All right. Well, as soon as the sun comes up I'm heading out. I won't be gone long; I just need to beg a little fuel and some water from the neighbours. I'm running bone dry."

"It's going to rain."

I laughed at that. "They've been saying that for weeks and I haven't seen so much as a drop."

You laid your head back on the pillow. "It's going to rain," you said, quietly now, a voice on the precipice of sleep. Your eyes were closed. "Not now, but soon. Can't you smell it?"

The air smelled of stale cigarette smoke, the ripe rust stink of blood. "I won't be gone long," I said. "An hour, maybe. I don't usually get visitors but I'll lock the door just in case. You'll be safe here till I get back. You should rest until then."

I rose from my chair. You were already asleep, or perhaps you were pretending. I imagined you were watching me as I left, peering through barely-parted lids. It was difficult to tell in the dark. I pulled the front door shut as I passed through the hall, turning the lock with a barely audible pop. I hadn't locked my door in years. I resented you for this sudden uncertainty.

The bedroom window framed a nascent sunrise; rose gold blooming slowly outward. I lay back on the bed, fighting sleep. You were at the periphery of my vision, utterly still. You might have been dead, and in that moment I might not have minded.

I laced my hands behind my skull and waited for morning.

You were asleep when I left. I decided against locking the door behind me; it felt like imprisonment, shutting you inside that tiny house in the gathering heat of the day. And part of me hoped you'd be gone by the time I returned. That you'd wake up to an unlocked door and smell freedom.

It was barely six AM and already the chill of the night had dissipated, a thick heat building behind the blanket of cloud overhead. I set out with a five-litre bottle under one arm, a jerry can in my free hand. The Burnetts lived out towards the hills. They'd been out here a long time, had raised and home-schooled their kids and were now alone, enjoying the solitude of their retirement. The kids moved to San Francisco, got jobs in tech startups and organic bakeries and never came back to visit. I imagined they must still dream about sand; hear the whisper of the wind along the dunes even in the depths of sleep.

The Burnetts' home was brick-built, a chimera made from parts scavenged over the best part of a decade and extended over and over, a tumorous mass expanding slowly into the scrub. They tolerated my presence; I was far enough away and suitably unobtrusive, not even a smudge on their wide blue horizon. I did not intrude upon their isolation.

Peggy was in the yard as I approached. High-waisted blue jeans slung on motherly hips, skin the shade and texture of old hide. "What brings you up here so early, Sadie?" She'd affected a perfect neutrality, but she glanced briefly down at the water bottle under my arm the way a rich man might glance at a beggar's bowl.

"Real sorry to trouble you, Peggy," I said. Humility was not my strong suit, but the shame that bowed my head was genuine. I had, after all, failed to prepare. I explained the situation without once mentioning you; as I spoke, the contortions of her face and haughty arch of her eyebrow reminded me so much of my mother it almost hurt. Serves you right, I imagined her saying, mouth twisted in spite. You'll die of thirst, lazy girl. The Rapture will catch you with your pants down and your engine dry, and then you'll be sorry.

She didn't. She listened, and did not say a word until I was done. And when I was, she beckoned me wordlessly to the back of the house. Six blue water barrels sat lined up in the shade. A far larger rain barrel was just visible beyond the curve of the far wall.

"Don't tell Dan about this," Peggy said, taking the water bottle from me. I heard her knees creak as she squatted. I thought about offering to help and knew she'd be offended. "Lord knows he means well. He's a big believer in tough love, you know? Says it's a harsh world out there and young folks have got to learn to fend for themselves, 'cause it's only gonna get harsher." Water spilled out of the tap, into the bottle. I realised then just how parched my throat was. "No doubt he's right, but that don't mean you can't lend a hand every now and again. It's about compassion, ain't it? That's what it's all about in the end." She shut off the tap, screwed the cap onto the bottle. A spattering of droplets fell from the tap, sinking without trace into the dust. Peggy stood, grimacing as her knees stretched out. "Smart girl like you, you'll do better next time, won't you?"

"I will, Peggy. Thank you."

"There's a little gas in the shed out back. Dan won't notice it's gone. Mostly it's me who drives these days, you know, since my boys moved away." She smiled then, and there was sorrow in the crease of her eyes, the starburst of wrinkles etched into her face. "Do you see much of your mother, Sadie?"

I blinked. In the two years since I'd shacked up in the desert Peggy had never once asked me anything about my life before. I thought about all the tinned food my mama had sent me over the years, always on the brink of expiration, piling up in the spare bedroom of my San Diego apartment because old habits died hard. "She passed away," I said. "Eight years ago."

"Oh." She looked down at her feet. Then, with sudden brightness: "Well, let me get you that gasoline. I'm sure you've got better things to be doing than standing around, listening to me harp on."

I stood in the shade as she went to the shed, gait slow and careful. I

Laura Mauro

wondered if she might be lonely out here, with only wild beasts and a
taciturn husband for company; whether perhaps the blissful isolation the
Burnetts had worked so hard for was everything they'd built it up to be.

By the time I got back the sun was up high, and you were gone.

You'd folded the blanket and left it atop the pillow, streaked rust-brown
with dried blood. It was the only sign you'd ever been there, and even that
seemed vague, as though that carefully-folded bundle might have been my
own doing. I picked it up. The scent of you clung to the blanket: sweat, faintly
sour but not entirely unpleasant. The sharp, animal smell of your hair. I
realised I was a little worried about you – out there, exposed to the rising heat,
weak and fatigued. The wound was still fresh. It might fester, the stitches
might split, anything might happen to you and I had abandoned you. I
swallowed down guilt as I put the blanket in the wash basket. I knew nothing
about you except that someone had hurt you, and that you had been afraid,
and that I had let you go. I hadn't even asked your name.

I set the water bottle down in a pool of shade outside the house.
Inside, I fished out a yellow legal pad from the stash under the couch;
there was a half-written article scrawled in upward slanting script, and a
deadline for the end of the week. I'd hand-write articles and drive over the
state border into Nevada, where Jackie Emery would lend me the use of
his computer and internet connection for five bucks an hour. A few
articles a month would keep me in fuel and supplies. I'd come to live the
kind of pared-down, uncomplicated life my parents might have considered
too sparse and therefore doomed, ultimately, to fail.

Pen hovered over paper. Through drooping eyes, my handwriting warped
into inscrutable hieroglyphs, marks without form or meaning. I hadn't slept in
over twenty-four hours and my eyes were heavy with grit. Just a nap, I told
myself, curling up on the couch. The cushions smelled of warm, old dust, and
faintly of you. Empirical evidence of your invasion, a stranger's presence yet to
be erased. Strange, then, that I didn't seem to mind.

A jaundiced afternoon light cast the room in shades of faded bruise. I'd
slept longer than I'd intended. My damaged ribs seemed to groan as I
stretched out. A glance at the clock on the windowsill revealed that despite
the gloom it was just past three o'clock.

Outside, the sky sweltered behind still clouds. The water bottle was
warm to the touch. I poured a little out, washing the sweat from my face
and neck; cool water wound a slow path down my spine, coursing down
my arms. There was no breeze, no movement; it seemed that the world

182

had stopped without warning and curled in on itself, interminably paused, waiting for something terrible. There was only the mechanical whirr of cicadas in the long grass, the air as still and silent as a held breath.

The first raindrop hit the ground hard, like a thrown penny.

And then the rain came, violently, and all at once. I found myself soaked and winded; the curves and concavities of my face became a waterfall, hair clinging to my face like black kelp, the shock of water in my nostrils, my open mouth. A premature twilight fell and in that sudden darkness I saw you. You were a silhouette against the deluge, growing darker, gaining corporeal form; you were unhurried as you tracked barefoot across the gleaming hardpan, dangling something unseen in your left hand.

I finally found the wherewithal to retreat into the house. My boots left great puddles on the linoleum as I shoved into the tiny shower room, retrieving the only two towels I owned. When I returned you were at the doorway, expectant but still, as though awaiting an invite. In your sodden state you seemed very small, as though the meat of you had been washed away; as though beneath it you had only ever been an imitation of a girl, fashioned from wire and draped in skin. Your smile was almost shy as you handed me your prize – a pair of skinned jackrabbits, rose-quartz flesh wet and glistening.

"I was right," you said, pointing to the sky. Your wounded shoulder drooped. You must have been in pain, but your face betrayed no hint of weakness; your lips retained a hint of a smile, a feral Mona Lisa.

"What's your name?" I asked.

"June."

Your name conjured up vibrant wildflower meadows, a cobalt sky reflected in a smooth, still lake. A Pacific Northwest spring. "As in the month?"

You smiled again, baring bone-white teeth. "As in the month. But I was born in November."

"Come inside," I said. "You'll drown out here."

So you did.

I didn't want you in my home. Except that somewhere along the way – pulling needle and thread through your open skin, perhaps, or your quiet belligerence, when you were hurt and afraid but still defiant – somewhere in among all of it I felt myself beginning to relent; a palpable sense that something inside of me had opened a little, exposing a glimpse of viscera, the hint of a rib. I hadn't wanted you there, but there you were anyway, my borrowed t-shirt hanging loose from your shoulders, wound cleaned and freshly bandaged. Your hair hung half-dried and leonine: dark honey shot through with silver, though you could surely be no older than twenty-five.

"A boy got killed up in Wildrose," I said.

You stared at the rain running down the window, silver rivulets like molten metal. "I heard an animal tore his throat out."

"Do you believe that?"

You turned your head. Your confusion was tempered with a narrow-eyed wariness; an inherent mistrust of the path I might be leading you down. "Shouldn't I?"

I sighed. "I know that man shot you, June. And he would've killed you if I hadn't found you first. What kind of a man hurts a woman the way he did? What kind of man hunts a woman down like an animal? You think someone like that would flinch at harming a child?"

I saw the flinch in your limbs, the way you folded in on yourself; I saw the defiance bleed slowly from you and felt an answering ache in my chest. "Don't," you murmured. "Please."

"What happened to you?" I wanted to grab you by the shoulders and shake you until the answers tumbled out. I wanted to hold you and soothe your ragged nerves. "It's your business, June, I know that, and maybe I don't have the right to ask questions of you. But I've never seen a person look as scared as you did that night."

"Okay." You had the look of a hunted thing, hunched and ready to bolt, but there was steel in the rigid set of your spine. "Ask me one question. Just one. But then you have to drop it, okay? Because I don't want to talk about this any more. I want it to go away."

You're in my house, I thought. If you're in danger then I might be too. I deserve to know. Rain clattered relentlessly against the windows, washing away seven weeks of dust. Pouring into the rain barrels, better late than never. I should have felt trapped in that small room, forced by the elements into your sullen vicinity; I should have resented every inch of space your body occupied. "Why you?"

You smiled then, though there was no joy in it; you drew your knees up, planting bare feet on the couch cushions. A hint of slender ankle, of downy dark-gold hair. "Because he thought I was somebody else," you said. The rain thrummed like an arrhythmia against the roof shingles. You closed your eyes and said nothing more.

Every morning I woke to find you gone. You were meticulous in your absence; the couch cushions were carefully rearranged, the blankets folded and replaced in the hall closet. You moved like a ghost, silent despite the creaking floorboards; the sun would rise, and you would already be gone.

In the first few days I would linger at the windows, squinting through the heat haze at distorted shapes; I would sit smoking on the porch as the sun crawled across the sky, watching shadows shift and lengthen. I didn't know if you would come back, at least in those first days; I found myself luxuriating in the space you left behind, glad of the silence but aware, unexpectedly, that something vital was missing. I would look up from my work and expect to feel your eyes on me; I would listen out for the hiss of your feet on dusty floorboards and hear only silence.

You returned as quietly as you left. The sun would slink behind the distant mountains and you would emerge from the deep shadows as though you'd been born there. I never saw you coming, no matter how long and how carefully I watched for you. You came in on the evening breeze, smiling that clever half-smile and you would pause at the door, an odd formality, waiting for me to invite you in. I always did.

I never asked you where you'd been.

We sat side by side on the porch, the air redolent with the musty wet-weather scent of the creosote bushes. Against a spilled-ink sky sat a spattered multitude of stars, their light guttering like faraway candles. I told you I could navigate using the stars as guidance; that it was one of the first things my father taught me as a young girl, my earliest lessons in preparedness.

I pointed up. "You locate the North Star," I said, plucking your hand from your lap. I guided your outstretched finger to where the North Star sat, bright and lonely. "You see? That's Polaris. And just across from there – those stars – that's the Big Dipper."

"The Great Bear," you said, and pulled my hand along with yours as you traced the shape in the sky, a wide, faltering oblong. "She's monstrous, bigger than any bear you've ever seen. And those four stars –" punctuating each one with the tip of your finger, as though they were mere yards away "– those are pissed-off mother coyotes chasing her across the sky. My mom told me that. She said that in those days, food was scarce, and the bear had grown so hungry that she would dig up coyote dens to eat the pups. And even though the coyotes were weak and hungry and scared to death of that bear, they vowed that they would fight to protect their babies. So when the Great Bear came sniffing around, they joined together, these four fierce coyote mothers, and they chased her. They chased her for so long and so far that when they stopped to catch their breath, they realised they'd run right up into the sky."

"I've never heard it told like that before."

"It was my mom's version." You drew your hands to your chest, long fingers forming a lattice across your heart. "My dumbass sisters never listened to her stories."

"You don't get on with your family?"

"My mom died. My sisters…We don't see eye to eye. I guess I don't like the way they live."

I let out a snort of bitter laughter. "I know how that feels."

"I listened to all my mom's stories. I liked that we saw the stars differently to everyone else. And I guess now…" You were dazzling in the dark, eyes like Baltic amber set into the pale bronze of your skin; you were a small and perfect sun, and I was willingly subsumed by your gravity. "I guess you do too, don't you?"

I smiled. I felt like you'd given me something of yourself then, a small gift by which I might begin know you. I looked up at the Great Bear, at the four coyote mothers chasing her in perpetuity through the heavens, and wondered who you were, where you'd been all this time, why you kept coming back to me.

The men came a few days later. They arrived in a rust-coloured station wagon, kicking up plumes of dust behind them like the tail of a comet. I stood out on the porch as they pulled up, piling out of the car in a tangle of identical plaid limbs and khaki vests.

I straightened my back, set my shoulders square. I didn't know any of them, though I had a vague sense that I'd seen one or two before – perhaps out at Wildrose, working the gas pumps or the campsite. Three of them, each with a rifle at their hip. Men on the hunt.

A tall, thin man stepped forward. "Afternoon, ma'am." He tipped his cap, an antiquated notion of politeness. Beneath it, a sparse rim of sandy hair traced an oasis of sun-pink skin. "You live out here by yourself?"

"Yes, I do." None of them were the man who'd shot you, but I was wary all the same. Men like that, they travelled in packs, associated closely with one another; they wore their guns like membership badges. I didn't like the nature of his question, the way all three of them ran their eyes the length of my body, assessing me as though I were a prize sow. "Can I ask what it is you want?"

"Sorry to disturb you, miss," the second man said, with a wide-eyed humbleness I knew was feigned. My palms itched. I wished I'd brought my gun out with me. I wished I'd never have to touch the damn thing again. "Only there's been a situation down at the campsite. Some sort of animal going round hurting folk. Rabid, maybe. Killed a couple kids…"

"A couple?"

"Yes, miss. Little girl got killed yesterday afternoon. Wandered out a little ways into the desert. Her momma never even knew she was gone till it was too late. Anyway, Bryson at the store said there was someone lived on her own out in the desert. He asked us to check on you, make sure you're able to protect yourself."

"I'm able," I said.

"We've seen coyotes heading out in this direction," the thin man said. "Could be there's a pack of them somewhere nearby. You'd best take care…"

"They say it's an animal," the third man said suddenly. "But nobody's got a lick of proof. Nobody's seen an animal do anything." His companions stared at him for a moment, uncertain how they ought to proceed; clearly, this was not the agreed story. "There's a lot of transients round here, is all I'm saying. It's damn near impossible to keep track of who's coming and going. You could do anything and nobody'd know so much as your name. You want my advice, ma'am, you'd be best off watching out for strangers."

I'm a grown woman, I thought, staring at the three of them, the earnest way they presented themselves; guns respectfully lowered, pink-cheeked and sweating like pigs beneath their heavy khakis. They thought me soft, I realised. They thought it a fluke that I'd survived this long. "I'll be careful," I told them. There was no acid in my voice; I burned with the desire to tell them to get the hell off my land, but I resisted. Better not to upset three armed men. "Thank you. I appreciate your good intentions. But you don't need to check up on me again. I've been looking after myself for a long time."

They scanned the distance as they piled back into the car, checking for motion, for shadows beneath the desert sun. I watched them leave, heading back the way they'd come, the car a bloodspot on the horizon. And I thought, better a pack of beasts than a pack of men with guns.

I didn't tell you about the men, but you knew anyway. You were quiet when you came back; you did not join me on the porch to smoke and stargaze, but curled up silent on the couch, blanket drawn over your head so that I could see only a vaguely human-shaped lump lying very still against the cushions.

The cloud cover was thick that night, the air heavy, foretelling rain. A dry wind had picked up, casting fistfuls of sand like a spiteful child. And I didn't feel safe out there on my own, staring into a distance whose edges I could not discern; in which anyone or anything might be hiding. I shucked off my shoes in the hallway, locked the door behind me. As I passed by the couch my fingers brushed the crest of the blanket, where I supposed your face might be.

"I don't know you very well, June, but for what it's worth, I know you've got a good heart. I can feel that much." I drew my hand away, honouring the privacy of your cocoon. "I know they have you mistaken. I just wanted you to know that."

Sometime in the night I felt you crawl into the bed beside me, slow but determined in your audacity. I lay perfectly still as you slipped beneath the sheet, each movement cautious; I sensed the breath held in your lungs as you curled a hand around my arm, your knees pressed gently behind my own. I felt the tension of your muscles: apprehensive, but bold enough to persevere. I turned to face you, pulling you closer with great care. I feared I might crush you with the slightest movement. Your ribcage was sharp against my abdomen, the planes and angles of you a stark contrast to my softness, my roundness.

"Be careful out there tomorrow," I said, as though this sudden easy intimacy were normal. "There're men with guns sniffing around."

Your mouth pressed against mine. You had glass shards for teeth, wire for bones; your lips tasted like copper. My father's voice distant in my mind: it is an abomination for a man to lay with another man. I traced the braille of your spine with the tips of my fingers. Joke's on you, Dad, I thought. Neither of us are men.

"Sadie, Sadie," you whispered, singsong. "Oh, Sadie, don't you know? I was born careful. I've been careful all my life."

Every day I feared your absence less and less; you were like the tide, receding into the gloaming, returning again as the sun set. I had not planned for the eventuality that, someday, you might not come back; curiously, I had no desire to prepare for it. It was as though after a life spent preparing fastidiously for a future that might never come, I had finally learned to absorb the present; you had taught me, somehow, that the sum total of my existence could not be pared down to numbers on a spreadsheet: how many tins, how many bullets, how fast I could run, how many weeks I might survive.

Sadie, you sang. I loved the way my name sounded in your mouth, the warm gravel of your voice lilting. I was born careful. Born lucky too, perhaps, because those men never found you, though I saw them on the road once or twice. They would nod, in greeting or in solidarity, and I would nod back, though I would sooner have driven on without acknowledgement.

"Can you run?" you asked me one night, perhaps a week after the men had stopped by. You were wrapped in a knitted blanket; a sharp breeze swept in from the mountains, a familiar whistling in the eaves, heralding the very beginnings of winter.

A cigarette stub glowed between the tips of my fingers, heat licking at the calluses. "When I was ten," I said, propping myself up against the headboard, "I was so physically fit I could do five hundred pushups in one session. I could run a mile in six minutes. I'd even go to bed with my sneakers on in case the world went to shit in the middle of the night and I'd have to run for my life."

"That's kind of fucked up."

"Yeah," I said. "Yeah, it is."

"But how about now?" You indicated the dying cigarette at my lips; you glossed over the heaviness of my thighs, the thickness of my waist, though they must have crossed your mind. "Could you run now? If you had to, I mean?"

The question sat heavy on my tongue, forbidden but always present. A ghost between us. Your face was drawn, eyes wide and anxious and beautiful. "June," I said, crushing the remnants of my cigarette between thumb and forefinger. Ash scattered the bedsheet, a thin grey snowfall. "What is it they think you've done?"

There came a strangled cry from outside, the sound of an animal caught unaware; the back of my neck prickled. We both turned our heads, staring out of the window at the darkened scrub. "Not what I've done," you murmured. "What I am."

"I don't understand."

"Listen." Your hands clasped my face, urgent. "I need you to know that what you see, right here – this is the truth. This is what's real. Do you believe me?"

You were so close I could see myself reflected in the black of your pupils. "June –"

"Whatever else I may be. Whatever anyone says. This –" You drew my head gently towards you; your lips were velvet against my forehead, your teeth hard behind them. "– all of this. I swear, Sadie. I'd give everything away just to keep this."

Everything you were to me had been pieced together; you were a loose-stitched patchwork of intuition, of little stories and guesswork. And I loved you, somehow, despite your insubstantiality; you cast no shadow, left no footprints, but the warmth of your body and the salt taste of your skin mattered far more. I wrapped my arms around you, the curve of your skull delicate beneath my chin. Your hair smelled like gasoline. I wondered where you'd been. "I see you, June," I said, after a time. "I believe you."

"It's not their fault." Barely audible. "My poor sisters. They're so hungry."

I smoothed your hair back, glancing down at your face. "Your sisters?" I asked, but you said nothing more. Your eyes were closed, your mouth a slack, sleepy line. Perhaps you'd been dreaming aloud.

The bed sagged a little under our combined weight; I lay quietly, listening to your breathing deepen; my beloved stranger, dreaming strange, sunlit dreams. I held your bones close and let my eyes slip shut.

I will always remember the look on your face when I saw you standing there, neck stretched, pulse throbbing in that vital spot beneath your jaw; the edge of a knife pressed against your throat just hard enough to break the skin. The man's grip tight on your arm, fingers buried deep in your flesh. I will always remember the spark in your eye: not fear but fury, acute as any knife-edge. It was barely dawn. I stood helpless, desperate to tear you from his grip but unarmed, unprepared.

"I said you ought to be careful." The .204 Ruger hung from his left shoulder; his right hand held the knife against your carotid. "Said there were vicious animals out there. Do you have the faintest clue what you've let into your home?"

"What I know is none of your goddamn business." I'd woken to the sound of shattering glass, a door being kicked in; your scream still echoed in my skull, ricocheting back and forth. I thought I'd lost you. I knew I still might. "I don't know where you get off hurting women –"

He spat. "She ain't a woman. Ain't even a person. What, she never told you?" Lips pulled back, a rictus sneer. His free hand yanked a clump of your hair, snapping your head sharply back; you let out a pained yelp. "Never even told your friend here the truth? What you and your bitch sisters have done?"

"Let her alone –"

"Watch," he said, brow knotted in disgust. "You just watch."

I could do nothing else. I watched as he dragged you by the hair, pulled you towards the shattered window, your bare feet dancing over broken glass; you shrank away from the sunlight, writhing wildly in his grip, and for the briefest of moments his balance faltered. Barely a second, but it was enough. Your teeth tore into his thick white throat; your fingers anchored in his hair, pulling him down, dragging him through the open doorway and onto the porch. He fought, but you were terrible in your persistence; his fingers spasmed, clutching ineffectually at your hair, your face. The knife clattered to the floor. In the darkness you were a girl, a furious girl with blood spilling like water from your mouth; in the sunlight I saw the truth. You were a thin, ragged animal, a starving coyote tearing the throat of a grown man as easy as paper. As you moved through that sun-dappled room you were liquid: shadow-girl, sun-dog; your pelt shone russet in the warm light, your skin smooth in the shade. Hot blood streamed from crimson lips, glistened on sharp ivory teeth, changing and warping as the sun rose, illuminating the truth of you.

At last, he slumped to the ground, and he did not move again.

In a pool of shade you stood up, all torn feet and trembling legs. You wiped your mouth with the back of your hand, streaking gore down your face, into your hair. I imagined I could hear the railroad clatter of your heart.

"Do you see me, Sadie?"

You were wild-eyed and trembling, but you were not afraid. You were a world away from the frightened, wounded girl I'd met outside Wildrose. You held your palms out to me. This is what's real: you, sleeping in my arms; your legs wrapped around mine, skin slick with sweat, your lips grazing my jaw. The sound of my name in your mouth. I swallowed, thick-throated. "I see you," I said.

There came the low hum of a car engine approaching. I turned. The rust-red station wagon was coming up the dirt road.

"Run with me," you said.

And we ran. You weaved through the shadows, into the light; you were a girl on torn feet, a swift coyote with the wind in your pelt. The hardpan stung my bare soles, the sun hot already at my back; my lungs burned with the effort and still there was such a long way to go. We had no plan, no destination, and perhaps we would fail, but for now we would run, and it seemed to me – breathless, exhilarated – that nothing in my life had been as pure, as perfect as this singular moment of freedom.

DISPOSSESSION

Nicholas Royle

Three months ago I moved to a new place and, while my new flat more than meets my needs, I'm finding that the old one is increasingly on my mind. I can't dismiss this as nostalgia, because I really wasn't ever happy there, but I can't stop thinking about the old place. The other night I even dreamed about it.

For a number of reasons, I was glad to move. I was moving from a rented studio, which was too small for me to have my children to stay, into a three-bedroom flat that I was buying. My children, who had never used the keys I had had cut for them for the old place, would get a bedroom each, which they would use two nights a week and alternate weekends, according to the agreement with my ex, and I would be able to get the rest of my stuff out of storage.

The flat is on the top floor of a three-storey development dating from the 1950s. There are a number of blocks, each comprising six or ten or a dozen flats, separated by communal gardens. I've filled the flat with cheap units and shelved my books according to size, doubling up where possible. I don't need to know how to find particular titles. I haven't read a book in two years. Yet I can't bring myself to give them away. I've bought new clothes for the children and these are stored in drawers in their respective bedrooms.

My son's bedroom is situated at the back of the flat, his windows offering a view across a courtyard to the rear of another block. You get the same view from the bathroom, if you open the frosted windows, and the kitchen, which is where I keep my binoculars, in an eye-level cupboard to the right of the sink. The flat opposite mine has been empty for a week, the soft outlines of shampoo bottles removed from the bathroom window ledge. Two days ago I watched a man painting woodwork in the kitchen. Since then, nothing.

After I moved, I would occasionally walk past my old place on the way to the shops, but, at first, I barely gave it a second glance. Then one day the letting agents rang me to say that the new tenant was having difficulties with the phone company and would I be kind enough to give them my old number, so they could give it to her and she could tell the phone company what it was. It seemed a funny way round to do things, but I looked it up. A couple of days later they called again, wanting to know if I had had broadband installed in the old flat without encountering any major difficulties. I said that I had and I named the provider.

The thing about the letting agents was that we had parted on bad terms. They had complained about the state of the flat when I moved out and surrendered my keys. Citing patches of peeling paint on the walls, soot on the ceiling and stubborn stains on the carpet, they had refused to return my deposit in its entirety and had informed me of their intention to deduct certain amounts, which were itemised on a memo that came attached to a tetchy email. I challenged their proposal, pointing out that the paint had peeled from the walls only where it had been behind furniture, which suggested to me that either damp or poor decorating was to blame. Also, although I had not told them this, when I had emptied the flat, I had gone round covering up the nail holes in the walls with TippEx. I hadn't anticipated any problems with the refunding of the deposit.

After an exchange of unfriendly emails, they agreed to reduce by a half the amount they intended to charge for cleaning and redecorating. I felt by that point that I had no choice but to give in.

So, when the agents started phoning me with regard to the difficulties the new tenant was experiencing, I didn't particularly welcome the contact. I felt like offering to be put directly in touch with her.

But it got me thinking and it reminded me of how I'd felt when I had just moved in, two years earlier. The flat had been unfurnished, superficially clean, but I had found myself wanting there to be some kind of trace left by the previous tenant, some clue to his or her identity. I didn't feel that he or she could be held accountable for the curtain rail that became detached from its fittings if you opened the curtain too far on one side, or for the lumpy lino in the kitchen. I found the trace I was looking for in the wardrobe cupboard in the hall. In it I found a number of empty hangers from mid-range high street fashion stores, some marked 14, others 16. I imagined a young woman, her weight fluctuating over the months or years that she lived there. I wondered what she might have looked like. I wondered where she might have gone to. I wondered if she ever gave a thought to the place she had left behind.

I was grateful for her clothes hangers, having brought few with me from the house I had shared with my ex. I remember the estate agent who showed me round. It takes special skill to show someone round a studio flat. But this studio was the best of a fairly bad bunch that I had viewed over the previous week. I remember looking at him when he had shown me a smaller one, where the kitchen was so small the position of the cooker prevented two of the cupboard doors from being opened.

The landlord will remove the cooker if you don't want it, the estate agent said.

I said nothing in response to this.

It will get harder to find a good place in the New Year, he said.

Why's that, I asked?

Because couples struggle through Christmas together, he explained, and realise they can't do it any more. Come January the men are out looking for flats.

I studied the expression on his face – scorn? Despair? – and tried to work out if he, too, was living in a rented studio. He hadn't once looked me in the eye.

I took the next flat he showed me – the studio with the clothes hangers whose previous owner had, I imagined, jumped from size 14 to size 16 as she had become unhappier, alone in the flat and perhaps alone in the world, and then back to 14 once she had made up her mind to move out.

I put up a picture in my daughter's room. A framed collage of images of butterflies cut out of magazines that she made in Year 9. I also have a go at fixing the window blind, which has been catching on one side. I open the top drawer of her chest of drawers and look through her tights and socks and underwear. I take out a pair of tights and hold them to my nose – they smell only of fabric softener – then drop them on the floor.

In my son's room, I go through his football shirts. I take one out and unfold it on his bed.

The intercom buzzes and I go to the door to pick up.

Post, says a voice.

I press the button and hear the door open down below in the communal hallway. I wait until I hear it shut again and then open my door and go down to see if there's anything for me or if, as is usually the case, I was simply the only one at home to let in the postman. In my pigeonhole I find a padded envelope.

In the kitchen I put the package down on the table while I get out bread, chopping board and bread knife, and cheese from the fridge, and

Nicholas Royle

make myself a sandwich. While I eat this, I open the padded envelope to reveal a proof copy of a forthcoming novel. I take the book into the living room and find room for it on a shelf full of similar-sized books. My eye briefly lingers on the spines of the books. Novels, short story collections, a non-fiction book about the night, an anthology of sea stories. An academic study of a certain school of French literature. A book about underground films. All they have in common is size.

In the old flat, there had been room for no more than two bookcases. I had taken books relating to what I was working on at the time, plus a couple of series for teenagers that I was in the process of collecting. I had bought one or two of those titles originally, secondhand, for my son, as I had enjoyed them at his age, but he had lost interest in reading, so I had carried on buying them, from charity shops and secondhand bookshops, partly out of nostalgia and partly out of a dimly understood need to collect them on my son's behalf, even though he had no interest in them.

Sometimes I would hear voices in the old flat. The first time I heard them, I couldn't figure out where they were coming from. My first thought was from beyond the wall behind my bed, but when I worked out that that was outside – and my flat was at the top of the converted house – I ruled that out. Then I thought I could hear them better if I approached the wall where my desk was, but I pretty soon ruled that out, too. I only figured it out by accident. I opened the door to the boiler cupboard to get the vacuum cleaner out and there I heard voices. I realised they were the same voices, still quite muffled, but I could hear them better in the boiler cupboard than anywhere else in the flat. So, from that point on, I kept the vacuum cleaner under my desk, leaving enough room in the boiler cupboard for me to stand in there and close the door behind me.

One of my then neighbours – either the woman in her forties from the floor below or the younger woman from the flat just down the half-landing from mine – was talking to a man. They sounded like a couple. The conversations were banal, but I found the cadences of their speech, the rhythms of their dialogue, soothing, lulling. I could spend up to an hour in there at a time, sometimes longer.

I'm in the kitchen bending down in front of the washing machine, loading it with my few items of laundry. I shake powder into the tray, then add conditioner, and close everything up. I pause a moment before pressing the start button. My knees pop as I stand up. I go to my bedroom and have a quick look around, but it doesn't appear as if I have missed anything. In my daughter's room I pick up a pair of tights from the floor and there's a football shirt on my son's bed that could do with a wash. Back in the kitchen I open the machine, add these items, slam the door and set it going.

I stand up again and look out of the window. The windows opposite are bathed in wintry sunlight. In the ground-floor flat directly across from mine – two below the empty flat – a young man and a woman are standing in the kitchen facing each other. His upper body is leaning forward, while she backs off slightly. He points, jabbing at the air between them, his shirt buttoned at the cuff. But he is the one who leaves the room. She remains where she is, rocking slightly to and fro, then turns on her heel towards the sink and the window. She rests her hands on the edge of the sink. I lower the binoculars for a moment to check that my kitchen light isn't switched on and when I lift them back up again she is pouring herself a glass of water from the tap.

In the kitchen of our family house, the four of us had sat down at the kitchen table. My wife and I – was she already my ex? Effectively, yes. I had told her. We had talked. It had been a few weeks – my ex and our two children.

I heard myself saying banal and unspeakable things.

Everything else will stay the same, I finished.

I stressed this point. We both did, my ex backing me up for the sake of the children.

My daughter looked faintly embarrassed, while my son's expression darkened quickly. I had never seen such a swift and dramatic transformation in a person's face. Something fluttered inside my chest. Desperate hopes revealed as vain. The worst that could happen, now happening. I was destroying my life and possibly theirs. My son got up and walked out of the room.

The washing machine signals the end of its cycle with a high-pitched beep. I open the door and pull the wet clothes out and drop them into the basket. I drape shirts, T-shirts and my son's football top on hangers and hang these on door handles around the flat, a 14 here, a 16 there. Smaller items, including my daughter's tights, I fold neatly over the radiators.

Job done, I pull out my phone and look at it. I realise I'm frowning.

I text my ex, reminding her it's a Thursday and I'm wondering where the children are.

She doesn't reply.

I call her.

What do you want?

It's Thursday, I say.

Don't, she says. Just stop it.

She hangs up.

I go into the children's rooms. They are very tidy. Really very tidy.

I find myself back in the kitchen looking at the flats opposite. The top flat is still empty. The middle flat is in darkness. In the kitchen of the ground-floor flat a single glass sits on the worktop.

I look around my own kitchen. The bread left out, going stale. The bread board. The bread knife.

I turn to the kitchen drawers and open the second one down. I rummage around and come up with the keys I'd had cut for the children and hadn't handed in to the letting agents.

I walk over to the old flat, the contents of my bag rattling with each step. I look up at the window, which is dark. Maybe she is out in one of the local bars or restaurants, or at work, or studying in a university library, or away for a spell. I press the buzzer and wait for a response, which doesn't come. I use my key to gain entry. The entrance hall looks the same. I see some junk mail addressed to me lying on the floor beneath the pigeonholes and I leave it there as I head for the stairs. On the half-landings I pass doors that were once familiar to me. A television can be heard behind one of them; cooking smells emanate from another. When I reach the top of the building I stand with my ear to my door. It still feels like my door. The key turns in the lock and I enter.

The flat is warm. She can't be far away. It doesn't look like it did in my dream; the bed is smaller, but it's in the same place. She has a cheap white desk where I used to have my sofa and coffee table. Her TV is where my desk was.

I hear footsteps on the stairs, a key in the lock. I cross the ten feet to the boiler cupboard in the time it takes her to open the door, and while she is closing the door to the flat I close the door to the boiler cupboard behind me.

I hear her moving around, even above the suddenly deafening sound of my heartbeat. I can also hear voices coming from behind the boiler. In my dream there had been a large window in the kitchen allowing access to a grassy slope. I had jumped from tussock to tussock, feeling buoyant and free.

I close my hands around the contents of my bag and try to listen only to the voices.

SHELL BABY

V.H. Leslie

The croft house stood stark white in the diminishing light, dark waves breaking against the shore in the distance. Elspeth looked past Donal toward the churning waters. It was desolate at this Northern edge, even the seagulls crooned melancholically as they soared overhead.

'You have to be crazy to move here,' Donal said, handing over the keys.

Elspeth nodded and pulled up the collar of her coat. The wind blustered past, obscuring what Donal said next.

'Pardon?'

'Would you like me to help with your things?' he repeated louder, looking toward the car. Elspeth had brought a ridiculous amount of provisions; the back seats full with food, the boot already overloaded with suitcases and clothing. She'd brought as much as she could physically carry. She was loath to make the journey across on the ferry to the supermarket on the Orkney mainland more than was absolutely necessary. She was ready to hunker down and forget all about the rest of the world.

'I'll be fine,' she said, shaking Donal's hand and walking decisively toward the front door. Though it would take her longer on her own to unload the car, she was reluctant for Donal to enter what was now her space. Though technically he owned the croft house, it was hers for the foreseeable future and she wanted to ensure it remained untainted by others.

She heard the sound of a car door slam behind her as she placed the keys in the lock, followed by the rumble of the engine. She took her time with the keys and waited until Donal was back on the road before she opened the door.

The croft house looked much the same as the photos on the tourist website. It was traditionally furnished, slightly outdated in parts with chintz ornaments and horseshoes nailed to the beams. But it was the view that had drawn her, as it did now. Sitting on a small window seat beside the hearth, she could see the sea, girded by a stretch of shingle beach. It was the sea, vast and inexhaustible, combined with the knowledge that there were no other homesteads for miles and miles that restored a peace within her. She was finally on her own.

She'd craved being on her own for such a long time. Over the years, she'd become increasingly frustrated with people, with the relentless noise they made. Even in the relative quiet of her flower shop, noise persisted, her customers' verbal outpourings stifling her roses and lilacs, their inane conversations drawing all the air out of the room and leaving her gasping. She could only spend so long in the little side alley, among the rotting vegetal remains before having to return to serve another patron, the shrill ringing of the doorbell summoning her back to the fray.

She didn't have to serve anyone now but herself. She watched the waves continue their unyielding assault against the shore and thought of the life she'd left behind. It was more than just an idle fancy, this quest for isolation. She'd felt a change over the last year, as though she had misplaced a part of herself somewhere, in the way she would lose her scissors beneath the debris of leaves and stalks on the counter or under the copious buds of hydrangeas or delphiniums.

She called it a kind of quiet madness, this descent, this slippage in herself. She was aware of how far she could plunge if she left it unchecked. She had imagined herself shouting at her customers, yelling profanities, striking vases, flowers tumbling about the room. Or worse, she would recede into herself, losing her grasp of reality entirely and begin talking to the azaleas and orchids.

She knew she had to go away. Somewhere where she would be alone. Where there was no one to witness her decline.

It would have been different if she'd had a child, someone to look after her in her old age, to accommodate this change in her. A daughter would have been best. Daughters are always better than sons at caring for their ailing parents. Elspeth wondered why that was. Were men only able to satisfy one woman in their lives? Maybe women were just more compassionate, dutiful.

She knew she was unusual; she'd never wanted a partner – a mate. Sex was a fleeting appetite that reared its head from time to time, not enough of a motivation to consider a life-long commitment to another person. But she craved a child.

The sea was disappearing into the encroaching darkness but she could still hear the reassuring hiss of the waves against the shore. And she thought of her former fantasies about discovering a foundling; a gurgling baby nestled amongst her blooms or left in a terracotta pot in lieu of a crib, as if it had grown overnight from the rich soil.

It took her well into the night to finish unpacking. It took her longer because every few minutes she was drawn seaward. Nestled on the window seat, she'd scrutinise the grey surface, waiting for something to disrupt the steady to and fro of the waves – perhaps the appearance of a seal, a trawler in the distance – but the waters remained unchanged, vacant.

Night fell early on the island and as Elspeth made the journey to and from the car, she was struck by the absolute black of the sky. Laden with bags, she could still smell the salt reek of the sea. It was on the last trip to the car that she noticed the green shimmer and, placing the bags back down, she leant against the bonnet of the car, realising what it was she was looking at.

In the supermarket earlier that day she'd told the curious cashier that it was the Northern Lights that had brought her to the islands. People don't typically head to the edge of the world in winter, when the days are short and harsh. It was why she'd got such a good deal on the croft house. She needed a ready excuse and it seemed the most plausible. But the Northern Lights held no more appeal than the orcas and porpoises that inhabited the waters in the summer months. Yet now, looking up at the strange green spectacle, Elspeth felt a twisting, sinking sensation in her stomach, a giddy trepidation that made her short of breath.

She made her way down to the shore, the swelling green sky lighting her way. She needed to be close to the sea, to see the cosmic light dance off the black water. She felt the crunch of shingle underfoot and wondered briefly when the beach had last been walked upon. But she didn't look down. She couldn't take her eyes away from the eerie luminosity.

It was loud at the sea's edge. Not the lazy lapping of the waves as she'd imagined but the violent crash of water against rock. And then there was the wind, whipping past her, drowning out even the sound of the sea, pushing her toward the surf. She was aware at some point that her feet were wet, that the water had crept up on her without her realising. Though her feet were cold, it wasn't unwelcome. In fact, despite being deep midwinter, with the wind buffeting her with icy gusts, she felt strangely unaffected by the temperature. She'd left her coat indoors and now considered recklessly casting off the remainder of her clothes, struck by an overwhelming desire to feel the icy bite of the water on her skin.

It was the kind of crazy behaviour she'd never indulge back home, but here at the edge of the world she could do as she pleased. She removed her clothes hastily, in case she changed her mind and, pausing to glance up at the green sky once more, she stepped out into the sea.

Elspeth rolled over in bed, stretching her limbs as if she were underwater. The memory of the sea forced her upright and into wakefulness and she realised that she was naked. Pulling the bedclothes tighter, she felt the shame of her younger self; of the times she'd woken unclothed beside a stranger, barely recalling much of the night before. There was no one beside her now, though her memories of the previous evening had the same vague quality about them. When she closed her eyes, a green haze filled her mind, interrupted by brief, half-formed recollections.

She remembered the initial shock of the ocean but later a curious, comforting warmth, as if the water was charged with the aurora's energy. And then there were the strange darting motions in the water, phosphorescence perhaps, snaking through the current towards her: potent rays of light seeking her out in the darkness.

Elspeth pulled the covers aside, looking around for her clothes. She couldn't remember anything beyond swimming. She must have stumbled back to the croft house at some point, making her way, naked and wet, to her bed; her clothes still cast down on the beach or else washed away by the tide.

She rose and made her way downstairs. Though she wanted to head straight for the beach, to confront the strange experience of the night before, she delayed, putting on the coffee machine, stirring porridge slowly in a pan. What she needed right now was some semblance of normality. After she washed and dressed, slipping her coat on this time and a scarf for good measure, she made her way down to the shore.

She didn't expect her clothes to still be there. She'd imagined them drifting away upon salt waters. But there they were in the distance, heaped like a cairn. She hadn't seen much of the beach the night before, only what the green light permitted. It had seemed a mystical place then, of light and shadows, the sea shimmering – primordial. In the daylight, it looked much like any other shoreline. The shingle underfoot was unremarkable, interspersed with driftwood; the hull of a rowboat stood rotting in the distance, while the ocean was flat and grey, the same bleak colour as the sky.

The magic had gone. She watched the horizon for a few moments longer before stooping to retrieve her clothes. They were wet and heavy from the sand and surf. Her shawl had separated itself from the bundle and lay stretched upon the shore. Lifting it, Elspeth was aware of a sticky residue coating the fibres and then she saw what was underneath.

It looked like some kind of membrane, gelatinous and almost translucent but for a pinkish tinge in the middle. Perhaps it was some kind of jellyfish, though there were no tentacles or muscular parts. It was just an empty sac, like a deflated balloon. It put her in mind of a caul.

Elspeth thought briefly about casting it into the sea but she didn't want to touch it. So, heaping up the clothes in her arms, she made her way back to the croft house.

Life on her lonely promontory suited her. She'd walk most days, skirting her way along the beach, or drifting further along the headland. She'd head back in the early afternoon, aware that the dark was creeping in. The days were short here, brief interludes in the drawn-out nights. She read old stories by the fireside – the bookshelves crammed with texts on local folklore and mythology, left by enthusiastic holidaymakers – while she listened to the familiar creaking of the wind through the house. Her memories of the flower shop were an ocean away.

She hadn't thought much more about the night in the water, about the cold lure of the sea. She was unwilling to seek an explanation for her behaviour any more than that she would try to understand the strange phenomenon that made the sky glow. But later, as she walked along the shore, keeping her eyes downcast to avoid the assault of the wind, she happened to glance upon the strange caul-like form in the surf.

It was larger now, if indeed it was the same thing, and pinker. In its centre a curious growth had appeared, a rose-coloured protuberance that almost resembled a starfish, though it had only four limbs. Elspeth knelt beside it and reached out a tentative finger. The membrane was slimy with sea-foam and salt. The pink swelling in the middle undulated with the movement of the tide or perhaps from some kind of internal pulsation. Was it alive?

Elspeth took a step back. She didn't know what to make of it. The thing didn't resemble any marine life she was familiar with. But then she didn't know what strange creatures thrived in these cold waters. For all she knew, this was a common organism in these parts. Again she wondered whether she should push it back into the open water but something stopped her from doing so, and turning slowly from the sea, she made her way homeward.

The next day it was even bigger. The membrane was now taut and the fleshy star had accrued a halo of seaweed, which appeared to be enmeshed in the translucent bubble that surrounded it. It was certainly alive; Elspeth could see pink darting rays coursing along the body of the creature like blood through an artery.

She thought about calling Donal and telling him about the thing she'd found on the shore. Perhaps it was an endangered species, an aquatic wonder particular to these shores. But she didn't want anyone to disrupt the peaceful silence of her new life, the dark, embryonic stillness of her world. She'd rejoiced at news on the radio that the ferry connecting the island to the Orkney mainland would most likely be cancelled due to inclement weather. The idea of being completely cut off, utterly inaccessible, gave her the same giddying feeling she'd experienced the night she saw the green lights in the sky. She felt empowered at the idea of her solitude and at the same time, utterly dependent on forces she didn't fully understand.

Elspeth knew something was wrong as soon as she set foot on the shore. She was becoming accustomed to the sounds of the island; the whistling of the wind, the roar of the surf, the croon of the gannets flying overhead but this was something she hadn't heard before. It sounded like a series of high-pitched cries, a multitudinous screeching and wailing, carrying with it a sense of frenzy and desperation. Elspeth walked faster toward the din, breaking into a run when she saw the host of seagulls ahead, converging on one spot, fighting against each other to get at the thing in the surf.

Elspeth raced toward them, waving her arms wildly and shouting loudly to compete with their noise. As she drew closer, they took slowly to the air, squawking irritably at being denied their meal.

The thing in the surf looked pitiful. The torn remains of the membrane curled about its pink flesh, red in parts from the seagulls' assault. Elspeth knelt beside it and looked over its injuries, seeping red from exposed, raw tissue.

'There, there,' she said, gently touching the creature's centre, its texture mollusc-like and slimy. She felt it recoil at her touch. She gathered seawater in her palms instead and gently poured it onto the creature, washing its wounds, hoping that the salt-water would restore it.

She could hear the seagulls circling above. She picked up a stone and threw it into the air. Then, shrieking loudly as she went, she walked toward what remained of the old rowboat, and began to drag it across the shoreline, stopping intermittently to scream at opportunistic gulls swooping low, or to fling another stone skyward.

The sea-battered hull was the perfect enclosure. She lowered it over the creature, sad that she would be denying it the light, though it would mean its survival. And she thought of her own existence, the absence of light in these long dark days that marked her time on the island, and how much she had thrived.

The creature healed well within the dark interior of the boat. It acquired a carapace of shell and shingle; seaweed adhered to the parts that had been most exposed by the seagulls' attack, compensating for the flesh it had lost. Though it didn't resemble any amphibious life Elspeth was aware of, it looked strangely appropriate on the shore, like a mollusc beneath its shell amid a net of kelp.

It grew in size, too. About the length of a newborn now, it squirmed in the surf in much the same way. Elspeth made her way down to the shore at first light each morning and would gently lift the driftwood from the creature so it could see the sky, though it had no discernible eyes. Often she'd take a blanket to sit upon, sometimes a flask and her breakfast so she could stay beside it as long as she pleased. She wondered as she watched the pink flesh stir whether it needed to be fed too, or if it absorbed the nutrients it required from the surf. She tried dangling a variety of food in front of it but, with no recognisable mouth, it was hard to know how it would feed if indeed it possessed an appetite.

She thought often of milk, of how most mammals are weaned by their mothers. She tried splashing it with a little cow's milk but it just ran off its surface and into the spume. She didn't suppose she had anything to worry about. The creature was growing in size each day and, though it didn't appear similar to any established form of life she knew, it looked healthy and strong in its own way. But she wanted to exert some kind of influence on its growth.

She began to tell it stories. First the stories she knew from her childhood, fairy tales with moral instructions, then the stories she read in the evenings beside the fire – stories from the island. Tales of creatures that appeared human, living in vast underwater kingdoms and monstrous creatures that inhabited the land: giants and trows, water horses that drowned their riders. She wanted the creature to know the stories of the land it was being born into.

One time, after talking of the impious trows – dwarf-like mischievous sprites, who crept into houses after dark to torment the inhabitants – she placed her finger against the soft pink belly of the creature and stroked it softly until it began to purr.

'This island breeds monsters,' she whispered, wondering if it possessed enough sentience to recognise her voice.

And just as she was about to withdraw her hand, she felt a sharp stab of pain and looking down saw the beading of blood on her fingertip.

Elspeth stood by the window watching the man beside the boat. She could almost fancy he was a sailor, presumed lost, the wreckage of his vessel at his feet. Or else one of the Finfolk from her stories, returned from the sea, dressed in a magical sealskin coat.

In the half-light, it certainly looked like a man. She'd fashioned him from driftwood and twine and dressed him in her oilskins. From a distance you wouldn't know that the figure was actually her mediocre attempt at constructing a scarecrow.

It seemed a good idea to create a sentinel. She couldn't watch the creature day and night and she worried about predators lurking nearby. She hoped it would be enough of a deterrent, though its purpose was perhaps to pacify her mind more than anything else.

Elspeth closed the curtains and sat beside the hearth. She thought of what she had told the creature. That islands like this one breed monsters. Maybe it was because things were more extreme here, the climate harsher, more severe, the land constantly besieged by the sea. After all, who knew what dark forces the sea harboured, perhaps from time to time spitting out these peculiarities to accumulate on the shore like flotsam.

Strange things thrived in the darkness, wasn't that right? So this was the perfect place to raise them. It was on a windswept island, much the same as this one, that Victor Frankenstein in Mary Shelley's novel retired to build his second creation. A female this time, at the behest of his first creature. Why did he choose such a lonely place to bring her into being? And what did he create her from anyway, far from the mortuaries and graveyards he'd plundered back in Ingolstadt to build his first monster piecemeal? Was she made from the shingle and spume like the creature on the shore?

Maybe it was something to do with femininity and wild places. Frankenstein's monster was the product of the civilised world, but the female, she could only be engendered in the wilderness.

Elspeth made her way back toward the window and peered out from behind the curtain. It was darker now, but she could still see the scarecrow's silhouette and the dark outline of the boat. She could imagine the creature within, pink and engorged, sleeping softly to the sound of the surf and she knew then, with a strange certainty, that the half-formed thing was more like her than she'd realised. The creature was female.

She'd always wanted a girl and here she was, brought in with the tide. The goddess Aphrodite had been born of the sea, formed on the foam after her father's castrated genitals were flung into the surf. It was an odd parentage; Aphrodite's existence was dependent on her father's emasculation, and her mother, according to this genealogy – was the sea.

The sea. Elspeth thought of that night in the luminous green water. Of the energy she felt charging through the current.

She would name her child Aphrodite.

Elspeth smiled and returned to her place by the fire. After all, it's a fine line between monsters and gods, a vague boundary like the shoreline itself where neither the land nor the sea hold dominion.

The next day Aphrodite began to crawl. She was now the size of a baby seal and moved in a similar lumbering way, pulling herself up on her fleshy stumps. Elspeth stood next to the driftwood man and clapped feverishly. Proud parents.

'Well done, Aphrodite. Well done,' she called.

And Aphrodite basked at the applause, though Elspeth could only surmise as much from the quickening of her movements, the excited writhing of her form. She still had no perceptible features; she was just a mass of pink flesh, like an oversized starfish, though the two lower limbs were less developed. When Aphrodite rested, reclining against the rocks, she almost resembled a human torso. Lying in the surf, dotted with sand and shingle, she gave the impression of a drowned person brought in by the tide. The only discernible thing about her was the shell carapace and the seaweed mane that trailed behind her when she moved.

The fact she was no longer bound to one spot filled Elspeth with hope. There was the prospect of her holding her, maybe taking her home to nurse and raise, perhaps even tucking her into a cot like a regular child. But there was nothing regular about Aphrodite. Her need for seawater would prohibit a normal home life. It would be more likely to nestle her into a bathtub than a crib. And then there was her diet to consider.

Elspeth stopped the train of her thoughts before they gained momentum. She didn't want to ruin this moment by worrying about how Aphrodite would fit into the world around her. It was enough that she was growing stronger, taking her first steps boldly along the shore. She watched Aphrodite amble toward her, her movements slower now as if she were fatigued. Or hungry. Elspeth knelt beside her and Aphrodite placed a stumpy oily limb on her leg.

Elspeth knew what she wanted and was happy to comply. Aphrodite deserved to be rewarded for such an achievement. Under the gaze of the driftwood man, she lifted up her sleeve, exposing the flesh of her wrist and let Aphrodite's cold, wet skin envelop her.

Elspeth found she adapted to motherhood well. She took pleasure bathing Aphrodite in the surf, plaiting her seaweed tresses. She even enjoyed the night feeds, untroubled by the lack of sleep. She could anticipate now when Aphrodite would call her, distinguishing her cry from the similar sound of the gulls. And wrapping a shawl about her shoulders she'd hasten to the shore and lift Aphrodite onto her lap. Then she'd pull up her sleeve and feel Aphrodite's cold, moist flesh coil itself around her in the way she imagined an octopus would fasten itself to its prey.

She hadn't expected to feel this kind of joy so late in life, this deep sense of contentment as she nursed Aphrodite. She wondered if all mothers felt such a bond. It didn't matter to her that it was blood instead of milk, she was feeding this nascent life with a part of herself and that was all that mattered.

The flower shop didn't even come close to this feeling, though it was the single product of her life's labour and though it had sucked out her energy and time in much the same way. It was just a shadow compared to the living thing in her arms and Elspeth felt a pang of regret that she had not arrived at motherhood earlier.

In the moonlight Aphrodite's shell-skin shone the colour of pearl. Elspeth took to identifying the seashells that made up her mantle as she rocked her: dog whelks and cockles, tellins and periwinkles. Interspersed with these empty shells, the exoskeletons of long-dead molluscs, clusters of barnacles grew in abundance and rock lice flitted along the surface, burrowing into the crevices and hollows left vacant.

Aphrodite pulled in time with the lapping of the waves and Elspeth withdrew her arm. Would it just be barnacles and isopods that would crowd Aphrodite's carapace, or would she, one day, sprout other more curious life forms, creatures as mysterious and strange as she was? Elspeth couldn't help but think how unfair it was that Aphrodite could generate life so readily, when it had taken her all her life to acquire a child. But how would she cope, with all this life to support, crouching along the shoreline with her monstrous children on her back?

The next morning there were two men beside the boat. Elspeth rubbed her eyes and made her way closer to the window, hoping she had conjured a second driftwood man from her sleep-addled mind. But there he was, a real man, slightly shorter than her creation though dressed in matching oilskins, stooping slightly to examine the boat.

Elspeth bolted toward the door, struggling with her shoes and coat before racing out onto the beach. If he looked beneath the driftwood, what would he make of Aphrodite? He'd flee, surely, perhaps report her to the authorities and they would take Aphrodite away to prod and examine. Or maybe out of revulsion or fear, he would attack her. What chance would she have, barely able to walk, let alone run from an assailant? She might retreat into the sea and perhaps disappear forever. Elspeth ran harder, with a speed and agility to her movements that belied her age. She needed to reach her child, to protect her from the man and the world he brought with him.

But as she made her way closer, she saw that he had disappeared. She scanned the scene ahead, looking for the slick, rubberised fabric, wondering briefly if she had imagined the intruder after all.

And then she saw his walking boots, sticking out from behind the boat, at the end of two narrow ankles that disappeared from view. Rounding the boat, she saw the whole hideous spectacle.

Aphrodite had pinned him to the ground, spreading her bulk across his chest. Her surface area was wider than normal as if she had elongated herself somehow, the effect being that more of her pink body was exposed beneath her shell exterior than normal. Elspeth edged closer, confused as to where Aphrodite's flesh ended and the man's began. She made the same gentle purring sound she made when Elspeth fed her.

'Aphrodite!' Elspeth said, summoning the voice she heard parents use when chastising their children in her shop. She repeated it again, more loudly this time, noticing how Aphrodite's body had spread over the man's face, perhaps obstructing his breathing. She began to consider a way to prise her off, looking about for some kind of stick or tool rather than touch her with her bare hands, possessed by some instinctive knowledge that physical contact at this moment would be precarious. Her gaze settled upon the driftwood man – his blank expression seemed to convey the same sense of bemusement she felt – when Aphrodite relinquished her grasp and slid back to her place beside the boat.

Elspeth wished she hadn't moved because now she could see what Aphrodite had done to the man. He was bloodied and disfigured; an Aphrodite-shaped hollow where she had lain on top, the man's face and torso reduced to a fleshy, red depression. Elspeth moved forward tentatively, watching the waves lap against his body, filling the concave that was completely devoid of organs and entrails.

She stumbled back to shore and fell against the shingle. She could see Aphrodite purring contentedly beside the upturned boat and a next to that, the man's backpack bobbed back and forth with the tide.

Elspeth sat on the shore for a long time. At one point she lay back against the rocks, hardly caring if Aphrodite crept silently toward her and up onto her prostrate body as she had done with the backpacker. She studied the grey sky, whorls of black clouds swelling like the dark undercurrents of the ocean and thought of the green spectacle on the night of Aphrodite's conception.

Because, in her mind, that strange light was responsible. It had compelled her into the sea, charging the water with its mysterious energy. It was inconceivable to Elspeth now that Aphrodite was merely washed in with the tide, transported from some place far or deep. No, she'd come to feel that Aphrodite was part of her. Not just because she fed her from time to time but because she had engendered her that night in the glowing water. Aphrodite was the fruit of her loins and the sea, a surrogate womb, had carried her and deposited her, newly-formed, on the shore.

Maybe that was why she experienced this feeling of disappointment more acutely. Even when Aphrodite did crawl toward her later, nuzzling her wet and bloodied body against her skin, Elspeth did not stroke her seaweed mane, nor caress her seashell skin, but lay there tight-lipped and unmoving, denying her the stories and songs she'd previously given so freely. Aphrodite reached out her slimy appendage and placed it against Elspeth's cheek, meaning perhaps to wipe away the tears.

As the radio had forecast, the weather worsened as the week progressed and Elspeth had a convenient excuse not to leave the croft house. She watched the sea from the window, tumultuous and wild, and thought of Aphrodite alone on the shore. In her more compassionate moments, she considered bringing Aphrodite out of the rain and wind and into the house but then she'd remember the backpacker's mutilated body and didn't know how she would ever forgive her.

She knew if Aphrodite didn't already have a ready supply of food – with regard to the remainder of the backpacker's body – she would have found a way to feed her, though the idea of personally nursing her as she had done was suddenly repugnant. Likewise, though she wanted to punish Aphrodite, her protective impulse was stronger, convincing her of the need to conceal the evidence, filling the man's backpack with stones and casting it out deep into the ocean.

As for his body, it was diminishing day by day. What Aphrodite didn't eat, the sea washed away, as if both Aphrodite's mothers were complicit in covering her crime.

Elspeth had found the first few days the hardest. She had turned up the radio to drown out the sound of Aphrodite's cries. There was no mistaking her high-pitched squall for the sound of the gulls anymore, for since Aphrodite had killed the backpacker the birds kept their distance. Where oystercatchers and seagulls used to converge on the surf, the gannets on the roof of the croft, now they avoided the beach altogether.

Lately, though, either the wind was more riotous or Aphrodite called for her less. Elspeth suspected it was the latter; Aphrodite was certainly becoming more independent. Without the driftwood boat to contain her, she roamed the shore unimpeded, her movements confident and agile. Watching her progress through binoculars, Elspeth saw that she delighted in chasing crabs or collecting debris from the beach, decorating the prow of the boat with nets of kelp as if constructing a lair. At some point she had pushed the driftwood man forward, so that he fell pitifully against the boat, his oilskins gaping open to form a tarpaulin enclosure. Even within this makeshift den, when the wind and rain was particularly ferocious, Aphrodite dug herself into the sand, so that only her shell exterior was visible.

And when she disappeared beneath the earth like this, Elspeth thought of the flower shop and the seeds she planted in the rich soil, wondering if when Aphrodite re-emerged she would have grown into something else. Perhaps something more beautiful.

Elspeth woke to a scratching outside her window. She lay staring into the darkness for a long time, unsure whether she was imagining things. Just as she was ready to dismiss it, the sound resumed with renewed fervour. There was something outside in the darkness, scratching eagerly at the pane.

Curiously, Elspeth's first thoughts were of the trows from the island's folk stories before she even considered Aphrodite. She imagined the impish sprites emerging from their hollows and mounds, climbing up onto the roof and dancing wildly to plague her peace of mind. And she wondered if the original owners of the house had adhered to superstition, leaving water outside for them, sweeping the hearth on a Saturday as was the custom, to appease their troublesome natures. But as the scratching became more feverish, she realised that the monster outside her window

211

was of her own making.

Elspeth made her way slowly to the window, thankful that she had
pulled the curtains, not wanting to see Aphrodite's pearlised exterior in the
moonlight. Moreover, the fact she had crawled all the way to the croft
house was alarming. Though she was becoming increasingly strong, she
had never covered so much ground. And she had never left the shore. Yet
here she was curled up outside Elspeth's window, drumming her shell-clad
mantle against the pane.

'Go away,' Elsepth called.

And softly, within the whistling of the wind she thought she heard the
creature emit a deep, growling exhalation,

'Die…'

Elspeth edged closer, her heart beating faster.

'Die-ty', the voice repeated and Elspeth realised she was trying to say
her name.

'Aphrodite,' Elspeth called, as if correcting her, 'go back to the shore.'

And with that she heard a low shuffling, a scrapping sound against the
shingle path, the sound diminishing as Aphrodite retreated into the
distance.

Elspeth made her way back to bed, Aphrodite's words swimming in
her head. It was miraculous, incredible that she could communicate.

Die. Die-ty. But it was the word deity that she thought about the
longest.

At dawn, Elspeth made her way down to the beach. It had been a week
since the death of the backpacker, an inordinate amount of time in
Aphrodite's brief lifetime to experience solitude. But, arriving at her lair,
Elspeth saw that Aphrodite was not there, though the place on the shore
looked more inhabited than ever before. Lifting the oilskin roof, she
peered into the darkness, the ground strewn with the remains of crabs and
cuttlefish. Seaweed hung from the spine of the driftwood man and
entangled within it were human bones and the torn shreds of the
backpacker's clothing.

Elspeth backed away, aware of the smell of decay. She had only
thought of the shore bringing life, not death. What had prompted
Aphrodite to build such a place, to nest among dead things? Maybe it was
for comfort, a way to cope with the sudden isolation; being among the
dead was better than being completely alone. Or maybe they were trophies.

Elspeth turned to make her way back, spying a protrusion in the sand
up ahead. She watched as the sand bulged upward, growing mound-like, a

sandy hillock existing suddenly where none had stood before. Then she saw the flail of seaweed, the chitinous carapace before the serpentine body coiled itself out of the sand.

Aphrodite was much bigger. She no longer crawled across the sand but seemed to glide, on limbs that appeared slender and long. As she got closer, Elspeth could see tatters of the backpacker's oilskin enmeshed within her seaweed train and as she sidled up alongside her, Elspeth noted the other curious development.

She had grown hair. Thick dark hair sprouting from the edge of her seashell skin, emerging from the pink fleshy parts of her body.

Elspeth reached out a tentative hand. The backpacker's hair had been dark. There had been no other identifiable features left after Aphrodite's attack. But his hair had fanned out upon the waves, moving like seagrass through the water. Had Aphrodite appropriated his hair as she had done his clothes? How could they grow so naturally from her flesh?

Aphrodite let Elspeth rest her hand against her skin. The texture was reassuringly cold and slimy, as it always had been.

'There, there Aphrodite,' Elspeth cooed.

But as she withdrew her hand she saw that the flesh of her palm had been eaten away. She clutched the gaping wound with her other hand, stumbling back bewildered.

'Die-ty, die-ty,' Aphrodite called as Elspeth ran from the creature on the shore.

'You were right,' Elspeth's voice wavered, 'I am crazy to stay here. Please come.' She spoke the last words softly into the receiver, still unsure whether inviting someone else in was the right thing to do. Though Elspeth was her mother, Aphrodite was still a creature of the island and maybe an islander would be better equipped to deal with her. She listened to the beep of Donal's voice recording, longing to hear a human voice, before hanging up.

She'd bandaged her hand, applied antiseptic to the lesion, surprised to see that it didn't gush blood as she would have suspected from a wound of its kind. It was as if it had been cauterised at the same time the flesh had been torn, or else the blood had been sucked away. Elspeth felt faint thinking about it and sat down heavily on her chair beside the hearth.

It had taken all her energy to barricade herself inside the croft house. All the doors were locked, the curtains pulled in case Aphrodite crept toward the window once more, to clink her seashell bulk against the pane. She'd thought about driving to the ferry in the hope that it was running.

Even waiting in her car, miles from the shore would be better than being stuck inside the croft house with Aphrodite lurking outside. But she couldn't drive with her hand the way it was and she worried about passing out at the wheel, feeling drowsy already from the cocktail of painkillers she'd taken.

Her hand still throbbed, her body broadcasting the loss of its flesh. She reached for the whisky bottle on the table and poured herself a generous measure. Beside it was the compendium of mythology, where she had read about Aphrodite's namesake. The goddess Aphrodite wasn't the only thing conceived when Uranus' genitals had been cast into the sea. From his blood had come the Furies, hideous hags with snakes for hair. Elspeth thought of the creature on the shore and of which set of sisters she resembled most. Maybe it had been foolish of her to think that her Aphrodite was made of the stuff of gods. She should have accepted her monstrous nature from the beginning.

Elspeth rose slowly and made her way to the window. Pulling the curtain aside, she could see Aphrodite slithering across the shore, scurrying into the sand in pursuit of crabs. In the diminishing light she looked even more surreal, like some mythical sea serpent from the pages of a medieval bestiary. A creature constructed from the imagination, rather than of flesh and shell.

Frankenstein had killed his she-monster, torn her apart with his bare hands in front of his first creation, fearing his monsters would procreate and fill the world with their hideous progeny. Elspeth thought of Aphrodite's body, of the living mantle on her back, wondering if she would be able to grow her own children one day. Would she be able to produce life asexually, sprouting her offspring as easily as the hair follicles she'd assimilated from the backpacker, or would she need a mate, a creature as strange as she was, to fertilise her somehow?

Elspeth felt tired. She had not thought of the future, of Aphrodite's legacy. She imagined the croft house surrounded by an army of eerie shell creatures, crawling onto the windowsills to bang their shell-limbs against the glass, or scurrying up onto the roof to dance like the trows. All of them baying for human blood, needing to be fed.

She realised then what a mistake it had been to call Donal. How could he possibly know what to expect or how to deal with such a creature. Besides, Aphrodite was stronger and faster than she'd been since her encounter with the backpacker. Donal wouldn't stand a chance; she'd make a meal of him in no time at all.

Elspeth poured herself another whisky and drank it quickly before she could change her mind, then she went to the front door and opened it wide, welcoming the darkness in. She stood for a moment on the threshold, seeking the aurora's luminescence in the sky, a twinkle of green above the water. But it was black. On her way to the bedroom, she stopped by the kitchen and found a long, sharp knife in the drawer.

She waited a long time. Such a long time that she lay back on the bed and closed her eyes. She could see the green haze then, dancing in her mind's eye as it had done that night in the water and then just before she let herself drift into it entirely, she heard a scrapping sound on the shingle path, the clinking of shell against shell that signalled Aphrodite's approach.

She had always wanted to bring Aphrodite into her world. To give her a home, a place to let her grow but now, the sound of her progress up the stone steps and into the hallway, the scratching of shell against the hardwood floor, made her uneasy. She could hear the crash of Aphrodite's body against the chair and table legs, the slick slither of her seaweed mane against the polished surfaces. And then she was purring outside her bedroom door.

'Die. Die-ty'.

Yet she entered the room soundlessly and crawled up onto the bed with similar stealthy dexterity, so that Elspeth was almost surprised to see her shadowed outline at the foot of the bed. It was too dark to see her clearly, to make out her slippery form beneath the husk of shell. Besides, her mind was still glowing green, the green of new life, of waxy seedlings pushing their heads out of the earth. And she thought of her flower shop and the life cycle of plants.

Often asexual reproduction involved the annihilation of the parent. Daffodils and potato plants grew their replacements beneath the earth, a lateral bulb forming when the old plant died. Maybe this was the natural order of things, Elspeth thought as Aphrodite climbed up on to her. And it wasn't as if she'd be forgotten. In the same way Aphrodite had assimilated the backpacker, perhaps something of her would become reproduced in Aphrodite's malleable flesh. She would live on in her daughter, part of her monstrous inheritance, unless of course she raised the knife and aimed it beneath the rim of seashell.

The purring became more contented as Aphrodite slid up Elspeth's body, her seaweed tresses licking her skin. She could smell the sea and the iron-reek of blood as she welcomed her shell baby to her breast.

THE UNWISH

Claire Dean

One step inside and Amy knew there was something she'd forgotten. She heaved her rucksack over the threshold and counted the carrier bags she'd lugged up from the Co-op in the town. Four, which was right. There might not be enough wine, though. With the front door key between her teeth – metallic tang on her tongue – she dragged the bags inside and stopped. The room hadn't changed at all. She'd been eleven when they last stayed here. She'd never been back. How could it have changed so little in twenty years? She placed the key on the table and heaped the bags beneath it. Her boots were caked with mud. She tiptoed towards the kettle rather than battle with the filthy laces to get them off.

She cradled her tea on the bench by the front door. The river was insistent in her ears, though it was hidden by the trees. The opposite valley-side shifted with the wind, the trees forming an agitated creature that could not rest. The wood of the bench had warmed in the spring sunshine, but clouds were collecting now. A narrow path beside the cottage climbed to the road. She watched for the arrival of her sister and parents. They'd have to leave their cars further up the hill and carry everything down. A goldfinch perched on the gate for just a breath before lifting off again. She'd reached for her phone to take a picture, but the moment had gone. She couldn't get a signal to send it to him anyway. And he'd be here before too long. They could sit on the bench together. The goldfinch might return.

Her cup was empty but still warm. She let it rest against her collarbone. She picked up her phone again and read through their last messages: 'Can't wait to see you tomorrow x,' she'd sent from the village. 'See you soon,' he'd replied. No kiss. She tackled her laces and dirt powdered the flagstones. There was a hole in her left sock. It was a good job she'd worn that pair today. She left her boots beneath the bench and headed inside to unpack.

Her parents would take the main bedroom in the front. Should she claim the other decent-sized one? Sara had it when they'd stayed here as kids. They'd fought over it but Sara won, as always. Amy had ended up in the tiny room off the kitchen downstairs. Dad said it was like having her own den. But there was another room upstairs, she realised now. She pushed open the door at the end of the hall. How had she forgotten it? It was single-sized, but a double bed and narrow set of drawers had been squeezed in. Blue blankets on the bed lapped against the window wall. Beech leaves pressed against the glass and green light filled the room. She climbed up onto the bed and unlatched the window, letting the sounds of leaves and the river into the room. Sara could keep the big room. It would be cosy in here when he arrived. She emptied all her clothes out of her rucksack onto the bed. Ordinarily, she'd leave them balled inside her bag and extract them as she needed them, but she didn't want him to see she was messy. She folded her creased T-shirts and the two lace nighties she'd brought. Maybe she should have brought pyjamas as well. She'd be cold that night in bed alone. She kept her stuff to one side in the drawers, leaving space for him. She put her washbag on top and then hid it back in her rucksack. He didn't need to see all that crap.

Lying on the bed, she tried to imagine him into the room. His arms around her. She read his last text over and over. Why had there been no kiss?

'Bolognese, really?' Sara set her grey leather weekend bag down on the table.

'Nice to see you too,' Amy said.

'Is that mince organic at least? You know, turkey mince is so much better for you.' Sara leaned over the pan and sniffed. 'I'll cook tomorrow night. Are Mum and Dad here yet? Mum, Dad, hellooo!'

Amy stabbed the mince with the spatula, trying to separate the claggy brown clumps. 'They're not here yet,' she said.

'And when's what's-he-called-again arriving?'

'Aidan will be here tomorrow night. He couldn't get time off today.'

Sara raised her eyebrows and lifted her bag off the table. 'I really don't know why we had to come back here.'

'Dad wanted to come. Mum said he was insistent about it.' Amy turned back to the mince as her sister pounded up the stairs. She tipped a tin of tomatoes into the pan and attempted to liquidise them with a potato masher. She sloshed a little red wine into the pan and more into her glass.

When her parents finally burst through the door in a flurry of bags and arms and kisses, the bottle was empty.

Sara picked it up. 'Do we have recycling here?' she said.

'Sorry we're late,' Mum said. 'Your dad got us lost.'

'I didn't get us lost. They've changed the road layout up in the village.'

'You got us lost.' Mum upended her handbag on the table and retrieved her tablets from a mound of tissues.

'Let us get the bags for you,' said Sara. 'Let's go and get comfy and light a fire. Do you remember how Amy used to hide the wood so we couldn't burn it? She said it screamed. Amy, can you take all the bags upstairs?'

Amy hadn't bought dessert. She never had dessert at home. Didn't wine count as dessert? Apparently not. They were already dangerously close to the end of the second bottle and Sara had barely touched her glass.

Mum started to clear the plates. 'It doesn't matter. I couldn't eat another thing anyway.'

'Pasta can sit so heavily, can't it, Mum?' Sara said. 'I'll go out in the car and find the nearest Waitrose tomorrow. Get us properly stocked up.'

'Shall we play a game?' Dad headed off into the snug as Mum began to clear the plates.

The Scrabble set still had old score sheets inside. People had made a palimpsest of them over the years. Sara pored over them. 'See I won,' she said finally. 'I always got the triple word scores.'

'You were older than me,' Amy said, looking over her shoulder at the sheet.

'I'm still older than you. It's not an excuse for losing.'

'Actually, who's K? It looks like they won,' Amy said.

'That's someone else's game.'

Amy lifted a battered Trivial Pursuit box down from the shelf. 'There were pieces of pie missing when we last played this.'

'You replaced them with beech nuts you'd all collected,' Dad said.

Now there were just the empty pies. Amy put the lid back on the box.

'So you'll have to face me at Scrabble,' Sara said, dishing out the tiles on the coffee table.

Dad pushed his back. 'Actually, just you two play. I'm happier watching.'

Mum came through from the kitchen, glass in hand, and pulled a Danielle Steel novel from the shelf. She crumpled into the armchair and took another of her tablets with the last of the wine. 'I probably read this last time,' she said. 'Good job I never remember how things end.'

There were other books on the shelf: a Ruth Rendell, some hardbacked

Dickens, a couple of Catherine Cooksons. 'Do you remember that book that was here, full of weird fairy tales?' Amy said. 'It was small, had a brown cover. There was that horrible story about the cat mother in it and –'

'No,' Sara said as she placed five tiles on the board. 'T.R.I.C.K., with the K on a double letter score. That makes 16.'

Amy placed an O beneath the C. If only she had a W. She added a D instead. 'C.O.D. That's 6,' she said.

Dad stood up. 'I've left the map in the car.'

'Well you don't need it now,' Mum said without looking up from her book. 'We're here.'

'I'd like to have a look at it. See what's going on with those roads in the village.'

'Get it in the morning.'

'It'll only take a minute.' He was already getting his boots on.

'D.E.U.X.' Sara placed each tile with emphasis.

'You can't have that,' Amy said.

'Of course I can. And the X is on a triple letter score, so that's 28 for me.'

Amy shuffled her tiles about as though it would make a difference to how useless she was at seeing words in the random letters. The fire guttered as cold air flooded the room. Dad mustn't have shut the door properly. Amy shuffled her tiles again. What was she going to do with two Fs? 'I'll go with Dad,' she said.

'Thanks, sweetheart,' Mum said.

'Well, I'll come too then,' Sara said.

'Good girls.' Mum sipped her wine and went back to her book.

Bluebells held on to the twilight. Tree branches reached up into the falling dark. Amy walked quickly, until the air was sharp in her chest, but there was no sign of Dad.

'So are you sure it's going to work out with this one?' Sara said from behind her.

Amy focused on trying to follow the lighter stones that made the path.

'Because you're not getting any younger. And after Gareth…' Sara let the memories out in a studied exhalation. The same way she used to blow smoke rings when they were teenagers and leave them to hang in the air.

'Mum said he's married,' she said.

'He's been separated for a long time. They're getting a divorce.'

'But he's still married?'

The stones were all mud-slick now. Amy stopped looking for the path and just kept heading upwards. They had to reach the road at some point.

And Dad. How could he have got ahead so fast?

'So what is it he's doing that couldn't be put off?'

'He had to work. I already told you that. Where's Richard anyway?'

'Closing a deal. The partners needed him there. Anyway, he's arranged a special meal for Mum and Dad at The Cottingdale when they come to stay with us at the end of the month. We'll have a lot to celebrate.'

'Great,' Amy said. There was a scuttering overhead as birds swapped places on the branches. She stopped.

'It's only the birds, Amy. God you're still scared of everything.'

'In that fairy tale book there was a story where all the leaves were really birds and they flew down all at once and trapped the children. And they had to live for years in a house of wings. Do you remember?'

Sara overtook her. 'Come on, we're never going to catch up with Dad.'

'And there was that story about the sisters. They were trying to collect wishes from... was it from a tree? Do you remember?'

'No. I don't.'

'But that one was your favourite. You made us act it out. There was a hollow tree down by the river... I'd completely forgotten about it until now, but there was a tree down there that we used to hide things in.'

'I don't remember.'

'There were three sisters and the eldest –'

'You're making things up again,' Sara said.

A shuffling and cracking ahead announced their father. In the last light he could have been a badger, stooped in his worn grey coat.

'I left a... I left something in the car. Went up to get it,' he said. He didn't have anything in his hands.

The morning was cold against her shoulder. Amy huddled under the blankets and watched shadow leaves flitter on the wall. Tomorrow she'd get to wake up beside him. It was worth having to put up with a few days of Sara for that. She hadn't actually spent a whole night with him yet. He said it was too difficult to get to work from her house. When he rolled out of her bed before midnight to retrieve his clothes the extra space was crushing. The smell of him never lasted long enough on her pillows.

She couldn't hear anyone else up. She dressed and crept downstairs. The front door was wide open. Dad's boots were gone. She headed out down the hill. The bluebells were still the colour of twilight. The river sounded heavy and urgent in the trees, drowning out any birdsong.

Dad was on the small stone bridge, curled over its side, staring down into the water. She watched as he turned, then crouched to the ground, crossed to the other side of the bridge and rushed back to his starting position like a creaky old automaton.

'Morning, Dad,' she said. The dank mouth of the bridge held ferns and boulders and old bricks tumbled until their corners were gone. The water that frothed through it all looked more like bitter. She pressed her fingers into the moss growing on the stone, expecting it to be cool and damp, but it was warm and dry.

Dad scrabbled for more leaves. One, two, three, he let them go. 'You always enjoyed playing this with your sisters,' he said.

Sister, she corrected in her head, but she let it go. He seemed fragile. Something wasn't right.

Two oak leaves raced through. The third must have got caught.

'Are you coming back to the cottage, Dad? I can make you some breakfast.'

'I'm waiting,' he said, 'for the other one.'

'It's got stuck, Dad, come on.'

Sara had already laid the table for breakfast and arranged several pans on the hob, but she'd disappeared upstairs to the bathroom. Amy took over and had served a full fry-up to Mum and Dad before Sara came down.

'Would you like some?' Amy asked.

'No, thanks.' Sara sat at the far end of the table.

Amy filled her own plate and sat right next to her.

'What's the plan today then?' Sara got up and leaned against the sink.

'I don't want to go out there,' Mum said. 'I mean, I would like to stay here and finish that book by the fire.'

'I need to go food shopping, of course,' Sara said. 'What time's your new boyfriend arriving, Amy?'

'Sixish. Although he said it could get to seven.'

'I'll do a late dinner then, if he can't be sure.'

'I'm going to go for a walk today,' Amy said.

'You've just been for a walk,' Sara said.

'A longer one. Maybe cross the river and climb the hill on the other side.'

'There's a good view from the top,' Dad said. 'You all loved it up there when you were younger.'

Each barely-there filament of the feather added to its delicate Rorschach pattern. Amy twirled it between finger and thumb as she set off down the hill. She might give it to him when he arrived. What would he do with it, though? Would he keep it because she'd given it to him? What if he just discarded it? She wanted to tell him she loved him when they went to bed that night. The words had been in her mouth so many times, but she'd been too nervous to let them out. What if he didn't say it back? He'd said he needed to take things slowly after his marriage. Did the fact he'd already been married mean he wouldn't want to do all that again? She'd never fantasised about a big fancy wedding like Sara's, but still. She let the feather fall back to the ground.

He didn't like to hold her hand. He'd never said that, but she could feel it when she let hers touch his as they walked. He never took it. It was a small thing really. But did it mean he didn't like her enough, or that he was still in love with his ex? Maybe he would never want to hold her hand. Would that matter? As she stumbled down the slope she couldn't pull apart the rush of wind in the leaves from the sound of the water. For a moment she felt as though she was walking beneath the water, and its surface was up above the branches. She might drown in the trees. She had to stop. She leaned against a tree and then sank to the ground between its roots. He thought it was fine for them to not see each other all week. She felt a longing for him that scared her. She checked her phone for him constantly. Every message from friends and every marketing email she'd never signed up for hurt, because she believed for a split second it was going to be from him.

Damp was seeping through her jeans, but the leaves around her felt dry beneath her hands. She stood up and looked at where she'd been sitting. There was a deep crevice, not much more than a hand's width, in the trunk. It was the hollow tree. She slipped her hand inside and pulled out mounds of desiccated leaves. With her face against the bark she reached in further. There was a smell of wet soil and something sickly. She dislodged an object deep inside the tree. Twisting her wrist, she managed to pull out an old ice cream tub. The label on the lid had disintegrated but there were initials scratched into its sky-blue plastic sides, SP, AP, KP. Inside there were seven ring pulls tied to a length of string, a rusty needle and the book. The fairy tale book they'd taken from the cottage. The text block came away from its sodden cover in her hands. The page edges were mildewed and it was difficult to prise them apart with her nails, but when she did, the printed words were remarkably intact. 'The Cat Mother', 'The Bird House', 'Devil's Bridge', 'Three Green Baskets', 'The Fox and the Leaf'. There were pages missing where the final story should have been; only its last page remained:

The last wish, the un-, had to be hidden from the world. The good sister folded it up and asked me to put it into this story. And a fine story it makes too, but, dear child, take heed; it must never be taken from here.

Amy shoved the book back into the tree. She stuffed the tub and lid after it, scraping her arm on unseen ridges. She remembered finding a tiny bone in the tree and pretending it was a key from one of the stories. Was that before, or after? They'd been playing in the woods. She remembered being piggy in the middle. She was always piggy in the middle. She remembered following a tangle of red thread through the trees. That was after. They found a little cairn of white pick-up sticks by the river. Sara threw stones at it. There were other parts, not attached to their names, that lay swollen and shining like jewels in the mud. There had been three of them. But by the time Dad had called them back for lunch they were two. There had been nothing left of her little sister: no bones, no eyes, no heart. The woods were empty of her. Before she was gone it was like her body had tried to hold on to the world, to make itself so viciously present they could never forget it. Forget her. But they had forgotten. What was her name?

Sara was making the dessert, stirring a thick chocolatey mess in a bowl. Mum and Dad were sitting at the table drinking tea in silence. They all looked so normal.

'Your boots are filthy,' Sara said.

It was you, Amy thought. It was you, it was you, it was you. You unwished her.

'Cup of tea, love?'

'No, thanks, Mum.'

She sat and fought with her mud-thick laces. We had a sister. We had a sister. We had a sister. Maybe if she kept saying it to herself she could stop it falling out of her mind again. She tried to picture her, but couldn't see her for the river water and leaves.

'Look at the state of me!' Sara laughed and wiggled her chocolatey fingers.

Amy watched Sara wash her hands and pat them dry on a towel before letting them rest lightly on her belly. A baby, Amy thought. Sara's going to have a baby. Of course she was. She always had to be the centre of attention.

'Are you okay, love?' Mum asked.

'I'm going to have a bath,' Amy said.

'Yes, best to make yourself presentable for your new boyfriend.' Sara's hand remained on her belly.

The water ran in a scorching stream. She tried to imagine her little sister into being, but every time her thoughts got close to the edge of her, her mind pulled away. She wiped the steamed-up mirror with her sleeve. Her face was streaked with tears, eyelids thickening. She'd look a mess when he arrived. She needed him to arrive. To hold her. Things would feel okay in his arms.

She folded her clothes neatly in a pile on the floor. How would she explain all this to him? Would he think she was mad? Would he let her cry? Gareth had always hated it when she cried, said she should go on tablets like her mum. Sara was having a baby. A baby. She shouldn't think about the baby. She couldn't breathe. Her skin was burning. She added more cold. What would he think of her, a beetroot with puffy eyes? He'd never seen her like this, or first thing in the morning, or kissed her morning mouth. Would she be what he wanted? Maybe he'd leave her too. She remembered the pages of the book washing under the bridge. Was that before, or after? She tried to imagine he was with her. Why wouldn't he hold her hand? Did he still love his wife? It was all her fault. How could she think he'd love her?

There were candles and napkins on the table. 'We waited,' Sara said.

'Sorry.'

It was raining outside. They ate their lamb steaks in silence. Sara made no pretence with the wine and poured herself a glass of orange juice instead. After dinner, Amy washed up. In Scrabble she got F.O.U.N.D. on a triple word score and wondered why it made her want to cry.

Green light leaked into the room. Amy shivered and hugged the blankets around herself. At least she was going home today. Stuffing her clothes back into her rucksack she wondered why she'd bothered unpacking in the first place. She had so little stuff with her that it only took up half the space in each drawer.

A DAY WITH THE DELUSIONISTS

Reggie Oliver

"I usually have a Creme de Menthe and a Mars Bar at about this time," said Dr. Soper "Would you care to join me?"

I declined the Mars Bar but accepted the Creme de Menthe which he served *frappé*, crushing the ice expertly in a little machine of his own invention. Dr Soper had been the Dean of my college, a genial, liberal spirit who had always seemed more like a friend than a figure in authority. After leaving Oxford I had occasionally corresponded with him. He would invite me to dine with him in college; I would have him down to London to be my guest at the Garrick. Even before he retired, however, he always insisted on our dining early so that he could get the 9 p.m train back to Oxford and sleep in his own bed. Dr. Soper's many eccentricities never went to the extent of denying himself the homely comforts of his bachelor existence. On retirement he had gone to live in luxurious "sheltered accommodation" on the Iffley Road, despite the fact that he was in no way infirm. From this pampered citadel he would venture out to the theatre, or to Bridge with a gaggle of female dons from Somerville, or, once a year, on a well organised cruise of cultural or historic interest. That afternoon as I watched him preparing my Creme de Menthe frappé he seemed to my eyes barely altered after forty years and I remarked on the fact.

"Good! Splendid!" he said. "Picture in the attic still rendering sterling service, I'm glad to say!" and he gave that curious braying laugh which brought back times past with the effectiveness of a Proustian Madeleine.

He was the same as ever, as were his rooms to all intents and purposes. The walls were still adorned with steel engravings of Castlereagh and Canning alongside framed photographic studies of Myrna Loy, Greta Garbo and other Hollywood luminaries. On his bookshelves were his own books on early nineteenth century British politics, jostling alongside the complete works of Noel Coward and Terence Rattigan. There was Walter Bagehot and Burke, the Pleiade editions of Proust and Mallarmé and a rare signed and limited edition of The Collected Limericks of Maurice Bowra. Memories came back in a torrent.

"It doesn't seem like forty years," I said fatuously.

"It does to me," said Dr. Soper, "but then I'm an historian. I know what a fickle jade Time is. Just think back to the seventies and you'll become aware how remote those times are. No Internet, no twitter, no mobile phones, precious little media coverage for the young and talentless."

"No women."

"No women in college, you mean? No, not officially. That still gives me rather a shock. There they are hanging around the quad, texting each other as if they own the place which of course they do; sitting down on the floor with their backs to the bars of the Shelley Memorial and eating flavoured yoghurt out of little pots. Gone are the times when you would watch them creep furtively out of an undergraduate's rooms in the early dawn and wonder if this was the moment to have an earnest talk with the gentleman in question. I took my duties as Dean seriously in those days, you know. Ah, *ou sont les neiges d'antan*? In those days, as they used to say on the wireless, we made our own amusements."

"Talking of which, do you remember the Delusionists? And the Delusionists' dinner?"

"Do I? Of course I do! How could I forget?"

It was a strange business, that one dinner of the Delusionists, with its shocking and sinister aftermath.

In the summer of my second year my friend Sarath Rajasinha, then a fellow undergraduate, now a habitué of the Sri Lankan corridors of power, invited me to join a dining club of his called the Delusionists. In those days Rajasinha was much given to theorising about the nature of human identity, before the hard business of politics knocked all that nonsense out of him. His theory was that we all search for our identity by trying on a series of masks until we finally discover the one that fits. We must all therefore be deluded in order to become undeluded and we look for these delusions through the lives of others. That was his theory anyway; but maybe it was just an excuse for dressing up and having fun.

Before one sets up a dining club one needs, or used to need, the sponsorship (and attendance) of one of the fellows of this college and to this end Rajasinha approached Dr. Soper who was, as it happened enthusiastic about the project. It was decided that the Delusionists would spend a whole day dressed as their favourite delusion and in the evening would dine together in the Arlington Rooms. It was Dr. Soper, I believe, who proposed a theme for these delusions and he suggested that for our first day we should choose the poets we most admired or would like to be. I was currently under the influence of Swinburne so I went as the Sage of Putney, despite not having red hair nor an addiction to beer and babies. Matthew Plowman, the would-be actor, went, rather predictably, as Shakespeare; and Sproole, the future Tory cabinet minister, had to be dissuaded by Dr. Soper from choosing Sylvia Plath (too suicidal), so went instead as Wordsworth because Dr. Soper insisted that both he and the great Lakelander both looked like elderly sheep. Rajasinha, with characteristic perversity, had set his heart on Emily Dickinson which meant his parading round all day in a skirt he had borrowed from the OUDS wardrobe and a curious hat with a feather in it. That Miss Dickinson wore a skirt, I have no doubt, but scholarly research has yet to come up with anything definite about the Belle of Amherst's preferred headgear. Dr. Soper had fairly early on chosen Lord Byron as his man and he found a black cloak with a blue silk lining which, he said, made him a dead ringer for the incestuous peer. Perhaps his gold-rimmed spectacles slightly detracted from the effect, but this is was a minor cavil.

There were about a dozen of us altogether and I forget who the rest came as but I do remember Rupert Stilling because he chose to come as himself. In spite of Rajasinha's protest that this went utterly against the spirit of the whole event, Stilling was insistent. He was, after all, already a published poet. Even in those days one tended to give way to Rupert Stilling.

Rupert Stilling was tall, golden haired, fine featured, a young Apollo, but his vanity was of a discreet order. He was not at all flamboyant in his costume, favouring soft pastel colours and quite conventional jackets and trousers, even ties on occasion. It was simply the way he carried himself that made one aware of a formidable presence. "There! Look! That's Poetry in Motion," we would say as he wafted his way, head held high around Oxford. Voltaire once remarked that "the vanity of little men consists in talking only of themselves; the vanity of the great consists in never doing so." If this is true, then Rupert Stilling undoubtedly belonged to the second category. There was no need for him to draw attention to himself: he simply knew that all eyes would be upon him.

"Ah, yes! Rupert Stilling," said Dr. Soper when I reminded him. "A coming man in those days. Hadn't quite come, but acted as if he had. Always wore powder blue or beige. *Ou sont les beiges d'antan?* Ah... A career poet, if ever there was one. Was one of the first undergraduates to befriend A. H. Weston, if I remember rightly."

A. H. Weston, the great radical poet of the 1930s had come, after decades of wandering, to spend his last years in Oxford and had been granted rooms at the college of which he and his fellow poet of an earlier generation, Shelley, had been alumni. Both had left the college under something of a cloud, Shelley for atheism, Weston for something even less metaphysical, but both had been, in their different ways welcomed back into its bosom. Weston had been granted some handsome rooms in the Radcliffe Quad and Shelley a cold marble fishmonger's slab behind an elegant wrought iron cage, there to be imprisoned forever by the authorities who had once expelled him.

"I often think," said Dr. Soper, "that what did for poor old Percy Bysshe was his dogmatism. It had to be 'The Necessity of Atheism,' you see. Now had it been The Possibiliity or even the Probability of Atheism, that would have been more in line with the spirit of our college. We have always prided ourselves on our tolerance. But can you, or should you tolerate intolerance? That is the question that we historians of the liberal mind perpetually ask ourselves. And, characteristically, we come to no definite conclusion."

Weston would hold court most mornings in a café in the High Street called Jack's and there one would go to sit at his feet, and watch him spill cappuccino down his front and stub out endless cigarettes into his saucer. (Yes, you were allowed to smoke in those days.) He had one of those deeply etched faces which are described as "lived in." This may once have been true, but I had my doubts as to whether it was now permanently occupied. To most people, including myself, he would deliver a set routine of anecdotes and aphorisms which never varied and if one encountered him after two o'clock in the afternoon he was usually too drunk even to recognise you.

He made one exception to this rather lifeless demeanour and that was with regard to Rupert Stilling. Whenever Stilling entered Jack's, perhaps with a fresh poem for Weston to inspect the rest of us would feel utterly superfluous. We knew that all of Weston's attention would be directed towards Stilling, and not half-heartedly. There was a steeliness in both of them which recognised mutual interest and ambition as well as mutual talent. They looked well together and, I am sure, knew it: Weston the baggy and battered old mariner of uncharted seas, Stilling the fresh-faced, golden young adventurer. What a subject for a Victorian painter they would have made.

My memories of the Delusionists' dinner are distinctly patchy, but Dr. Soper was able to fill in the gaps. "On these occasions, the trick is always to keep your glass at least half full," said Dr. Soper. "That way you never drink too much. And have plenty of water with it. I have given this piece of advice to countless generations of undergraduates, but they never take heed. Also, a nice cup of Horlicks before and after to line the stomach is an excellent wheeze."

I remember giving an impassioned and, I am sure, inaccurate rendering of Swinburne's Dolores (Our Lady of Pain), and Rajasinha tripping over his skirt while trying to remember "Because I could not stop for Death." Then there was a long and animated argument with Dr. Soper who insisted that Swinburne's and Lord Melbourne's obsession with corporal punishment was entirely due to their Etonian education. I tried to defend Eton, but did not succeed. I kept saying: "look at me. Perfectly normal! Perfectly normal!" which did not help. At each repetition Dr. Soper brayed with laughter. I was a little drunk.

Towards the end of the dinner, at the Sauternes, perhaps even the Port stage, Stilling said: "Arthur Weston said he might drop in on us." This news was greeted with some enthusiasm. Stilling till now had been rather stiff and aloof, particularly during the early part of the evening, but the wine had finally got to him. He began telling us that Weston was a great genius and that he, Stilling, was the only one who truly understood him. Almost to a man we agreed that this was so, though how we knew this was a mystery.

I think someone was throwing Brazil nuts about and Dr. Soper was calling him to order when Weston finally arrived. He was carrying a pile of books under his arm and looked even more dilapidated than usual. We offered him Port which he rejected with an expression of disgust and demanded whisky. Somehow the whisky was procured. He had obviously been drinking for some time before his arrival.

The books he had been carrying were copies of his most recent book of verse *Minos and Narcissus* which had been delivered to him that day by the publishers. He insisted that, in celebration of this, every one of us should have a copy. Fortunately, there were just enough copies to go round. Then we began to clamour for them to be signed by him. Several of us had pens in our pockets and we produced them for him. He stared at the pens with bewilderment and then revulsion.

"No! No!" He said. "I couldn't possibly. I couldn't write anything with those disgusting modern things: biros and felt tips and other such rubbish. Out of the question. I have a pen in my room... I have a pen which old Tom Eliot gave me on the publication of my first volume Angelus. He told me that the pen had once belonged to Browning. Great chap, but, oh dear he does go on, doesn't he? Browning, I mean, not Tom Eliot, though come to think of it.... Where was I? No. I will sign your books, but only with Browning's pen. That'll be something to tell the grandchildren, eh? Back in two shakes of a Lamb's Tale from Shakespeare."

And with that Weston rose very unsteadily to his feet and staggered out of the room. My recollections after that are again hazy, but I know that some of us waited a considerable while for Weston to return with Browning's pen, but he never did. Eventually, at Dr. Soper's prompting we dispersed.

And that would have been that, rather an anticlimax, but for one thing. The following morning Weston was found dead in his rooms in the Radcliffe Quad.. There were signs of a struggle and Weston had received the fatal blow to the back of his head from it having been banged against the marble chimney piece. For several days the college swarmed with police and we were interrogated repeatedly. Dr. Soper seemed a ubiquitous and calming influence at that time. He had that curious historian's ability for seeing things from a longer perspective.

"Was that business ever resolved?" I asked him. "Was anyone arrested? I really don't remember."

"Officially the case remains open. No one was arrested, let alone charged." Something in the way Dr. Soper said this suggested that he knew more than he was letting on. I decided to provoke him.

I said: "Everyone thought Weston had gone off and picked up some rough trade in the town, brought him back to his rooms and there was a quarrel over money or something."

"Ah! Rough Trade. The Love That Dare Not Spell Its Name. No, I knew it couldn't be that. You see, I checked with George at the Porter's Lodge and Weston had not left college that night, nor had anyone alien come in. The Police took George to be an unreliable witness, mainly because of the colour of his language, and his rather farouche manners, but I knew him to be scrupulously observant about such things. So, really it had to be one of the Delusionists."

"But why? Which one? It wasn't me," I said feeling a sudden and wholly irrational access of guilt. "And it couldn't have been Rajasinha. He was far too drunk and still wearing a skirt."

"Oh, I found out who did it a couple of days after the killing," he said.

"Good God! How? And what proof have you got?"

"Fetch me that book," said Dr. Soper pointing to the bookcase. "The one just to the right of The Collected Limericks of Maurice Bowra"

I took down a slim volume in a drab paper cover. It was Minos and

Narcissus by A. H. Weston.

"Now look at the flyleaf."

I looked. In spidery writing was written the words: With Browning's pen May 1973 A. H. Weston.

"But it's signed!" I said.

"Precisely," said Dr. Soper.

"That's impossible. Weston didn't come back to sign our books. He just disappeared,"

"Yes, but I had a feeling that one of you went to his rooms to get the book signed. I just needed to find out which one."

"You mean you searched all the Delusionists' rooms?"

"I was the Dean, you know. But actually I only had to search one set of rooms. It was the first one I tried. I had guessed which one of you it was, and I guessed correctly."

This time it was my turn to guess: "Rupert Stilling?"

"Precisely. The only man who came to the Delusionists' Dinner as himself. That bespeaks an egoism which makes a man capable of anything. You see, undergraduates divide roughly into two categories. There were those like you who were still floundering around, tasting the delights on offer and not quite sure what they were going to do with their lives, but open to possibilities. Then there were the ones like Rupert who thought they knew precisely where they were going and were prepared to exploit Oxford for all it was worth to that end. I tend to admire the latter but prefer the company of the former. I had the feeling that Rupert was not one of those people who give up on getting a first edition Weston signed. Moreover, he would want it signed there and then. He was that sort of person. After I had found his copy, I summoned him to my rooms for sherry and macaroons and had it out with him. After a lot of nonsense he eventually admitted that he had gone to Weston's rooms to get the book signed. Weston in his inebriated state had become amorous with Young Apollo and insisted on his *droit de seigneur*. Rupert resisted rather too strenuously and a struggle ensued with fatal results for the older poet. Rupert broke down and begged me not to tell the police. I told him that our conversation was confidential and my Dean's duties did not include snitching – is that the word: 'snitching'? – to the police. Of course I told him he should not make a habit of this sort of thing. Ah... I kept his signed copy of the Weston book so it wouldn't incriminate him, and as a memento. *Memento mori*, I suppose. Since then I have watched Rupert Stilling's career with interest. It would appear to have been blameless."

"So you let him off."

"Had the police come close to the truth, I would not have stood in their way. But I was not going to be the pram in the hallway to his undoubted promise. Besides, in one way or another we are all of us serving a life sentence for what we've done in the past. Rupert gave up poetry and has become, as you know, a well-known novelist. He was kind enough to send me a copy of his Booker Prize Winning work last year, charmingly inscribed too. Very worthy: not a bundle of laughs, but that's Rupert. I feel my decision not to shop him has paid off though. Every Oxford Undergraduate should be allowed to get away with one murder... Now then, about this time I usually partake of a cup of Horlicks and a cucumber sandwich. Ah... Would you care to join me?"

WE WHO SING BENEATH THE GROUND

Mark Morris

The village school was not quite at the highest point of the steep main street, but it was elevated and isolated enough for Stacy to see the sea through the chain-link fence that bordered the far side of the playground. She could smell the sea from here too, crisp and salty, especially on a day like today, when a brisk November wind bowled up and over the hill, unimpeded by the buildings and patches of woodland that proliferated further inland.

She'd always wanted to live in Cornwall. She'd been in love with the place since spending family holidays here as a kid with her parents and her elder brother Paul. She had such happy memories of Fowey – Daphne Du Maurier's house, and the annual regatta with its carnival procession and its hilarious pasty-eating contest, Looe Beach, where the seagulls would steal the food right out of your hand if you didn't remain vigilant at all times, and beautiful fishing villages like Mousehole and Polperro, which to her had seemed deliciously mysterious with their tales of smugglers and pirates.

Carl hadn't been keen on moving so far south, but after their divorce two years ago she'd thought: *What's to stop me?* They had no children to complicate matters – when things had initially started going wrong between them she'd blamed her own inability to conceive, but with hindsight she realised that Carl's increasing lack of consideration and reliability had been far more pertinent factors – and so she had started looking for teaching jobs in the area.

It had taken nine months, but eventually she'd been offered the deputy headship of the little primary school in Porthfarrow (only thirty eight pupils and five members of staff). Accepting the job had entailed her biting the bullet and taking a twenty per cent wage drop, but in her opinion the positives of her new life far outweighed the negatives. Life was slower here, and less stressful, and more community-minded, all of which suited her down to the ground. She could walk to and from work instead of having to negotiate the nerve-shredding hassle of the Manchester rush hour, which meant she not only saved on petrol but was fitter than she'd been since she was a teenager.

Okay, so she might not have the dating opportunities here that Manchester offered, but that was something that bothered Stacy's mum more than Stacy herself. And small though the village was, it wasn't as if she hadn't turned a few heads since buying her little white cottage just a couple of turns off the High Street. Cliff Monroe, who owned the hardware store, had taken her out to dinner a couple of times, and although he hadn't exactly set her pulse a-fluttering, he was a nice guy with a nice smile – and interesting too. Although he'd been born in the village, and had confessed to her that he'd probably die in it, he'd travelled the world a bit before putting down his roots. Plus he owned a boat. Not that she was particularly materialistic. In fact, she'd become far less so since leaving the city – and Carl – behind.

The little yellow bus, with its daily contingent of more than half the school's pupil population, crept into view at the bottom of the winding, leaf-strewn hill. There had been a couple of days last winter when the icy roads had proved too treacherous for the ancient vehicle, as a result of which those pupils who relied on it – most of whom lived in isolated farmhouses and remote cottages out in the sticks – had had to stay home.

As the bus wheezed to a halt and disgorged its twenty or so passengers, Stacy crossed the playground and opened the little iron gate to admit the chattering hordes. On Friday she had announced that today would be Show and Tell day, and so she was pleased to see that most of the children were carrying something other than their school bags. Richard Charlton had a skateboard, Maisie Flynn had a photo album, and Kylie Kendall, who was crazy about gymnastics and often had to be stopped from cartwheeling about the playground in case she did somebody a mischief, had a large plastic wallet stuffed with certificates and rosettes. Little Adam North, whose black and permanently tousled hair was like an ink dab above his pale, secretive, mole-like face, was clutching something long and curved, wrapped in newspaper.

"What have you got there, Adam?" Stacy asked. "I hope it's not a Samurai sword?"

She had made it an ambition to get Adam to smile – he was a solitary soul who barely spoke unless spoken to, and who hardly ever showed emotion, be it anger, unhappiness, mirth or joy. If she had been a betting woman, Stacy would have put money on Adam turning up today with nothing to show the class, and so she was secretly delighted that her idea, although not a particularly original one, had at least motivated him to make an effort.

As always he responded to her flippant comment with deadly seriousness. "No, miss."

"Well, that's good," she said, and laughed more heartily than the occasion merited. "We wouldn't want you to…"

She'd been about to say 'slice off any heads', but at the last second it occurred to her that the phrase was inappropriate, given the terrorist atrocities that turned the news into a rolling account of seemingly ceaseless depravity and horror every day. She hesitated a little too long, glanced again at the sea as if seeking inspiration, and in the end muttered lamely, "…do any damage, would we?"

Adam regarded her with a deadpan expression. "No, miss," he said again, and followed his fellow pupils into the school.

Show and Tell, which took place between morning break and lunchtime, turned out, on the whole, to be a great success. Most of the children were loquacious and enthusiastic, and Daniel Roberts' account of his recently departed grandfather's heroism during the Second World War, as he held up the old man's medals, was so poignant that Stacy felt tears pricking at the backs of her eyes.

As each child finished his or her turn in the spotlight, a mass of increasingly fewer hands would shoot up and a chorus of "Please, miss! Me next!" would fill the classroom.

Perhaps inevitably, the only child who didn't stick up his hand was Adam. He sat near the back, his face expressionless, the strange, curved, newspaper-wrapped object held protectively against his body. Stacy thought he might have remained there all day, if, with six or seven children still to take their turn, she hadn't said, "What about you, Adam? Do you want to go next?"

He blinked. Shrugged. Made no move to rise from his seat.

"Come on," she said gently, beckoning him forward. "Show us what you've brought."

The other children turned to look at Adam as if they'd only just noticed he was among them. Looking neither intimidated nor resigned, he rose slowly from his seat and ambled to the front of the class. He turned to face his fellow pupils and for a moment just stood there, holding his newspaper-wrapped bundle. They stared back at him silently.

"Do you want me to help you unwrap it? Is it fragile?" Stacy coaxed.

Adam glanced at her, then unceremoniously pulled away the sheets of newspaper and dropped them on the floor.

Revealed beneath was a curved half-moon of what appeared to be a pearly, shell-like substance. It was smooth on one side and serrated, or ragged, on the other. It was perhaps a metre long, and Stacy's first thought was that it was a large boomerang, her second that it was something organic – part of the exoskeleton of some sea creature, perhaps. The children craned forward, their faces puzzled. Stacy held out her hand.

"May I see?"

Adam hesitated for just a second, then handed the object over.

It was lighter than she had expected, and there was a rime of what appeared to be dirt on one side of it.

"What is it, miss?" Caroline Fairley asked.

Stacy had no idea. She turned to Adam with a smile. "Perhaps Adam can tell us?"

He looked at her blankly.

"Don't you know?" one of the boys – it might have been Luke Cooke – sneered.

"You shouldn't have brought it in if you don't know," another boy, who was yet to be summoned to the front of the class, piped up sulkily.

"Shhh," Stacy said. "Don't interrupt when it's not your turn to speak. It's rude." The class quietened down. She glanced again at Adam. "If you can't tell us what it is, Adam, can you tell us where it's from?"

Quietly Adam said, "Found it."

"You found it?" Stacy repeated it loudly, for the benefit of those who hadn't heard. "Where did you find it? On the beach?"

He shook his head. "Farm."

"The farm where you live, you mean?"

He nodded.

"And whereabouts on the farm did you find it?"

His eyes narrowed, as though he was wondering how much he ought to reveal. "Field."

"I see. And was it lying in the field?"

He hesitated, then shook his head. "Was buried."

"And you dug it up?"

So quietly she wasn't sure she'd heard him correctly, he said, "Came up by itself."

"What did he say, miss?" one of the girls chirruped, and Stacy was about to reply that the buried object had worked its way to the surface of the soil, before realising she wasn't sure entirely how that process would work. To avoid having to explain it she held up the object and said, "So what do we think this is, class? Hands up. No shouting out."

The hands went up, and Stacy pointed to each in turn.

"An alien sword!"

"A shark's jaw!"

"A dinosaur bone!"

"A hockey stick for a caveman!"

Some of the suggestions made the children hoot with laughter, and Stacy laughed along with them. At one point she glanced at Adam, who was still standing silently beside her, and saw that he wasn't joining in with the laughter. He was gazing at his classmates, or at least gave the impression that he was doing so. Looking at his unfocused eyes, though, Stacy couldn't help wondering whether he was staring at something else entirely.

The next day, Tuesday, Adam didn't turn up for school. Between registration and morning assembly, Stacy popped her head into the office.

"Have Adam North's parents rung to explain why he's absent today?"

Moira, the school secretary, a blowsy, middle-aged woman who wore a lot of orange, scowled as if Stacy was accusing her of not doing her job.

"Not yet. I was about to call them. It's on my list."

"I'll do it," said Stacy.

"You don't have to."

"No, but I want to. So could you please give me the number?"

She didn't know why she felt compelled to take personal action. Was it because the boy was such an enigma? She told herself it might be useful to speak to Adam's parents anyway, regardless of his absenteeism, perhaps call them in for a chat. She tried to remember whether she'd met them at any of the three Parents' Evenings she'd attended since arriving in Porthfarrow, and couldn't recall. Not that that was entirely unusual. Some parents were simply too busy.

Moira gave her the number with a disapproving huff, and Stacy punched it in. The phone rang out at the other end. She let it ring fifteen times before replacing the receiver.

Moira looked almost triumphant. "The Norths are farmers. They'll be busy during the day."

Out in the fields, digging up alien swords, Stacy thought, and said, "They're bound to be in at some point. Keep trying, will you?"

Moira sniffed.

Next day was the same story. Adam was a no-show; his parents didn't call; their phone rang out, unanswered.

"Shall I write them a letter?" Moira offered, albeit in a tone that suggested she thought the action onerous and unnecessary.

Stacy shook her head. "No, I'll take a drive out there after school, see what's what."

Moira pulled a face. "Are you sure? It's a long way."

"It's fifteen miles at the most."

"Like I said, a long way. Pardon me for saying so, but don't you think you're making a fuss?"

"No I don't. I happen to be worried about Adam."

"He's only one boy."

"And he's the one who's currently causing me worry. I'm his teacher and he's not attending school. It's my job to be concerned."

Moira sighed. She conveyed an awful lot in that sigh. "They won't thank you for it."

"Who won't?"

"The Norths. They're a funny lot. Keep themselves to themselves. Always have. The only reason Adam's not in school is because John North'll have him helping out on the farm. They've never been big on education, that lot."

"Well, I'll just have to point out the error of their ways to them then, won't I?" Stacy said.

Moira rolled her eyes. "Rather you than me."

At 4:15 that afternoon, Stacy found herself driving along a narrow country road between high hedges that her sat nav was trying to convince her didn't exist. The wind had picked up considerably in the past few hours, and was making a high-pitched whining sound as it attempted to squeeze through the doorframe gaps of her little Ford Fiesta. The sky was deepening to a muddy blue blotched with muddier clouds, and leaves which had been red and gold when she had set off, but which now looked black, swirled in mad flocks through the twin beams of her headlights.

"Make a U-turn when necessary," her sat nav instructed her.

"Shut the fuck up!" Stacy retorted and jabbed at the button to silence it as savagely as if it was the speaker's eye. Distracted, she only registered the dark opening on her left, and the lopsided sign beside it, after she had passed them by. She hit the brakes, and then, hoping that nothing was beetling along the narrow, winding lane behind her, put the car into reverse.

And there it was. An opening in the hedge marked by a pair of rotting gateposts. Sagging from the left-hand post, the paint faded, was the sign she'd seen: North Field Farm.

"Hallelujah," she muttered, and manoeuvred the car around in the lane until it was in a position to nose its way between the posts and on to the dirt track beyond. Flanking the track were huge, flat, muddy fields, bordered in the distance by stunted trees. After the narrow confines of the country lanes the sudden space was almost bewildering. Ahead of her, perhaps five hundred metres away at the far end of the track, she spied her destination: a huddle of buildings that were little more than silhouettes in the encroaching twilight.

Wondering whether the Norths had gone away for a while (*Do farmers go away? If so, who looked after their livestock?*) she began to meander along the track. It was muddy and rutted, and she took it slowly, keeping the car in second gear. Above the grumble of the engine and the whistling of the wind, she could hear the sustained screeching of what sounded like crows coming from somewhere on her left and glanced in that direction. Jutting from the centre of the field, perhaps a hundred and fifty metres away, she saw five lopsided standing stones, above and around which were indeed a flock of crows, flapping and cawing.

Her eyes were swivelling to face front again when one of the stones moved. Or at least, she thought it did; in truth, the impression was both slight and fleeting. It was enough, though, to make Stacy stamp on the brake and bring the car to a jolting halt. As the seatbelt locked across her chest she gasped. By the time she had settled back into her seat she was aware her heart was beating rapidly.

She turned to look again at the stones. Stared at them for a full ten seconds. They were motionless. Yet one of them had seemed to... What? Lean over? Bend in the middle? The idea was ludicrous. It must have been a trick of the fading light, perhaps exacerbated by the constant whirlwind of swirling leaves and circling crows.

She shuddered, as though sloughing off the vagaries of her own imagination, faced front again, and put the car into gear. The dark buildings loomed larger as she approached them, until eventually they filled enough of her windscreen to mostly blot out a sky that was now the colour of slightly faded denim. She passed through another set of equally rotten gateposts and in to a yard of slick, uneven cobbles, across which was strewn a combination of rubble, muddy straw and sizeable clumps of either mud or manure.

Peering at the farmhouse bathed in the glow of her headlights, and at the shadowy buildings set back on either side of it – the most prominent of which appeared to be a barn on the right, which was twice the height of the house itself – Stacy found herself hoping, for the first time, that the Norths *wouldn't* be home, after all. The farm where Adam lived with his parents was a *dismal* place. Not just run-down, but squalid enough to be unsettling. There were tiles missing from the farmhouse roof, the windows were filthy, and the stonework was black and crumbling. Against the side of the house were stacked rotting planks, rusting machinery, stone slabs and large, white plastic bags, many of which were split and leaking what might have been grain or sand or rubble.

For a good minute, Stacy sat in her car, the engine running and the heater on, her hands gripping the steering wheel so tightly that her forearms ached. Despite having come all this way, she thought about turning the car round and driving all the way home again – thought very seriously about it. Then she muttered, "Fuck it," and cut the engine.

As she did so, the headlights cut out too, and she was plunged into blackness. But then, as her eyes adjusted to the dim light still bleeding from the darkening sky, her surroundings acquired a sketchy definition. Pushing the driver's door open and placing one foot on the muddy ground, she felt the wind biting into her. She was leaning forward when an extra strong gust buffeted the door and tried to slam it shut on her leg. She caught it just in time, heaving it back open as she stood up. Instantly her dark reddish hair began to whip about her head. Stepping away from the car she found she didn't even have to push the door shut again; the wind did it for her.

"Hello?" she shouted, but the wind whipped her voice away. She picked her way across the filthy yard towards the farmhouse. Why, if the Norths were here, was there not a light showing in any of the windows? She reached the door and used the metal knocker, in the shape of a fox's head, to rap on it four times. Faintly she could still hear the crows in the field screeching and cawing. The sound reminded her of a full-blooded, drunken family argument, like the ones they always had on *EastEnders* at Christmas.

There was no answer to her knock. *I'll try once more*, she thought, *then I'll go home.*

But after the next four raps had elicited no response, she found herself trying the doorknob. It felt greasy beneath her grip, but it turned. The door opened.

Tentatively she stepped forward, edging into the widening gap. "Hello?" she called. "Anyone home?" She wrinkled her nose. The house smelled… mouldy. As if food had been left out. As if the building's occupants had been cooped up for too long without a wash or a change of clothes.

Was that *all* it was? She hovered on the threshold, unsure whether to go further. Slipping her hand into her pocket, she gripped the reassuring shape of her mobile. Should she call the police? But what would she tell them? That she had found a dark and empty house? No, she had to have more evidence before her claim that something was wrong here would be taken seriously.

Her arm snaked out to the left, fingers stretching for a light switch. For a horrible moment she imagined touching a face in the darkness, then she found what she was looking for. The light switch depressed with a chunky click; for a split-second she was convinced that nothing would happen, that the power would be off. Then she was screwing up her eyes, blinded by the light that filled the room.

Slowly her vision adjusted. Squinting, she looked around. The door had opened directly into a big farmhouse kitchen. It was a tip, the work surfaces and the big wooden table covered with dirty dishes, empty tins, food that had been left out. There was a broken mug on the floor, the spillage from which was a sticky-looking stain. In one corner were a jumble of clothes and muddy boots.

Stacy's eyes widened as she noticed Adam's school bag dumped on a chair. Above it, on the table, between a bowl that held a detritus of brown sludge and the evidence of what that sludge consisted of – an open Coco Pops packet and a half-empty bottle of milk – was the strange curved object of pearly-white, shell-like material that Adam had brought to school a couple of days before.

"Adam?" Stacy called. Her voice echoed, as if the house was hollow, or at least devoid of carpets. "Mr and Mrs North?"

A door leading out of the kitchen on the far side of the room was standing ajar. Stacy glanced at it, then up at the ceiling, as if anticipating the creak of movement. But there was nothing. And all at once she knew instinctively that the house was empty – of life, at least. So where –?

From outside came a hideous, high wailing sound.

Instantly Stacy felt as though her body had been doused in freezing water. She hunched her shoulders to her ears, opened her eyes wide and released a shocked gasp. The wailing continued for three or four seconds, then died away. It sounded forlorn, even despairing. It also sounded utterly chilling – and utterly inhuman.

For a moment Stacy couldn't – didn't want to – move. She considered slamming the door of the farmhouse, sliding into place any bolts that she could find. Then she thought of what it would be like to spend a night inside the building while the wailing thing, whatever it was, prowled the darkness outside. And rather than face that prospect she found herself instead calculating how many running steps it might take to reach her car, how many seconds after that it would be before she could turn the car round in the rutted yard and hightail it out of there.

The door to the farmhouse creaked open a little, and she jumped – but it was only the wind. Oddly, it was this that broke the rising spiral of fear inside her, enabled her to view what she had heard more logically – or at least less hysterically.

Perhaps it had simply been the wind, rushing through the buildings to the rear of the farmhouse, warping wood and even metal with its strength and making it screech in protest. Or if not the wind, then an animal, or several animals, in distress. Hungry pigs maybe? Cows that needed milking?

Should she check? She didn't want to leave animals to suffer. Neither could she drive away from here without finding out... well, *something*. Because at the moment there was no guarantee that the police would investigate if she reported what she'd found – or rather, hadn't.

She took a deep breath, then stepped back out of the house and closed the door behind her. The wind lashed at her body, intermittently blinding her with her own hair. She wished she had something to tie it back with, but she didn't. Dead leaves swirled and swooped, making a rat-like scuttling as they swept across the ground. She looked longingly at her car, then turned away from it and headed towards the looming shape of the barn behind the farmhouse.

She'd gone no more than half a dozen steps when she stopped. Something large and bulky, further up the track, was squatting beside the wall of the barn, or perhaps leaning on it. She held her flapping hair away from her face, vowing that the instant the thing moved she would turn and bolt for her car. Then she realised what it was. A tractor. Nothing but a common-or garden tractor. Now that she had identified it, she wondered how she could ever have imagined it was anything else. *Get a grip, girl,* she told herself, and laughed, though almost immediately she swallowed the sound with a grimace, because it hadn't sounded like a laugh at all; it had sounded like a sob.

She resumed walking, keeping to the ridge between the channels where the wheels of the tractor and perhaps other farm vehicles had compressed the ground. The large door of the barn was facing her, the wood dark grey in the twilight. The black line between the edge of the door and the squared-off arch of wooden wall into which it was set was wide enough for her to realise that the door was slightly ajar. As she came to within five metres of the barn an extra-strong gust of wind plucked the door a little further open. As it widened with a grinding creak, Stacy saw a glimmer of light from within.

Her heartbeat quickened. She couldn't decide whether the glow was a welcome sight or the opposite. It was a sign of life, at least, but that didn't stop her from feeling wary; didn't stop a little internal voice from whispering that the light might be a lure. She opened her mouth to call out, then closed it again. Perhaps in this instance discretion might be the better part of valour. Her hair was still whipping around her head and she could feel the tiny hairs on her arms prickling as they rose.

By the time she reached the barn door she was creeping like a burglar. The glow from within was dim but steady. Not a candle flame then, which would have flickered, but certainly something that didn't cast much light – a lantern of some sort, perhaps.

The gap between door and frame was wide enough for her to slip through. As she did so, her eyes darted everywhere, her senses alert for attack. The lamp was on a wooden box just inside the door, its area of illumination fairly minimal. Certainly the majority of the vast space in front of her was in shadow, dwindling even further back to a darkness so impenetrable she couldn't see the far wall.

There was a smell in the barn, hot and… what was the word? *Visceral.* Yes, that was it. Not rank, exactly, but unpleasant all the same, like the thick, lingering odour of someone's meaty belch after a rich meal. Could it be the smell of animals? Horses or pigs? Or maybe it was silage? Some sort of organic matter used on the crops?

Her eyes continued to dart left and right as she listened. If there were stealthy movements in the barn she couldn't hear them beneath the shuddering and creaking of the wooden walls as the wind battered against them. After a few seconds she moved forward, her steps light and tentative, her weight shifting carefully on to each probing foot to lessen its impact with the ground. Something loud enough to be heard above the wind suddenly shifted in front of her. A rustle of straw? If so, caused by what? A rat – or something heavier?

Oh, for God's sake! she thought, and almost before she had decided she was going to do it, she barked, "Who's there?"

She was answered not by a voice, but a sound – a deep and oddly wistful groan. It sounded like the involuntary sound a child might make turning over in its sleep, albeit amplified a hundredfold. Yet, although it was loud, the sound was fleeting, and tangled up in the still-howling wind, and therefore impossible to identify. It was disquieting enough, though, to set off a jittering in her belly, to make her feel suddenly claustrophobic, trapped by the dark. All at once the urge to see what was in front of her overwhelmed her natural caution, her desire to remain undetected. With a trembling hand she snatched her phone from her pocket and switched on the 'Torch' app, shining it in front of her.

She couldn't help it – she let out a gasp that was sharp enough to emerge as a breathy scream. No more than two metres away was a circular pit that, as far as she could tell, stretched from one wall of the barn to the other. She thought of animal traps, in the bottom of which might be sharpened stakes designed to pierce the animal's body as it fell. *Oh God, oh God.* Was that what this was? She tilted her phone down, shining it into the hole.

It wasn't black down there, as she had expected. It was red.

Blood red.

And she could see something moving. Something huge and glistening and slug-like.

She jerked back so quickly she stumbled and almost fell. Her fingers sprang open, an involuntary defence mechanism, and her phone flew out of her hand and into the hole. She watched in horror as it dropped out of reach, briefly illuminating the wet red walls of the pit, before bouncing on the glistening, slowly uncoiling thing at the bottom and winking out.

Now she was in darkness, and she could smell the thing, its meaty, burpy stench, as it rose towards her. At least, she *imagined* it was rising towards her. Imagined it adhering to the walls, hauling its bulk upwards, extruding tentacles to coil around her limbs to ensnare her, pull her down.

"Won't hurt you," said a voice.

She whirled round with a scream. Squatting in the corner of the barn to the right of the door, just out of the reach of the lamplight, was a small figure. Her heart thumping, she stared at it, and then in a flinty voice she said, "Adam?"

The figure rose and stepped forward. Now the lamplight illuminated it from below, transforming its small, pale face into a skull-like mask. Stacy saw that Adam's hands were red. Blood red. Like the colour of the pit.

"It's old, but it's just a baby," he said. "Got no teeth. Likes meat, though."

Disjointed and staccato though his words were, Stacy thought this was the most she had ever heard him speak in one go. She glanced behind her, in the direction of the pit.

"What is it?" she asked.

"Told you. Just a baby."

"That thing in the pit is a *baby*?"

She saw shadows rushing into the creases his frown made.

"Ain't a pit," he said. "That's its mouth."

For a moment she couldn't make sense of his words. Then all at once she was hit by a revelation. The glistening thing in the red pit wasn't a creature. It was a *tongue*.

"Its mouth," she breathed. "You mean... there's more of it?"

"Lots more. Found its hand first. Came up through the soil. Then it started singing to me. In my head. Told me where to find its mouth, where to dig. Told me how to feed it."

Its hand... came up through the soil... Stacy thought of the standing stones in the field, how she could have sworn one of them had moved. She thought of the curved, shell-like object Adam had brought to school.

"Oh my God," she said. "Show and tell. That was one of its fingernails, wasn't it?"

He shrugged.

Her mind was whirling. "How big..." she breathed. "How big is this thing?"

"Big," he said, and frowned again. "Ain't a thing. It's a giant."

A giant. Cornish folklore was full of tales of giants. But none of them could possibly be true, could they?

A hysterical giggle bubbled its way into her throat. But she thought if she let it loose, if she gave rein to it, it might become something else. Might become terrified, helpless sobbing. She had to hold it together. Had to get back to her car and inform the authorities. Let them deal with this.

Sliding a glance from Adam's motionless figure to the barn door, she asked, "Where are your parents, Adam? Your mum and dad?"

For a moment Adam looked anguished. Then his face cleared. "He sang to me. He was hungry. I couldn't say no. It was quick. I used poison. Lots of it. On the animals too. But he's still hungry."

Oh God, oh God. Her mind kept repeating it, two panicked syllables, over and over. The jittering in her belly had extended to her limbs and she was shaking badly. Her mouth had gone so dry she couldn't even lick her lips.

She made a mighty effort. Unpeeled her tongue from the bottom of her mouth. Forced herself to swallow. When she spoke her voice was a rasp.

"I'm going now," she said. "Are you going to stop me?"

His expression was bland. His red hands, his bloody hands, hung by his sides. "No, miss."

She nodded and edged towards the door, her eyes never leaving him. He was only a ten-year-old kid, and a smaller than average one at that, but what if he had a knife? Or even a gun? Farmers owned guns, didn't they? If he made a sudden move she'd jump him. She wouldn't hesitate. He might only be a child, but she'd do all she could to get away.

She reached the door. Still he hadn't moved. He was no more than two metres away from her now. She said, "What are you going to do?"

He shrugged. "He'll be hungry again soon. He's always hungry."

She nodded, as if she understood, and slipped out of the door. As soon as she was outside she started running.

The wind howled around her, buffeting her body as though trying to stop her from leaving. She slithered in the mud, went down on one knee, then picked herself up and stumbled on. She glanced back at the barn, expecting to see Adam coming after her, a shotgun in his hands, but there was no sign of him. She started to shake again. To shake so badly she could barely stand. Then she realised it wasn't her who was shaking. It was the ground.

She staggered from one side of the track to the other. She fell. What was this? An earthquake?

The land was wrapped in a deep, dusky grey, but it wasn't quite dark yet. The sun was still hovering on the horizon, providing just enough light to see by.

But all at once a huge shadow raced across the ground, smothering the farmhouse and the yard where her car was parked, blotting out what little light there was. She saw it coming, a tide of black. She looked up.

The shape was vast, vaster than vast, against the darkening sky. She thought of what Adam had said about the creature in the ground, the creature whose open, wailing mouth was in the barn, and whose fingers were jutting from the soil of a farmer's field.

Won't hurt you, he had said. *It's just a baby.*

The ground shook again. The shadow passed over her like a vast tide.

Only one word filled Stacy's mind.

Mummy.

ABOUT THE AUTHORS

Colette de Curzon was born in 1927. The daughter of the then French Consul General, she wrote "Paymon's Trio" in 1949 in Portsmouth, at the age of 22. Having no knowledge of available routes to publication, she tucked it away in a folder of her work, where it remained until 2016 and was published in 2017 by Nicholas Royle of Nightjar Press. Mother of four grown-up daughters and three grandchildren, Colette died in March 2018.

A.K. Benedict read English at Cambridge and Creative Writing at the University of Sussex. She writes in a room filled with mannequins, clowns and teapots. Her debut novel, *The Beauty of Murder* (Orion), was shortlisted for an eDunnit award and is in development for an 8-part TV series. Her second novel, *Jonathan Dark or The Evidence of Ghosts* (Orion), was published in February 2016 and *The Stone House*, a tie-in novel for Doctor Who spin-off *Class*, was published by BBC Books in 2017.

Her poems and short stories have featured in journals and anthologies including *Best British Short Stories*, *Magma*, *Scaremongrel*, and *Great British Horror*. She is currently writing scripts, short stories, a standalone psychological thriller and the sequel to *The Beauty of Murder*. She lives in St Leonards-on-Sea with her dog, Dame Margaret Rutherford.

'Departures' was originally published in *New Fears* (Titan)

Charlotte Bond is an author, ghostwriter, freelance editor, reviewer and podcaster. Under her own name she has written within the genres of horror and dark fantasy. As a ghostwriter, she's tackled everything from romance to cozy mystery stories and YA novels. She is a reviewer for the *Ginger Nuts of Horror* website, as well as the British Fantasy Society. Her articles have appeared in such places as Tor.com and *Writing Magazine*. She is a co-host of the podcast, *Breaking the Glass Slipper*. "The Lies We Tell" was originally published in *Great British Horror 2: Dark Satanic Mills*

Georgina Bruce is a writer and teacher based in Edinburgh. Her stories have been published in *Black Static, Interzone, Strange Horizons* and various other zines and anthologies. She keeps a sporadically updated journal at www.georginabruce.com and tweets as @monster_soup. She is currently working on a novel in which the concerns of Philip K Dick meet the sensibilities of the feminist gothic… on the moon. "Book of Dreems" was originally published in *Black Static* #61, Nov/Dec 2017.

Ray Cluley is a British Fantasy Award winner with stories published in various magazines and anthologies. Some of these have been reprinted in various 'best of' volumes. His work has been translated into French, Polish, and Hungarian, with a Chinese version of his award-winning 'Shark! Shark!' due soon and German translation of his novella *Water For Drowning* rumoured to be in the works. *Probably Monsters*, his debut collection, is available from ChiZine Publications "In the Light of St. Ives" was originally published in *Terror Tales of Cornwall* (Telos)

Claire Dean's short stories have been widely published and reprinted in *Best British Short Stories 2011, 2014 & 2017* (Salt). *Marionettes, Into the Penny Arcade, Bremen* and *The Unwish* have all been published as chapbooks by Nightjar Press. Her short story collection *The Museum of Shadows and Reflections* came out with Unsettling Wonder in 2016. Claire lives in the north of England with her family. 'The Unwish' was originally published as a chapbook by Nightjar Press.

James Everington is a writer from Nottingham. Most of what he writes is dark, supernatural fiction, although not necessarily 'horror' in the blood and guts sense. His main influences are writers like Ramsey Campbell, Shirley Jackson, and Robert Aickman. He enjoys the unexplained, the psychological, and the ambiguous in his fiction.James drinks Guinness, if anyone's offering. "The Affair" was originally published in *Nightscript III*

Paul Finch is a novelist, screenwriter, short story writer and journalist, whose published and broadcast work covers a wide spectrum of genres, including crime, thrillers, horror, fantasy and science fiction. He has seen enormous success with his *Terror Tales* anthologies and DC 'Heck' Heckenburg novels. "Tools of the Trade" was originally published in *Great British Horror 2: Dark Satanic Mills*

Cate Gardner is a horror and fantastical author with over a hundred short stories published. Several of those stories appear in her collection *Strange*

Men in Pinstripe Suits . She is also the author of five novellas: *Theatre of Curious Acts, Barbed Wire Hearts, In the Broken Birdcage of Kathleen Fair, This Foolish & Harmful Delight* and *The Bureau of Them*.
"Fragments of a Broken Doll" was originally published in *Great British Horror 2: Dark Satanic Mills*

V.H. Leslie's stories have appeared in a range of speculative publications, including *Black Static, Interzone* and *Shadows and Tall Trees* and have been reprinted in a range of "Year's Best" anthologies. Leslie's debut short story collection, *Skein and Bone*, garnered comparisons to M.R. James and Shirley Jackson and was nominated for both the World Fantasy Award and the British Fantasy Award. Her novel *Bodies of Water* was hailed a "feminist ghost story" and was published by Salt Publishing and has also been translated into French.
    "Shell Baby" was originally published in *Shadows and Small Trees* #7

Daniel McGachey's stories have been anthologised in *The Black Book of Horror* and *BHF Book of Horror Stories* series, while his radio plays aired as instalments of *Imagination Theatre*. Dark Regions Press published his collection *They That Dwell in Dark Places*, many of the stories featuring the folklorist Dr Lawrence. Also for Dark Regions, *Sherlock Holmes: The Impossible Cases* pits Holmes against the supernatural, while further adventures feature in *The MX Book of New Sherlock Holmes Stories*. He is a regular contributor to *The Ghosts and Scholars M.R. James Newsletter*, and is working on a new ghost story collection.
    "Ting-a-Ling-a-Ling" was published as a stand-alone chapbook that was included with the *The Ghosts and Scholars M.R. James Newsletter*.

Laura Mauro's work has featured in Black Static and has previously been nominated for two British Fantasy Awards, and was recently shortlisted for a Shirley Jackson award ('Sun Dogs' appears in this anthology) Laura was born south east London and currently live in Essex, under extreme duress. When she's not making things up she enjoys reading, travelling, watching wrestling, playing video games, collecting tattoos, dyeing her hair strange colours and making up nicknames for her cats. 'Sun Dogs' was originally published in Shadows and Small Trees #7

Mark Morris has written over thirty books, among which are the novels *Toady, Stitch, The Immaculate, The Secret of Anatomy, Fiddleback, The Deluge* and four books in the popular Doctor Who range. He is also the author of three short story collections, *Close to the Bone*, *Long Shadows*, *Nightmare Light* and *Wrapped In Skin*, and several novellas. He is also the editor of the *Spectral Book of Horror* (two volumes) and and, as editor, New Fears (two volumes). "We Who Sing Beneath The Ground" was originally published in *Terror Tales of Cornwall*.

Reggie Oliver, according to Ramsey Campbell '...quite possibly our finest modern writer of spectral tales,' is an actor, director, playwright, and an award-winning author of fiction. Published work includes six plays, three novels, seven volumes of short stories. His stories have appeared in over sixty anthologies. "Love and Death" originally published in *The Scarlet Soul, Stories for Dorian Gray* (Swan River Press). 'A Day with the Delusionists' originally published in *Holidays From Hell* (Tartarus)

Nicholas Royle is the author of seven novels, two novellas and three volumes of short fiction. He has edited twenty anthologies of short stories and is also a senior lecturer in creative writing at the Manchester Writing School at Manchester Metropolitan University. Nicholas is also a head judge of the Manchester Fiction Prize,and also runs Nightjar Press, publishing original short stories as signed, limited-edition chapbooks. He works as an editor for Salt Publishing. "Dispossession" was originally published in *Shadows and Small Trees #7*

Mark West first wrote a collection of short stories called *Strange Tales* of short horror stories from 1987 to 1989 but began writing in the genre again in 1998, when he discovered the small press. Since then, he's had over ninety short stories published, two collections, most recently *Things We Leave Behind* (2017). He has written two novels, a novelette, a chapbook, four novellas; one of which, *Drive,* was nominated for a British Fantasy Award. His latest novella, *Polly*, was published in 2017.

"The Taste of Her" was originally published in *Things We Leave Behind*.

EDITOR'S THANKS AND ACKNOWLEDGEMENTS

First of all to Ian Whates, a legend among legends – thanks for getting this series up and running again! To all of the publishers, authors and readers who make this book what it is. Finally, to family Mains, and my ever faithful hound, Biscuit - an interesting air 'freshener' if there ever was one...

Cover art by Vincent Sammy

NewCon Press Novellas, Set 2

Simon Clark – Case of the Bedevilled Poet

His life under threat, poet Jack Crofton flees through the streets of war-torn London. He seeks sanctuary in a pub and falls into company with two elderly gentlemen who claim to be the real Holmes and Watson. Unconvinced but desperate, Jack shares his story, and Holmes agrees to take his case…

Alison Littlewood – Cottingley

A century after the world was rocked by news that two young girls had photographed fairies in the sleepy village of Cottingley, we finally learn the true nature of these fey creatures. Correspondence has come to light; a harrowing account written by village resident Lawrence Fairclough that lays bare the fairies' sinister malevolence.

Sarah Lotz – Body in the Woods

When an old friend turns up on Claire's doorstep one foul night and begs for her help, she knows she should refuse, but she owes him and, despite her better judgement, finds herself helping to bury something in the woods. Will it stay buried, and can Claire live with the knowledge of what she did that night?

Jay Caselberg – The Wind

Having moved to Abbotsford six months ago, Gerry reckons he's getting used to country life and the rural veterinary practice he's taken on. Nothing has prepared him, though, for the strange wind that springs up to stir the leaves in unnatural fashion, nor for the strikingly beautiful woman the villagers are so reluctant to talk about…

Cover art by Ben Baldwin

NewCon Press Novella Set 4: Strange Tales

Gary Gibson – Ghost Frequencies

Do the odd sounds – snatches of random conversation and even music – that are hampering Susan MacDonalds attempts to perfect a revolutionary form of communication represent 'ghosts' as some claim, deliberate sabotage as suggested by others, or is there an even more sinister explanation?

Adam Roberts – The Lake Boy

Cynthia lives in a small village in Cumbria, where none suspect her blemished past. Then a ghostly scar-faced boy starts to appear to her and strange lights manifest over Blaswater. What of married mother of two Eliza, who sets Cynthia's heart so aflutter? What can any of this mean for her place in the world?

Ricardo Pinto – Matryoshka

Lost in Venice in the aftermath of the war, Cherenkov just wants to put his head down somewhere and sleep, but her copper hair snares his eye. Beguiled, he allows himself to be led through a quirky little shop and so to Eborius, a baroque land lost in time, where her family rule in ornate splendour…

Hal Duncan – The Land of Somewhere Safe

The Land of Somewhere Safe: where things go when you think, "I must put this somewhere safe," and then can never find them again. The Scruffians: street waifs Fixed by the Stamp to provide immortal slave labour. But now they've nicked the Stamp to prevent any more of their number being exploited. Hounded by occultish Nazi spies and demons, they leave London and the Blitz behind in search of somewhere safe to stow it…

Ten Tall Tales
And Twisted Limericks

Edited by Ian Whates

Ramsey Campbell
Sarah Pinborough
Michael Marshall
Smith
James Barclay
Maura McHugh
Edward Cox
Lynda E. Rucker
Simon Clark
Paul Kane
Andrew Hook
Mark West

Cover art by Sarah Anne Langton

Ten Tall Tales of horror, dark fantasy and dark science fiction, commissioned from some of the most twisted imaginations writing today. Each story is inter-leafed with a Twisted Limerick from that master of terror, Ramsey Campbell.

www.newconpress.co.uk

IMMANION PRESS

Purveyors of Speculative Fiction

Venus Burning: Realms by Tanith Lee

Tanith Lee wrote 15 stories for the acclaimed *Realms of Fantasy* magazine. This book collects all the stories in one volume for the first time, some of which only ever appeared in the magazine so will be new to some of Tanith's fans. These tales are among her best work, in which she takes myth and fairy tale tropes and turns them on their heads. Lush and lyrical, deep and literary, Tanith Lee created fresh poignant tales from familiar archetypes.
ISBN 978-1-907737-88-6, £11.99, $17.50 pbk

A Raven Bound with Lilies by Storm Constantine

The Wraeththu have captivated readers for three decades. This anthology of 15 tales collects all the published Wraeththu short stories into one volume, and also includes extra material, including the author's first explorations of the androgynous race. The tales range from the 'creation story' *Paragenesis*, through the bloody, brutal rise of the earliest tribes, and on into a future, where strange mutations are starting to emerge from hidden corners of the earth.
ISBN: 978-1-907737-80-0 £11.99, $15.50 pbk

The Lightbearer by Alan Richardson

Michael Horsett parachutes into Occupied France before the D-Day Invasion. Dropped in the wrong place, badly injured, he falls prey to two Thelemist women who have awaited the Hawk God's coming, attracts a group of First World War veterans who rally to what they imagine is his cause, is hunted by a troop of German Field Police, and has a climactic encounter with a mutilated priest who believes that Lucifer Incarnate has arrived...*The Lightbearer* is a unique gnostic thriller, dealing with the themes of Light and Darkness, Good and Evil, Matter and Spirit. ISBN 9781907737763 £11.99 $18.99

Voices of the Silicon Beyond by E. S. Wynn

Vaetta is not human, but far more than a mere robot. Her world is overcrowded, it resources at breaking point. The humans who govern this parallel Earth need a solution to these problems. Then a strange, androgynous visitor appears from an inexplicable portal to another world, also seeking help. His world is sparsely populated, following the demise of humankind and the rise of a civilization known as Wraeththu. Vaetta is chosen to scout this new world and begin preparations for invasion, but what waits for her on the other side of the portal doesn't make sense to her, until a fatal meeting through which she discovers a history with far-reaching implications covering all realities. (A novel set in Storm Constantine's Wraeththu Mythos.)
ISBN: 978-1-907737-97-8, £9.99, $14.99 pbk

Dark in the Day, Ed. by Storm Constantine & Paul Houghton

Weirdness lurks beyond the margins of the mundane, emerging to dismantle our assumptions of reality. Dark in the Day is an anthology of weird fiction, penned by established writers and also those new to the genre – the latter being authors who are, or were, students of Creative Writing at Staffordshire University, where editor Storm Constantine occasionally delivers guest lectures. Her co-editor, Paul Houghton, is the senior lecturer in Creative Writing at the university.
Contributors include: Martina Bellovičová, J. E. Bryant, Glynis Charlton, Storm Constantine, Louise Coquio, Elizabeth Counihan, Krishan Coupland, Elizabeth Davidson, Siân Davies, Paul Finch, Rosie Garland, Rhys Hughes, Kerry Fender, Andrew Hook, Paul Houghton, Tanith Lee, Tim Pratt, Nicholas Royle, Michael Marshall Smith, Paula Wakefield, Ian Whates and Liz Williams. ISBN: 978-1-907737-74-9 £11.99, $18.99

34 by Tanith Lee (writing as Esther Garber)

Tanith Lee 'co-wrote' *34* with Esther Garber – a fictional character (perhaps?). This is Esther's autobiography – but how much of it is true? What of the mysterious 'gentleman', who initiates her into forbidden pleasures of a Sapphic kind? Is she haunted or merely manipulated? Esther pursues her elusive tormentor into a fairy-tale version of the French countryside, to journey's end and revelation, but also further mystery. Sensual, thought-provoking, and with an unreliable narrator, who twists and turns within her own tortured story, *34* demonstrates that haunting comes in many forms.
ISBN: 978-1-907737-82-4 £10.99 $13.99

All these and more on our web site
www.immanion-press.com
info@immanion-press.com

Lightning Source UK Ltd.
Milton Keynes UK
UKHW04f2132081018

330212UK00002B/384/P